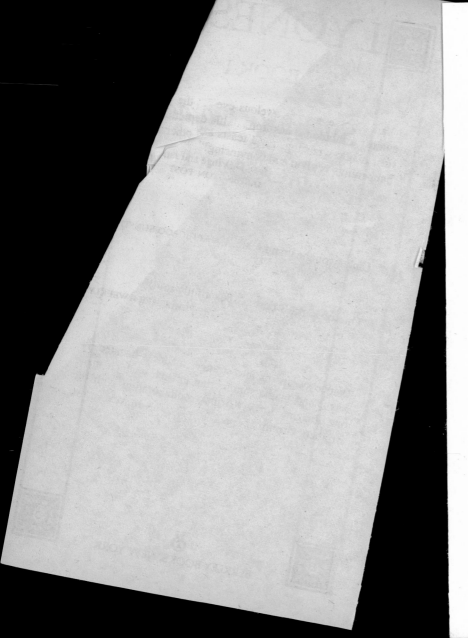

LYONESSE

BOOK I

Suldrun's Garden

JACK VANCE

BERKLEY BOOKS, NEW YORK

To Norma:

WIFE AND COLLEAGUE

LYONESSE

A Berkley Book / published by arrangement with
the author

PRINTING HISTORY
Berkley trade paperback edition / April 1983
Berkley edition / June 1984

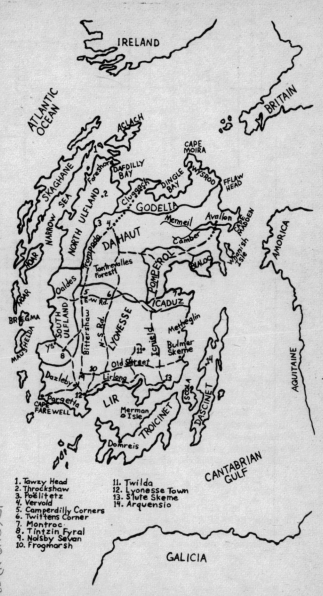

1. Tawzy Head
2. Throckshaw
3. Poëllitetz
4. Vervold
5. Camperdilly Corners
6. Twittens Corner
7. Montroc
8. Tintzin Fyral
9. Nolsby Sevan
10. Frogmarsh
11. Twilda
12. Lyonesse Town
13. Slute Skeme
14. Arquensio

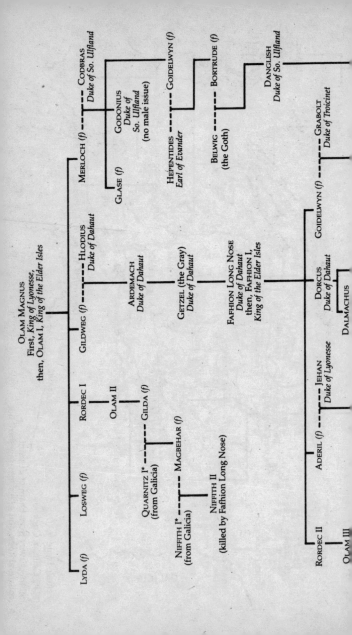

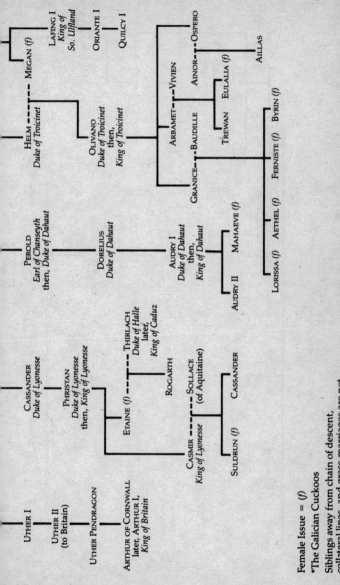

UTHER I

UTHER II
(to Britain)

UTHER PENDRAGON

ARTHUR OF CORNWALL
later, ARTHUR I,
King of Britain

CASSANDER
Duke of Lyonesse

PHRISTAN
Duke of Lyonesse,
then, King of Lyonesse

ETAINE (f) ---- THIRLACH
Duke of Halle
later, King of Caduz

ROGARTH

CASMIR ---- SOLLACE
King of Lyonesse   (of Aquitaine)

SULDRUN (f)   CASSANDER

PEROLD
Earl of Chanseyth
then, Duke of Dahaut

DORELIUS
Duke of Dahaut

AUDRY I
Duke of Dahaut,
then, King of Dahaut

AUDRY II   MAHAEVE (f)

LORISSA (f)   AETHEL (f)   FERNISTE (f)   BYRIN (f)

MEGAN (f) ---- HELM
Duke of Troicinet

LAFING I
King of So. Ulfland

ORIANTE I

QUILCY I

OLIVANO
Duke of Troicinet
then, King of Troicinet

ARBAMET ---- VIVIEN

AINOR ---- OSPERO

AILLAS

GRANICE ---- BAUDILLE

TREWAN   EULALIA (f)

Female Issue = (f)

*The Galician Cuckoos

Siblings away from chain of descent,
collateral lines, and grass-marriages are not
indicated to avoid over-complexity.

◆ PRELIMINARY ◆

The Elder Isles and its peoples: a brief survey, which, while not altogether tedious, may be neglected by the reader impatient with facts.

The Elder Isles, now sunk beneath the Atlantic, in olden times were located across the Cantabrian Gulf (now the Bay of Biscay) from Old Gaul.

Christian chroniclers have little to say regarding the Elder Isles. Gildas and Nennius both make references to Hybras, though Bede is silent. Geoffrey of Monmouth alludes both to Lyonesse and Avallon, and perhaps other places and events which can less certainly be identified. Chrétien of Troyes rhapsodizes upon Ys and its pleasures; and Ys is also the frequent locale of early Armorican folk-tales. Irish references are numerous but confusing and contradictory.* St. Bresabius of Cardiff propounds a rather fanciful list of the Kings of Lyonesse; St. Columba inveighs against the "heretics, witches, idolators and Druids" of the island he calls "Hy Brasill," the medieval term for "Hybras." Otherwise the record is quiet.

Greeks and Phoenicians traded with the Elder Isles. Romans visited Hybras and many settled there, leaving behind aqueducts, roads, villas and temples. In the waning days of the Empire Christian dignitaries landed at Avallon amid vast pomp and panoply. They established bishoprics, appointed appropriate officials and spent good Roman gold to build their basilicas, none of which prospered. The bishops strove mightily against the olden gods, halflings and magicians alike, but few dared enter the Forest of Tantrevalles. Aspergillums, thuribles and

*See Glossary, I.

curses proved futile against such as Dankvin the giant, Taudry the Weasoning, the fairies* of Pithpenny Shee. Dozens of missionaries, exalted through faith, paid terrible prices for their zeal. Saint Elric marched barefoot to Smoorish Rock where he intended to subdue the ogre Magre and bring him to the Faith. According to subsequent tale-tellers, Saint Elric arrived at noon and Magre politely agreed to hear his declaration. Elric spoke a mighty sermon, while Magre started the fire in his pit. Elric expounded, recited Scripture and sang the glories of the Faith. When he came to an end and declared his final "Hallelujah!," Magre gave him a stoup of ale to ease his throat. Sharpening a knife he complimented Elric upon the fervor of his rhetoric. Then he smote off Elric's head, cut, drew, spitted, cooked and devoured the sanctified morsel with a garnish of leeks and cabbages. Saint Uldine attempted the baptism of a troll in the waters of Black Meira Tarn. She was indefatigable; he raped her four times during her efforts, until at last she despaired. In due course she gave birth to four imps. The first of these, Ignaldus, became father to the eery knight Sir Sacrontine who could not sleep of nights until he had killed a Christian. Saint Uldine's other children were Drathe, Alleia and Bazille.* In Godelia Druids never paused in the worship of Lug the Sun, Matrona the Moon, Adonis the Beautiful, Kernuun the Stag, Mokous the Boar, Kai the Dark, Sheah the Graceful, and innumerable local half-gods.

During this period Olam Magnus of Lyonesse, aided by Persilian, his so-called "Magic Mirror," brought all the Elder Isles (excepting Skaghane and Godelia) under his rule. Styling himself Olam I, he enjoyed a long and prosperous reign and was succeeded by Rordec I, Olam II, then, briefly, by the "Galician Cuckoos," Quarnitz I and Niffith I. Then Fafhion Long-nose reasserted the old blood line. He sired Olam III, who moved his throne Evandig and that great table known as Cairbra an Meadhan, the "Board of Notables,"* from Lyonesse Town to Avallon in the Duchy of Dahaut. When Olam III's grandson Uther II fled to Britain (there to sire Uther Pendragon, father of Arthur, King

*See Glossary, II.

*The deeds of the four have been chronicled in a rare volume, "Saint Uldine's Children."

*The Round Table of King Arthur was later inspired by the Cairbra an Meadhan.

of Cornwall), the land fragmented to become ten kingdoms: Dahaut, Lyonesse, North Ulfland, South Ulfland, Godelia, Blaloc, Caduz, Pomperol, Dascinet and Troicinet.

The new kings found many pretexts for contention, and the Elder Isles entered a time of trouble. North and South Ulfland, exposed to the Ska,* became lawless wastes, occupied by robber knights and dire beasts. Only the Vale Evander, guarded to the east by the castle Tintzin Fyral and to the west by the city Ys, remained a realm of tranquility.

King Audry I of Dahaut at last took a fateful step. He declared that since he sat on the throne Evandig, he must be acknowledged King of the Elder Isles.

King Phristan of Lyonesse at once challenged him. Audry assembled a great army and marched down Icnield Way through Pomperol and into Lyonesse. King Phristan led his army north. At the Battle of Orm Hill the armies fought for two days and finally separated in mutual exhaustion. Both Phristan and Audry died in combat and both armies retired. Audry II failed to press his father's claim; effectively Phristan had won the battle.

Twenty years pass. The Ska have made serious inroads into North Ulfland and have taken to themselves a section known as the North Foreshore. King Gax, old, half-blind and helpless has gone into hiding. The Ska do not even trouble to search for him. The king of South Ulfland is Oriante, who resides at Castle Sfan Sfeg near the town Oäldes. His single son, Prince Quilcy, is feeble-minded and spends his days playing with fanciful dolls and doll-houses. Audry II is King of Dahaut and Casmir is King of Lyonesse, and both intend to become King of the Elder Isles and sit rightfully on the throne Evandig.

*See Glossary, III.

1

ON A DREARY WINTER'S DAY, with rain sweeping across Lyonesse Town, Queen Sollace went into labor. She was taken to the lying-in room and attended by two midwives, four maids, Balhamel the physician and the crone named Dyldra, who was profound in the lore of herbs, and by some considered a witch. Dyldra was present by the wish of Queen Sollace, who found more comfort in faith than logic.

King Casmir made an appearance. Sollace's whimpers became moans and she clawed at her thick blonde hair with clenched fingers. Casmir watched from across the room. He wore a simple scarlet robe with a purple sash; a gold coronet confined his ruddy blond hair. He spoke to Balhamel. "What are the signs?"

"Sire, there are none as yet."

"There is no way to divine the sex?"

"To my knowledge, none."

Standing in the doorway, legs somewhat apart, hands behind his back, Casmir seemed the very embodiment of stern and kingly majesty. And, indeed, this was an attitude which accompanied him everywhere, so that kitchen-maids, tittering and giggling, often wondered if Casmir wore his crown to the nuptial bed. He inspected Sollace from under frowning eyebrows. "It would seem that she feels pain."

"Her pain is not so much, sire, as might be. Not yet, at any rate. Remember, fear magnifies that pain which actually exists."

To this observation Casmir made no response. He noticed, in the shadows to the side of the room, Dyldra the crone, where she crouched over a brazier. He pointed with his finger: "Why is the witch here?"

"Sire," whispered the chief midwife, "she came at the behest of Queen Sollace!"

Casmir grunted. "She'll bring a wrack to the child."

Dyldra only crouched the lower over the brazier. She threw a handful of herbs on the coals; a waft of acrid smoke drifted across the room and touched Casmir's face; he coughed, backed away, and departed the room.

The maid drew hangings across the wet landscape and set the bronze lanterns alight. On the couch Sollace lay taut, legs outthrust, head thrown back, her regal bulk fascinating the attention of those who stood tending her.

The pangs became sharp; Sollace cried out, first for pain, then for rage that she should suffer like a common woman.

Two hours later the child was born: a girl, of no great size. Sollace closed her eyes and lay back. When the child was brought to her she waved it away and presently relaxed into a stupor.

The celebration attendant upon the birth of Princess Suldrun was muted. King Casmir issued no jubilant proclamation and Queen Sollace refused audience to all save a certain Ewaldo Idra, Adept of the Caucasian Mysteries. Finally, and only, so it seemed, that he might not contravene custom, King Casmir ordained a gala procession.

On a day of brittle white sunlight, cold wind and high hurrying clouds, the gates before Castle Haidion opened. Four heralds in white satin marched forth, at a stately step-halt-step. From their clarions depended gonfalons of white silk, embroidered with the emblem of Lyonesse: a black Tree of Life, on which grew twelve scarlet pomegranates.* They marched forty yards, halted, raised clarions and blew the "Gladsome Tidings" fanfare. From the palace yard, on snorting white horses, rode four noblemen: Cypris, Duke of Skroy; Bannoy, Duke of Tremblance; Odo, Duke of Folize and Sir Garnel, Knight Banneret of Castle Swange, nephew to the King. Next came the royal carriage, drawn by four white unicorns. Queen Sollace sat swathed in green robes, holding Suldrun on a crimson pillow; King Casmir rode his great black horse, Sheuvan, beside the carriage. Behind marched the Elite Guard, each of noble blood, carrying ceremonial silver halberds. At the rear rolled a wagon from which a pair of maidens tossed handfuls of pennies into the throng.

---

*The usages of heraldry, as well as the theory and practice of chivalry, were still simple and fresh. They would not attain their full baroque extravagance for centuries to come.

The procession descended the Sfer Arct, the central avenue of Lyonesse Town, to the Chale, the road which followed the semi-circle of the harbor. At the Chale, the procession circled the fish market and returned up the Sfer Arct to Haidion. Outside the gate, booths offered the king's pickled fish and biscuits to all who hungered; and ale to those who might wish to drink health to the new princess.

During the months of winter and spring King Casmir looked only twice at the infant princess, in each case, standing back in cool disinterest. She had thwarted his royal will by coming female into the world. He could not immediately punish her for the act, no more could he extend the full beneficence of his favor.

Sollace grew sulky because Casmir was displeased and, with a set of petulant flourishes, banished the child from her sight.

Ehirme, a raw-boned peasant girl, and niece to an undergardener, had lost her own infant son to the yellow bloat. With an amplitude of both milk and solicitude she became Suldrun's wet-nurse.

Centuries in the past, at that middle-distant time when legend and history start to blur, Blausreddin the pirate built a fortress at the back of a stony semi-circular harbor. His concern was not so much assault from the sea, but surprise attacks down from the pinnacles and gorges of the mountains, to the north of the harbor.

A century later the Danaan king, Tabbro, enclosed the harbor behind a remarkable breakwater, and added the Old Hall, new kitchens and a set of sleeping chambers to the fortress. His son, Zoltra Bright Star, constructed a massive stone pier and dredged the harbor so that any ship in the world might moor at the pier.*

Zoltra further augmented the old fortress, adding the Great Hall and the West Tower, though he died before completion of the work, which continued through the reigns of Palaemon I, Edvarius I and Palaemon II.

The Haidion of King Casmir held aloft five major towers: the East Tower, the King's Tower, the Tall Tower (also known as

---

*According to legend both Tabbro and Zoltra Bright Star engaged Joald, a submarine giant, to aid in their undertakings, for an unknown compensation.

the Eyrie), the Tower of Palaemon and the West Tower. There were five major halls: the Great Hall; the Hall of Honors; the Old Hall; the Clod an Dach Nair, or the Banquet Hall; and the Small Refectory. Of these, the Great Hall was remarkable for its ponderous majesty, which seemed to transcend the scope of human effort. The proportions, the spaces and masses, the contrasts of shadow and light, which changed from morning to evening and again to the moving illumination of flamboys, all acted together to awe the senses. The entrances were almost afterthoughts; in any case no one could achieve a dramatic entrance into the Great Hall. At one end a portal entered upon a narrow stage from which six wide steps descended into the hall, beside columns so massive that a pair of men, arms outstretched, could not enclasp them. To one side a row of high windows, glazed with thick glass now lavender with age, admitted a watery half-light. At night, flamboys in iron brackets seemed to cast as much black shadow as light. Twelve Mauretanian rugs eased the harshness of the stone floor.

A pair of iron doors opened into the Hall of Honors, which in scope and proportion resembled the nave of a cathedral. A heavy dark red carpet ran down the center from entrance to royal throne. Around the walls ranged fifty-four massive chairs, each signified by an emblem of nobility hanging on the wall above. On these chairs, for ceremonial occasions, sat the grandees of Lyonesse, each under the emblem of his ancestors. The royal throne, had been Evandig until Olam III moved it to Avallon, along with the round table Cairbra an Meadhan. The table where the noblest of the noble might discover their named places, had occupied the center of the hall.

The Hall of Honors had been added by King Carles, last of the Methewen Dynasty. Chlowod the Red, first of the Tyrrhenians,* extended Haidion's precincts to the east of Zoltra's Wall. He paved the Urquial, Zoltra's old parade ground, and to the back built the massive Peinhador, in which were housed infirmary, barracks and penitentiary. The dungeons under the old armory fell into disuse, with the ancient cages, racks, griddles, wheels, strappado lofts, presses, punches and twisting machines left to molder in the damp.

The kings proceeded to rule, one by one, and each augmented Haidion's halls, passages, prospects, galleries, towers and tur-

---

*Chlowod's grandfather had been a Balearic Etruscan.

rets, as if each, brooding on mortality, sought to make himself part of ageless Haidion.

For those who lived there, Haidion was a small universe indifferent to the events of elsewhere, though the membrane of separation was not impermeable. There were rumors from abroad, notices of the changing seasons, arrivals and excursions, an occasional novelty or alarm; but these were muffled murmurs, dim images, which barely stirred the organs of the palace. A comet flaring across the sky? Marvelous!—but forgotten when Shilk the pot-boy kicks the undercook's cat. The Ska have ravaged North Ulfland? The Ska are like wild animals; but this morning, after eating cream on her porridge, the Duchess of Skroy found a dead mouse in the cream jug, and here was emotion raw and stark, what with her outcries and shoes thrown at the maids!

The laws which ruled the small universe were exact. Status was graduated with the finest of discrimination, from high degree to lowest of the low. Each knew his quality and understood the delicate distinction between next highest (to be minimized) and next lowest (to be enforced and emphasized). Some encroached beyond their station, generating tension; the sharp stench of rancor hung in the air. Each scrutinized the conduct of those above, while concealing his own affairs from those below. The royal personages were watched with care; their habits were discussed and analyzed a dozen times a day. Queen Sollace showed great cordiality to religious zealots and priests, and found much of interest in their creeds. She was thought to be sexually cold and never took lovers. King Casmir made connubial visits to her bed regularly, once each month, and they coupled with stately ponderosity, like the mating of elephants.

Princess Suldrun occupied a peculiar place in the social structure of the palace. The indifference of King Casmir and Queen Sollace were duly noted; petty discourtesies therefore might be visited upon Suldrun with impunity.

The years passed and, without any notice being taken, Suldrun became a quiet child with long soft blonde hair. Because no one saw fit to arrange otherwise, Ehirme made the leap in status from wet-nurse to the private maid of the princess.

Ehirme, untrained in etiquette and not greatly gifted in other ways, had assimilated lore from her Celtic grandfather, which across the seasons and over the years she communicated to Suldrun: tales and fables, the perils of far places, dints against the mischief of fairies, the language of flowers, precautions while walking out at midnight and the avoidance of ghosts, the knowledge of good trees and bad trees.

Suldrun learned of lands which lay beyond the castle. "Two roads lead from Lyonesse Town," said Ehirme. "You may go north through the mountains along the Sfer Arct, or you go east through Zoltra's Gate and across the Urquial. Presently you come to my little cottage and our three fields where we grow cabbages, turnips and hay for the beasts; then the road forks. To the right you follow the shore of the Lir all the way to Slute Skeme. To the left you fare north and join the Old Street which runs beside the Forest of Tantrevalles where the fairies live. Two roads pass through the forest, north to south and east to west."

"Tell what happens where they meet!" Suldrun already knew but she enjoyed the zest of Ehirme's descriptions.

Ehirme warned her: "I've never fared so far, you understand! But what grandfather says is this: in the old times the crossroads would move about, because the place was enchanted and never knew peace. This might be well enough for the traveler, because, after all, he would put one foot ahead of him and then the other and the road would at last be won, and the traveler none the wiser that he had seen twice as much forest as he had bargained for. The most troubled were the folk who sold their goods each year at the Goblin Fair, and where was that but at the crossroads! The folk for the fair were most put out, because the fair should be at the crossroads on Midsummer Night, but when they arrived at the crossroads it had shifted two miles and a half, and nowhere a fair to be seen.

"About this time the magicians vied in awful conflict. Murgen proved the strongest and defeated Twitten, whose father was a halfling, his mother a bald priestess at Kai Kang, under the Atlas Mountains. What to do with the defeated magician, who seethed with evil and hate? Murgen rolled him up and forged him into a stout iron post, ten-foot long and thick as my leg. Then Murgen took this enchanted post to the crossroads and waited till it shifted to the proper place, then he drove the iron post down deep in the center, fixing the crossroads so it no longer could move, and all the folk at the Goblin Fair were glad, and spoke well of Murgen."

"Tell about Goblin Fair!"

"Well then, it's the place and time when the halflings and men can meet and none will harm the other, so long as he stays

6

polite. The folk set up booths and sell all manner of fine things: cobweb cloth and wine of violets in silver bottles, books of fairy-skein, written with words that you can't get out of your head once they're in. You'll see all kinds of halflings: fairies and goblins, trolls and merrihews, and even an odd falloy, though they show themselves seldom, out of shyness, despite being the most beautiful of all. You'll hear songs and music and much chinking of fairy-gold, which they squeeze from buttercups. Oh they're a rare folk, the fairies!"

"Tell how you saw them!"

"Oh indeed! It was five years ago when I was with my sister who married the cobbler in Frogmarsh Village. One time, just at gloaming, I sat by the stile to rest my bones and watch while evening came over the meadow. I heard *tink-a-tink-tinkle*, and I looked and listened. Again: *tink-a-tink-tinkle*, and there, not twenty paces distant came a little fellow with a lantern that gave green light. From the beak of his cap hung a silver bell that went *tink-a-tink-tinkle* as he jumped along. I sat quiet as a post, till he was gone with his bell and green lantern, and that's all there is to it."

"Tell about the ogre!"

"No, that's quite enough for today."

"Do tell, please."

"Well, in truth I know not all that much. There are different sorts among the halflings, different as fox from bear, so that fairy and ogre and goblin and skite are different. All are enemies each to each, except at the Goblin Fair. The ogres live deep in the forest, and it's true, they'll take children and roast them on spits. So never you run too far into the forest for berries, lest you be lost."

"I'll be careful. Now tell me—"

"It's time for your porridge. And today, who knows? There might be a nice rosy apple in my bag yonder..."

Suldrun took lunch in her small sitting-room, or, if the weather were fine, in the orangery: delicately nibbling and sipping while Ehirme held the spoon to her mouth. In due course, she fed herself, with careful movements and sober concentration, as if the most important thing in the world was eating daintily, without mess.

Ehirme found the habit both absurd and endearing, and sometimes she would come up behind Suldrun, and say 'Boo!' in her ear, just as Suldrun opened her mouth for a spoonful of soup. Suldrun pretended to be outraged and reproached Ehirme: "That is a naughty trick!" Then she once more commenced to eat, watching Ehirme carefully from the corner of her eye.

Away from Suldrun's chambers Ehirme moved as unobtrusively as possible, but gradually the fact emerged that Ehirme the peasant girl had stolen a march on her betters. The matter was referred to Dame Boudetta, Mistress of the Household, a severe and uncompromising lady, born into the petty gentility. Her duties were manifold: she supervised the female servants, monitored their virtue, arbitrated questions of propriety. She knew the special conventions of the palace. She was a compendium of genealogical information and even greater masses of scandal.

Bianca, an upper-chamber maid, first brought complaint of Ehirme. "She's an outsider and doesn't even live at the palace. She comes in smelling of pigs and now she's taken to all manner of airs just because she sweeps out little Suldrun's bedchamber."

"Yes, yes," said Dame Boudetta, speaking through her long high-bridged nose. "I know all about it."

"Another thing!" Bianca now spoke with sly emphasis. "Princess Suldrun, as we all know, has little to say, and may be just a trifle backward—"

"Bianca! That is quite enough!"

"—but when she does speak, her accent is atrocious! What when King Casmir decides to converse with the princess and hears the voice of a stable-boy?"

"Your point is well taken," said Dame Boudetta loftily. "Still, I have already given the matter thought."

"Remember, I am well suited to the office of personal maid and my accent is excellent, and I am thoroughly conversant with details of deportment and dress."

"I will keep this in mind."

In the end Dame Boudetta appointed a gentlewoman of middle quality to the post: in fact, her cousin Dame Maugelin, to whom she owed a favor. Ehirme was forthwith discharged and sent trudging home with hanging head.

Suldrun, at this time, was four years old, and ordinarily docile, gentle and easy of disposition, if somewhat remote and pensive. Upon learning of the change she stood transfixed in shock. Ehirme was the single living object in the world whom she loved.

Suldrun made no outcry. She climbed to her chamber, and

8

for ten minutes stood looking down over the town. Then she wrapped her doll into a kerchief, pulled on her hooded cloak of soft gray lamb's-wool and quietly departed the palace.

She ran up the arcade which flanked the east wing of Haidion, and slipped under Zoltra's Wall by a dank passage twenty feet long. She ran across the Urquial, ignoring the grim Peinhador and the gallows on the roof, from which dangled a pair of corpses.

With the Urquial behind, Suldrun trotted along the road until she was tired, then walked. Suldrun knew the way well enough: along the road to the first lane, left along the lane to the first cottage.

She shyly pushed open the door, to find Ehirme sitting glumly at a table, paring turnips for the supper soup.

Ehirme stared in astonishment. "And what are you doing here?"

"I don't like Dame Maugelin. I've come to live with you."

"Ah, little princess, but that won't do! Come, we must get you back before there's an outcry. Who saw you leave?"

"No one."

"Come then; quickly now. If any should ask, we're just out for the air."

"I don't want to stay there alone!"

"Suldrun, my dearest, you must! You're a royal princess, and you may never forget it! That means you do as you're told. Come along now!"

"But I won't do as I'm told, if it means that you'll be gone."

"Well, we'll see. Let's hurry; maybe we can slip in with none the wiser."

But Suldrun already had been missed. While her presence at Haidion meant nothing particular to anyone, her absence was a matter of great import. Dame Maugelin had searched the entire East Tower, from the garret under the roof-slates, which Suldrun was known to visit (Skulking and hiding, the secret little imp! thought Dame Maugelin), down through the observatory where King Casmir came to assess the harbor beyond, down through the chambers on the next floor, which included Suldrun's rooms. Finally, hot, tired and apprehensive, she descended to the main floor, to halt in mingled relief and fury to see Suldrun and Ehirme push open the heavy door and come quietly into the foyer at the end of the main gallery. In an angry swirl of robes Dame Maugelin descended the last three stairs and advanced upon

9

the two. "Where have you been? We are all in a state of supreme anxiety! Come; we must find Dame Boudetta; the matter is in her hands!"

Dame Maugelin marched off down the gallery and along a side corridor to Dame Boudetta's office, with Suldrun and Ehirme following apprehensively behind.

Dame Boudetta heard Dame Maugelin's excited report and looked back and forth between Suldrun and Ehirme. The matter seemed of no great moment; in fact, trivial and tiresome. Still, it represented a certain amount of insubordination and so must be dealt with, briskly and decisively. The question of fault was irrelevant; Dame Boudetta ranked Suldrun's intelligence, sluggish though it might be, about on a par with the moony peasant stupidity of Ehirme. Suldrun, of course, could not be punished; even Sollace would rise in wrath, to learn that royal flesh had been scourged.

Dame Boudetta dealt practically with the affair. She turned a cold gaze upon Ehirme. "Now then, woman, what have you done?"

Ehirme, whose mind indeed was not agile, looked blankly at Dame Boudetta. "I have done nothing, my Lady." Then, hoping to ease matters for Suldrun, she blundered on: "It was just one of our little walks we were having. Wasn't it, Princess dear?"

Suldrun, looking from hawk-like Dame Boudetta to portly Dame Maugelin, discovered only expressions of cold dislike. She said: "I went for a walk; that is true."

Dame Boudetta turned upon Ehirme. "How dare you take such liberties upon yourself! Were you not dismissed from your post?"

"Yes, my Lady, but it wasn't like that at all—"

"Tush, no more. I will hear no excuses." Boudetta signaled to a footman. "Take this woman to the yard and assemble the staff."

Sobbing in bewilderment Ehirme was led to the service yard beside the kitchen, and a gaoler was summoned down from the Peinhador. The palace staff was marshaled to watch, while Ehirme was bent over a trestle by a pair of footmen in Haidion livery. The gaoler came forward: a burly black-bearded man with a pallid, almost lavender, skin. He stood idly by, staring at the maids and twitching his scourge of willow-withes.

Dame Boudetta stood on a balcony, with Dame Maugelin and

Suldrun. In a clear nasal voice she cried out: "Attention, staff! I cite this woman, Ehirme, for malfeasance! Through folly and carelessness she sequestered the person of beloved Princess Suldrun, to cause us grief and consternation. Woman, can you now claim contrition?"

Suldrun cried out: "She didn't do anything! She brought me home!"

Beset by that peculiar passion which attends those at an execution, Dame Maugelin dared so far as to pinch Suldrun's arm and drew her roughly back. "Silence!" she hissed.

Ehirme bawled: "I'm shamed if I did wrong! I only walked the Princess home, in haste."

Dame Boudetta suddenly, in all clarity, perceived the truth of the matter. Her mouth sagged. She stepped forward. Events had gone too far; her dignity was at stake. No doubt Ehirme had escaped punishment for other offenses. There was always her presumptuous behavior to be paid off.

Dame Boudetta raised her hand. "For all, a lesson to be learned! Work dutifully! Never presume! Respect your superiors! Watch and take heed! Warden! Eight strokes, stringent but just."

The gaoler stood back, pulled a black executioner's mask over his face, then advanced upon Ehirme. He threw her brown furze skirt up over her shoulders, exposing a pair of ample white buttocks. He raised the switches high. *Thwish-wack!* A gasping cry from Ehirme. From the onlookers, a mingling of indrawn breaths and titters.

Dame Boudetta looked on impassively. Dame Maugelin showed a pursing mindless smile. Suldrun stood silently, biting her lower lip. With self-critical deliberation the gaoler wielded the scourge. While not a kindly man, he had no taste for pain and today he was in good humor. He contrived a mighty effort, swinging his shoulders, lurching, grunting, but laid small actual weight into his strokes and took away no skin. Ehirme nevertheless bellowed with each stroke, and all were awed by the severity of her thrashing.

"...seven...eight. Enough," declared Dame Boudetta. "Trinthe, Molotta; attend the woman; dress her body with good oil, and send her home. The rest of you: return to your work!"

Dame Boudetta turned, marched from the balcony into a parlor for high-caste servants, such as herself, the seneschal, the bursar, the sergeant of the palace guards and the master steward, where they could take refreshment and confer. Dame Maugelin and Suldrun followed.

Dame Boudetta faced Suldrun, to find her already halfway to the door. "Child! Princess Suldrun! Where are you going?"

Dame Maugelin ran heavy-legged to stand in Suldrun's way.

Suldrun halted, and looked from woman to woman, her eyes glinting with tears.

"Please give me your attention, Princess," said Dame Boudetta. "We are starting something new, which perhaps has been delayed too long: your education. You must learn to be a lady of esteem and dignity. Dame Maugelin will instruct you."

"I don't want her."

"Nevertheless, you shall have her, by particular order of gracious Queen Sollace."

Suldrun looked up full into Dame Boudetta's face. "Someday I will be Queen. Then you will be whipped."

Dame Boudetta opened her mouth, then shut it again. She took a quick step toward Suldrun, who stood half-passive, half-defiant. Dame Boudetta halted. Dame Maugelin, grinning mirthlessly, watched from the side, eyes looking in several directions.

Dame Boudetta spoke in a croaking voice, painfully gentle. "Now then, Princess Suldrun, I act only from devotion to yourself. It is not meet for either queen or princess to use peevish vindictiveness."

From Dame Maugelin came an unctuous corroboration: "So it is indeed. Remember the same for Dame Maugelin!"

"The punishment is now accomplished," declared Dame Boudetta, still using a careful and strained voice. "Everyone will surely be the better for it; now we must put it from our minds. You are the precious Princess Suldrun, and honest Dame Maugelin will instruct you in the proprieties."

"I do not want her. I want Ehirme."

"Tush now, be complaisant."

Suldrun was taken to her chamber. Dame Maugelin plumped herself in a chair, and began to work embroidery. Suldrun went to the window and stared out across the harbor.

Dame Maugelin trudged up the circular stone steps to Dame Boudetta's apartments, hips rolling and thrusting under her dark brown gown. On the third floor she halted to pant, then went to an arched door of fitted timbers, bound with black iron straps.

The door stood ajar. Dame Maugelin pushed it somewhat more open, with a creaking of iron hinges, so that she could pass her amplitude through the gap. She advanced to stand in the doorway, eyes darting to all corners of the room at once.

Dame Boudetta sat at a table, tendering rape-seed on the tip of a long thin forefinger to a caged tom-tit. "Peck, Dicco, peck! Like a gallant bird! Ah! That was a good one."

Dame Maugelin crept a pace or two forward, and at last Dame Boudetta looked up. "What is it now?"

Dame Maugelin shook her head, wrung her hands and licked her pursing lips. "The child is like a stone. I can do nothing with her."

Dame Boudetta made a short brittle sound. "You must be brisk! Arrange a schedule! Insist on obedience!"

Dame Maugelin held her arms wide, and spoke a single poignant word: "How?"

Dame Boudetta gave an annoyed snap of tongue against teeth. She turned back to the bird cage. "Dicco? Twit, twit, Dicco! One more peck and that is all...No more!" Dame Boudetta rose to her feet, and with Dame Maugelin in her wake, went downstairs and up to Suldrun's chambers. She opened the door, looked into the sitting room.

"Princess?"

Suldrun made no response and, indeed, was nowhere to be seen.

The two advanced into the room. "Princess?" called Dame Boudetta. "Are you hiding from us? Come now; don't be naughty."

Dame Maugelin moaned in a sad contralto: "Where is the perverse little thing? I gave stern instructions that she must sit in her chair."

Dame Boudetta looked into the bedchamber. "Princess Suldrun! Where are you?"

She cocked her head sidewise to listen, but heard nothing. The chambers were empty. Dame Maugelin muttered: "She's gone off again to the stour-woman."

Dame Boudetta went to the window thinking to overlook a view to the east, but the way was concealed by the slanting tiled roof over the arcade and the moldering bulk of Zoltra's Wall. Below was the orangery. To the side, half-hidden under dark green foliage, she noted the glimmer of Suldrun's white frock.

Silent and grim she stalked from the room, followed by Dame Maugelin, hissing and muttering furious phrases under her breath.

They descended the stairs, went out and around to the orangery.

Suldrun sat on a bench playing with a wisp of grass. She noted the approach of the two women without emotion, and returned her attention to the grass.

Dame Boudetta halted and stood looking down at the small blonde head. Anger surged up within her, but she was too clever and too wary to allow it tangible scope. Behind stood Dame Maugelin, mouth puckered in excitement, hoping that Dame Boudetta would deal roughly with the Princess: a shake, a pinch, a slap on the firm little buttocks.

Princess Suldrun raised her eyes and for a moment stared up at Dame Boudetta. Then, as if in boredom or apathy, she looked away, and Dame Boudetta was left with a strange sensation that she was seeing ahead, down long years of the future.

Dame Boudetta spoke in a voice grating with effort: "Princess Suldrun, you are not happy with Dame Maugelin's instruction?"

"I don't like her."

"But you like Ehirme?"

Suldrun merely twitched the grass stalk.

"Very well," said Dame Boudetta grandly. "So it will be. We cannot have our precious Princess unhappy."

A quick glance upward, which seemed to read Dame Boudetta through and through.

Dame Boudetta thought with bitter amusement: If that's the way it is, let it be. At least we understand each other.

To salvage face she said sternly: "Ehirme shall return, but you must heed Dame Maugelin, who will instruct your deportment."

2

EHIRME RETURNED, and Dame Maugelin continued her attempts to instruct Suldrun, with success no greater than before. Suldrun was not so much insubordinate as remote; rather than spend effort in defying Dame Maugelin, she simply ignored her.

Dame Maugelin was placed in an irksome predicament; if she admitted her incapacity, Dame Boudetta might put her to even less pleasant employment. So daily Dame Maugelin presented herself to Suldrun's chambers, where Ehirme was already on hand.

The two might or might not acknowledge her presence. Dame Maugelin, then, wearing a moony grin and looking in all directions at once, would wander about the room, pretending to put things to rights.

At last she would advance upon Suldrun, in breezy and lightsome confidence. "Now, Princess, today we must think about making a fine court lady out of you. To start, show me your best curtsy."

Suldrun had been tentatively instructed in six curtsies of varying formality, mainly by Dame Maugelin's ponderous demonstrations, over and over again, joints creaking audibly, until Suldrun, taking pity, might make an attempt at the exercise.

After the noon meal, which would be served either in Suldrun's chambers, or in the orangery if the weather were fine, Ehirme returned home to manage her own household, while Dame Maugelin laid herself down for an afternoon nap. Suldrun also was expected to sleep, but as soon as Dame Maugelin's throat began to rattle Suldrun was out of her bed, into her shoes and away along the hall and down the stairs, to wander the fastnesses of the ancient palace.

During the slow hours of the afternoon the palace itself seemed

15

to drowse, and the small frail shape moved along the galleries and through the tall chambers like a dream-wisp.

In sunny weather she might visit the orangery, to play pensive games in the shade of sixteen old orange trees; more often she went by unobtrusive ways to the Great Hall and thence to the Hall of Honors beyond, where fifty-four great chairs, ranking the walls to right and left, represented the fifty-four most noble houses of Lyonesse.

The emblem above each chair, for Suldrun, told the innate nature of the chair: qualities distinctive, vivid and complex. One chair was characterized by a shifting sidelong deceit, but pretended graceful charm; another exhibited a doomed and reckless bravery. Suldrun recognized a dozen varieties of menace and cruelty, and as many nameless affections which could not be described or worded, which caused her a churning of the bowels, or thrills along her skin, or erotic sensations, transient, pleasant but very strange. Certain chairs loved Suldrun and gave her protection; others were heavy with danger. Moving among these massive entities, Suldrun felt subdued and tentative. She walked with slow steps, listening for inaudible sounds and watching for movement or shifting of the muted colors. Sitting half-drowsing, half-alert, in the arms of a chair who loved her, Suldrun became receptive. The murmuring unheard voices approached the audible, as tragedies and triumphs were told and retold: the colloquy of the chairs.

At the end of the room a dark red gonfalon, embroidered with a Tree of Life, hung from the beams to the floor. A split in the fabric allowed access to a retiring chamber: a room dark and dingy, smelling of ancient dust. In this room were stored ceremonial oddments: a bowl carved from alabaster, chalices, bundles of cloth. Suldrun disliked the room; it seemed a cruel little place where cruel deeds had been planned and perhaps accomplished, leaving a subliminal quiver in the air.

Occasionally the Halls lacked zest, then Suldrun might go out along the parapets of the Old Keep, where always there were interesting sights to be seen along the Sfer Arct: travelers coming and going; wagons loaded high with barrels, bales, and baskets; vagabond knights in dented armor; grandees with their retinues; mendicants, wandering scholars, priests and pilgrims of a dozen sects; country gentry come to buy good cloth, spices, trifles of this and that.

To the north the Sfer Arct passed between the crags Maegher

and Yax: petrified giants who had helped King Zoltra Bright Star dredge Lyonesse Harbor; becoming obstreperous, they had been transformed into stone by Amber the sorcerer: so the story went.

From the parapets Suldrun could see the harbor and wonderful ships from far lands creaking at their moorings. They were unattainable; to venture so far would arouse storms of reproach from Dame Maugelin; she might be taken in disgrace before Queen Sollace, or even into the awesome presence of King Casmir. She had no wish to see either: Queen Sollace was little more than an imperious voice from a billow of splendid robes; King Casmir, to Suldrun, meant a stern face with prominent blue eyes, golden curls and a golden crown on top, and a fringe of golden beard below.

To risk confrontation with either Queen Sollace or King Casmir was not to be considered. Suldrun confined her adventures to the precincts of Haidion.

When Suldrun was seven, Queen Sollace once more grew big and on this occasion gave birth to a boy. Sollace had lost some of her fear, and as a consequence suffered far less than she had with Suldrun. The baby was named Cassander; in due course he would become Cassander V. He was born during the fine weather of summer, and the festivals attending his birth continued a week.

Haidion hosted notable guests from across the Elder Isles. From Dascinet came Prince Othmar and his Aquitanian spouse Princess Eulinette, the Dukes Athebanas, Helingas, and Outrimadax, with their retinues. From Troicinet King Granice sent his princely brothers Arbamet and Ospero, Arbamet's son Trewan and Ospero's son Aillas. From South Ulfland came Grand Duke Erwig, with a birth-gift: a magnificent mahogany chest inlaid with red chert and blue turquoise. King Gax of North Ulfland, beleaguered by the Ska, made no representation. King Audry of Dahaut sent a delegation of nobles and a dozen elephants carved from ivory...And so it went.

At the name-giving ceremony in the Great Hall, Princess Suldrun sat demurely with six daughters of the upper nobility; opposite sat the princelings Trewan and Aillas of Troicinet, Bellath of Caduz, and the three young dukes of Dascinet. For the occasion Suldrun wore a gown of pale blue velvet, and a fillet studded with moonstones confined her soft pale hair. She was clearly well-favored, and attracted the thoughtful attention of many persons who previously had paid her little heed, including King Casmir himself. He thought: "She is pretty, certainly, if somewhat thin and peaked. She has a solitary look about her; perhaps she keeps too much to herself... Well, all this can be remedied. She will grow to be a desirable match." And Casmir, who ever more fervently yearned to restore the ancient grandeur of Lyonesse, went on to reflect: "It is certainly not too early to think along these lines."

He cast his mind across the possibilities. Dahaut was of course the great obstacle to his plans and King Audry was his dedicated if covert enemy. Someday the old war must continue, but rather than attack Dahaut on the east, through Pomperol, where Audry's lines of operation were short (which had been King Phristan's grim mistake), Casmir hoped to attack through South Ulfland, to gnaw at Dahaut's exposed western flanks. And King Casmir mused upon South Ulfland.

King Oriante, a pallid round-headed little man, was ineffectual, shrill and waspish. He reigned at his castle Sfan Sfeg, near the town Oäldes, but could not rule the fiercely independent barons of mountain and moor. His queen, Behus, was both tall and corpulent and she had borne him a single son, Quilcy, now five years old, somewhat lack-witted and unable to control the flow of saliva from his mouth. A match between Quilcy and Suldrun could bring great advantage. Much depended upon how much influence Suldrun could exert over a feeble-minded spouse. If Quilcy were as tractable as report suggested, a clever woman should find no difficulty with him.

Such were King Casmir's reflections as he stood in the Great Hall at the name-day of his son Cassander.

Suldrun felt her father's eyes upon her. The intensity of his gaze made her uncomfortable, and for a moment she feared that she had aroused his disapproval. But presently he looked away, and to her relief paid her no more heed.

Directly opposite sat the princelings from Troicinet. Trewan was fourteen years old, tall and strong for his age. His dark hair was cut low and square across the forehead and hung thick at the sides past his ears. His features were perhaps a trifle heavy but he was by no means ill-favored; indeed, he already had made his presence felt among the housemaids at Zarcone, the manor house of Prince Arbamet, his father. His eyes rested often upon Suldrun, in a way she found disturbing.

The second Troice princeling was Aillas, two or three years

younger than Trewan. He was slender of hip and square in the shoulder. His straight light-brown hair was cropped into a cap covering the top of his ears. His nose was short and even; the line of his jaw showed clean and definite. He seemed not to notice Suldrun, which prompted in her an absurd little quiver of vexation, even though she had disapproved of the other prince's boldness... Her attention was distracted by the coming of four gaunt Druid priests.

They wore long robes of brown furze, belted and hooded to hide their faces, and each carried an oak branch from their sacred grove. They shuffled forward, their long white feet appearing and disappearing below the robes, and arranged themselves to north, south, east and west of the cradle.

The Druid to the north held the oak branch over the child and touched his forehead with a wooden periapt, then spoke: "The Dagda blesses you and gives you the benefit of your name Cassander."

The Druid to the west extended his oak branch. "Brigit, first daughter of the Dagda, blesses you and gives you the benefit of poetry, and names you Cassander."

The Druid to the south extended his oak branch. "Brigit, second daughter of Dagda, blesses you and gives the benefit of strong health and powers of healing, and calls you Cassander."

The Druid to the east extended his oak branch. "Brigit, third daughter of the Dagda, blesses you and gives the benefit of iron, in sword and shield, in sickle and plough, and calls you Cassander."

All held their branches to form a leafy ceiling over the child. "May the light of Lug warm your body; may the dark of Ogma improve your prospects; may Lir support your ships; may the Dagda forever hold you in grace."

They turned and moved on slow bare feet from the hall.

Pages in scarlet puff-pantaloons raised clarions and blew the *Queen's Honor*. The company stood in murmurous near-silence as Queen Sollace retired on the arm of Lady Lenore, while Lady Desdea supervised the removal of the infant prince.

Musicians appeared on the high gallery, with dulcimer, pipes, lute, and a cadwal (this a single-stringed fiddle apt for the playing of jigs). The center of the hall was cleared; the pages blew a second fanfare: *Lo! the Jocund King!*

King Casmir addressed himself to the Lady Arresme, Duchess of Slahan; the musicians produced a stately concord and King

Casmir led Lady Arresme forth for the pavanne, followed by the lords and ladies of the realm, in a pageant of magnificent costumes of every color, with every gesture, every step, every bow and position of head, hand and wrist ordained by etiquette. Suldrun watched in fascination: slow-step, pause, little bow and swing of the arms in graceful style, then another step, and shimmer of silk, the rustle of petticoats to the careful sonorities of the music. How stern and stately seemed her father, even engaged in the frivolity of dancing the pavanne!

The pavanne ended, and the company removed to the Clod an Dach Nair, and found their places at the banquet table. The most rigid rules of precedence applied; the chief herald and an ordinator had worked with enormous pains, making the most subtle of discriminations. Suldrun was seated directly to the right of King Casmir, in that chair usually occupied by the queen. Tonight Queen Sollace was unwell, and lay in her bed, where she ate to repletion of sweet curd tarts, while Suldrun for the first time dined at the same table with her father the king.

Three months after the birth of Prince Cassander, the circumstances of Suldrun's life altered. Ehirme, already mother to a pair of sons, gave birth to twins. Her sister, who had managed the household while Ehirme was at the palace, married a fisherman, and Ehirme could no longer serve Suldrun.

Almost coincidentally, Dame Boudetta announced that by the wishes of King Casmir, Suldrun must be schooled in deportment, dancing, and all other skills and graces appropriate to a royal princess.

Suldrun resigned herself to the program, which was rendered by various ladies of the court. As before, Suldrun used the soporific hours of early afternoon to wander quietly abroad: out into the orangery, or the library, or the Hall of Honors. From the orangery the way led along an arcade, up to Zoltra's Wall, through a vaulted tunnel and out upon the Urquial. Suldrun ventured so far as the tunnel, and stood in the shadows watching the men-at-arms as they drilled with pikes and swords. They made a gallant spectacle, thought Suldrun, stamping, shouting, lunging forward, falling back...To the right a crumbling wall flanked the Urquial. Almost hidden behind a sprawling old larch a heavy wooden door, dessicated with age, led through the wall. Suldrun slipped from the tunnel and into the shadows behind the larch. She peered through a crack in the door, then pulled at a bolt which held the warped timbers in place. She exerted all her strength, to no avail. She found a rock and used it as a hammer. The rivets parted; the bolt sagged aside. Suldrun pushed; the door creaked and shuddered. She turned around and bumped it with her round little buttocks. The door protested with an almost human voice, and moved ajar.

Suldrun squeezed through the gap and found herself at the head of a ravine which seemed to descend all the way to the sea. Greatly daring, she ventured a few steps down an old path. She stopped to listen...no sound. She was alone. She went another fifty feet and came upon a small structure of weathered stone, now desolate and empty: apparently an ancient fane.

Suldrun dared go no farther; she would be missed and Dame Boudetta would scold her. She craned her neck to look down the ravine and glimpsed the foliage of trees. Reluctantly she turned and went back the way she had come.

An autumn storm brought four days of rain and mist to Lyonesse Town, and Suldrun was pent within Haidion. On the fifth day the clouds broke, and shafts of sunlight struck down through the rents at various angles. By noon the sky was half blue space, half hurrying cloud-wrack.

At first opportunity Suldrun ran up the arcade, through the tunnel under Zoltra's Wall; then, after a precautionary glance around the Urquial, under the larch and through the old wooden door. She closed the door behind her and stood tingling with a sense of isolation from all the rest of the world.

She descended the old path to the fane: an octagonal stone structure perched on a stone shelf, with the ridge rising steeply behind. Suldrun looked through the low arched door. Four long steps would take her to the back wall, where the symbol of Mithra overlooked a low stone altar. To each side a narrow window admitted light; slate tiles covered the roof. A drift of dead leaves had blown through the doorway; otherwise the fane was empty. The atmosphere carried a dank clammy-sweet odor, faint but unpleasant. Suldrun twitched her nose and backed away.

The ravine descended steeply; the ridges to either side assumed the semblance of low irregular cliffs. The path angled this way and that: through stones, clumps of wild thyme, asphodel and thistles and out upon a terrace where the soil lay deep. Two massive oaks, almost filling the ravine, stood sentinel over the ancient garden below, and Suldrun felt like an explorer discovering a new land.

To the left the cliff rose high. An irregular copse of yew, laurel, hornbeam and myrtle shaded an undergrowth of shrubs and flowers: violets, ferns, harebells, forget-me-nots, anemones; banks of heliotrope scented the air. On the right hand the cliff, almost equally tall, trapped sunlight. Below grew rosemary, asphodel, foxglove, wild geranium, lemon verbena; slim black-green cypress and a dozen enormous olive trees, gnarled, twisted, the fresh gray-green foliage in contrast with the age-worn trunks.

Where the ravine widened Suldrun came upon the ruins of a Roman villa. Nothing remained but a cracked marble floor, a half-toppled colonnade, a tumble of marble blocks among weeds and thistles. At the edge of the terrace grew a single old lime tree with a heavy trunk and sprawling boughs. Below, the path led down to a narrow beach of shingle, curving between a pair of capes where the cliffs on either hand thrust into the sea.

The wind had eased to a near-calm, but swells from the storm continued to bend around the headlands and break upon the shingle. For a time Suldrun watched the sunlight sparkling on the sea, then turned and looked back up the ravine. The old garden doubtless was enchanted, she thought, with a magic evidently benign; she felt only peace. The trees basked in the sunlight and paid her no heed. The flowers all loved her, except the proud asphodel, which loved only itself. Melancholy memories stirred among the ruins, but they were insubstantial, less than wisps, and they had no voices.

The sun moved across the sky; Suldrun reluctantly turned to go. She would be missed if she stayed longer. Up through the garden she went, out the old door and back down the arcade to Haidion.

3

SULDRUN AWOKE TO A COLD GRAY ROOM and a dismal wet light from outside her windows: the rains had returned and the chambermaid had neglected to build up the fires. Suldrun waited a few minutes, then resignedly slid from her bed and with shanks shivering to the chill, dressed herself and combed out her hair.

The maid at last appeared, and hurriedly built the fires, fearful lest Suldrun might denounce her to Dame Boudetta, but the lapse had already slipped from Suldrun's mind.

She went to stand by the window. Rain blurred the panorama; the harbor was a rain-puddle; the tiled roofs of the town were ten thousand shapes in many tones of gray. Where had the color gone? Color! What peculiar stuff! It glowed in the sunlight, but in the dimness of rain it faded: most peculiar. Suldrun's breakfast arrived and as she ate she pondered the paradoxes of color. Red and blue, green and purple, yellow and orange, brown and black: each with its character and special quality, yet impalpable...

Suldrun went down to the library for her lessons. Her tutor was now Master Jaimes, archivist, scholar, and librarian to the court of King Casmir. Suldrun had at first found him a daunting figure of severity and precision, for he was tall and thin, and a great thin beak of a nose gave him the look of a predatory bird. Master Jaimes was a few years past the first wild urgencies of youth, but not yet old nor even middle-aged. His coarse black hair was cut level with his mid-forehead clear around the scalp, to hang in a shelf over his ears; his skin was parchment pale; his arms and legs were long and as gaunt as his torso; nevertheless he carried himself with dignity and even an odd ungainly grace. He was sixth son to Sir Crinsey of Hredec, an estate comprising thirty acres of stony hillside, and had gained nothing

23

from his father but gentle birth. He resolved to teach Princess Suldrun with dispassionate formality, but Suldrun quickly learned how to charm and befuddle him. He fell hopelessly in love with her, though he pretended that the emotion was no more than easy tolerance. Suldrun who was perceptive when she put her mind to it, saw through his attempts at airy detachment and took charge of the learning process, as when Master Jaimes frowned at her writing and said: "These A's and G's look quite alike. We must do them all over, in a careful hand."

"But the quill is broken!"

"Then sharpen it! Carefully now, do not cut yourself. It is a knack you must learn."

"Oo-ow—oo!"

"Did you cut yourself?"

"No. I was just practicing in case I did."

"You need not practice. Cries of pain come quite easily and naturally."

"How far have you traveled?"

"What has that to do with cutting a quill?"

"I wonder if the students in far places, like Africa, cut their quills differently."

"As to that I can't say."

"How far have you traveled?"

"Oh—not too far. I studied at the university in Avallon, and also at Metheglin. Once I visited Aquitania."

"What is the farthest place of the whole world?"

"Hmn. That is hard to say. Cathay? The far side of Africa?"

"That can't be the proper answer!"

"Oh? In that case, please instruct me."

"There is no such place; something farther always lies beyond."

"Yes. Perhaps so. Let me cut the quill. There, just so. Now as to the A's and G's..."

On the rainy morning when Suldrun went into the library for lessons, she found Master Jaimes already on hand, with a dozen quills cut and ready. "Today," said Master Jaimes, "you must write your name, in whole and full, and with such exquisite skill that I will exclaim in surprise."

"I will do my best," said Suldrun. "These are beautiful quills."

"Excellent indeed."

"The plumes are all white."

"I believe that is true."

"This ink is black. I think black plumes would be better for black ink."

"I don't think the difference is noticeable."

"We could try white ink with these white plumes."

"I have no white ink, nor yet black parchment. So now—"

"Master Jaimes, this morning I wondered about colors. Where do they come from? What are they?"

Master Jaimes blinked and tilted his head to the side. "Colors? They exist. Everywhere we see color."

"But they come and go. What are they?"

"Well, truthfully, I don't know. How clever of you to ask the question. Red things are red and green things are green, and that would seem to be that."

Suldrun smilingly shook her head. "Sometimes, Master Jaimes, I think I know as much as you."

"Do not reproach me. Do you see those books yonder? Plato and Cnessus and Rohan and Herodotus—I have read them all, and I have learned only how much I do not know."

"What of the magicians? Do they know everything?"

Master Jaimes slouched his awkward length back in his chair and gave up all hopes for a formal and correct atmosphere. He looked out the library window, and presently said: "When I still lived at Hredec—I was little more than a lad—I became friendly with a magician." Glancing at Suldrun he saw that he had captured her attention. "His name was Shimrod. One day I visited his house Trilda, and forgot all about time. Night came and I was far from home. Shimrod caught a mouse and changed it into a fine horse. 'Ride home at speed,' he told me. 'Do not dismount or touch the ground before your destination, for as soon as your foot touches ground, the horse is once more a mouse!'

"And so it was. I rode in style, to the envy of those who saw me, and I took care to dismount behind the stable, so that none would know that I had been riding a mouse.

"Alas! We are wasting time." He straightened up in his chair. "Now then, take up your pen, dip ink, and inscribe me a good R, as you will need to write your name."

"But you have not answered my question!"

"'Do magicians know everything?' The answer is no. Now: the characters, in a fine square hand."

"Oh Master Jaimes, today I am bored with writing. Teach me magic instead."

"Ha! If I knew magic, would I be frousting here at two florins a week? No, no, my princess, I have better schemes in mind! I would take two fine mice and change them to a pair of beautiful horses and I would become a handsome young prince not much older than you, and we would go riding away over hill and dale to a wonderful castle in the clouds, and there we would dine on strawberries and cream and listen to the music of harps and fairy bells. Alas, I know no magic. I am the wretched Master Jaimes, and you are sweet mischievous Suldrun who won't learn her letters."

"No," said Suldrun in sudden decision. "I'll work very hard so that I can read and write, and do you know why? So that I may learn magic, and you need only learn to catch mice."

Master Jaimes uttered a queer choked laugh. He reached across the table and took her two hands. "Suldrun, you already know magic."

For a moment they smiled at each other, then in sudden embarrassment, Suldrun bowed her head over her work.

The rains continued. Master Jaimes, walking abroad in the cold and wet, caught a fever and could not teach. No one troubled to notify Suldrun and she went down to the library to find it empty.

For a time she practiced writing, and looked through a leather-bound book brought down from Northumbria, illuminated with exquisite depictions of saints in landscapes wrought in vivid inks.

At last Suldrun put the book aside and went out into the hall. The time was now mid-morning, and servants were busy in the Long Gallery. Undermaids polished the flagstones with beeswax and lamb-skin; a footman stalking on ten-foot stilts replenished the sconces with oil of nenuphar. From outside the palace, muffled by the intervening walls, came the blare of clarions, announcing the arrival of notables. Looking along the gallery, Suldrun saw them enter the reception hall: three grandees, stamping and shaking the rain from their garments. Footmen hastened forward to relieve them of their cloaks, helmets and swords. From the side a herald raised his voice to its most resonant pitch. "From the Realm of Dahaut, three noble personages! I declare their identities: Lenard, Duke of Mech! Milliflor, Duke of Cadwy and Josselm! Imphal, Marquis of the Celtic March!"

King Casmir stepped forward. "Sirs, I give you welcome to Haidion!"

The three grandees performed a ritual genuflection, bobbing their right knees toward the floor, rising to hold hands out from the sides with head and shoulders still bent. The circumstances indicated an occasion of formal but less than ceremonial import.

King Casmir returned them a gracious wave of the hand. "Sirs, for now I suggest that you make haste to your chambers, where warm fires and dry clothing will bring you comfort. In due course we will exchange our counsels."

Sir Milliflor responded: "Thank you, King Casmir. In truth we are wet; the cursed rain has allowed us no respite!"

The visitors were ushered away. King Casmir turned down the gallery. He noticed Suldrun and stopped short. "Eh then, what's this? Why are you not at lessons?"

Suldrun thought to gloss over Master Jaimes' absence from his duties. "I have only just finished my work for the day. I can write all the characters well, and I can use them to make up words. This morning I read a great book about the Christians."

"Ha, so read you did? Characters and all?"

"Not all the characters, Father. They were uncial and the language was Latin. I have trouble with both. But I scanned the pictures carefully, and Master Jaimes tells me that I am doing well."

"That is good to hear. Still, you must learn proper comportment and not go strolling up and down the gallery unattended."

Suldrun spoke in apprehension: "Father, sometimes I prefer to be alone."

Casmir, faintly frowning, stood with feet apart and hands behind his back. He disliked opposition to his judgments, especially from a girl so small and inexperienced. In a measured voice intended to define the facts with exactitude and finality he said: "Your preference must on occasion yield to the forces of reality."

"Yes, Father."

"You must hold in mind your importance. You are the Princess Suldrun of Lyonesse! Soon the quality of the world will be coming to woo you in marriage, and you must not seem a hoyden. We want to pick and choose, for the best advantage to yourself and the kingdom!"

Suldrun said uncertainly, "Father, marriage is nothing I care to think about."

Casimir narrowed his eyes. Again: the hint of wilfulness! In reply he used a voice of bluff jocularity. "I should hope not! You are only just a child! Still, you are never too young to be conscious of position. Do you understand the word 'diplomacy'?"

"No, Father."

"It means dealing with other countries. Diplomacy is a delicate game, like a dance. Troicinet, Dahaut, Lyonesse, the Ska and the Celts, all in pirouettes, all ready to join in threes or fours to deal the outsiders their death-blow. I must ensure that Lyonesse is not excluded from the quadrille. Do you understand my meaning?"

Suldrun considered. "I think so. I'm happy that I must not do any such dancing."

Casimir stood back, wondering whether she might have perceived his meaning all too well. He said shortly: "That's all for now; be off with you to your proper quarters! I will speak to Lady Desdea; she will find you a suitable set of companions."

Suldrun started to explain that she needed no new companions, but glancing up into King Casimir's face, she held her tongue and turned away.

In order to obey King Casimir's command in its exact and literal sense, Suldrun ascended to her chambers in the East Tower. Dame Maugelin sat snoring in a chair, with her head thrown back.

Suldrun looked out the window, to discover the steady fall of rain. She thought a moment, then slipped past Dame Maugelin into her dressing-room and changed into a frock woven from dark green linen. With a final demure over-the-shoulder glance toward Dame Maugelin she left the chambers. King Casimir's order had been obeyed; if he chanced to see her she could demonstrate as much by her change of garments.

Daintily, step by step, she descended the stairs to the Octagon. Here she halted to look and listen. The Long Gallery was empty; no sound. She wandered an enchanted palace where everyone drowsed.

Suldrun ran to the Great Hall. The gray light which managed to seep through the high windows was lost in the shadows. On silent feet, she went to a tall narrow portal in the long wall, looked over her shoulder, mouth twitching up at the corners. Then she tugged open the massive door and slipped into the Hall of Honors.

The light, as in the Great Hall, was gray and dim, and the

solemnity of the chamber was enhanced. As always, fifty-four tall chairs ranged the walls to left and right and all seemed to stare in brooding disdain at the table which, with four attendant and lesser chairs, had been placed at the center of the room.

Suldrun surveyed the interloping furniture with equal disapproval. It intruded into the space between the tall chairs, and impeded their easy intercourse. Why would anyone do so clumsy a deed? No doubt the arrival of the three grandees had dictated the arrangement. The thought stopped Suldrun in her tracks. She decided to depart the Hall of Honors at once... But not quickly enough. From outside the door: voices. Suldrun, startled, froze into a statue. Then she ran back and forth in confusion, and finally darted behind the throne.

At her back lay the dark red gonfalon. Suldrun slipped through the slit in the fabric into the storage room. By standing close to the hanging and twitching open the slit, Suldrun watched a pair of footmen enter the hall. Today they wore splendid ceremonial livery: scarlet puff-pantaloons, black and red striped hose, black shoes with curled tips, ocher tabards embroidered with the Tree of Life. They paced around the room setting alight the wall sconces. Two other footmen carried in a pair of heavy black iron candelabra, which they set on the table. The candles, each two inches thick and molded from bayberry wax, were also set alight; Suldrun had never seen the Hall of Honors so resplendent.

She began to feel annoyed with herself. She was the Princess Suldrun and need not hide from footmen; still, she remained in concealment. News traveled quickly among the corridors of Haidion; if the footmen saw her, soon Dame Maugelin would know, then Dame Boudetta, and who knows how high the story might rise?

The footmen completed their preparations and retired from the room, leaving the doors open.

Suldrun stepped out into the chamber. Beside the throne she paused to listen, face slantwise, fragile and pale, alive with excitement. Suddenly bold, she ran out across the chamber. She heard new sounds: the jingle of metal, the tramp of heavy footsteps; in a panic she turned and ran back behind the throne. Looking over her shoulder she glimpsed King Casmir in full panoply of might and majesty. He marched into the Hall of Honors, head high, chin and short blond beard jutting. The flames from the sconces reflected from his crown: a simple gold band under a circlet of silver laurel leaves. He wore a long black

29

cape trailing almost to his heels, black and brown doublet, black trousers, black ankle-boots. He carried no weapon and wore no ornament. His face as usual was cold and impassive. To Suldrun he seemed the embodiment of awful pomp; she dropped to her hands and knees and crawled under the gonfalon into the back room. Finally she dared to stand erect and peer through the slit.

King Casmir had failed to notice a twitching of the gonfalon. He stood by the table with his back to Suldrun, hands on the chair in front of him.

Heralds entered the room, two by two, to the number of eight, each bearing a standard displaying the Lyonesse Tree of Life. They took positions along the back wall. Into the room marched the three grandees who had arrived earlier in the day.

King Casmir stood waiting until the three had separated to stand by their chairs, then seated himself, followed by his three guests.

Stewards placed beside each man a silver chalice which the chief steward filled with dark red wine from an alabaster pitcher. He then bowed and departed the room, and after him, the footmen and then the heralds. The four sat alone at the table.

King Casmir held aloft his chalice. "I propose joy to our hearts, fulfillment to our needs and success to those goals which we hold in mutuality."

The four men drank wine. King Casmir said: "Now then, to our affairs. We sit in informality and privacy; let us speak in candor, without restraint. Such a discussion will yield benefit to us all."

"We will take you at your word," spoke Sir Milliflor. He smiled a thin smile. "Still, I doubt if our hearts' desires run quite so closely in conjunction as you envision."

"Let me define a position which all of us must endorse," said King Casmir. "I cite the memory of the olden times, when a single rule maintained a halcyon peace. Since then we have known incursions, pillage, war and suspicion. The two Ulflands are poisonous wastes, where only the Ska, robbers and wild beasts dare walk abroad. The Celts are suppressed only by dint of constant vigilance, as Sir Imphal will attest."

"I do so attest," said Sir Imphal.

"Then I will put the matter into simple terms," said King Casmir. "Dahaut and Lyonesse must work in concert. With this combined force under a single command, we can drive the Ska out of the Ulflands, and subdue the Celts. Next Dascinet, then

Troicinet; and the Elder Isles are once more whole. First: the merging of our two lands."

Sir Milliflor spoke. "Your statements are beyond debate. We are halted by a set of questions: Who becomes preeminent? Who leads the armies? Who rules the realm?"

"These are blunt questions," said King Casmir. "Let the answers wait until we are agreed in principle, then we will examine such possibilities."

Sir Milliflor said: "We are agreed on the principles. Let us now explore the real issues. King Audry sits on the ancient throne Evandig; will you concede his preeminence?"

"I cannot do so. Still, we can rule in tandem as equals. Neither King Audry nor Prince Dorcas are stern soldiers. I will command the armies; King Audry shall conduct the diplomacy."

Sir Lenard uttered a grim laugh. "At the first difference of opinion the armies might well overcome the diplomats."

King Casmir also laughed. "That condition need not arise. Let King Audry rule supreme until his death. Then I will rule until my death. Prince Dorcas shall succeed me. In the event that he breeds no sons, Prince Cassander will be next in line."

"That is an interesting concept," said Sir Milliflor drily. "King Audry is old, and you are relatively young; need I remind you? Prince Dorcas might wait thirty years for his crown."

"Possibly so," said King Casmir without interest.

"King Audry has instructed us," said Sir Milliflor. "His anxieties are similar to yours, but he is wary of your notorious ambitions. He suggests that you would like Dahaut to engage the Ska, thereby allowing you to attack Troicinet."

King Casmir sat silent a moment, then stirred and spoke. "Will Audry agree to a joint effort against the Ska?"

"He will indeed, if the armies are under his command."

"Has he no alternate proposals?"

"He notes that the Princess Suldrun will soon arrive at marriageable age. He suggests the possibility of betrothal between Princess Suldrun and Prince Whemus of Dahaut."

King Casmir leaned back in his chair. "Whemus is his third son?"

"That is true, your Majesty."*

*The honorifics of the time are modified by a hundred special cases. It is impossible to translate them into contemporary terms with both crispness and accuracy; they will therefore be rendered in more familiar, if simplistic, terms.

King Casmir smiled and touched his short blond beard. "Let us, rather, unite his first daughter, the Princess Cloire, with my nephew Sir Nonus Roman."

"We will dutifully convey your suggestion to the court at Avallon."

King Casmir drank from the chalice; the emissaries courteously drank as well. King Casmir looked from face to face. "Are you then merely messengers? Or in truth can you negotiate?"

Sir Milliflor said: "We may negotiate within the limits set by our instructions. Would you care to rephrase your proposal in the simplest way, without euphemism?"

King Casmir picked up the chalice in his two hands, held it to chin level, and turned his pale blue eyes over the top. "I propose that the assembled might of Lyonesse and Dahaut, under my command, attack the Ska and drive them back out across the Atlantic, and that next we subdue the Celts. I propose that we join our kingdoms not only through cooperation but also through marriage. Either Audry or I will die first. The survivor shall thereupon rule the joint kingdoms, to be known as the Kingdom of The Elder Isles, in the old fashion. My daughter Princess Suldrun shall marry the Prince Dorcas. My son Prince Cassander shall marry—suitably. So much I propose."

"The proposal has much in common with our position," said Sir Lenard. "King Audry prefers that military operations conducted on the soil of Dahaut be commanded by himself. Secondly—"

The negotiations proceeded another hour, but only emphasized the mutual inflexibility. Since nothing more had been expected the conversations ended on a polite basis. The envoys departed the Hall of Honors, that they might rest before the evening's banquet, while King Casmir remained brooding alone at the table. In the back room Suldrun watched in fascination, then in panic as King Casmir picked up one of the candelabra, turned and with heavy steps walked toward the back chamber.

Suldrun stood paralyzed. Her presence was known! She turned, darted to the side, ducked into the corner beside a storage case, and pulled a fragment of old rag over her shining hair.

The hangings parted; candlelight flickered through the chamber. Suldrun crouched, awaiting the voice of King Casmir. But he stood in silence, nostrils dilated, perhaps sensing the fragrance of the lavender sachet in which Suldrun's clothes were

32

laid. He looked over his shoulder, then went to the back wall. From a crevice he took a thin iron rod, which he pushed into a small hole at the level of his knee, then into another somewhat higher. A door opened, emitting a light quivering and almost palpable, like a flickering alternation of purple and green. Out from the room flowed the thrilling tingle of magic. A pair of high-pitched voices produced a babbling outcry.

"Silence," said King Casmir. He entered the room and closed the door.

Suldrun jumped from the corner and departed the room. She ran across the Hall of Honors, slipped out into the Great Hall and thence to the Long Gallery. Once more, she went sedately to her rooms, where Dame Maugelin scolded her for soiled clothes and a dirty face.

Suldrun bathed, dressed in a warm robe. She went to the window with her lute and pretended to practice, making such energetic discords that Dame Maugelin threw up her hands and went elsewhere.

Suldrun was left alone. She put the lute aside and sat looking across the landscape. The time was late afternoon; the weather had broken; sunlight glistened on the wet roofs of Lyonesse Town.

Slowly, incident by incident, Suldrun reviewed the events of the day.

The three envoys from Dahaut interested her little, except that they wanted to take her away to Avallon and marry her to a strange man. Never! She would run away; she would become a peasant, or a minstrel girl, or gather mushrooms in the woods!

The secret room behind the Hall of Honors in itself seemed neither extraordinary nor remarkable. In fact, it only corroborated certain of her half-formed suspicions regarding King Casmir, who wielded such absolute and awful power!

Dame Maugelin returned to the room, panting in haste and excitement. "Your father commands you to the banquet. He wishes you to be everything a beautiful princess of Lyonesse should be. Do you hear? You may wear your blue velvet gown and your moonstones. At all times remember court etiquette! Don't spill your food; drink very little wine. Speak only when you are addressed, then respond with courtesy and without chewing your words. Neither titter, nor scratch yourself, nor wriggle in your chair as if your bottom itched. Do not belch, gurgle or gulp. If someone breaks wind, do not stare or point or attempt to place the blame. Naturally you will control yourself as well; nothing is more conspicuous than a farting princess. Come! I must brush your hair."

In the morning Suldrun went to take her lessons in the library, but again Master Jaimes was not on hand, nor on the day after, nor the day after. Suldrun became a trifle miffed. Surely Master Jaimes might have communicated with her despite his indisposition. For an entire week she ostentatiously absented herself from the library, but still no word from Master Jaimes!

In sudden alarm Suldrun sought out Dame Boudetta, who sent a footman to Master Jaimes' bleak little cell in the West Tower. The footman discovered Master Jaimes outstretched and dead on his pallet. His fever had become pneumonia, and he had died with no one the wiser.

4

ONE MORNING OF THE SUMMER before Suldrun's tenth birthday she went to the third floor parlor in the squat old Tower of Owls for her dancing lesson. The room itself she thought perhaps the finest of all Haidion. A well-waxed birch parquetry floor reflected light from three windows draped with a pearl-gray satin. Furniture upholstered in pale gray and scarlet ranged the walls; and Mistress Laletta made sure that fresh flowers were to be found on all the tables. The students included eight boys and eight girls of high degree, ranging in age from eight to twelve. Suldrun judged them a mixed lot: some agreeable, others tiresome and dull.

Mistress Laletta, a slender dark-eyed young woman of gentle birth but few prospects, taught competently and showed no favoritism; Suldrun neither liked nor disliked her.

On this morning Mistress Laletta was indisposed and could not teach. Suldrun returned to her chambers to discover Dame Maugelin lying grandly naked on Suldrun's bed, mounted by a hearty young footman named Lopus.

Suldrun watched in startled fascination until Dame Maugelin caught sight of her and uttered a horrified cry.

"Disgusting!" said Suldrun. "And in my bed!"

Lopus, sheepishly disengaging himself, drew on his breeches and departed. Dame Maugelin dressed herself no less hastily, meanwhile making jovial small-talk. "Back so soon from dancing, my dear Princess? Well, then, did you have a good lesson? What you saw was nothing of moment, just a bit of play. Better, far better, if no one knew—" Suldrun spoke in annoyance: "You've soiled my bed!"

"Now then, dear Princess—"

35

"Take all the bedding out—no, first go wash yourself, then bring in all clean bedding and air the room well!"

"Yes, dear Princess." Dame Maugelin hastened to obey, and Suldrun ran off down the stairs, with a lift of the spirits, a skip and a gleeful laugh. Dame Maugelin's strictures might now be dismissed, and Suldrun could do as she pleased.

Suldrun ran up the arcade, scanned the Urquial to make sure that no one watched, then ducked under the old larch and thrust open the groaning old gate. She squeezed through, shut the gate and descended the winding path past the fane and into the garden.

The day was bright and sunny; the air smelled sweet of heliotrope and fresh green leaves. Suldrun surveyed the garden with satisfaction. She had uprooted all those weeds she considered rank and crass, including all the nettles and most of the thistles; the garden now was almost orderly. She had swept leaves and dirt from the tessellated floor of the old villa, and had cleared detritus from the bed of a little stream which trickled down one side of the ravine. There was still much to do, but not today.

Standing in the shadow of a column, she opened the clasp at her shoulder, let her gown drop around her ankles and stepped away naked. Sunlight tingled on her skin; cool air produced a delicious contrast of sensations.

She moved down through the garden. Just so must a dryad feel, thought Suldrun; just so must it move, in just such a hush, with no sound but the sigh of the wind in the leaves.

She halted in the shade of the solitary old lime tree, then continued down to the beach to see what the waves had brought in. When the wind blew from the southwest, as was often the case, the currents swung around the headland and curled into her little cove, bringing all manner of stuff to the beach until the next high tide, when the same current lifted the articles and took them away once more. Today the beach was clean. Suldrun ran back and forth, skirting the surf as it moved along the coarse sand. She halted to scrutinize a rock fifty yards out under the headland, where she once had discovered a pair of young mermaids. They had seen her and called out, but they used a slow strange language Suldrun could not understand. Their olive-green hair hung about their pale shoulders; their lips and the nipples of their breasts were also a pale green. One waved and Suldrun saw the webbing between her fingers. Both turned and looked offshore to where a bearded merman reared from the waves. He called out in a hoarse windy voice; the mermaids slipped from the rocks and disappeared.

Today the rocks were bare. Suldrun turned and walked slowly up into the garden.

She dressed in her rumpled frock and returned to the top of the ravine. First a peek through the gateway to make sure no one watched, then quickly through and a run, hop and skip back down the arcade, past the orangery and once more into Haidion.

A summer storm blowing in from the Atlantic brought a soft rain to Lyonesse Town. Suldrun was confined to Haidion. One afternoon she wandered into the Hall of Honors.

Haidion was quiet; the castle seemed to hold its breath. Suldrun walked slowly around the room, examining each of the great chairs as if to appraise its strength. The chairs in turn considered her. Some stood proud and aloof; others were surly. Some were dark and sinister, others benevolent. At the throne of King Casmir Suldrun surveyed the dark red gonfalon which concealed the back room. Nothing, she told herself, could induce her to venture within; not with magic so close.

Stepping to the side she evaded the purview of the throne and felt more at ease. There, not ten feet from her face, hung the gonfalon. Naturally she dared not enter, nor even approach, the back room... Still, to look would cause no harm.

On soft feet she sidled close to the hanging, and gently pulled it aside. Light from the high windows passed over her shoulder to fall on the far stone wall. There: in a crevice, the iron rod. There: the upper and lower lock-holes. And beyond, the room where only King Casmir might go... Suldrun let the panels come together. She turned away and, in a sober mood, departed the Hall of Honors.

Relations between Lyonesse and Troicinet, never warm, had become strained, for a variety of reasons, which, trifle by trifle, acted to create hostility. The ambitions of King Casmir excluded neither Troicinet nor Dascinet, and his spies pervaded every level of Troice society.

King Casmir was handicapped in his program by the absence of a navy. Despite a long coastline, Lyonesse lacked easy access to the sea, with blue-water ports only at Slute Skeme, Bulmer

Skeme, Lyonesse Town and Pargetta behind Cape Farewell. The indented coast of Troicinet created dozens of sheltered harbors, each with piers, yards and ways. There was an amplitude both of skilled shipwrights and good timber: hackberry and larch for knees, oak for frames, stands of young pinhead spruce for masts, and a dense resinous pine for planking. Troice merchant ships ranged north to Jutland, Britain and Ireland, south down the Atlantic to Mauretania, and the Kingdom of the Blue Men, east past Tingis and into the Mediterranean.

King Casmir considered himself a master of intrigue and sought incessantly for some trifling advantage which he might exploit. On one occasion a heavily laden Troice cog, inching along the coast of Dascinet in a dense fog ran aground on a sand bank. Yvar Excelsus, the irascible King of Dascinet, instantly claimed the vessel and its cargo, citing maritime law, and sent lighters to unload the cargo. A pair of Troice warships appeared, repelled what was now a swarming flotilla of half-piratical Dasce, and at high tide pulled the cog into deep water.

In a fury King Yvar Excelsus sent an abusive message to King Granice at Alceinor demanding reparations, upon pain of punitive action.

King Granice, who well knew the temperament of Yvar Excelsus, ignored the message, exasperating the Dasce king almost to a state of incandescence.

King Casmir now dispatched a secret emissary to Dascinet, urging attack upon Troicinet, and promising full assistance. Troice spies intercepted the envoy and took him with his documents to Alceinor.

A week later a cask was delivered to King Casmir at Haidion, in which he discovered the body of his envoy with the documents crammed into his mouth.

Meanwhile King Yvar Excelsus became distracted by another matter, and his threats against Troicinet came to nothing.

King Granice made no further remonstrance to King Casmir, but began seriously to consider the possibility of an unwelcome war. Troicinet, with a population half that of Lyonesse, could never expect to win such a war and hence had nothing to gain and everything to lose.

From the town Pargetta, close by Cape Farewell, came ill reports of pillage and slaughter by the Ska. Two black ships, arriving at dawn, discharged troops who looted the town with a dispassionate precision more terrifying than savagery. All who interfered were killed. The Ska took crocks of olive oil, saffron, wine, gold from the Mithraic temple, tin and silver ingots, flasks of quicksilver. They took away no captives, put torches to no buildings, committed no rape or torture, and killed only those folk who impeded their robbery.

Two weeks later a Troice cog, putting into Lyonesse Town with a cargo of Irish flax, reported a disabled Ska ship in the Sea of Tethra, west of Cape Farewell. The Troice cog had put in close to discover forty Ska sitting at their benches too weak to row. The Troice had offered a tow, but the Ska refused to take a line, and the cog sailed away.

King Casmir instantly despatched three war-galleys to the area, where they found the long black ship wallowing dismasted in the swells.

The galleys drew up alongside, to discover disaster, anguish and death. A storm had broken the vessel's back-stay; the mast had collapsed upon the forepeak, crushing the water casks, and half the ship's complement already had succumbed to thirst.

Nineteen men survived; too weak to offer resistance, they were taken aboard the Lyonesse ships and given water. A line was made fast to the long-ship; the corpses were thrown overboard and all returned to Lyonesse Town, and the Ska were jailed in an old fort at the west end of the harbor. King Casmir, riding his horse Sheuvan, went down to the harbor to inspect the long-ship. The contents of the forward and after cargo holds had been conveyed to the dock: a case of gold and silver temple adornments, glass jars of saffron gathered from the sheltered valleys behind Cape Farewell, pottery urns stamped with the symbol of the Bulmer Skeme press.

King Casmir inspected the loot and the long-ship, then rode Sheuvan around the Chale to the fortress. At his command the prisoners were brought out and ranked before him, to stand blinking into the sunlight: tall dark-haired men, pale of complexion, thin and sinewy rather than massive. They looked about them with the easy curiosity of honored guests, and spoke to each other in soft measured voices.

King Casmir addressed the group. "Which among you is captain of the vessel?"

The Ska turned to look at him, politely enough, but no one answered.

King Casmir pointed to a man in the front rank. "Which man

among you is in authority? Point him out."

"The captain is dead. We are all 'dead.' Authority is gone, and everything else of life."

"To me you appear quite alive," said Casmir, smiling coldly.

"We reckon ourselves dead."

"Because you expect to be killed? Suppose I allowed you ransom?"

"Who would ransom a dead man?"

King Casmir made an impatient gesture. "I want information, not garble and cant." He looked through the group and in one man, somewhat older than the others, thought to recognize the quality of authority. "You will remain here." He signaled the guards. "Take the others back to confinement."

King Casmir took the man he had selected aside. "Are you also 'dead'?"

"I am no longer among the living Ska. To my family, my comrades and myself, I am dead."

"Tell me this: Suppose I wished to confer with your king, would he come to Lyonesse under guarantees of protection?"

"Naturally not." The Ska seemed amused.

"Suppose I wished to explore the possibility of an alliance?"

"To what end?"

"The Ska navy and the seven Lyonesse armies, acting in concert, might be invincible."

"'Invincible'? Against whom?"

King Casmir disliked anyone who pretended to more acuity than himself. "Against all others of the Elder Isles! Whom else?"

"You imagine the Ska assisting you against your enemies? The idea is preposterous. If I were alive I would laugh. The Ska are at war with all the world, including Lyonesse."

"That is no vindication. I am about to adjudge you a pirate."

The Ska looked up at the sun, around the sky and out over the sea. "Do as you like. We are dead."

King Casmir showed a grim smile. "Dead or not, your fate shall serve to daunt other murderers, and the time shall be noon tomorrow."

Along the breakwater nineteen frames were erected. The night passed; the day dawned bright and clear. By mid-morning crowds had assembled along the Chale, including folk from coastal villages, peasants in clean smocks and bell-hats, vendors of sausages and dried fish. On the rocks west of the Chale crawled cripples, lepers and the weak-minded, in accordance with the statutes of Lyonesse.

The sun reached the zenith. The Ska were led from the fortress. Each was spread-eagled naked to a frame and hung upside down, facing out to sea. Down from the Peinhador came Zerling, the Chief Executioner. He walked along the row, stopped by each man, slit the abdomen, drew out the intestines with a double-pronged hook, so that they fell over the chest and head, then moved on to the next. A black and yellow flag was hoisted at the entrance to the harbor, and the dying men were left to themselves.

Dame Maugelin pulled an embroidered bonnet over her head and went down to the Chale. Suldrun thought that she might be left to herself, but Dame Boudetta took her to the balcony outside the Queen's bedchamber, where ladies of the court gathered to watch the execution. At noon the conversations halted and all pressed to the balustrade to view the proceedings. As Zerling went about his duties, the ladies sighed and made murmuring sounds. Suldrun was lifted to the balustrade the better that she might learn the fate accorded to outlaws. In fascinated revulsion she watched Zerling saunter from man to man, but distance concealed the details of his work.

Few of the ladies present spoke favorably of the occasion. For Lady Duisane and Lady Ermoly who suffered poor vision, the distances were too great. Lady Spaneis pronounced the affair simply dull. "It was like butcher's work upon dead animals; the Ska showed neither fear nor penitence; what kind of execution is that?" Queen Sollace grumbled: "Worst of all, the wind blows directly across the harbor and into our windows. In three days the stink will drive us off to Sarris."

Suldrun listened in hope and excitement; Sarris was the summer palace, some forty miles to the east beside the river Glame.

But there was no instant removal to Sarris, despite the inclinations of Queen Sollace. The corpses were quickly scavenged by carrion birds. King Casmir became bored with the frames and the fragments of bone and gristle hanging at odd angles, and ordered the display dismantled.

Haidion was quiet. Dame Maugelin, suffering from swollen legs, lay moaning in her chamber, high in the Tower of Owls. Suldrun, alone in her room, became restless, but a blustering wind, raw and cold, dissuaded her from the secret garden.

Suldrun stood looking from the window, troubled by a sweet sad malaise. Oh! for a magic steed to carry her away through the air! How far she would fly, across the white clouds, over the Land of the Silver River, to the mountains at the edge of the world.

For a breathless moment she thought how it would be to don her cloak, slip from the palace and be away: up the Sfer Arct to Old Street, with all the wide land before her! She sighed and smiled a wan smile for the folly of her fancies. The vagabonds she had seen from the parapets were by and large a disreputable lot, hungry and dirty and sometimes rather crass in their habits. Such a life lacked appeal, and now, as she considered the matter, Suldrun decided that she very much enjoyed shelter from the wind and rain and nice clean clothes and the dignity of her person.

If only she had a magic carriage which at night became a little cottage where she could dine on the things she liked and sleep in a snug bed!

She sighed once more. An idea came into her mind. She licked her lips at the audacity. Dared she? What harm could be done, if she were extremely careful? She thought a moment, lips pursed and head tilted sideways: the definitive image of a girl planning mischief.

At the hearth Suldrun put flame to the candle in her night-lamp and drew down the hood. Carrying the candle she descended the stairs.

The Hall of Honors was dim and dreary, and quiet as the grave. Suldrun entered the chamber with exaggerated stealth. Today the great chairs gave her small attention. The unfriendly chairs maintained a stony reserve; the kind chairs seemed absorbed in their own affairs. Very well, let them ignore her. Today she would ignore them as well.

Suldrun went around the throne to the back wall, where she slid the hood from her candle. Just one look; that was all she intended. She was far too wise a girl to venture into danger. She pushed aside the hanging. Candlelight illuminated the room, and the stone wall to the rear.

Suldrun hurriedly found the iron rod; if she hesitated her daring might desert her. Quick then! She pushed the rod into the holes, bottom and top, and returned the iron to its place.

The door shuddered open, releasing a plane of purple-green

light. Suldrun moved a tentative step forward; no more than a peep or two! Wary now, and slow! Magic had its entrapments: so much she knew.

She eased the door open. The room swam in layers of colored light: green, purple, persimmon red. To one side was a table supporting a peculiar instrument of glass and carved black wood. Flasks, bottles and squat stoneware pots were ranged on shelves, as well as books, librams, touch-stones and mogrifiers. Suldrun came a cautious pace forward. A soft throaty voice called out: "Who comes to see us, quiet as a mouse, a nose at a time, with small white fingers and the smell of flowers?"

A second voice said: "Come in, come in! Perhaps you will do a kind service, to earn our blessings and our rewards."

On the table Suldrun saw a green glass bottle of a size to hold a gallon. The mouth fitted tightly about the neck of a double-headed homunculus, so that only its two small heads protruded. These were squat, no larger than cat-size, with wrinkled bald pates, snapping black eyes, a nose and oral apparatus of tough brown horn. The body was obscured by the glass and a dark liquid, like strong beer. The heads craned to look at Suldrun, and both spoke: "Ah, what a pretty girl!" "And kind-hearted as well!" "Yes, that's Princess Suldrun; already she is known for good works." "Have you heard how she nursed a little sparrow back to its health?" "Come a bit closer, my dear, so that we may enjoy your beauty."

Suldrun remained where she stood. Other objects claimed her attention, but all seemed curious and items to excite amazement rather than functional equipment. An urn exuded the colored light which like liquid flowed down or drifted up to its proper level. On the wall hung an octagonal mirror in a frame of tarnished wood. Farther along, pegs supported a quasi-human skeleton of black bones, slender as withes. From the shoulder blades protruded a pair of curving pinions, punctured with dozens of sockets, from which might have grown feathers, or scales. The skeleton of a demon? Looking into the eye sockets Suldrun felt an eery conviction that the creature had never flown the air of Earth.

The imps called out in hearty tones: "Suldrun, beautiful princess! Step forward!" "Give us the benefit of your presence!"

Suldrun moved a step farther into the room. She bent to examine a plumb-bob suspended over a dish of roiling quicksilver. On the wall above a leaden tablet displayed a set of crabbed black characters which altered as she watched: a remarkable object indeed! Suldrun wondered what the characters portended; they were like none she had seen before.

A voice issued from the mirror, and Suldrun saw that a lower section of the frame had been shaped to represent a wide mouth, curled up at the corners. "The characters read thus: 'Suldrun, sweet Suldrun, leave this room before harm arrives upon you!'"

Suldrun looked about her. "What would harm me?"

"Let the bottled imps clamp your hair or your fingers and you will learn the meaning of harm."

The two heads spoke at the same time: "What a wicked remark! We are as faithful as doves." "Oh! It is bitter to be maligned, when we cannot seek redress for the wrong!"

Suldrun shrank even farther to the side. She turned to the mirror. "Who is it that is speaking?"

"Persilian."

"You are kind to warn me."

"Perhaps. Perversity moves me from time to time."

Suldrun came cautiously forward. "May I look in the mirror?"

"Yes, but be warned: what you see you may not like!"

Suldrun paused to reflect. What might she not wish to see? If anything the concept twitched at her curiosity. She slid a three-legged stool across the room and climbed upon it, so that she looked into the mirror. "Persilian; I see nothing. It is like looking into the sky."

The surface of the mirror moved; for an instant a face looked into her own: a man's face. Dark hair curled down past a flawless complexion; fine eyebrows curved over lustrous dark eyes; a straight nose complemented a full supple mouth...The magic faded. Suldrun again stared into a void. In a thoughtful voice she asked: "Who was that?"

"If ever you meet him, he will pronounce his name. If you see him never again, then his name will serve you no purpose."

"Persilian, you mock me."

"Perhaps. From time to time I demonstrate the inconceivable, or mock the innocent, or give truth to liars, or shred the poses of virtue—all as perversity strikes me. Now I am silent; this is my mood."

Suldrun climbed down from the stool, blinking at tears which had come to her eyes. She felt confused and depressed...The two-headed goblin suddenly stretched one of its necks and with its beak seized at Suldrun's hair. It caught only a few strands which it snatched out by the roots. Suldrun stumbled from the room. She started to close the door, then remembered her candle. She ran back into the room, snatched the candle and left. The jeering cries of the two-headed goblin were muffled by the closing of the door.

5

ON THE DAY OF BELTANE, in the spring of the year following Suldrun's eleventh birthday, occurred the ancient rite known as Blodfadh, or "Coming into Flower." With twenty-three other girls of noble lineage, Suldrun stepped through a circlet of white roses, and then led a pavanne with Prince Bellath of Caduz for a partner. Bellath, at the age of sixteen years was spare rather than sturdy. His features were crisp, well-shaped if somewhat austere; his manners were precisely correct and pleasantly modest. In certain qualities he reminded Suldrun of someone else she had known. Who could it be? She searched her mind in vain. As they stepped the careful measures of the pavanne, she studied his face, to discover that he was giving her a similar scrutiny.

Suldrun had decided that she liked Bellath. She laughed self-consciously. "Why do you watch me so intently?"

Bellath asked half-apologetically, "Shall I tell you the truth?"

"Of course."

"Very well, but you must control your anguish. I have been told that you and I are eventually to marry."

Suldrun could find nothing to say. In silence they performed the stately evolutions of the dance.

Bellath finally spoke in anxiety: "I hope that you are not disturbed by what I said?"

"No...I must marry one day—so I suppose. I am not ready to think about it."

Later that night, as she lay in her bed considering the events of the day, Suldrun recalled of whom Prince Bellath reminded her: it was none other than Master Jaimes.

Blodfadh brought changes to Suldrun's life. Despite her inclinations she was moved from her dear and familiar chambers

47

in the East Tower to more commodious quarters on the next floor below, and Prince Cassander moved into Suldrun's old rooms.

Two months previously, Dame Maugelin had died of the dropsy. Her place was taken by a seamstress and a pair of maids.

To Dame Boudetta was given supervision of Prince Cassander. The new archivist, a wizened little pedant names Julias Sagamundus, became Suldrun's instructor in orthography, history and calculation with numbers. For the enhancement of her maidenly graces Suldrun was given into the charge of the Lady Desdea, widow of Queen Sollace's brother, who resided permanently at Haidion and performed genteel duties at the languid behest of Queen Sollace. Forty years old, without property, large-boned, tall, with over-large features and bad breath, Lady Desdea had no prospects whatever; still, she beguiled herself with impossible fantasies. She primped, powdered and perfumed herself; she dressed her chestnut hair in high style, with a complicated bun at the back and twin sponsons of crisp curls confined in nets over her ears.

Suldrun's fresh young beauty and easy absentminded habits rasped the most sensitive fibers of Lady Desdea's disposition. Suldrun's visits to the old garden had now become generally known. Lady Desdea automatically disapproved. For a high-born maiden—or any other kind of maiden—the desire for privacy was not only eccentric; it was absolutely suspicious. Suldrun was somewhat too young to have taken to herself a lover. And yet... The idea was absurd. Her breasts were but nubbins. Still, might she have been beguiled by a faun, who were known to be partial to the tart-sweet charms of young maidens?

So went Lady Desdea's thinking. One day she blandly suggested that Suldrun escort her through the garden. Suldrun tried to evade the issue. "You wouldn't like the place. The path goes over rocks, and there is nothing much to see."

"Still, I think I would like to visit this place."

Suldrun studiously said nothing, but Lady Desdea persisted. "The weather is fine. Suppose we take our little walk now."

"You must excuse me, my lady," said Suldrun politely. "This is a place where I go only when I am alone."

Lady Desdea raised high her thin chestnut eyebrows. "'Alone'? It is not seemly that young ladies of your place should wander alone through remote areas."

Suldrun spoke in a placid and offhand manner, as if enunciating a known truth. "There is no harm enjoying one's private garden."

Lady Desdea could find nothing to say. Later she reported Suldrun's obstinacy to Queen Sollace, who at the moment was testing a new pomade formulated from the wax of lilies. "I've heard something of this," said Queen Sollace, rubbing a gobbet of white cream along her wrist. "She is a strange creature. At her age I had eyes for several gallant lads, but as for Suldrun such ideas never enter her odd little head... Ha! This offers a rich scent! Feel the unction!"

On the next day the sun shone fair among small high cloud-tufts. Reluctantly to her lessons with Julias Sagamundus went Suldrun wearing a prim little lavender and white striped gown gathered high up under her breasts and trimmed with lace at hem and collar. Perched on a stool, Suldrun dutifully wrote the ornate Lyonesse script with a gray goose-quill, so fine and long that the tip twitched a foot above her head. Suldrun found herself gazing out the window ever more frequently, and the characters began to straggle.

Julias Sagamundus, seeing how the wind blew, sighed once or twice, but without emphasis. He took the quill from Suldrun's fingers, packed his exercise books, quills, inks and parchments, and went off about his own affairs. Suldrun climbed down from the stool and stood rapt by the window, as if listening to far music. She turned and left the library.

Lady Desdea emerged into the gallery from the Green Parlor, where King Casmir had instructed her in careful detail. She was only just in time to notice the lavender and white flutter of Suldrun's dress as she disappeared into the Octagon.

Lady Desdea hurried after, heavy with King Casmir's instructions. She went into the Octagon, looked right and left, then went outside, to glimpse Suldrun already at the end of the arcade.

"Ah, Miss Sly-boots!" said Lady Desdea to herself. "Now we shall see. But presently, presently!" She tapped her mouth with her finger, then went up to Suldrun's chambers, and there put inquiries to the maids. Neither knew Suldrun's whereabouts. "No matter," said Lady Desdea. "I know where to find her. Now then, lay out her pale blue afternoon gown with the lace bodice, and all to match, and draw her a bath."

Lady Desdea descended to the gallery and for half an hour sauntered here and there. At last she turned back up the Long Gallery. "Now," she told herself, "now we shall see."

She ascended the arcade and passed through the tunnel out upon the parade ground. To her right wild plum and larch shadowed an old stone wall, in which she spied a dilapidated timber door. She marched forward, ducked under the larch, pushed open the door. A path led away and down through juts and shoulders of rock.

Clutching skirts above ankles, Lady Desdea picked her way down irregular stone steps, which angled first right then left, past an old stone fane. She proceeded, taking great care not to stumble and fall, which would certainly compromise her dignity.

The walls of the ravine spread apart; Lady Desdea overlooked the garden. Step by step she descended the path, and were she not so alert for mischief, she might have noticed the banks of flowers and pleasant herbs, the small stream flowing into artful pools, then tinkling down from stone to stone and into yet another pool. Lady Desdea saw only an area of rocky wasteland, uncomfortable of access, dank and unpleasantly isolated. She stumbled, hurt her foot and cursed, angry at the circumstances which had brought her so far from Haidion, and now she saw Suldrun, thirty feet along the path, quite alone (as Lady Desdea had known she must be; she had only hoped for scandal).

Suldrun heard the steps and looked up. Her eyes glowed blue in a face pale and furious.

Lady Desdea spoke peevishly: "I've hurt my foot on the stones; it's truly a shame."

Suldrun's mouth moved; she could not find words to express herself.

Lady Desdea heaved a sigh of resignation and pretended to look around her. She spoke in a voice of whimsical condescension. "So, my dear Princess, this is your little retreat." She gave an exaggerated shudder, hunching her shoulders. "Aren't you at all sensitive to the air? I feel such a dank waft; it must come from the sea." Again she looked about her, mouth pursed in amused disapproval. "Still, it's a wild little nook, like the world must have been before men appeared. Come, child, show me about."

Fury contorted Suldrun's face, so that teeth showed through her clenched mouth. She raised her hand and pointed. "Go! Go away from here!"

Lady Desdea drew herself up. "My dear child, you are rude. I am only concerned with your welfare and I do not deserve your spite."

Suldrun spoke wildly: "I don't want you here! I don't want you around me at all! Go away!"

Lady Desdea stood back, her face an ugly mask. She seethed with conflicting impulses. Most urgently she wanted to find a switch, lift the impudent child's skirt and lay half a dozen goodly stripes across her bottom: an act in which she dared not indulge herself. Backing away a few steps, she spoke in dreary reproach: "You are the most ungrateful of children. Do you think it pleasure to instruct you in all that is noble and good, and guide your innocence through the pitfalls of the court, when you fail to respect me? I look for love and trust; I find rancor. Is this my reward? I struggle to do my duty; I am told to go away." Her voice became a ponderous drone. Suldrun turned half-away and gave her attention to the flight of a rock-swallow, then another. She watched ocean swells crashing through the offshore rocks, then come twinkling and foaming up to her beach. Lady Desdea spoke on. "I must make clear: not for my benefit do I clamber through rock and thistle to notify you of duties such as today's important reception, as I now have done. No, I must accept the role of meddlesome Lady Desdea. You have been instructed and I can do no more."

Lady Desdea swung around her haunches, trudged up the path and departed the garden. Suldrun watched her go with brooding gaze. There had been an indefinable air of satisfaction in the swing of her arms and the poise of her head. Suldrun wondered what it meant.

The better to protect King Deuel of Pomperol and his retinue from the sun, a canopy of red and yellow silk, the colors of Pomperol, had been erected across the great courtyard at Haidion. Under this canopy King Casmir, King Deuel, and various persons of high degree came to take their pleasure at an informal banquet.

King Deuel, a thin sinewy man of middle years, carried himself with mercurial energy and zest. He had brought only a small entourage: his only son, Prince Kestrel; four knights, sundry aides and lackeys; so that, as King Deuel expressed it, "we are free as birds, those blessed creatures who soar the air, to go where we wish, at our own speed and pleasure!"

Prince Kestrel had achieved his fifteenth year and resembled his father only in his ginger-colored hair. Otherwise he was staid and phlegmatic, with a fleshy torso and a placid expression. King Casmir nonetheless thought of Kestrel as a possible match for the Princess Suldrun, if options more advantageous were not open, and so arranged that a place for Suldrun be laid at the banquet table.

When the place remained vacant, King Casmir spoke sharply aside to Queen Sollace: "Where is Suldrun?"

Queen Sollace gave her marmoreal shoulders a slow shrug. "I can't say. She is unpredictable. I find it easiest to leave her to her own devices."

"All well and good. Nevertheless, I commanded her presence!"

Queen Sollace shrugged once more and reached for a sugarplum. "In that case Lady Desdea must inform us."

King Casmir looked over his shoulder to a footman. "Bring here the Lady Desdea."

King Deuel meanwhile enjoyed the antics of trained animals, which King Casmir had ordained for his pleasure. Bears in blue cocked hats tossed balls back and forth; four wolves in costumes of pink and yellow satin danced a quadrille; six herons with as many crows marched in formation.

King Deuel applauded the spectacle, and was especially enthusiastic in regard to the birds: "Splendid! Are they not worthy creatures, stately and wise? Notice the grace of their marching! A pace: so! Another pace: just so!"

King Casmir acknowledged the compliment with a stately gesture. "I take it that you are partial to birds?"

"I consider them remarkably fine. They fly with an easy courage and a grace far exceeding our own capabilities!"

"Exactly true...Excuse me, I must have a word with Lady Desdea. King Casmir turned aside. "Where is Suldrun?"

Lady Desdea feigned puzzlement. "Is she not here? Most odd! She is stubborn, and perhaps a bit wayward, but I cannot believe her to be wilfully disobedient."

"Where is she then?"

Lady Desdea made a facetious grimace and waved her fingers. "As I say, she is a headstrong child and given to vagaries. Now she has taken a fancy to an old garden under the Urquial. I have tried to dissuade her, but she makes it her favored resort."

King Casmir spoke brusquely. "And she is there now? Un-attended?"

"Your Majesty, she permits no one in the garden but herself, or so it would seem. I spoke to her and communicated Your Majesty's wishes. She would not listen and sent me away. I assume she remains still in the garden."

King Deuel sat enthralled by the performance of a trained ape walking a tightrope. King Casmir murmured an excuse, and strode away. Lady Desdea went about her own affairs with a pleasant sense of achievement.

King Casmir had not set foot in the old garden for twenty years. He descended along a path paved with pebbles set into sand, among trees, herbs and flowers. Halfway to the beach he came upon Suldrun. She knelt in the path, working pebbles into the sand.

Suldrun looked up without surprise. King Casmir silently surveyed the garden, then looked down at Suldrun, who slowly rose to her feet. King Casmir spoke in a flat voice. "Why did you not heed my orders?"

Suldrun stared in slack-jawed puzzlement. "What orders?"

"I required your attendance upon King Deuel of Pomperol and his son Prince Kestrel."

Suldrun cast back into her memory and now recovered the echo of Lady Desdea's voice. Squinting off toward the sea she said: "Lady Desdea might have said something. She talks so much that I seldom listen."

King Casmir allowed a wintry smile to enliven his face. He also felt that Lady Desdea spoke at unnecessary length. Once more he inspected the garden. "Why do you come here?"

Suldrun said haltingly: "I am alone here. No one troubles me."

"But, are you not lonely?"

"No. I pretend that the flowers talk to me."

King Casmir grunted. Such fancies in a princess were un-necessary and impractical. Perhaps she was indeed eccentric. "Should you not entertain yourself among other maids of your station?"

"Father, I do so, at my dancing lessons."

King Casmir examined her dispassionately. She had tucked a small white flower into her gleaming dusty-gold hair; her features were regular and delicate. For the first time King Casmir

53

saw his daughter as something other than a beautiful absent-minded child. "Come along," he said gruffly. "We shall go at once to the reception. Your costume is far from adequate but neither King Deuel nor Kestrel will think the worse of you." He noticed Suldrun's melancholy expression. "Well then, are you reluctant for a banquet?"

"Father, these are strangers; why must I meet them today?"

"Because in due course you must marry and Kestrel might be the most advantageous match."

Suldrun's face fell even further. "I thought that I was to marry Prince Bellath of Caduz."

King Casmir's face became hard. "Where did you hear that?"

"Prince Bellath told me himself."

King Casmir voiced a harsh laugh. "Three weeks ago, Bellath became betrothed to Princess Mahaeve of Dahaut."

Suldrun's mouth sagged. "Is she not already a grown woman?"

"She is nineteen years old and ill-favored to boot. But no matter; he obeyed his father the king, who chose Dahaut over Lyonesse, to his great folly as he will learn... So you became fond of Bellath?"

"I liked him well enough."

"It's of no consequence now. We need both Pomperol and Caduz; if we make a match with Deuel, we'll have them both. Come along, and mind you, show courtesy to Prince Kestrel." He turned on his heel. Suldrun followed him up the path on laggard feet.

At the reception she was seated beside Prince Kestrel, who practiced lofty airs upon her. Suldrun failed to notice. Both Kestrel and the circumstances bored her.

In the autumn of the year King Quairt of Caduz and Prince Bellath went to hunt in the Long Hills. They were set upon by masked bandits and killed. Caduz was thereby plunged into confusion, forboding and doubt.

In Lyonesse King Casmir discovered a claim to the throne of Caduz, stemming from his grandfather Duke Cassander, brother to Queen Lydia of Caduz.

The claim, based upon the flow of lineage from sister to brother, thence to a descendant twice removed, while legal (with qualifications) in Lyonesse and also in the Ulflands, ran counter to the strictly patrilinear customs of Dahaut. The laws of Caduz itself were ambiguous.

The better to press his claim, Casmir rode to Montroc, capital of Caduz, at the head of a hundred knights, which instantly aroused King Audry of Dahaut. He warned that under no circumstances might Casmir so easily annex Caduz to his crown, and began to mobilize a great army.

The dukes and earls of Caduz, thus emboldened, began to express distaste for Casmir, and many wondered, ever more pointedly, as to the identity of bandits so swift, so deadly and so anonymous in a countryside ordinarily so placid.

Casmir saw the way the wind was blowing. One stormy afternoon, as the nobles of Caduz sat in conclave, a weird-woman dressed in white entered the chamber holding high a glass vessel which exuded a flux of colors swirling behind her like smoke. As if in a trance she picked up the crown, set it on the head of Duke Thirlach, husband to Etaine, younger sister to Casmir. The woman in white departed the chamber and was seen no more. After some contention, the omen was accepted at face value and Thirlach was enthroned as the new king. Casmir rode home with his knights, satisfied that he had done all possible to augment his interests, and indeed his sister Etaine, now Queen of Caduz, was a woman of redoubtable personality.

Suldrun was fourteen years old and marriageable. The rumor of her beauty had traveled far, and to Haidion came a succession of young grandees, and others not so young, to judge the fabulous Princess Suldrun for themselves.

King Casmir extended to all an equal hospitality, but was in no hurry to encourage a match until all of his options were clear to him.

Suldrun's life became increasingly complex, what with balls and banquets, fêtes and follies. Some of the visitors she found pleasing, others less so. King Casmir, however, never asked her opinion, which in any case was of no interest to him.

A different sort of visitor arrived at Lyonesse Town: Brother Umphred, a portly round-faced evangelist, originally from Aquitania, who had arrived at Lyonesse by way of Whanish Isle and the Diocese of Skro.

With an instinct as certain and sure as that which takes a ferret to the rabbit's throat, Brother Umphred found the ear of Queen Sollace. Brother Umphred used an insistent mellifluous voice and Queen Sollace became a convert to Christianity.

Brother Umphred established a chapel in the Tower of Palaemon only a few steps from Queen Sollace's chambers.

At Brother Umphred's suggestion, Cassander and Suldrun were baptized and required to attend early morning mass in the chapel.

Brother Umphred attempted next to convert King Casmir, and far overstepped himself.

"Exactly what is your purpose here?" demanded King Casmir. "Are you a spy for Rome?"

"I am a humble servant of the one and all-powerful God," said Brother Umphred. "I carry his message of hope and love to all folk, despite hardship and tribulation; no more."

King Casmir uttered a derisive laugh. "What of the great cathedrals at Avallon and Taciel? Did 'God' supply the money? No. It was milked from peasants."

"Your Majesty, humbly we accept alms."

"It would seem far easier for all-powerful God to create the money...No further proselytizing! If you accept a single farthing from anyone in Lyonesse you will be whipped from here to Port Fader and shipped back to Rome in a sack."

Brother Umphred bowed without visible resentment. "It shall be as you command."

Suldrun found Brother Umphred's doctrines incomprehensible and his manner over-familiar. She stopped attending mass and so incurred her mother's displeasure.

Suldrun found little time for herself. Noble maidens attended most of her waking hours, to chatter and gossip, to plan small intrigues, to discuss gowns and manners, and to analyze the persons who came courting to Haidion. Suldrun found little solitude and few occasions to visit the old garden.

Early one summer morning the sun shone so sweetly and the thrush sang such plaintive songs in the orangery, that Suldrun felt impelled to leave the palace. She pretended indisposition to avoid her maids-in-waiting and furtively, lest someone notice and suspect a lover's tryst, she ran up the arcade, through the old portal and into the garden.

Something had changed. She felt as if she were seeing the garden for the first time, even though every detail, every tree and flower was familiar and dear. She looked about her in sadness for the lost vision of childhood. She saw evidence of neglect: harebells, anemones and violets growing modestly in the shade had been challenged by insolent tufts of rank grass. Opposite, among the cypresses and olive trees, nettles had risen more proudly than the asphodel. The path she had so diligently paved with beach pebbles had been broken by rain.

Suldrun went slowly down to the old lime tree, under which she had passed many dreaming hours...The garden seemed smaller. Ordinary sunlight suffused the air, rather than the old enchantment which had gathered in this place alone, and surely the wild roses had given a richer fragrance when first she had entered the garden? At a crunch of footsteps she looked about to discover a beaming Brother Umphred. He wore a brown cassock tied with a black cord. The cowl hung down between his plump shoulders; his tonsured baldness shone pink.

Brother Umphred, after a quick glance to left and right, bowed and clasped his hands before him. "Blessed princess, surely you have not come so far without escort?"

"Exactly so, since I have come here for solitude." Suldrun's voice was devoid of warmth. "It pleases me to be alone."

Brother Umphred, still smiling, again surveyed the garden. "This is a tranquil retreat. I, too, enjoy solitude; is it possible that we two are cut from the same cloth?" Brother Umphred moved forward, halting no more than a yard from Suldrun. "It is a great pleasure to find you here. I have long wanted to talk to you, in all earnestness."

Suldrun spoke in an even colder voice. "I do not care to talk to you, or anyone else. I came to be alone."

Brother Umphred gave a wry jocular grimace. "I will go at once. Still, do you think it proper to venture alone into a place so secluded? How tongues would wag, were it known! All would wonder whom you favored with such intimacy."

Suldrun turned her back in icy silence. Brother Umphred performed another comical grimace, shrugged, and ambled back up the path.

Suldrun seated herself beside the lime tree. Brother Umphred, so she suspected, had gone up to wait among the rocks, hoping to discover who came to keep rendezvous.

At last she arose and started back up the path. The outrage of Brother Umphred's presence had restored something of the garden's charm, and Suldrun stopped to pull weeds. Perhaps tomorrow morning she would come to uproot the nettles.

Brother Umphred spoke to Queen Sollace, and made a number of suggestions. Sollace reflected, then in a spirit of cold and deliberate malice—she had long decided that she did not particularly care for Suldrun—she gave appropriate orders.

Several weeks passed before Suldrun, despite her resolution, returned to the garden. Upon passing through the old timber door, she discovered a gang of masons at work upon the old fane. They had enlarged the windows, installed a door and broken open the back to expand the interior, and had added an altar. In consternation Suldrun asked the master mason: "What are you building here?"

"Your Highness, we build a churchlet, or a chapel, as it might be called, that the Christian priest may conduct his rituals."

Suldrun could hardly speak. "But—who gave such orders?"

"It was Queen Sollace herself, your Highness, for her ease and convenience during her devotions."

# 6

BETWEEN DASCINET AND TROICINET was Scola, an island of crags and cliffs twenty miles across, inhabited by the Skyls. At the center a volcanic peak, Kro, reminded all of its presence with an occasional rumbling of the guts, a wisp of steam or a bubble of sulfur. From Kro radiated four steep ridges, dividing the island into four duchies: Sadaracx to the north, Corso to the east, Rhamnanthus to the south and Malvang to the west, nominally ruled by dukes who in turn gave fealty to King Yvar Excelsus of Dascinet.

In practice the Skyls, a dark crafty race of unknown origin, were uncontrollable. They lived isolated in mountain glens, emerging only when the time came for dreadful deeds. Vendetta, revenge and counter-revenge ruled their lives. The Skyls' virtues were stealth, reckless elan, blood-lust and stoicism under torment; his word, be it promise, guarantee or threat might be equated with certainty; indeed the Skyl's exact adherence to his pledge often verged upon the absurd. From birth to death his life was a succession of murders, captivities, escapes, wild flights, daring rescues: deeds incongruous in a landscape of Arcadian beauty.

On days of festival truce might be called; then merry-making and reveling exceeded rational bounds. Everything was to excess: tables groaned under the weight of food; fabulous feats of wine drinking were performed; there was passionate music and wild dancing. In sudden spasms of sentiment, ancient enmities might be resolved and feuds of a hundred murders put to rest. Old friendships were made whole, amid tears and reminiscences. Beautiful maidens and gallant lads met and loved, or met and parted. There were rapture and despair, seductions and abductions, pursuits, tragic deaths, virtue blighted and fuel for new vendettas.

The clansmen along the west coast, when the mood came on them, crossed the channel to Troicinet, where they performed mischiefs, including pillage, rape, murder and kidnap.

King Granice had long and often protested the acts to King Yvar Excelsus, who replied in effect that the incursions represented little more than youthful exuberance. He implied that in his opinion the better part of dignity was simply to ignore the nuisances and that, in any event, King Yvar Excelsus knew no practical method of abatement.

Port Mel, at the eastern tip of Troicinet, each year celebrated the summer solstice with a three-day festival and a Grand Pageant. Retherd, the young and foolish Duke of Malvang, in the company of three roistering friends, visited the festival incognito. At the Grand Pageant, they agreed that the maidens who represented the Seven Graces were remarkably charming, but could form no consensus as to which was supreme. They discussed the matter well into the evening over wine, and at last, to resolve the matter in a practical way, kidnapped all seven of the maidens and took them across the water to Malvang.

Duke Retherd was recognized and the news swiftly reached King Granice.

Wasting no time in a new complaint to King Yvar Excelsus, King Granice landed an army of a thousand warriors on Scola, destroyed Retherd's castle, rescued the maidens, gelded the duke and his cronies, then, for good measure, burned a dozen coastal villages.

The three remaining dukes assembled an army of three thousand and attacked the Troice encampment. King Granice had secretly reinforced his expeditionary army with two hundred knights and four hundred heavy cavalry. The undisciplined clansmen were routed; the three dukes were captured and King Granice controlled Scola.

Yvar Excelsus issued an intemperate ultimatum: King Granice must withdraw all troops, pay an indemnity of one hundred pounds of gold, rebuild Malvang Castle and put a bond of another hundred pounds of gold to insure no further offenses against the Kingdom of Dascinet.

King Granice not only rejected the ultimatum but decreed annexation of Scola to Troicinet. King Yvar Excelsus raged, expostulated, then declared war. He might not have acted so strongly had he not recently signed a treaty of mutual assistance with King Casmir of Lyonesse.

At the time King Casmir had thought only to strengthen himself for his eventual confrontation with Dahaut, never expecting to be embroiled in trouble not of his own choosing, especially a war with Troicinet.

King Casmir might have extricated himself by one pretext or another had not the war, upon due reflection, seemed to promise advantage.

King Casmir weighed all aspects of the situation. Allied with Dascinet he might base his armies on Dascinet, then thrust with all force across Scola against Troicinet, and thereby neutralize Troice sea-power, which was otherwise invulnerable.

King Casmir made a fateful decision. He commanded seven of his twelve armies to Bulmer Skeme. Then, citing past sovereignty, present complaints and his treaty with King Yvar Excelsus, he declared war upon King Granice of Troicinet.

King Yvar Excelsus had acted in a fit of fury and drunken bravado. When he became sober he perceived the error of his strategy, which neglected an elemental fact: he was outmatched by the Troice in every category: numbers, ships, military skills and fighting spirit. He could take comfort only in his treaty with Lyonesse, and was correspondingly cheered by King Casmir's ready participation in the war.

The marine transport of Lyonesse and Dascinet assembled at Bulmer Skeme; and there, at midnight, the armies of Lyonesse embarked and sailed for Dascinet. They discovered, first, contrary winds; then at dawn, a fleet of Troice warships.

In the space of two hours half of the overloaded ships of Lyonesse and Dascinet were either sunk or broken on the rocks, with a loss of two thousand men. The lucky half fled back downwind to Bulmer Skeme and grounded on the beach.

Meanwhile a miscellaneous flotilla of Troice merchant ships, coastal cogs and fishing vessels, loaded with Troice troops, put into Arquensio, where they were hailed as Lyonesse troops. By the time the mistake was discovered, the castle had been taken and King Yvar Excelsus captured.

The war with Dascinet was over. Granice declared himself

King of the Outer Islands, a realm still not so populous as either Lyonesse or Dahaut, but which held in total control the Lir and the Cantabrian Gulf.

The war between Troicinet and Lyonesse was now an embarrassment for King Casmir. He proposed a cessation of hostilities and King Granice agreed, subject to certain terms: Lyonesse must cede the Duchy of Tremblance, at the far west of Lyonesse, beyond the Troagh, and undertake to build no warships by which it might again threaten Troicinet.

King Casmir predictably rejected such harsh conditions, and warned of bitter consequences if King Granice persisted in his unreasonable hostility.

King Granice responded, "Let it be remembered: I, Granice, instituted no war upon you. You, Casmir, made wanton war upon me. You were dealt a great and just defeat. Now you must suffer the consequences. You have heard my terms. Accept them or continue a war which you cannot win and which will cost you dearly in men, resources and humiliation. My terms are realistic. I require the Duchy of Tremblance to protect my ships from the Ska. I can land a great force at Cape Farewell when so I choose; be warned."

King Casmir responded in tones of menace: "On the basis of a small and temporary success, you challenge the might of Lyonesse. You are as foolish as you are arrogant. Do you think that you can outmatch our great power? I now declare a proscription against you and all your lineage; you will be hunted as criminals and killed on sight. I have no more words for you."

King Granice replied to the message with the force of his navy. He blockaded the coast of Lyonesse so that not so much as a fishing boat could safely navigate the Lir. Lyonesse took its subsistence from the land, and the blockade meant only nuisance and a continuing affront which King Casmir was powerless to rebuff.

In his turn, King Granice could inflict no great damage upon Lyonesse. Harbors were few and well-defended. Additionally, Casmir maintained a vigilant shore-watch and employed spies, in both Dascinet and Troicinet. Meanwhile, Casmir assembled a council of shipwrights, and charged them to build swiftly and well a fleet of warships to defeat the Troice.

In the estuary of the River Sime, the best natural harbor of all Lyonesse, twelve keels went on the ways, and as many more at smaller yards on the shores of Balt Bay in the Duchy of Fetz.

One moonless night along the Sime, when the ships were framed, planked and ready for launching, six Troice galleys stealthily entered the estuary and, despite fortifications, garrisons and watches, burned the shipyards. Simultaneously Troice raiders landed in small boats along the shores of Balt Bay, burning shipyards, boats on the ways, and a great stock of timber planks. Casmir's plans for a quick armada went glimmering.

In the Green Parlor at Haidion King Casmir breakfasted alone on pickled eel, boiled eggs and scones, then leaned back to ponder his many affairs. The defeat at Bulmer Skeme and its anguish had receded; he was able to assess the aftermath with at least a degree of dispassion.

All in all, there seemed to be scope for cautious optimism. The blockade was a provocation and an insult which for the nonce, in the interests of dignity, he must passively accept. In due course he would inflict harsh retribution, but for the present he must proceed with his grand design: in short, the defeat of King Audry and restoration of the throne Evandig to Haidion.

Dahaut was most vulnerable to attack from the west: so to bypass the line of forts along the Pomperol border. The avenue of such an invasion led north from Nolsby Sevan, past the castle Tintzin Fyral, then north along that road known as the Trompada, into Dahaut. The route was blocked by two staunch fortresses: Kaul Bocach, at the Gates of Cerberus, and Tintzin Fyral itself. A South Ulfish garrison guarded Kaul Bocach, but King Oriante of South Ulfland, in fear of Casmir's displeasure, had already granted Casmir and his armies freedom of passage.

Tintzin Fyral alone stood athwart Casmir's ambition. Tintzin Fyral reared high above two gorges and controlled both the Trompada and the way through Vale Evander into South Ulfland. Faude Carfilhiot, who ruled Vale Evander from his impregnable eyrie, in vanity and arrogance, recognized no master, least of all his nominal sovereign King Oriante.

An under-chamberlain entered the Green Parlor. He bowed before King Casmir. "Sir, a person waits upon your pleasure. He names himself Shimrod and is here, so he declares, at your Majesty's orders."

Casmir straightened in his chair. "Bring him here."

The under-chamberlain retired, to return with a tall young man of spare physique, wearing a smock and trousers of good cloth, low boots and a dark green cap which he doffed to reveal thick dust-colored hair, cut at ear-level after the fashion of the day. His features were regular, if somewhat gaunt: a thin nose, a bony jaw and chin, with a wide crooked mouth and bright gray eyes which gave him a look of droll and easy self-possession, in which there was perhaps not quite enough reverence and abnegation to please King Casmir.

"Sir," said Shimrod, "I am here in response to your urgent request."

Casmir surveyed Shimrod with compressed mouth and head skeptically aslant. "For a fact, you are not as I expected you to be."

Shimrod made a polite gesture, disclaiming responsibility for King Casmir's perplexity.

King Casmir pointed to a chair. "Be seated, if you will." He himself rose and went to stand with his back to the fire. "I am told that you are trained in magic."

Shimrod nodded. "Tongues will wag, at every departure from the ordinary."

Casmir smiled somewhat thinly. "Well then: are these reports accurate?"

"Your majesty, magic is a taxing discipline. Some persons have easy and natural abilities; I am not one of them. I am a careful student of the techniques, but that is not necessarily a measure of my competence."

"What then is your competence?"

"Compared to that of the adepts, the ratio is, let us say, one to thirty."

"You are acquainted with Murgen?"

"I know him well."

"And he has trained you?"

"To a certain extent."

King Casmir kept his impatience under control. Shimrod's airy mannerisms skirted safely around the far edge of insolence; still, Casmir found them irritating, and his response to questions with precise but minimal information made conversation tiresome. Casmir spoke on in an even voice.

"As you must know, our coast is blockaded by the Troice. Can you suggest how I might break this blockade?"

Shimrod reflected a moment. "Everything considered, the simplest way is to make peace."

"No doubt." King Casmir pulled at his beard; magicians were odd folk. "I prefer a method, possibly more complicated, which will advance the interests of Lyonesse."

"You would have to counter the blockade with a superior force."

"Exactly so. That is the crux of my difficulty. I have thought to enlist the Ska as allies, and I wish you to foretell the consequences of such an act."

Shimrod smilingly shook his head. "Your Majesty, few magicians can read the future. I am not one of them. Speaking as a man of ordinary common sense, I would advise you against such an act. The Ska have known ten thousand years of travail; they are a harsh folk. Like you, they intend to dominate the Elder Isles. Invite them into the Lir, give them bases, and they will never depart. So much is obvious."

King Casmir's gaze narrowed; he was seldom dealt with so briskly. Still, so he reasoned, Shimrod's manner might well be a measure of his candor; no one attempting to dissemble would use quite so easy a tone. He asked in a carefully neutral voice: "What do you know of Tintzin Fyral the castle?"

"This is a place I have never seen. It is said to be impregnable, as I am sure you already know."

King Casmir gave a crisp nod. "I have also heard that magic is part of its defense."

"As to that I can't say. It was built by a lesser magician, Ugo Golias, so that he might rule Vale Evander, secure from the syndics of Ys."

"Then how did Carfilhiot gain the property?"

"In this regard I can only repeat rumor."

King Casmir, with an impassive gesture, indicated that Shimrod was to proceed.

"Carfilhiot's own lineage is a matter of doubt," said Shimrod. "It's quite possible that he was sired by the sorcerer Tamurello upon the witch Desmëi. Still, nothing is known certainly except that first Desmëi disappeared, then Ugo Golias, with all of his staff, as if devils had snatched them away, and the castle was empty until Carfilhiot arrived with a troop of soldiers and took possession."

"It would seem that he also is a magician."

"I think not. A magician would conduct himself differently."

"Then you are acquainted with him?"

"Not at all. I have never seen him."

"Still, you appear to be familiar with his background and personality."

"Magicians are as prone to gossip as anyone else, especially when the subject is as notorious as Carfilhiot."

King Casmir pulled a bell-cord; two footmen entered the parlor with wine, nuts and sweetmeats which they arranged upon the table. King Casmir seated himself across the table from Shimrod. He poured two goblets of wine, one of which he tendered to Shimrod.

"My best respects to your Majesty," said Shimrod.

King Casmir sat looking into the fire. He spoke thoughtfully. "Shimrod, my ambitions are perhaps no secret. A magician such as yourself could provide me invaluable aid. You would find my gratitude commensurate."

Shimrod twirled the goblet of wine and watched the spin of the dark liquid. "King Audry of Dahaut has made the same approach to Tamurello. King Yvar Excelsus sought the aid of Noumique. All refused, by reason of Murgen's great edict, which applies no less to me."

"Pah!" snapped King Casmir. "Does Murgen's authority transcend all other?"

"In this regard—yes."

King Casmir grunted. "Still you have spoken without any apparent restraint."

"I have only advised you as might any reasonable man."

King Casmir rose abruptly to his feet. He tossed a purse upon the table. "That will reimburse your service."

Shimrod turned out the purse. Five golden crowns rolled forth. They became five golden butterflies which fluttered into the air and circled the parlor. The five became ten, twenty, fifty, a hundred. All at once they dropped to cluster upon the table, where they became a hundred gold crowns.

Shimrod took five of the coins, returned them to the purse, which he placed in his pouch. "I thank your Majesty."

He bowed and departed the chamber.

Odo, Duke of Folize, rode with a small company north through the Troagh, a dreary land of crags and chasms, into South Ulfland, past Kaul Bocach where opposing cliffs pressed so close together that three men could not ride abreast.

A fan of small waterfalls fell into the defile to become the south fork of the Evander River; road and river proceeded north side by side. Ahead rose a massive crag: the Tooth of Cronus, or the Tac Tor. Down through a gorge came the north fork of the Evander. The two forks joined and passed between the Tac Tor and the crag which supported the castle Tintzin Fyral.

Duke Odo announced himself at a gate and was conducted up a zig-zag road into the presence of Faude Carfilhiot.

Two days later he departed and returned the way he had come to Lyonesse Town. He alighted in the Armory yard, shook the dust from his cloak and went directly to an audience with King Casmir.

Haidion, at all times an echo chamber of rumor, immediately reverberated to the impending visit of an important grandee, the remarkable lord of a hundred mysteries: Faude Carfilhiot of Tintzin Fyral.

SULDRUN SAT IN THE ORANGERY with her two favorite maids-in-waiting: Lia, daughter to Tandre, Duke of Sondbehar; and Tuissany, daughter to the Earl of Merce. Lia already had heard much talk of Carfilhiot. "He is tall and strong, and is proud as a demigod! His gaze is said to fascinate all who look upon him!"

"He would seem an imposing man," said Tuissany, and both girls looked sidewise at Suldrun, who twitched her fingers.

"Imposing men take themselves too seriously," said Suldrun. "Their talk is mostly orders and complaints."

"There is much else!" declared Lia. "It comes from my seamstress, who heard the conversation of Lady Pedreia. It seems that Faude Carfilhiot is the most romantic of men. Each evening he sits in a high tower watching the stars rise, pining."

"'Pining'? For what?"

"For love."

"And who is the haughty maiden who causes him such pain?"

"That is the curious part. She is imaginary. He worships this maiden of his dreams."

"I find this hard to believe," said Tuissany. "I suspect that he spends more time in bed with real maidens."

"As to that I cannot say. After all, the reports may be exaggerated."

"It will be interesting to discover the truth," said Tuissany. "But here is your father, the king."

Lia rose to her feet as did Tuissany and more slowly Suldrun. All performed a formal curtsy.

King Casmir sauntered forward. "Maidens, I wish to speak with the princess on a private affair; please allow us a few moments alone."

Lia and Tuissany withdrew. King Casmir surveyed Suldrun

a long moment. Suldrun turned half-away, a chill of apprehension at the pit of her stomach.

King Casmir gave a small slow nod of the head, as if in corroboration of some private concept. He spoke in a portentous voice. "You must know that we are expecting the visit of an important person: Duke Carfilhiot of Vale Evander."

"I have heard so much, yes."

"You have come to marriageable age and should Duke Carfilhiot find you pleasing, I would look favorably upon the match, and I shall impart so much to him."

Suldrun raised her eyes to the golden-bearded face. "Father, I am not ready for such an event. I have not the slightest yearning to share a man's bed."

King Casmir nodded. "That is sentiment properly to be expected in a maiden chaste and innocent. I am not displeased. Still, such qualms must bend before affairs of state. The friendship of Duke Carfilhiot is vital to our interests. You will quickly become accustomed to the idea. Now then, your conduct toward Duke Carfilhiot must be amiable and gracious, yet neither fulsome nor exaggerated. Do not press your company upon him; a man like Carfilhiot is stimulated by reserve and reluctance. Still, be neither coy nor cold."

Suldrun cried in distress: "Father, I will not need to feign reluctance! I am not ready for marriage! Perhaps I never shall be!"

"Tush now." King Casmir's voice sharpened. "Modesty is all very well in moderation, even appealing. Still, when exercised to excess it becomes tiresome. Carfilhiot must not think you a prig. These are my wishes; are they quite clear?"

"Father, I understand your wishes very well."

"Good. Make certain that they influence your conduct."

A cavalcade of twenty knights and men-at-arms came down the Sfer Arct and into Lyonesse Town. At their head rode Duke Carfilhiot, erect and easy: a man with black curling hair cropped at his ears, a fair skin, features regular and fine, if somewhat austere, save for the mouth, which was that of a sentimental poet.

In the Armory yard the company halted. Carfilhiot dismounted and his horse was led away by a pair of grooms in the lavender and green of Haidion. His retinue likewise dismounted and ranged themselves behind him.

King Casmir descended from the upper terrace and crossed the yard. Duke Carfilhiot performed a bow of conventional courtesy, as did his company.

"Welcome!" spoke King Casmir. "Welcome to Haidion!"

"I am honored by your hospitality." Carfilhiot spoke in a voice firm, rich and well-modulated but lacking timbre.

"I introduce to you my seneschal, Sir Mungo. He will show you to your rooms. A collation is being laid and when you are refreshed we will take an informal repast on the terrace."

An hour later Carfilhiot stepped out on the terrace. He had changed to a robe of gray and black striped silk, with black trousers and black shoes: an unusual garment which enhanced his already dramatic presence.

King Casmir awaited him by the balustrade. Carfilhiot approached and bowed. "King Casmir, already I am finding pleasure in my visit. The palace Haidion is the most splendid of the Elder Isles. Its prospect over city and sea is without parallel."

King Casmir spoke with stately affability. "I hope that your visit will often be repeated. We are, after all, the closest of neighbors."

"Precisely so!" said Carfilhiot. "Unluckily I am vexed with problems which keep me preoccupied at home; problems happily unknown to Lyonesse."

King Casmir raised his eyebrows. "Problems? We are by no means immune! I count as many problems as there are Troice in Troicinet!"

Carfilhiot laughed politely. "In due course we must exchange commiserations."

"I would as lief exchange problems."

"My robbers, footpads and renegade barons for your blockade of warships? It would seem a bad bargain for both of us."

"As an inducement you might wish to include a thousand of your Ska."

"Gladly, were they my Ska. For some odd reason they avoid South Ulfland, though they rampage across the North blithely enough."

A pair of heralds blew a shrill sweet fanfare, to signal the appearance of Queen Sollace and a train of her ladies.

King Casmir and Carfilhiot turned to meet her. King Casmir presented his guest. Queen Sollace acknowledged Carfilhiot's compliments with a bland stare, which Carfilhiot graciously ignored.

Time passed. King Casmir became restive. He glanced over his shoulder toward the palace ever more frequently. Finally he muttered a few words to a footman, and another five minutes passed.

The heralds raised their clarions and blew another fanfare. Out upon the terrace came Suldrun at a lurching run, as if she had been pushed; in the shadows behind her the contorted face of Lady Desdea showed for an instant.

With a grave face Suldrun approached the table. Her gown, of a soft pink stuff, clung close to her figure; from beneath a round white cap soft golden curls hung to her shoulders.

Slowly Suldrun came forward, followed by Lia and Tuissany. She paused, looked across the terrace, brushing Carfilhiot with her gaze. A steward approached with a tray; Suldrun and her maids took goblets of wine, then went modestly apart, where they stood murmuring together.

King Casmir watched under lowering brows and at last turned to Sir Mungo, his seneschal. "Inform the princess that we wait upon her attendance."

Sir Mungo delivered the message. Suldrun listened with a drooping mouth. She seemed to sigh, then crossed the terrace, halted in front of her father, and performed a somber curtsy.

In his richest tones Sir Mungo declared: "Princess Suldrun, I am honored to introduce to you Duke Faude Carfilhiot of Vale Evander!"

Suldrun inclined her head; Carfilhiot smilingly bowed and kissed her hand. Then raising his head and looking into her face he said: "Rumors of Princess Suldrun's grace and beauty have crossed the mountains to Tintzin Fyral. I see that they were not exaggerated."

Suldrun responded in a colorless voice. "I hope you have not heeded these rumors. I'm sure they would give me no pleasure if I heard them."

King Casmir leaned quickly forward with lowering brows, but Carfilhiot spoke first. "Indeed? How so?"

Suldrun refused to look toward her father. "I am made out to be something I do not choose to be."

"You do not enjoy the admiration of men?"

"I have done nothing admirable."

"Nor has a rose, nor a sapphire of many facets."

"They are ornaments; they have no life of their own."

"Beauty is not ignoble," said King Casmir heavily. "It is a gift bestowed to only a few. Would anyone—even the princess Suldrun—prefer to be ugly?"

Suldrun opened her mouth to say: "I would prefer, first of all, to be somewhere other than here." She thought better of the remark and closed her mouth.

"Beauty is a most peculiar attribute," Carfilhiot declared. "Who was the first poet? It was he who invented the concept of beauty."

King Casmir gave an indifferent shrug and drank from his purple glass goblet.

Carfilhiot continued, his voice easy and musical: "Our world is a place terrible and wonderful, where the passionate poet who yearns to realize the ideal of beauty is almost always frustrated."

Suldrun, her hands clasped together, studied her fingertips. Carfilhiot said, "It would seem that you have reservations?"

"Your 'passionate poet' might well be a very tiresome companion."

Carfilhiot clapped his hand to his forehead in mock-outrage. "You are as heartless as Diana herself. Have you no sympathy for our passionate poet, this poor moon-struck adventurer?"

"Probably not. He seems over-emotional and self-centered, at the very least. The emperor Nero of Rome, who danced to the flames of his burning city, was perhaps such a 'passionate poet.'"

King Casmir made a restive movement; this sort of conversation seemed a pointless frivolity... Still, Carfilhiot appeared to be enjoying himself. Was it possible that timid reclusive Suldrun was cleverer than he had supposed?

Carfilhiot addressed himself to Suldrun: "I find this conversation most interesting. I hope that we can continue it another time?"

Suldrun replied in her most formal voice: "Truly, Duke Carfilhiot, my ideas are not at all profound. I would be embarrassed to discuss them with a person of your experience."

"It shall be as you wish," said Carfilhiot. "Still, please allow me the simple pleasure of your company."

King Casmir hastened to intervene before Suldrun's unpredictable tongue gave offense. "Duke Carfilhiot, I notice certain grandees of the realm who wait to be introduced."

Later King Casmir took Suldrun aside. "I am surprised by your conduct in regard to Duke Carfilhiot! You do more harm

73

than you know; his good will is indispensable to our plans!"

Standing before the majestic bulk of her father, Suldrun felt limp and helpless. She cried out in a plaintive soft voice: "Father, please do not force me upon Duke Carfilhiot! I am frightened by his company!"

King Casmir had prepared himself against piteous appeals. His response was inexorable: "Bah! You are silly and unreasonable. There are far worse matches than Duke Carfilhiot, I assure you. It shall be as I decide."

Suldrun stood with down-turned face. She apparently had no more to say. King Casmir swung away, marched off down the Long Gallery and up the stairs to his chambers. Suldrun stood looking after him, hands clenched and pressed to her sides. She turned and ran down the gallery, out into the fading light of afternoon, up the arcade, through the old gate and down into the garden. The sun, hanging low in the sky, sent a somber light under a tall bank of clouds; the garden seemed cool and remote.

Suldrun wandered down the path, past the ruins, and settled herself under the old lime tree, arms clasped around her knees, and considered the fate which seemed to be advancing upon her. Beyond doubt, or so it seemed to her, Carfilhiot would choose to wed her, take her away to Tintzin Fyral, there, at his own good time, to explore the secrets of her body and her mind... The sun sank into clouds; the wind blew cold. Suldrun shivered. Rising, she returned the way she had come, slowly, with eyes downcast. She climbed to her chambers where Lady Desdea gave her a fretful scolding.

"Where have you been? By the queen's command I must array you in fine garments; there is to be a banquet and dancing. Your bath is ready."

Suldrun passively stepped out of her clothes and into a wide marble basin, brimming with warm water. Her maids rubbed her with soap of olive oil and ash of aloe, then rinsed her in water scented with lemon verbena, and dried her with soft cotton towels. Her hair was brushed till it shone. She was dressed in a dark blue gown and a fillet of silver, set with tablets of lapis lazuli, was placed on her head.

Lady Desdea drew back. "That's the best I can do with you. No doubt but what you are well-favored. Still, something is lacking. You must use a bit of flirtation—not to excess, mind you! Let him know that you understand what he has in mind.

Mischief in a girl is like salt on meat...Now, tincture of foxglove, to sparkle your eyes!"

Suldrun jerked back. "I want none of it!"

Lady Desdea had learned the futility of argument with Suldrun. "You are the most obstinate creature alive! As usual, you shall do as you please."

Suldrun laughed bitterly. "If I did as I pleased, I would not be going to the ball."

"La, then, you saucy mince." Lady Desdea kissed Suldrun on the forehead. "I hope that life will dance to your tune...Come now, to the banquet. I pray you, be civil to Duke Carfilhiot, since your father hopes for a betrothal."

At the banquet King Casmir and Queen Sollace sat at the head of the great table, with Suldrun at her father's right and Carfilhiot to the left of Queen Sollace.

Covertly Suldrun studied Carfilhiot. What with his clear skin, thick black hair and lustrous eyes he was undeniably handsome: almost to an excess. He ate and drank gracefully; his conversation was courteous; perhaps his only affectation was modesty: he spoke little of himself. Yet, Suldrun found herself unable to meet his gaze, and when she spoke to him, as occasion compelled, words came with difficulty.

Carfilhiot sensed her aversion, so she divined, and it only seemed to stimulate his interest. He became even more fulsome, as if he sought to overcome her antipathy by sheer perfection of gallantry. All the while, like a chill on the air, Suldrun felt the careful attention of her father, to such an extent that she began to lose her composure. She bent her head over her plate, but found herself unable to eat.

She reached for her goblet, and chanced to meet Carfilhiot's eyes. For a moment she stared transfixed. He knows what I think, went her thoughts. He knows—and now he smiles, as if already he owned me...Suldrun wrenched her gaze down to her plate. Still smiling, Carfilhiot turned to listen to the remarks of Queen Sollace.

At the ball, Suldrun thought to evade notice by mingling with her maids-in-waiting, but to no effect. Sir Eschar, the underseneschal, came to seek her out and took her into the presence of King Casmir, Queen Sollace, and Duke Carfilhiot, and other high dignitaries. When the music started, she was convenient to the arm of Duke Carfilhiot and dared not refuse.

In silence they stepped the measures, back and forth, bowing, turning with graceful gesture, among colored silks and sighing satins. A thousand candles in six massive candelabra suffused the chamber with mellow light.

When the music stopped, Carfilhiot led Suldrun to the side of the room, and somewhat apart. "I hardly know what to say to you," Carfilhiot remarked. "Your manner is so glacial as to seem menacing."

Suldrun replied in her most formal voice: "Sir, I am unaccustomed to grand affairs, and in all truth they do not amuse me."

"So that you would prefer to be elsewhere?"

Suldrun looked across the chamber to where Casmir stood among the grandees of his court. "My preferences, whatever they may be, seem to be of consequence only to myself. So I have been given to understand."

"Surely you are mistaken! I, for one, am interested in your preferences. In fact I find you most unusual."

Suldrun's only response was an indifferent shrug and Carfilhiot's airy whimsicality for a brief moment became strained, even a trifle sharp. "Meanwhile, your opinion of me is a person ordinary, drab and perhaps something of a bore?" So much said in the hope of exciting a tumble of embarrassed disclaimers.

Suldrun, looking off across the room, responded in an absentminded voice: "Sir, you are my father's guest; I would not presume to form such an opinion, or any opinion whatever."

Carfilhiot uttered a soft strange laugh, so that Suldrun turned in startled puzzlement, to look as through a rift into Carfilhiot's soul, which quickly made itself whole. Once more debonair, Carfilhiot held out his hands, to express polite and humorous frustration. "Must you be so aloof? Am I truly deplorable?"

Suldrun once more used cool formality. "Sir, certainly you have given me no reason to form such judgments."

"But is that not an artificial pose? You must know that you are admired. I for one am anxious to gain your favorable opinion."

"Sir, my father wants to marry me away. That is well-known. He pushes me faster than I want to go; I know nothing of love or loving."

Carfilhiot took both of her hands and compelled her to face him. "I will reveal some arcane facts. Princesses seldom marry their lovers. As for loving, I would willingly teach a pupil so innocent, and so beautiful. You would learn overnight, so to speak."

Suldrun pulled her hands away. "Let us rejoin the others."

Carfilhiot escorted Suldrun to her place. A few minutes later she informed Queen Sollace that she felt unwell, and slipped quietly from the chamber. King Casmir, elevated by drink, failed to notice.

On Derfwy Meadow, two miles south of Lyonesse Town, King Casmir ordained a pageant and pleasure fair, to celebrate the presence of his honored guest: Faude Carfilhiot, Duke of Vale Evander and Lord of Tintzin Fyral. Preparations were elaborate and bountiful. Bullocks had been turning over coals since the preceding day, with good bastings of oil, onion juice, garlic and syrup of tamarind; now they were done to a turn and exuded a tantalizing waft across all the meadow. Trays nearby were heaped high with loaves of white bread, and to the side six tuns of wine awaited only a starting of the bungs.

Villages of the neighborhood had sent young men and women in festival costumes; to the music of drums and pipes, they danced jigs and kick-steps, until sweat beaded their foreheads. At noon clowns fought with bladders and wooden swords; and somewhat later, knights of the royal court jousted* with lances tipped with leather pillows.

Meanwhile, the roast meat had been lifted to the carving table, cut into slices and chunks and taken away on half-loaves of bread by all who chose to partake of the king's bounty, while wine bubbled happily through the spigots.

King Casmir and Carfilhiot watched the jousting from a raised platform, in company with Queen Sollace, Princess Suldrun, Prince Cassander and a dozen others of rank. King Casmir and Carfilhiot then strolled across the meadow to watch an archery contest, and conversed to the hiss and *chunk* of arrow striking into butt. Two from Carfilhiot's retinue had entered the contest and were shooting with such proficiency that King Casmir was moved to comment.

Carfilhiot responded: "I command a relatively small force, and all must excel with their weapons. I reckon each soldier the

---

*The tournament in which armored knights jousted with lances, or fought mock battles, had not yet evolved. Contests of this time and place were relatively mild events: competitions at wrestling, horse-racing, vaulting: events in which the aristocracy seldom if ever competed.

equal of ten ordinaries. He lives and dies by steel. Nonetheless, I envy you your twelve great armies."

King Casmir gave a dour grunt. "Twelve armies are a fine thing to command, and King Audry sleeps poorly on their account. Still, twelve armies are useless against the Troice. They sail back and forth along my shores; they laugh and joke; they pull up beside my harbor and show me their naked backsides."

"Well beyond bow-shot, no doubt."

"Fifty yards beyond bow-shot."

"Most vexing."

King Casmir spoke weightily: "My ambitions are no secret. I must reduce Dahaut, subdue the Ska, and defeat the Troice. I will bring the throne Evandig and the table Cairbra an Meadhan to their rightful places and once more the Elder Isles will be ruled by a single king."

"That is a noble ambition," said Carfilhiot graciously. "Were I King of Lyonesse I would strive no differently."

"The strategies are not easy. I can work south against the Troice, with the Ska as allies; or into the Ulflands, presupposing that the Duke of Vale Evander allows me thoroughfare past Tintzin Fyral. Then my armies drive the Ska from the Foreshore, overawe the Godelians and turn eastward into Dahaut for the climactic campaign. With a flotilla of a thousand ships I overwhelm Troicinet, and the Elder Isles are once more a single kingdom, with the Duke of Vale Evander, now Duke of South Ulfland."

"It is a pretty concept; and, I would think, feasible. My own ambitions are not affected; indeed I am content with Vale Evander. I have yearnings of quite a different sort. In all candor, I have become enamored of the Princess Suldrun. I find her the most beautiful of living creatures. Would you consider me presumptuous if I asked her hand in marriage?"

"I would consider it a most suitable and auspicious match."

"I am happy to hear your approval. What of Princess Suldrun? She has allowed me no conspicuous favor."

"She is somewhat fanciful. I will have a word with her. To-morrow you and she shall take your betrothal vows in a ceremonial rite, and nuptials will follow in due course."

"This is a joyful prospect, for myself and, so I hope, the Princess Suldrun as well."

* * *

Late in the afternoon the royal carriage returned to Haidion, with King Casmir, Queen Sollace and Princess Suldrun. Riding on horseback beside were Carfilhiot and young Prince Cassander.

King Casmir spoke to Suldrun in a ponderous voice: "Today I have conferred with Duke Carfilhiot, and he declares himself enamored of you. The match is advantageous and I agreed to your betrothal."

Suldrun stared aghast, her worst apprehensions realized. Finally she found her tongue. "Sir, can you not believe me? I want no marriage now, least of all to Carfilhiot! He does not suit me at all!"

King Casmir brought the full impact of his round-eyed blue gaze to bear on Suldrun. "This is niminy-piminy petulance; I will not hear of it. Carfilhiot is a noble and handsome man! Your qualms are over-nice. Tomorrow at noon you will pledge troth with Carfilhiot. In three months you shall marry. There is no more to be said."

Suldrun subsided into the cushions. The carriage rumbled along the road, swaying on springs of layered hornbeam. Poplars beside the road passed in front of the sun. Through tears Suldrun watched lights and shadows playing across her father's face. In a soft broken voice she essayed a final plea: "Father, do not force this marriage on me!"

King Casmir listened stolidly, and turning his face away, made no reply.

In anguish Suldrun looked to her mother for support, but saw only waxen dislike. Queen Sollace said tartly: "You are marriageable, as anyone with eyes can see. It is time you were away from Haidion. With your vapors and vagaries you have brought us no joy."

King Casmir spoke. "As a princess of Lyonesse you know neither toil nor care. You dress in soft silk and enjoy luxuries beyond the hopes of ordinary women. As a princess of Lyonesse you also must bend to the dictates of policy, even as I. The marriage will proceed. Have done with this petty diffidence and approach Duke Carfilhiot with amiability. I will hear no more on the subject."

Upon arrival at Haidion, Suldrun went directly to her chambers. An hour later, Lady Desdea found her staring into the fire.

"Come now," said Lady Desdea. "Moping causes the flesh to sag and yellows the skin. Be of good cheer then! The king desires your presence at the evening meal, in an hour's time."

"I prefer not to go."

"Still, you must! The king has given his order. So hey nonny no! To supper we shall go. You shall wear the dark green velvet which becomes you so that every other woman looks a dead fish. Were I younger I would gnash my teeth for jealousy. I cannot understand why you sulk."

"I have no taste for Duke Carfilhiot."

"Tush. In marriage all things alter. You may come to dote on him; then you will laugh to think of your foolish whims. Now then—off with your clothes! Heigh ho! Think how it will be when Duke Carfilhiot gives the command! Sosia! Where is that flibbet of a maid? Sosia! Brush the princess's hair, a hundred strokes to either side. Tonight it must glisten like a river of gold!"

At the supper Suldrun tried to achieve an impersonal manner. She tasted a morsel of stewed pigeon; she drank half a glass of pale wine. When remarks were addressed to her she responded politely, but clearly her thoughts were elsewhere. Once, looking up, she met Carfilhiot's gaze, and for a moment stared into his lambent eyes like a fascinated bird.

She shifted her gaze and broodingly studied her plate. Carfilhiot was undeniably gallant, brave and handsome: Why then her antipathy? She knew her instincts to be accurate. Carfilhiot was involuted; his mind teemed with strange rancors and peculiar inclinations. Words entered her mind as if from another source: *For Carfilhiot beauty was not to be cherished and loved, but something to be plundered and hurt.*

The ladies left for the queen's drawing-room; Suldrun quickly ran off to her own chambers.

Early in the morning a brief rain swept in from the sea, to wash the greenery and settle the dust. By midmorning the sun shone through broken clouds, and sent hurrying shadows across the city. Lady Desdea arrayed Suldrun in a white gown with a white surcoat, embroidered in pink, yellow and green; and a small white cap inside a golden diadem studded with garnets.

On the terrace, four precious rugs had been laid end to end, from Haidion's ponderous main entrance to a table draped with heavy white linen. Antique silver vases four feet tall overflowed with white roses; the table supported the sacred chalice of the Lyonesse kings: a silver vessel a foot tall, carved with characters no longer intelligible to Lyonesse.

As the sun rose toward noon, dignitaries began to appear, wearing ceremonial robes and ancient emblems.

At noon Queen Sollace arrived. She was escorted by King Casmir to her throne. Behind came Duke Carfilhiot, escorted by Duke Tandre of Sondbehar.

A moment passed. King Casmir looked toward the door, where the Princess Suldrun should now be appearing, on the arm of her aunt, the Lady Desdea. Instead, he glimpsed only a flutter of agitated motion. Presently he noted the beckoning arm of Lady Desdea.

King Casmir rose from the throne and strode back to the palace where Lady Desdea stood gesturing in confusion and bewilderment.

King Casmir looked around the foyer, then turned back to Lady Desdea. "Where is Princess Suldrun? Why do you cause this undignified delay?"

Lady Desdea blurted an explanation: "She was ready! She stood there beautiful as an angel. I led the way downstairs; she followed. I went along the gallery, and I had a strange feeling! I stopped and turned to look, and she stood there, pale as a lily. She called out something, but I could not quite hear; I think she said: 'I cannot! No, I cannot!' And then she was gone, out the side door and away up under the arcade! I called after her, to no avail. She would not look back!"

King Casmir turned and walked out on the terrace. He halted, looked around the half-circle of questioning faces. He spoke in a harsh monotone. "I beg the indulgence of those now assembled. The Princess Suldrun has suffered indisposition. The ceremony will not proceed. A collation has been laid out; please partake as you wish."

King Casmir turned and re-entered the palace. Lady Desdea stood to the side, hair in disorder, arms hanging like ropes.

King Casmir inspected her for five seconds, then stalked from the palace. Up the arcade, under Zoltra Bright Star's Wall, through the timber gate and down into the old garden, he strode. Here Suldrun sat, on a fallen column, elbows on knees and chin in her hands.

King Casmir halted twenty feet behind her. Slowly Suldrun looked around, eyes wide, mouth drooping.

King Casmir said: "You have come to this place in defiance of my command."

Suldrun nodded. "I did so: yes."

"You have marred the dignity of Duke Carfilhiot in a manner which can know no mitigation."

Suldrun's mouth moved, but no words came. King Casmir spoke on.

"For frivolous whim you have come here rather than in dutiful obedience to the place required by my command. Therefore, remain in this place, both night and day, until the great hurt you have done me is assuaged, or until you are dead. If you depart either boldly or by stealth, you shall be slave to whomever first lays claim to you, be he knight or peasant, loon or vagabond; no matter! You shall be his thing."

King Casmir turned, climbed the path, passed through the gate which closed hard behind him.

Suldrun turned slowly, face blank and almost serene. She looked out to sea, where rays of sunlight shot through gaps in the clouds and down at the water.

King Casmir found a silent group awaiting him on the terrace. He looked this way and that. "Where is Duke Carfilhiot?"

Duke Tandre of Sondbehar came forward. "Sire, upon your departure he waited one minute. Then he called for his horse, and with his company he rode from Haidion."

"What said he?" cried King Casmir. "Gave he no notice of any kind?"

Duke Tandre responded, "Sire, he spoke no word."

King Casmir cast one terrible glance around the terrace, then turned and walked on long strides back into the palace Haidion.

King Casmir brooded for a week, then uttered an angry expletive and set himself to the composition of a letter. The final version read:

> For The Notice Of
> The Noble Duke Faude Carfilhiot
> At Tintzin Fyral His Castle.

Noble Sir:
　　With difficulty I write these words, in reference to an incident which has given me great embarrassment. I can not properly apologize, since I am as much victim of the circumstances as yourself—perhaps even more. You suffered an affront which understandably caused you exasperation. Still, there is no doubt but what a dignity such

as yours is proof against the vapours of a captious and silly maiden. On the other hand, I have lost the privilege of uniting our houses through a marital link.

Despite all, I can convey my sorrow that this event occurred at Haidion and so, in this measure, marred my hospitality.

I trust that in the generous breadth of your tolerance you will continue to look upon me as your friend and ally in mutual endeavors of the future.

> *With my best regards, I am*
> Casmir,
> Lyonesse, the King.

An envoy carried the letter to Tintzin Fyral. In due course he returned with a response.

> For The Attention Of His August Majesty
> Casmir, Of Lyonesse, The King.

Revered Sir:

Be assured that the emotions I derived from the incident to which you refer, while they arose within me—understandably I hope—like a storm, subsided almost as quickly, and left me embarrassed for the narrow verges of my forbearance. I agree that our personal association should in no way be compromised by the unpredictabilities of a young maiden's fancy. As always, you may rely upon my sincere respect and my great hope that your proper and legitimate ambitions may be realized. Whenever the wish comes upon you to see something of Vale Evander, be assured that I shall welcome the opportunity to extend to you the hospitality of Tintzin Fyral.

> *I remain in all amiability,*
> *Your friend,*
> Carfilhiot.

King Casmir studied the letter with care. Carfilhiot apparently cherished no pangs of resentment; still, his declarations of good will, while hearty, might have gone somewhat further and been more specific.

# 8

KING GRANICE OF TROICINET was a man thin, grizzled and angular, abrupt of manner and notably terse until events went awry, whereupon he singed the air with expletives and curses. He had greatly desired a son and heir, but Queen Baudille gave him four daughters in succession, each born to the sound of Granice's furious complaints. The first daughter was Lorissa, the second Aethel, the third Ferniste, the fourth Byrin; then Baudille went barren and Granice's brother, Prince Arbamet, became heir-presumptive to the throne. Granice's second brother, Prince Ospero, a man of complicated personality and somewhat frail constitution, not only lacked ambition to the throne but so disliked the flavor of court life with its formality and artificial circumstances, that he stayed almost reclusively at his manor Watershade, at the center of the Ceald, Troicinet's inner plain. Ospero's spouse, Ainor, had died bearing his single son, Aillas, who in due course grew to be a strong broad-shouldered lad of middle stature, taut and sinewy rather than massive, with ear-length blond-brown hair and gray eyes.

Watershade occupied a pleasant place beside Janglin Water, a small lake with hills to the north and south and the Ceald stretching away to the west. Originally, Watershade had served to guard the Ceald, but three hundred years had passed since the last armed excursion through its gates, and the defenses had fallen into a state of picturesque disrepair. The armory was silent except for the forging of shovels and horseshoes; the drawbridge had not been raised within memory. The squat round towers of Watershade stood half in the water, half on the shore with trees overhanging the conical tiled roofs.

In the spring blackbirds flocked above the marsh and crows wheeled in the sky, calling "Caw! Caw! Caw!" across far distances. In the summer bees droned through the mulberry trees, and the air smelled of reeds and water-washed willow. At night cuckoos cried in the forest and in the morning brown trout and salmon struck at the bait almost as soon as it touched the water. Ospero, Aillas and their frequent guests took supper outdoors on the terrace and watched many a glorious sunset fade over Janglin Water. In fall the leaves turned color and the storehouses became chock-full with the yields of harvest. In winter fires burned in all the fireplaces and the white sunlight reflected in diamond sparkles from Janglin Water, while the salmon and trout lay close to the bottom and refused to strike at bait.

Ospero's temperament was poetic rather than practical. He took no great interest either in events at the royal palace Miraldra nor the war against Lyonesse. His bent was that of the scholar and antiquarian. For the education of Aillas he brought savants of high repute to Watershade; Aillas was instructed in mathematics, astronomy, music, geography, history and literature. Prince Ospero knew little of martial techniques, and delegated this phase of Aillas' education to Tauncy, his bailiff, a veteran of many campaigns. Aillas learned the use of bow, sword and that recondite art of the Galician bandits: knife-throwing. "This use of the knife," stated Tauncy, "is neither courteous nor knightly. It is, rather, the desperado's resource, a ploy of the man who must kill to survive the evening. The thrown knife suffices to a range of ten yards; beyond, the arrow excels. But in cramped conditions, a battery of knives is a most comfortable companion.

"Again, I prefer the small-sword to the heavy equipment favored by the mounted knight. With my small-sword I will maim a full-armored man in half a minute, or kill him if I choose. It is the supremacy of skill over brute mass. Here! Lift this two-hander, strike at me."

Aillas dubiously hefted the sword. "I fear that I might cut you in two parts."

"Stronger men than you have tried and who stands here to tell about it? So swing with a will!"

Aillas struck out; the blade was deflected. He tried once more; Tauncy wrenched and the sword flew from Aillas' hands. "Once more," said Tauncy. "See how it goes? Flick, slide, off, away! You may drive down the weapon with all your weight; I interpose, I twist! the sword leaves your grasp; I stab where your armor gaps; in goes the sword and out comes your life."

"That is a useful skill," said Aillas. "Especially against our chicken-thieves."

"Ha! you will not keep to Watershade all your days—not with the land at war. Leave the chicken-thieves to me. Now, to proceed. You are sauntering along the back streets of Avallon; you step into a tavern for a cup of wine. A great lummox claims that you have molested his wife; he takes up his cutlass and comes at you. So now! With your knife! Draw and throw! All in a single movement! You advance, pull your knife from the villain's neck, wipe it on his sleeve. If in fact you have molested the dead churl's wife, bid her begone! The episode has quite dampened your spirit. But you are attacked from another side by another husband. Quick!" So the lesson proceeded.

At the end, Tauncy said: "I consider the knife a most elegant weapon. Even apart from its efficacy, there is beauty in its flight, as it cleaves hard to its target; there is a spasm of pleasure as it strikes home deep and true."

In the springtime of his eighteenth year Aillas rode somberly forth from Watershade, never looking over his shoulder. The road took him beside the marshes which bordered the lake, across the Ceald and up through the hills to Green Man's Gap. Here Aillas turned to look back across the Ceald. Far in the distance, beside the glimmer of Janglin Water, a dark blot of trees concealed the squat towers of Watershade. Aillas sat a moment in contemplation of the dear familiar places he was leaving behind, and tears came to his eyes. Abruptly he reined his horse about, rode through the tree-shrouded gap and down Rundle River Valley.

Late in the afternoon he glimpsed the Lir ahead, and shortly before sunset arrived at Hag Harbor under Cape Haze. He went directly to the Sea Coral Inn where he was well-known to the landlord, and so was provided a good meal and a comfortable chamber for the night.

In the morning he rode westward along the coast road, and by early afternoon arrived at the city Domreis. He paused on the heights overlooking the city. The day was windy; the air seemed more than transparent, like a lens transmitting minute detail with clarity. Hob Hook, with a beard of foaming surf along its outer face, surrounded the harbor. At the base of Hob Hook stood Castle Miraldra, the seat of King Granice, with a long parapet extending to a lighthouse at the end of the hook. Originally a watch-tower, Miraldra, across the ages had been conjoined to an amazing complex of additions: halls, galleries, a dozen towers of apparently random mass and height.

Aillas rode down the hill, past the Palaeos, a temple sacred to Gaea, where a pair of twelve-year-old maidens in white kirtles tended a sacred flame. Aillas rode through the town, the hooves of his horse suddenly loud on the cobbled way. Past the docks, where a dozen ships were moored, past narrow-fronted shops and taverns, then out on the causeway to Castle Miraldra.

The outer walls loomed high above Aillas. They seemed almost unnecessarily massive and the entrance portal, flanked by a pair of barbicans, seemed disproportionately small. Two guards, wearing the dress maroon and gray of Miraldra with polished silver helmets and bright silver cuirasses, stood with halberds tilted at parade-rest. From the barbican Aillas was recognized; heralds blew a fanfare. The guards jerked the halberds into the erect "salute" position as Aillas passed through the portal.

In the courtyard Aillas dismounted and gave his horse over to a groom. Sir Este, the portly seneschal, coming to meet him, performed a gesture of surprise. "Prince Aillas! Have you come alone, without retinue?"

"By preference, Sir Este, I came alone."

Sir Este, who was notorious for his aphorisms, produced yet another comment upon the human condition: "Extraordinary that those who command the perquisites of place are those most ready to ignore them! It is as if the blessings of Providence are specious and notable only in their absence. Ah well, I refuse to speculate."

"You are well, I trust, and enjoying your own perquisites?"

"To the fullest! I have, you must know, this deep-seated fear that were I to neglect one of my little privileges, Providence might become peevish and whisk them away. Come now, I must see to your comfort. The king is away to Ardlemouth for the day; he inspects a new vessel which is said to be swift as a bird." He signaled to a footman. "Take Prince Aillas to his chamber, see to his bath and provide him garments suitable for the court."

Late in the afternoon King Granice returned to Miraldra. Aillas met him in the grand hall; the two embraced. "And how goes the health of my good brother Ospero?"

"He ventures seldom from Watershade. The outer air seems to bite at his throat. He tires easily and goes to hard gasping, so that I fear for his life!"

"All his years he has been frail! In any case, you seem sound enough!"

"Sir, you also seem to enjoy the best of health."

"True, lad, and I will share with you my little secret. Every day at this very hour I take a cup or two of good red wine. It enriches the blood, brightens the gaze, sweetens the breath and stiffens the frontal member. Magicians search high and low for the elixir of life, and they already hold it in their hands, if only they knew our little secret. Eh, lad?" And Granice clapped Aillas on the back. "Let us invigorate ourselves."

"With pleasure, sir."

Granice led the way into a parlor hung with banners, escutcheons and trophies of war. A fire blazed on the hearth; Granice warmed himself while a servant poured wine into silver cups.

Granice waved Aillas to a chair, and settled himself into a chair beside the fire. "I summoned you here for a reason. As a prince of the blood it is time that you acquainted yourself with affairs of state. The surest fact of this precarious existence is that one may never stand static. In this life everyone walks on ten-foot stilts; he must move and hop and cause an agitation; otherwise he topples. Fight or die! Swim or drown! Run or be trampled!" Granice drank down a cup of wine at a gulp.

"The placidity here at Miraldra then, is no more than an illusion?" Aillas suggested.

Granice gave vent to a grim chuckle. "'Placidity?' I know none of it. We are at war with Lyonesse and wicked King Casmir. It is the case of a small stopper holding back the contents of a tun. I will not recite the number of ships patrolling the Lyonesse coast; that number is a war secret, which Casmir's spies would be glad to learn, just as I would be glad to learn the number of Casmir's spies. They are everywhere, like flies in a barn. Just yesterday I hanged a pair, and their cadavers dangle high on Semaphore Hill. Naturally, I employ spies of my own. When Casmir launches a new ship I am notified, and my agents set it afire while it lies at dock, and Casmir gnashes his teeth to the gum. So goes the war: at a stalemate until the sluggish King Audry sees fit to intervene."

"And then?"

"'And then?' Battle and blood, sinking ships, burning castles. Casmir is astute, and more flexible then he might seem. He risks little unless the gain is great. When he could not strike at us, his thoughts went to the Ulflands. He tried to suborn the Duke of Vale Evander. The ploy failed. Relations between Casmir and Carfilhiot are now at best correct."

"So what will he do next?"

King Granice performed a cryptic gesture. "Ultimately, if we hold him off long enough, he must make peace with us, at our terms. Meanwhile, he struggles and squirms, and we try to read his mind. We puzzle over the despatches of our spies; we look at the world as it must appear from the parapets of Haidion. Well, enough for now, of plots and intrigue. Your cousin Trewan is somewhere at hand: a stern and earnest young man, but worthy, or so I hope, since one day, if events pursue their normal course, he will be king. Let us step into the dining hall, where no doubt we will discover more of this noble Voluspa."

At supper Aillas found himself seated beside Prince Trewan, who had grown to be a burly, darkly handsome young man, a trifle heavy in the face, with dark round eyes separated by a long patrician nose. Trewan dressed with care, in a style consonant with his rank; already he seemed to anticipate the day when he would become king: which would be upon the death of his father Arbamet, if Arbamet indeed succeeded Granice as king.

Ordinarily Aillas refused to take Trewan seriously, thus vexing Trewan and incurring his heavy disapproval. On this occasion Aillas restrained his levity, that he might learn as much as possible, and Trewan was more than ready to instruct his bucolic cousin.

"Truly," said Trewan, "it is a pleasure to see you down from Watershade, where time goes like a dream."

"We have little to startle us," agreed Aillas. "Last week a kitchen-maid went to pull greens in the garden and was stung by a bee. That was the most notable event of the week."

"Things go differently at Miraldra, I assure you. Today we inspected a great new ship, which we hope will augment our power, and cause Casmir a canker. Did you know that he wants to ally with the Ska and turn them against us?"

"It seems an extreme measure."

"Exactly so, and Casmir may not dare so greatly. Still, we must prepare for any eventuality, and this has been my point of view in the counsels."

"Tell me about the new ship."

"Well, its design comes from the seas under Arabia. The hull is wide at the deck and narrow at the water, so that it is very easy and stable. There are two short masts, each supporting a very long yard at its middle point. One end of the yard is brought down to the deck, the other lifts high to catch the upper wind. The ship should move at speed even in light airs, in any direction whatever. There will be catapults fore and aft and other contrivances to foil the Ska. As soon as possible after shake-down—mind you now, this is secret information—the King has required that I undertake a diplomatic mission of great importance. At the moment I can say no more. What brings you to Miraldra?"

"I am here at King Granice's command."

"For what purpose?"

"I'm not sure."

"Well, we shall see," said Trewan rather grandly. "I will put in a word for you during my next conference with King Granice. It may help your prospects and certainly can't hurt."

"That is good of you," said Aillas.

On the following day Granice, Trewan, Aillas and several others rode out from Miraldra, through Domreis, then two miles north along the shore to an isolated shipyard in the estuary of the Tumbling River. The group passed through a guarded gate, then walked along a trestle to a cove hidden from the sea by a bend of the river.

Granice told Aillas: "We attempt secrecy, but the spies refuse to oblige us. They come over the mountains to swarm among the shipwrights. Some come by boat, others think to swim. We only know of the ones we capture, but it is a good sign that they keep coming, which tells us something of Casmir's curiosity... There is the vessel itself. The Saracens call this type a felucca. Notice how low she floats! The hull is shaped like a fish and eases through the water without stirring a wake. The riggers are now stepping the masts." Granice pointed to a pole hanging from a derrick. "The mast is timberline spruce which is light and resilient. Yonder lie the yards, which are built of spruce poles scarfed, glued and seized with iron wire and pitch to make a very long spar tapered at each end. There are no better masts or yards on the face of the earth, and in a week we shall put them to test. It will be named *Smaadra* after the Bithne-Schasian* goddess of the sea. Let us go aboard."

Granice led the way to the after cabin. "We are not so com-

*One of the Third Era peoples to inhabit the Elder Isles.

modious as on a merchantman, but the quarters suffice. Now, sit you two yonder." Granice waved Aillas and Trewan to a bench. "Steward, bring Sir Famet here and you may also give us refreshment." Granice seated himself at the table and inspected the two young men. "Trewan, Aillas: listen now with all four of your ears. You are presently to make a voyage aboard the *Smaadra*. Ordinarily a new ship would be indulged with careful sea trials, and all its parts tested. We shall still do so, but very hastily."

Sir Famet entered the cabin: a sturdy white-haired man with a face chiseled from rough stone. He gave a laconic greeting to Granice and seated himself at the table.

Granice continued his exposition. "I have had recent advice from Lyonesse. It appears that King Casmir, writhing and casting about like a wounded snake, has sent a secret mission to Skaghane. He hopes for the use of a Ska fleet, if only to protect a landing of Lyonesse troops on Troicinet. The Ska so far have committed themselves to nothing. Neither, of course, trusts the other; each would want to emerge with advantage. But, evidently, Troicinet faces a grave danger. If we are defeated, so go the Elder Isles, either to Casmir, or worse, to the Ska."

Trewan said in a portentous voice, "That is menacing news."

"It is indeed, and we must take counter-measures. If the *Smaadra* behaves as we hope, six new hulls go on the ways at once. Second, I hope to bring pressure, both military and diplomatic, to bear against Casmir, though without any great optimism. Still, the effort can do no harm. To this end, as soon as possible, I will send the *Smaadra* with envoys first to Dahaut, Blaloc and Pomperol, then Godelia, and finally South Ulfland. Sir Famet will command the voyage; you, Aillas, and you, Trewan, shall be his aides. I intend that you make this voyage not for your health, nor personal satisfaction, nor the enhancement of your vanities, but for education. You, Trewan, are in direct line for the throne. You will need to learn a great deal about marine warfare, diplomacy and the quality of life around the Elder Isles. The same applies to Aillas, who must justify his rank and its perquisites by service to Troicinet."

"Sir, I shall do my best," said Aillas.

"And I, no less!" declared Trewan.

Granice nodded. "Very good; I expected no less. During this voyage, remember well, you are under the command of Sir Famet. Listen to him carefully, and profit by his wisdom. He will not require your advice, so please reserve your opinions and theories unless they are specifically required. In fact, on this voyage, forget that you are princes and conduct yourselves as cadets, unskilled and inexperienced but eager to learn. Do I make myself clear? Trewan?"

Trewan spoke in a surly voice: "I shall obey, of course. Still, I was under the impression—"

"Revise that impression. What of you, Aillas?"

Aillas could not help but grin. "I understand perfectly, sir. I shall do my best to learn."

"Excellent. Now look around the ship, the two of you, while I confer with Sir Famet."

 9

THE PRE-DAWN AIR WAS QUIET and cool; the sky showed the colors of citron, pearl, and apricot, which were reflected from the sea. Out from the Tumbling River estuary drifted the black ship *Smaadra*, propelled across the water by its sweeps. A mile off-shore, the sweeps were shipped. The yards were raised, sails sheeted taut and back-stays set up. With the sunrise came breeze; the ship glided quickly and quietly into the east, and presently Troicinet had become a shadow along the horizon.

Aillas, tiring of Trewan's company, went forward to the bow, but Trewan sauntered after him, and took occasion to explain the workings of the bow catapults. Aillas listened with polite detachment; exasperation and impatience were profitless exercises in dealing with Trewan.

"Essentially, these are no more than monstrous cross-bows," said Trewan in the voice of one providing insights of great interest to a respectful child. "Their range is functionally two hundred yards, though accuracy is compromised on a moving ship. The tensile member is laminated of steel, ash and hornbeam, assembled and glued in an expert and secret method. The instruments will hurl harpoons, stones or fireballs, and are highly effective. Eventually, and I shall see to it personally, if need be, we shall deploy a navy of a hundred ships such as this, equipped with ten larger and heavier catapults. There will also be supply ships, and an admiral's flagship, with proper accommodations. I am not particularly pleased with my present quarters. It is an absurd little place for one of my rank." Here Trewan referred to his cubbyhole beside the aft cabin. Aillas occupied a similar space opposite, with Sir Famet enjoying the relatively commodious aft cabin itself.

Aillas said in full gravity: "Perhaps Sir Famet might consider changing berths with you, if you put it to him in a reasonable manner."

Trewan merely spat over the rail; he found Aillas' humor at times a trifle tart, and for the rest of the day he had nothing to say.

At sundown the winds diminished to a near calm. Sir Famet, Trewan and Aillas took supper at a table on the rear deck, under the tall bronze stern-lantern. Over a beaker of red wine Sir Famet relaxed his taciturnity.

"Well then," he asked, almost expansively, "and how goes the voyage?"

Trewan at once brought forward a set of peevish complaints, while Aillas looked on and listened in slack-jawed wonder: how could Trewan be so insensitive? "Well enough, or so I suppose," said Trewan. "There is obvious room for improvement."

"Indeed?" asked Sir Famet without overmuch interest. "How so?"

"In the first place, my quarters are intolerably cramped. The ship's designer could well have done better. By adding ten or fifteen feet to the length of the ship, he might have provided two comfortable cabins instead of one; and certainly a pair of dignified privies."

"True," said Sir Famet, blinking over his wine. "With another thirty feet still, we might have brought valets, hairdressers and concubines. What else troubles you?"

Trewan, absorbed in his grievances, failed to heed the tenor of the remark. "I find the crew far too casual. They dress as they please; they lack smartness. They know nothing of punctilio; they take no account of my rank... Today while I was inspecting the ship I was told to 'Move aside, sir, you are in the way'— as if I were a squire."

No muscle of Sir Famet's hard face so much as twitched. He considered his words, then said: "At sea as on the battlefield, respect does not come automatically. It must be earned. You will be judged by your competence rather than your birth. It is a condition with which I for one am content. You will discover that the obsequious sailor, like the over-respectful soldier, is not the one you most want beside you in either a battle or a storm."

A trifle daunted, Trewan nevertheless argued his point. "Still, a proper deference is ultimately important! Otherwise all authority and order is lost, and we would live like wild animals."

"This is a picked crew. You will find them orderly indeed when the time comes for order." Sir Famet drew himself up in his chair. "Perhaps I should say something about our mission. The overt purpose is to negotiate a set of advantageous treaties. Both I and King Granice would be surprised if we did so. We will be dealing with persons of status exceeding our own, of the most various dispositions and all stubbornly controlled by their own conceptions. King Deuel of Pomperol is an ardent ornithologist, King Milo of Blaloc ordinarily consumes a gill of aquavit before he rises from bed in the morning. The court at Avallon seethes with erotic intrigues, and King Audry's chief catamite wields more influence than the Lord General Sir Ermice Propyrogeros. Our policy therefore is flexible. At minimum, we hope for polite interest and a perception of our power."

Trewan frowned and pursed his lips. "Why be content with modesty and half-measures? I would hope in my conversations to achieve something closer to the maximum. I suggest that we arrange our strategies more on these terms."

Sir Famet, tilting his head back, showed a cool thin smile to the evening sky and drank wine from his beaker. He set the vessel down with a thump. "King Granice and I have established both strategy and tactics, and we will adhere to these procedures."

"Of course. Still, two minds are better than one"—Trewan spoke past Aillas as if he were not present—"and there is clearly scope for variation in the arrangements."

"When circumstances warrant I shall consult with Prince Aillas and yourself. King Granice envisioned such training for you both. You may be present at certain discussions, in which case you shall listen, but at no time speak unless I direct you so to do. Is this clear, Prince Aillas?"

"Sir, absolutely."

"Prince Trewan?"

Trewan performed a curt bow, whose effect he at once attempted to ameliorate with a suave gesture. "Naturally, sir, we are under your orders. I will not put forward my personal views; still, I hope that you will keep me informed as to all negotiations and commitments, since, after all, it is I who eventually must deal with the aftermath."

Sir Famet responded with a cool smile. "In this regard, Prince Trewan, I will do my best to oblige you."

"In that case," declared Trewan in a hearty voice, "there is no more to be said."

Halfway through the morning an islet appeared off the port bow. A quarter-mile away, the sheets were eased and the ship lost way. Aillas went to the boatswain who stood by the rail. "Why are we stopping?"

"Yonder is Mlia, the mermen's isle. Look sharp; sometimes you will see them on the low rocks, or even on the beach."

A raft of scrap lumber was lifted on the cargo-boom; jars of honey, packets of raisins and dried apricots were stowed aboard; the raft was lowered into the sea and set adrift. Looking down through the clear water Aillas saw the flicker of pallid shapes, an upturned face with hair floating behind. It was a strange narrow face with limpid black eyes, a long thin nose, an expression wild, or avid, or excited, or gleeful: there were no precepts in Aillas' background for the comprehension of such an expression.

For a few minutes the *Smaadra* floated still in the water. The raft drifted slowly at first, then more purposefully and with small jerks and impulses moved toward the island.

Aillas put another question to the boatswain: "What if we went to the island with such gifts?"

"Sir, who can say? If you dared to row your boat yonder without such gifts, you would surely find misfortune. It is wise to deal politely with the merfolk. After all, the sea is theirs. Now then, time to be underway. Hoy, you yonder! Trim the sheets! Over with the helm! Let's kick up the spume!"

The days passed; landfalls were made and departures taken. Later Aillas recalled the events of the voyage as a collage of sounds, voices, music; faces and forms; helmets, armor, hats and garments; reeks, perfumes and airs; personalities and postures; ports, piers, anchorages and roadsteads. There were receptions, audiences; banquets and balls.

Aillas could not gauge the effect of their visits. They made, so he felt, a good impression: the integrity and strength of Sir Famet could not be mistaken, and Trewan, for the most part, held his tongue.

The kings were uniformly evasive, and would consider no commitments. Drunken King Milo of Blaloc was sober enough to point out: "Yonder stand the tall forts of Lyonesse, where the Troice navy exerts no strength!"

"Sir, it is our hope that, as allies, we may ease the threat of these forts."

King Milo responded only with a melancholy gesture and raised a tankard of aquavit to his mouth.

Mad King Deuel of Pomperol was equally indefinite. To obtain an audience, the Troice delegation traveled to the summer palace Alcantade, through a pleasant and prosperous land. The folk of Pomperol, far from resenting the obsessions of their monarch, enjoyed his antics; he was not only tolerated in his follies but encouraged.

King Deuel's madness was harmless enough; he felt an excessive partiality for birds, and indulged himself with absurd fancies, some of which, by virtue of his power, he was able to make real. He dubbed his ministers with such titles as Lord Goldfinch, Lord Snipe, Lord Peewit, Lord Bobolink, Lord Tanager. His dukes were Duke Bluejay, Duke Curlew, Duke Black Crested Tern, Duke Nightingale. His edicts proscribed the eating of eggs, as a "cruel and murderous delinquency, subject to punishment dire and stern."

Alcantade, the summer palace, had appeared to King Deuel in a dream. Upon awakening he called his architects and ordained the substance of his vision. As might be conjectured, Alcantade was an unusual structure, but nonetheless a place of curious charm: light, fragile, painted in gay colors, with tall roofs at various levels.

Arriving at Alcantade, Sir Famet, Aillas and Trewan discovered King Deuel resting aboard his swan-headed barge, which a dozen young girls clad in white feathers propelled slowly across the lake.

In due course King Deuel stepped ashore: a small sallow man of middle years. He greeted the envoys with cordiality. "Welcome, welcome! A pleasure to meet citizens of Troicinet, a land of which I have heard great things. The broad-billed grebe nests along the rocky shores in profusion, and the nuthatch dines to satiety upon the acorns of your splendid oaks. The great Troice horned owls are renowned everywhere for their majesty. I confess to a partiality for birds; they delight me with their grace and courage. But enough of my enthusiasms. What brings you to Alcantade?"

"Your Majesty, we are the envoys of King Granice and we bear his earnest message. When you are so disposed, I will speak it out before you."

"What better time than now? Steward, bring us refreshment! We will sit at yonder table. Speak now your message."

Sir Famet looked right and left at the courtiers who stood in polite proximity. "Sir, might you not prefer to hear me in private?"

"Not at all!" declared King Deuel. "At Alcantade we have no secrets. We are like birds in an orchard of ripe fruit, where everyone trills his happiest song. Speak on, Sir Famet."

"Very well, sir. I will cite certain events which disquiet King Granice of Troicinet."

Sir Famet spoke; King Deuel listened carefully, with head cocked to the side. Sir Famet finished his exposition. "These, sir, are the dangers which menace us all—in the not too distant future."

King Deuel grimaced. "Dangers, everywhere dangers! I am beset on all hands, so that often I hardly take rest of nights." King Deuel's voice became nasal and he twitched in his chair as he spoke. "Daily I hear a dozen pitiful cries for protection. We guard our entire north border against the cats, stoats, and weasels employed by King Audry. The Godelians are also a menace, even though their roosts lie a hundred leagues distant. They breed and train the cannibal falcons, each a traitor to his kind. To the west is an even more baleful threat, and I allude to Duke Faude Carfilhiot, who breathes green air. Like the Godelians he hunts with falcons, using bird against bird."

Sir Famet protested in a strained voice. "Still, you need fear no actual assault! Tintzin Fyral stands far beyond the forest!"

King Deuel shrugged. "It is admittedly a long day's flight. But we must face reality. I have named Carfilhiot a dastard; and he dared not retort, for fear of my mighty talons. Now he skulks in his toad-wallow planning the worst kinds of mischief."

Prince Trewan, ignoring Sir Famet's cold blue side-glance, spoke out briskly: "Why not place the strength of those same talons beside those of your fellow birds? Our flock shares your views in regard to Carfilhiot and his ally King Casmir. Together we can rebuff their attacks with great blows of talon and beak!"

"True. Someday we shall see the formation of just such a mighty force. In the meantime each must contribute where he can. I have cowed the squamous Carfilhiot and defied the Godelians; nor do I spare mercy upon Audry's bird-killers. You are thereby liberated to aid us against the Ska and sweep them from the sea. Each does his part: I through the air; you on the ocean wave."

The *Smaadra* arrived at Avallon, largest and oldest city of the Elder Isles: a place of great palaces, a university, theaters and an enormous public bath. There were a dozen temples erected to the glory of Mithra, Dis, Jupiter, Jehovah, Lug, Gaea, Enlil, Dagon, Baal, Cronus and three-headed Dion of the ancient Hybrasian pantheon. The Somrac lam Dor, a massive domed structure, housed the sacred throne Evandig and the table Cairbra an Meadhan, objects whose custody in olden days had legitimized the kings of Hybras.*

King Audry returned from his summer palace riding in a scarlet and gold carriage drawn by six white unicorns. On the same afternoon the Troice emissaries were allowed an audience. King Audry, a tall saturnine man, had a face of fascinating ugliness. He was noted for his amours and said to be perceptive, self-indulgent, vain and occasionally cruel. He greeted the Troice with urbanity and put them at their ease. Sir Famet delivered his message, while King Audry leaned back into his cushions, eyes half-closed, stroking the white cat which had jumped into his lap.

Sir Famet concluded his statement. "Sir, that is my message to you from King Granice."

King Audry nodded slowly. "It is a proposal with many sides and more edges. Yes! Of course! I dearly yearn for the subjugation of Casmir and the end of his ambitions. But before I can commit treasure, arms and blood to such a project I must secure my flanks. Were I to look away an instant, the Godelians would come pounding down on me looting, burning, taking slaves. North Ulfland is a wilderness, and the Ska have encroached upon the foreshore. If I embroiled myself in North Ulfland against the Ska, then Casmir would be upon me." King Audry reflected a moment, then: "Candor is such a poor policy that we all recoil

---

*The table, Cairbra an Meadhan, was divided into twenty-three segments, each carved with now unreadable glyphs, purportedly the names of twenty-two in the service of the fabulous King Mahadion. In years to come a table in the style of Cairbra an Meadhan would be celebrated as the Round Table of King Arthur.

automatically from the truth. In this case you might as well know the truth. It is to my best interests that Troicinet and Lyonesse maintain a stalemate."

"Daily the Ska grow stronger in North Ulfland. They too have ambitions."

"I hold them in check with my fort Poëlitetz. First the Godelians, then the Ska, then Casmir."

"Meanwhile, what if Casmir, with the help of the Ska, takes Troicinet?"

"A disaster for both of us. Fight well!"

Dartweg, King of the Godelian Celts, listened to Sir Famet with a ponderous and bland courtesy.

Sir Famet came to the end of his remarks. "That is the situation as it seems from Troicinet. If events go with King Casmir, he will move at last into Godelia and you will be destroyed."

King Dartweg pulled at his red beard. A Druid bent to mutter in his ear and Dartweg nodded. He rose to his feet. "We cannot spare the Dauts so that they may conquer Lyonesse. They would thereupon attack us with new strength. No! We must guard our interests!"

The *Smaadra* sailed on, through days bright with sunlight and nights sparkling with stars: across Dafdilly Bay, around Tawgy Head and into the Narrow Sea, with the wind dead fair and wake warbling up astern; then south, past Skaghane and Frehane, and smaller islands by the dozens: cliff-girt places of forest, moor and crag, exposed to all the winds of the Atlantic, inhabited by multitudes of sea-birds and the Ska. On various occasions Ska ships were sighted, and as many of the small trading cogs, Irish, Cornish, Troice or Aquitanian, which the Ska suffered to ply the Narrow Sea. The Ska ships made no effort to close, perhaps because the *Smaadra* clearly was able to outrun them down a fresh wind.

Oäldes, where ailing King Oriante maintained a semblance of a court, was passed by; the final port of call would be Ys at the mouth of the Evander, where the Forty Factors preserved the independence of Ys against Carfilhiot.

Six hours out of Ys the wind slackened and at this time a Ska long-ship, powered by sweeps and a red and black square sail came in view. Upon sighting the *Smaadra* it changed course. The *Smaadra*, unable to outrun the Ska ship, prepared for battle. The catapults were manned and armed, fire-pots prepared and slung to booms; arrow-screens raised above the bulwarks.

The battle went quickly. After a few arrow volleys the Ska moved in close and tried to grapple.

The Troice returned the arrow fire, then winged out a boom and slung a fire-pot accurately onto the long-ship, where it exploded in a terrible surprise of yellow flame. At a range of thirty yards the *Smaadra's* catapults in a leisurely fashion broke the long-ship apart. The *Smaadra* stood by to rescue survivors but the Ska made no attempt to swim from the wallowing hulk of their once-proud ship, which presently sank under the weight of its loot.

The Ska commander, a tall black-haired man in a three-pronged steel helmet and a white cap over the pangolin scales of his armor, stood immobile on the afterdeck and so sank with his ship.

Casualties aboard the *Smaadra* were slight; unfortunately they included Sir Famet, who, in the initial volley, took an arrow in the eye and now lay dead on the afterdeck, with the arrow shaft protruding from his head two feet into the air.

Prince Trewan, conceiving himself the second ranking member of the delegation, took command of the ship. "Into the sea with our honored dead," he told the captain. "The rites of mourning must wait upon our return to Domreis. We will proceed as before, to Ys."

The *Smaadra* approached Ys from the sea. At first nothing could be seen but a line of low hills parallel to the shore, then, like shadows looming through the haze, the high serrated outline of the Teach tac Teach* appeared.

A wide pale beach gleamed in the sunlight, with a glistening fringe of surf. Presently the mouth of the River Evander appeared beside an isolated white palace on the beach. Aillas' attention was caught by its air of seclusion and secrecy, and its unusual architecture, which was like none other of his experience.

The *Smaadra* entered the Evander estuary, and gaps in the dark foliage shrouding the hills revealed many more white palaces, on terrace above terrace: clearly Ys was a rich and ancient city.

*Literally: 'peak on peak' in one of the precursor tongues.

A stone jetty came into view, with ships moored alongside, and, behind, a row of shops: taverns, green-grocers' booths, and fish-mongers' stalls.

The *Smaadra* eased close to the jetty, made fast to wooden bollards carved to represent the torsos of mermen. Trewan, Aillas and a pair of ship's officers jumped ashore. No one took notice of their presence.

Trewan had long since placed himself thoroughly in command of the voyage. By various hints and signals he gave Aillas to understand that, in the context of the present business, Aillas and the ship's officers occupied an exactly equal standing as members of the retinue. Aillas, sourly amused, accepted the situation without comment. The voyage was almost over and Trewan in all probability, for better or worse, would be the future king of Troicinet.

At Trewan's behest, Aillas made inquiries, and the group was directed to the palace of Lord Shein, the First Factor of Ys. The route took them a quarter-mile at a slant up the hillside, from terrace to terrace, in the shade of tall samfire trees.

Lord Shein received the four Troice with neither surprise nor effusive demonstration. Trewan performed the introductions. "Sir, I am Trewan, Prince at the Court of Miraldra and nephew to King Granice of Troicinet. Here is Sir Leves, and Sir Elmoret, and here my cousin, Prince Aillas of Watershade."

Lord Shein acknowledged the introductions informally. "Please be seated." He indicated settees and signaled his servants to bring refreshment. He himself remained standing: a slender olive-skinned man of early maturity, dark-haired, who carried himself with the elegance of a mythical dawn-dancer. His intelligence was obvious; his manners were courteous but so in contrast to Trewan's sententiousness that he seemed almost frivolous.

Trewan explained the business of the delegation as he had heard Sir Famet put it on previous occasions: to Aillas' mind, an insensitive misreading of conditions at the city Ys, what with Faude Carfilhiot looming above Vale Evander only twenty miles east and Ska ships daily visible from the jetty.

Shein, half-smiling, shook his head and gave Trewan's proposals short shrift. "Understand, if you will, that Ys is something of a special case. Normally we are subject to the Duke of Vale Evander, who in equal measure is a dutiful vassal of King Oriante. Which is to say, we heed Carfilhiot's orders even less than he obeys King Oriante. Not at all, in sheer fact. We are detached from the politics of the Elder Isles. King Casmir, King Audry, King Granice: they are all beyond our concerns."

Trewan made an incredulous expostulation. "You would seem to be vulnerable on both sides, to Ska and Carfilhiot alike."

Shein, smiling, demolished Trewan's concept. "We are Trevenas, like all the folk of the vale. Carfilhiot has only a hundred men of his own. He could raise a thousand or even two thousand troops from the valley if a clear need arose, but never to attack Ys."

"Still, what of the Ska? On a moment's notice, they could overrun the city."

Shein once again demurred. "We Trevenas are an old race, as old as the Ska. They will never attack us."

"I cannot understand this," muttered Trewan. "Are you magicians?"

"Let us talk of other matters. You are returning to Troicinet?"

"At once."

Shein looked quizzically around the group. "With absolutely no offense intended, I am perplexed that King Granice sends what appears a rather junior group on affairs of so much consequence. Especially in view of his special interests here in South Ulfland."

"What special interests are these?"

"Are they not clear? If Prince Quilcy dies without issue, Granice is next in the lawful succession, through the line that starts with Danglish, Duke of South Ulfland, who was grandfather to Granice's father and also grandfather to Oriante. But surely you were well aware of all this?"

"Yes, of course," said Trewan. "Naturally we keep abreast of such matters."

Shein was now openly smiling. "And naturally you are aware of the new circumstances in Troicinet?"

"Naturally," said Trewan. "We are returning to Domreis at once." He rose to his feet and bowed stiffly. "I regret that you could not take a more positive attitude."

"Still, it will have to serve. I bid you a pleasant voyage home."

The Troice emissaries returned down through Ys to the jetty. Trewan muttered: "What could he mean 'new circumstances in Troicinet?'"

"Why didn't you ask him?" asked Aillas, in a studiously neutral voice.

"Because I chose not to do so," snapped Trewan.

Upon reaching the jetty they noticed a Troice cog, newly arrived and only just making its lines fast to the bollards.

Trewan stopped short. "I'll just have a word with the captain. You three prepare the *Smaadra* for immediate sailing."

The three returned aboard the *Smaadra*. Ten minutes later Trewan left the cog and came along the jetty, walking with a slow and thoughtful step. Before boarding, he turned and looked up Vale Evander. Then slowly he turned and boarded the *Smaadra*.

Aillas asked: "What were the new circumstances?"

"The captain could tell me nothing."

"You seem suddenly very glum."

Trewan compressed his lips but had no comment to make. He scanned the horizon. "The cog lookout sighted a pirate ship. We must be on the alert." Trewan turned away. "I am not altogether well; I must rest." He lurched away to the aft cabin which he had occupied since the death of Sir Famet.

The *Smaadra* departed the harbor. As they passed the white palace on the beach, Aillas, from the afterdeck, noticed a young woman who had come out upon the terrace. Distance blurred her features, but Aillas was able to make out her long black hair, and, by her carriage or some other attribute, he knew her to be well-favored, perhaps even beautiful. He raised his arm and waved to her, but she made no response and returned into the palace.

The *Smaadra* put out to sea. The lookouts scanned the horizon but reported no other shipping; the pirate vessel, if such indeed existed, was nowhere to be seen.

Trewan failed to reappear on deck until noon of the following day. His indisposition, whatever its source, had departed and Trewan seemed once more in sound health, if still somewhat gaunt and pale. Except for a few words with the captain as to the progress of the ship, he spoke to no one, and presently returned to his cabin, where the steward brought him a pot of boiled beef with leeks.

An hour before sunset Trewan once more stepped out on deck. He looked at the low sun and asked the captain: "Why do we sail this course?"

"Sir, we have made a bit too much easting. Should the wind rise or shift, we might well fall in peril of Tark, which I put yonder, just over the horizon."

"Then we are having a slow passage."

"Something slow, sir, but easy. I see no occasion to man the sweeps."

"Quite so."

Aillas took supper with Trewan, who suddenly became talkative and formulated a dozen grandiose plans. "When I am King, I shall make myself known as 'Monarch of the Seas!' I will build thirty warships, each with a complement of a hundred mariners." He went on to describe the projected ships in detail. "We will care never a fig whether Casmir allies himself with the Ska or the Tartars, or the Mamelukes of Araby."

"That is a noble prospect."

Trewan disclosed even more elaborate schemes. "Casmir intends to be King of the Elder Isles; he claims lineage from the first Olam. King Audry also pretends to the same throne; he has Evandig to validate his claim. I also can claim lineage from Olam, and if I were to make a great raid and take Evandig for my own, why should I not aspire to the same realm?"

"It is an ambitious concept," said Aillas. And many heads would be lopped before Trewan achieved his purpose, so thought Aillas.

Trewan glanced sidewise at Aillas from under his heavy brows. He drank a goblet of wine at a gulp and once more became taciturn. Presently Aillas went out on the afterdeck where he leaned on the taff-rail and watched the afterglow and its shifting reflections on the water. In another two days the voyage would be over, and he would be done with Trewan and his irritating habits: a joyful thought!...Aillas turned away from the taff-rail and went forward to where the off-watch crew sat under a flaring lamp, a few gambling dice, one singing mournful ballads to the chords of his lute. Aillas remained half an hour, then went aft to his cubbyhole.

Dawn found the *Smaadra* well into the Straits of Palisidra. At noon Cape Palisidra, the western tip of Troicinet, loomed into view, then disappeared, and the *Smaadra* now rode the waters of the Lir.

During the afternoon the wind died, and the *Smaadra* floated motionless, with spars rattling and sails flapping. Toward sunset the wind returned, but from a different quarter; the captain put the ship on a starboard tack, to sail almost due north. Trewan gave vent to his dissatisfaction. "We'll never make Domreis tomorrow on this course!"

The captain, who had adjusted to Trewan only with difficulty, gave an indifferent shrug. "Sir, the port tack takes us into the Twirles: 'the ships' graveyard.' The winds will drive us to Domreis tomorrow, if the currents do not throw us off."

"Well then, what of these currents?"

"They are unpredictable. The tide flows in and out of the Lir; the currents may swing us in any of four directions. They flow at speed; they eddy in the middle of the Lir; they have thrown many sound ships on the rocks."

"In that case, be vigilant! Double the lookout!"

"Sir, all that needs doing already has been done."

At sunset the wind died again and the *Smaadra* lay motionless.

The sun set into smoky orange haze, while Aillas dined with Trewan in the aft cabin. Trewan seemed preoccupied, and spoke hardly a word during the entire meal, so that Aillas was glad to depart the cabin.

The afterglow was lost in a bank of clouds; the night was dark. Overhead the stars shone with brilliance. A chilly breeze suddenly sprang up from the southeast; close-hauled the *Smaadra* beat to the east.

Aillas went forward, to where the off-watch entertained itself. Aillas joined the dice game. He lost a few coppers, then won them back, then finally lost all the coins in his pocket.

At midnight the watch changed; Aillas returned aft. Rather than immerse himself immediately in his cubbyhole he climbed up the ladder to the afterdeck. Breeze still filled the sails; wake, sparkling and streaked with phosphorescence, bubbled up astern. Leaning on the taff-rail Aillas watched the flickering lights.

A step behind him, a presence. Arms gripped his legs; he was lifted and flung into space. He knew a brief sensation of tilting sky and whirling stars, then struck into water. Down, down, into the tumble of wake, and his chief emotion was still astonishment. He rose to the surface. All directions were the same; where was the *Smaadra*? He opened his mouth to yell, and took a throatful of water. Gasping and coughing, Aillas called out once more but produced only a dismal croak. The next attempt was stronger, but thin and weak, hardly more than the cry of a sea-bird.

The ship was gone. Aillas floated alone, at the center of his private cosmos. Who had cast him into the sea? Trewan? Why should Trewan do such a deed? No reason whatever. Then:

who?...The speculations faded from his mind; they were irrelevant, part of another existence. His new identity was one with the stars and the waves...His legs felt heavy; he twisted in the water, removed his boots, and let them sink. He slipped out of his doublet, which was also heavy. Now he remained afloat with less effort. The wind blew from the south; Aillas swam with the wind at his back, which was more comfortable than with the waves breaking into his face. The waves lifted him, and carried him forward on their surge.

He felt at ease; his mood was almost exalted, even though the water, at first cold, then tolerable, once more seemed chilly. With disarming stealth, he began to feel comfortable again. Aillas felt at peace. It would be easy now to relax, to slide away into languor.

If he slept, he would never awaken. Worse, he would never discover who had thrown him into the sea. "I am Aillas of Watershade!"

He exerted himself; he moved his arms and legs to swim; and once again became uncomfortably cold. How long had he floated in this dark water? He looked up to the sky. The stars had shifted; Arcturus was gone and Vega hung low in the west...For a period the first level of consciousness departed and he knew only a bleary awareness which started to flicker and go out...Something disturbed him. A quiver of sentience returned. The eastern sky glowed yellow; dawn was at hand. The water around him was black as iron. Off to the side, a hundred yards away, water foamed around the base of a rock. He looked at it with sad interest, but wind and waves and current carried him past.

A roaring sound filled his ears; he felt a sudden harsh impact, then he was sucked away by a wave, picked up and thrown against something cruelly sharp. With numb arms and sodden fingers he tried to cling, but another surge pulled him away.

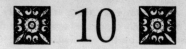

10

DURING THE REIGNS OF OLAM I, Great King of the Elder Isles, and his immediate successors, the throne Evandig and the sacred stone table Cairbra an Meadhan occupied place in Haidion. Olam III, "the Vain," moved throne and table to Avallon. This act and its consequences came about as an oblique result of discord among the arch-magicians of the land. At this time they numbered eight: Murgen, Sartzanek, Desmëi, Myolander, Baibalides, Widdefut, Coddefut and Noumique.* Murgen was reckoned first among his fellows, by no means to the satisfaction of all. Sartzanek in particular resented Murgen's austere inflexibility, while Desmëi deplored his strictures against meddling with affairs of the countryside, which was her sport.

Murgen made his residence at Swer Smod, a rambling stone manse in the northwest part of Lyonesse, where the Teach tac Teach sloped down into the Forest of Tantrevalles. He based his edict on the thesis that any assistance rendered to a favorite must sooner or later transgress upon the interests of other magicians.

Sartzanek, perhaps the most capricious and unpredictable of all the magicians, resided at Faroli, deep inside the forest, in the then Grand Duchy of Dahaut. He long had resented Murgen's

---

*Whenever the magicians met together, another appeared: a tall shape muffled in a long black cape, with a wide-brimmed black hat obscuring his features. He stood always back in the shadows and never spoke; when one or another of the magicians chanced to look into his face they saw black emptiness with a pair of far stars where his eyes might be. The presence of the ninth magician (if such he were) at first made for uneasiness, but in due course, since the presence seemed to affect nothing, he was ignored, save for occasional side-glances.

prohibitions, and contravened them as flagrantly as he dared.

Sartzanek occasionally conducted erotic experiments with the witch Desmëi. Stung by the derision of Widdefut, Sartzanek retaliated with the Spell of Total Enlightenment, so that Widdefut suddenly knew everything which might be known: the history of each atom of the universe, the devolvements of eight kinds of time, the possible phases of each succeeding instant; all the flavors, sounds, sights, smells of the world, as well as percepts relative to nine other more unusual senses. Widdefut became palsied and paralyzed and could not so much as feed himself. He stood trembling in confusion until he dessicated to a wisp and blew away on the wind.

Coddefut made an indignant protest, exciting Sartzanek to such a rage that he put by all caution and destroyed Coddefut with a plague of maggots. Coddefut's entire surface seethed under an inch-thick layer of worms, to such effect that Coddefut lost control of his wisdom and tore himself to pieces.

The surviving magicians, with the exception of Desmëi, invoked pressures which Sartzanek could not repugn. He was compressed into an iron post seven feet tall and four inches square, so that only upon careful scrutiny might his distorted features be noted. This post was similar to the post at Twitten's Corner. The Sartzanek post was implanted at the very peak of Mount Agon. Whenever lightning struck down, Sartzanek's etched features were said to twitch and quiver.

A certain Tamurello immediately took up residence in Sartzanek's manse, Faroli, and all understood him to be Sartzanek's *alter ego*, or scion: in certain respects an extension of Sartzanek himself.* Like Sartzanek, Tamurello was tall, heavy of physique, with black eyes, black curls, a full mouth, round chin, and a temperament which expressed itself in terms of vivid emotion.

The witch Desmëi, who had performed erotic conjunctions with Sartzanek, now amused herself with King Olam III. She appeared to him as a female clothed with a soft pelt of black fur and an oddly beautiful cat-like mask. This creature knew a thousand lascivious tricks; King Olam, befuddled and foolish, succumbed to her will. To spite Murgen, Desmëi persuaded Olam

---

*In just such a fashion Shimrod was known to be an extension, or *alter ego*, of Murgen, though their personalities had separated and they were different individuals.

to move his throne Evandig and the table Cairbra an Meadhan to Avallon.

The old tranquility was gone. The magicians were at odds, each suspicious of the other. Murgen, in cold disgust, isolated himself at Swer Smod.

Difficult times came upon the Elder Isles. King Olam, now deranged, attempted copulation with a leopard; he was savaged and died. His son, Uther I, a frail and timid stripling, no longer enjoyed the support of Murgen. Goths invaded the north coast of Dahaut and looted Whanish Isle, where they sacked the monastery and burned the great library.

Audry, Grand Duke of Dahaut, raised an army and destroyed the Goths at the Battle of Hax, but suffered such losses that the Celtic Godelians moved east and took the Wysrod Peninsula. King Uther, after months of indecision, marched his army against the Godelians only to meet disaster at the Battle of Wanwillow Ford, where he was killed. His son, Uther II fled north to England, where in due course he sired Uther Pendragon, father to King Arthur of Cornwall.

The dukes of the Elder Isles met at Avallon to choose a new king. Duke Phristan of Lyonesse claimed kingship by virtue of lineage, while the aging Duke Audry of Dahaut cited the throne of Evandig and the table Cairbra an Meadhan in support of his own claim; the conclave dissolved in acrimony. Each duke returned home and thereafter styled himself King of his own personal domain.

Instead of one there were now ten kingdoms: North Ulfland, South Ulfland, Dahaut, Caduz, Blaloc, Pomperol, Godelia, Troicinet, Dascinet and Lyonesse.

The new kingdoms found ample scope for contention. King Phristan of Lyonesse and his ally King Joel of Caduz went to war against Dahaut and Pomperol. At the Battle of Orm Hill, Phristan killed the old but stalwart Audry I and was himself killed by an arrow; the battle and the war ended indecisively, with each side charged with hatred for the other.

Prince Casmir, known as "the Popinjay," fought in the battle bravely but without recklessness and returned to Lyonesse Town as King. Immediately he abandoned his elegant postures for a hard practicality, and set himself to the task of strengthening his realm.

A year after Casmir became King, he married Princess Sollace of Aquitaine, a handsome blonde maiden with Gothic blood in her veins, whose stately mien disguised a stolid temperament.

Casmir considered himself a patron of the magical arts. In a secret chamber he kept a number of curios and magical adjuncts, including a book of incantations, indited in illegible script, but which glowed dimly in the dark. When Casmir ran his finger over the runes a sensation peculiar to each incantation suffused his mind. He could tolerate one such contact; twice caused him to sweat; thrice he dared not lest he lose control of himself. A griffin's claw reposed in an onyx case. A gallstone cast by the ogre Heulamides gave off a peculiar stench. A small yellow skak* sat in a bottle, resignedly awaiting his eventual release. On a wall hung an article of real power: Persilian, the so-called "Magic Mirror." This mirror would answer three questions to its owner, who then must relinquish it to another. Should the owner ask a fourth question, the mirror would make glad response, then dissolve into freedom. King Casmir had put three questions, and now reserved the fourth against emergency.

According to popular wisdom, the company of magicians was usually more bane than benefit. Though he well knew of Murgen's edicts, Casmir at various times solicited aid from archmagicians Baibalides and Noumique, and several other lesser magicians, to be everywhere rebuffed.

Casmir received news of the sorceress Desmëi, reputedly the enemy of Murgen. By reliable report she had taken herself to the Goblin Fair, an annual occasion which she enjoyed and never failed to patronize.

Casmir disguised himself under blue and iron-gray armor, and a shield displaying two dragons rampant. He named himself Sir Perdrax, knight errant, and, with a small retinue, rode into the Forest of Tantrevalles.

In due course he arrived at Twitten's Corner. The inn known as The Laughing Sun and The Crying Moon was filled to capacity; Casmir was forced to accept a place in the barn. A quarter-

---

*The least in the hierarchy of fairies. First in rank are fairies, then falloys, goblins, imps, finally skaks. In the nomenclature of Faerie, giants, ogres and trolls are also considered halflings, but of a different sort. In a third class are merrihews, willawen and hyslop, and also, by some reckonings, quists and darklings. Sandestins, most powerful of all, are in a class by themselves.

mile into the forest he found the Goblin Fair. Desmëi was no-where to be seen. Casmir wandered among the booths. He saw much to interest him and paid good gold for various oddments.

Late in the afternoon he noted a tall woman, somewhat gaunt of face and feature, her blue hair gathered into a silver cage. She wore a white tabard embroidered in black and red; she evoked in King Casmir (and all men who saw her) a curious disturbance: fascination mingled with revulsion. This was Des-mëi the sorceress.

Casmir approached her with caution, where she stood hag-gling with an old knave who kept a booth. The merchant's hair was yellow, his skin sallow; his nose was split and his eyes were like copper pellets; goblin blood flowed in his veins. He held up a feather for her inspection. "This feather," he said, "is indis-pensable to the conduct of daily affairs, in that it infallibly detects fraudulence."

"Astounding!" declared Desmëi in a voice of boredom.

"Would you say that here is an ordinary feather taken from the carcass of a dead blue jay?"

"Yes. Dead or even alive. So I would assume."

"You would be as wrong as an umpdoodle's trivet."

"Indeed. How is this miraculous feather used?"

"Nothing could be simpler. If you suspect a cheat, a liar or a swindler, touch him with the feather. If the feather turns yellow, your suspicions are confirmed."

"If the feather remains blue?"

"Then the person with whom you are dealing is staunch and true! This excellent feather is yours for six crowns of gold."

Desmëi uttered a metallic laugh. "Do you think me so gullible? It is almost insulting. Evidently you expect me to test you with the feather, then when it remains blue, I pay over to you my gold!"

"Precisely! The feather would verify my assertions!"

Desmëi took the feather and touched it to the split nose. Instantly the feather became bright yellow. Desmëi repeated her scornful laugh. "No less than I suspected! The feather declares you to be a cheat!"

"Ha ha! Does not the feather perform exactly as I have claimed? How can I be a cheat?"

Desmëi frowningly regarded the feather, then threw it back upon the counter. "I have no time for conundrums!" Haughtily she strolled away, to inspect the sale of a young harpy in a cage.

After a moment Casmir approached. "You are the sorceress Desmëi?"

Desmëi fixed her attention on him. "And who are you?"

"I call myself Sir Perdrax, knight errant from Aquitaine."

Desmëi smiled and nodded. "And what do you wish of me?"

"It is a delicate matter. May I count upon your discretion?"

"To a certain extent."

"I will express myself bluntly. I serve King Casmir of Lyonesse, who intends to restore the throne Evandig to its rightful place. To this end he implores your advice."

"The arch-magician Murgen forbids such involvement."

"Already you are at odds with Murgen. How long will you obey his precepts?"

"Not forever. How would Casmir reward me?"

"State your terms; I will communicate them."

Desmëi became suddenly fretful. "Tell Casmir to come in his own right to my palace at Ys. There I will talk to him."

Sir Perdrax bowed and Desmëi moved away. Presently she departed through the forest in a palanquin carried by six running shadows.

Before setting out for Ys, King Casmir brooded long and well; Desmëi was known for her bitter bargains.

At last he ordered out the royal galleass, and on a sparkling windy day sailed out past the breakwater, around Cape Farewell and so to Ys.

Casmir disembarked upon the stone jetty and walked down the beach to Desmëi's white palace.

Casmir found Desmëi on a seaward-facing terrace leaning on the balustrade, half in the shade of a tall marble urn, from which trailed the foliage of sweet arbutus.

A change had come over Desmëi. Casmir halted, wondering at her pallor, hollow cheeks and gaunt neck. Her fingers, thin and knobbed at the knuckles, hooked over the lip of the balustrade; her feet, in silver sandals, were long and frail and showed a net of purple veins.

Casmir stood slack-jawed and graceless, feeling himself in the presence of mysteries far beyond his understanding.

Desmëi glanced at him sidelong, showing neither surprise nor pleasure. "So you have come."

Casmir made a rather strained effort to regain the initiative which he felt should rightly be his. "Did you not expect me?"

Desmëi said only, "You are here too late."

"How so?" exclaimed Casmir in new concern.

"All things change. I have no more interest in the affairs of men. Your forays and wars are a trouble; they disturb the quiet of the countryside."

"There is no need for war! I want only Evandig! Give me magic or a mantle of stealth, so that I may take Evandig without war."

Desmëi laughed a soft wild laugh. "I am known for my bitter bargains. Would you pay my price?"

"What is your price?"

Desmëi looked out toward the sea's horizon. At last she spoke, so quietly that Casmir came a step closer to hear. "Listen! I will tell you this. Marry Suldrun well; her son will sit on Evandig. And what is my price for this presagement? Nothing whatever, for the knowledge will do you no service." Desmëi abruptly turned and walked through one in a line of tall archways into the shadows of her palace. Casmir watched the thin form become indistinct and disappear. He waited a moment, standing in the hot sunlight. No sound could be heard but the sigh of surf.

Casmir swung away and returned to his ship.

Desmëi watched the galleass dwindle across the blue sea. She was alone in her palace. For three months she had awaited Tamurello's visit; he had not come and the message of his absence was clear.

She went into her workroom, unclasped her gown and let it slip to the floor. She studied herself in the mirror, to see grim features, a body bony, lank, almost epicene. Coarse black hair matted her head; her arms and legs were lean and graceless. Such was her natural embodiment, a self in which she felt most easy. Other guises required concentration lest they become loose and dissolve.

Desmëi went to her cabinets and brought out a variety of instruments. Over a time of two hours she worked a great spell to sunder herself into a plasm which entered a vessel of three vents. The plasm churned, distilled, and emerged by the vents, to coalesce into three forms. The first was a maiden of exquisite conformation, with violet-blue eyes and black hair soft as midnight. She carried within her the fragrance of violets, and was named Melancthe.

The second form was male. Desmëi, still by a trick of time, a husk of sentience, quickly shrouded and covered it lest others (such as Tamurello) discover its existence.

The third form, a demented squeaking creature, served as sump for Desmëi's most repugnant aspects. Shaking with disgust Desmëi quelled the horrid thing and burnt it in a furnace, where it writhed and screamed. A green fume rose from the furnace; Melancthe shrank back but involuntarily gasped upon a wisp of the stench. The second form, shrouded behind a cloak, inhaled the stench with savor.

Vitality had drained from Desmëi. She faded to smoke and was gone. Of the three components she had yielded, only Melancthe, fresh with the subtle odor of violets, remained at the palace. The second, still shrouded, was taken to the castle Tintzin Fyral, at the head of Vale Evander. The third had become a handful of black ashes and a lingering stench in the workroom.

11

IN THE CHAPEL AT THE TOP of the garden Suldrun's bed had been arranged, and here a tall dour kitchen maid named Bagnold daily brought food, precisely at noon. Bagnold was half-deaf and might have been mute as well, for all her conversation. She was required to verify Suldrun's presence, and if Suldrun were not at the chapel Bagnold trudged angrily down into the garden to find her, which was almost every day, since Suldrun gave no heed to time. After a period Bagnold tired of the exertion and put the full basket on the chapel steps, picked up the empty basket of the day before and departed: an arrangement which suited both Suldrun and herself.

When Bagnold departed she dropped a heavy oaken beam into iron brackets thus to bar the door. Suldrun might easily have scaled the cliffs to either side of the garden, and someday, so she told herself, she would do so, to depart the garden forever.

So passed the seasons: spring and summer, and the garden was at its most beautiful, though haunted always by stillness and melancholy. Suldrun knew the garden at all hours: at gray dawn, when dew lay heavy and bird calls came clear and poignant, like sounds at the beginning of time. Late at night, when the full moon rode high above the clouds, she sat under the lime tree looking to sea while the surf rattled along the shingle.

One evening Brother Umphred appeared, his round face abeam with innocent good will. He carried a basket, which he placed upon the chapel steps. He looked Suldrun carefully up and down. "Marvelous! You are as beautiful as ever! Your hair shines, your skin glows; how do you keep so clean?"

"Don't you know?" asked Suldrun. "I bathe, in yonder basin."

Brother Umphred raised his hands in mock horror. "That is the font for holy water! You have done sacrilege!"

Suldrun merely shrugged and turned away.

With happy gestures Brother Umphred unpacked his basket. "Let us bring cheer to your life. Here is tawny wine; we will drink!"

"No. Please leave."

"Are you not bored and dissatisfied?"

"Not at all. Take your wine and go."

Silently Brother Umphred departed.

With the coming of autumn the leaves turned color and dusk came early. There was a succession of sad and glorious sunsets, then came the rains and the cold of winter, whereupon the chapel became bleak and chill. Suldrun piled stones to build a hearth and a chimney against one of the windows. The other she wadded tight with twigs and grass. Currents swinging around the cape cast driftwood up on the shingle, which Suldrun carried to the chapel to dry, and then burnt on the hearth.

The rains dwindled; sunlight burned bright through cold crisp air, and spring was at hand. Daffodils appeared among the flower beds and the trees put on new leaves. In the sky appeared the stars of spring: Capella, Arcturus, Denebola. On sunny mornings cumulus clouds towered high over the sea, and Suldrun's blood seemed to quicken. She felt a strange restlessness, which never before had troubled her.

The days became longer, and Suldrun's perceptions became more acute, and each day began to have its own quality, as if it were one of a limited number. A tension began to form, an imminence, and often Suldrun stayed awake all night long, so that she might know all to occur in her garden.

Brother Umphred paid another visit. He found Suldrun sitting on the stone steps of the chapel, sunning herself. Brother Umphred looked at her with curiosity. The sun had tanned her arms, legs and face, and lightened strands of her hair. She looked the picture of serene good health; in fact, thought Brother Umphred, she seemed almost happy.

The fact aroused his carnal suspicions; he wondered if she had taken a lover. "Dearest Suldrun, my heart bleeds when I think of you solitary and forlorn. Tell me; how do you fare?"

"Well enough," said Suldrun. "I like solitude. Please do not remain here on my account."

Brother Umphred gave a cheerful chuckle. He settled himself

beside her. "Ah, dearest Suldrun—" He put his hand on hers. Suldrun stared at the fat white fingers; they felt moist and over-amiable. She moved her hand; the fingers fell away reluctantly. "—I bring you not only Christian solace, but also a more human consolation. You must recognize that while I am a priest I am also a man, and susceptible to your beauty. Will you accept this friendship?" Umphred's voice became soft and unctuous. "Even though the emotion is warmer and dearer than simple friendship?"

Suldrun laughed drearily. She rose to her feet and pointed at the gate. "Sir, you have my leave to go. I hope that you will not return." She turned and descended into the garden. Brother Umphred muttered a curse and departed.

Suldrun sat beside the lime tree and looked out over the sea. "I wonder," she asked herself, "what will become of me? I am beautiful, so everyone says, but it has brought me only bane. Why am I punished, as if I had done wrong? Somehow I must bestir myself; I must make a change."

After her evening meal she wandered down to the ruined villa, where she liked best, on clear nights, to watch the stars. Tonight they showed an extraordinary brilliance and seemed to address themselves to her, like wonderful children brimming with secrets...She rose to her feet and stood listening. Imminence hung in the air; its meaning she could not decide.

The night breeze became cool; Suldrun retreated up through the garden. In the chapel, coals yet smouldered in the fireplace. Suldrun blew them ablaze; lay on dry driftwood and the room became warm.

In the morning, wakening very early, she went out into the dawn. Dew lay heavy on foliage and grass; the silence held a primitive quality. Suldrun went down through the garden, slow as a sleepwalker, down to the beach. Surf boomed up the shingle. The sun, rising, colored far clouds at the opposite horizon. At the southern curve of the beach, where currents brought driftwood, she noticed a human body which had floated in on the tide. Suldrun halted, then approached, step by step, and stared down in horror, which quickly became pity. What tragedy, that so cold a death had taken one so young, so wan, so comely...A wave stirred the young man's legs. His fingers spasmodically extended, clawed into the shingle. Suldrun dropped to her knees, pulled the body up from the water. She brushed back the sodden curls. The hands were bloody; the head was bruised. "Don't die," whispered Suldrun. "Please don't die!"

The eyelids flickered; eyes, glazed and filmed with sea-water, looked up at her, then closed.

Suldrun dragged the body up into dry sand. When she tugged the right shoulder he emitted a sad sound. Suldrun ran to the chapel, brought back coals and dry wood, and built up a fire. She wiped the cold face with a cloth. "Don't die," she said again and again.

His skin began to warm. Sunlight shone over the cliffs and down upon the beach. Aillas opened his eyes once more and wondered if indeed he had died, and now roamed the gardens of paradise with the most beautiful of all golden-haired angels to tend him.

Suldrun asked: "How do you feel?"

"My shoulder hurts." Aillas moved his arm. The twinge of pain assured him that he still lived. "Where is this place?"

"This is an old garden near Lyonesse Town. I am Suldrun." She touched his shoulder. "Do you think it's broken?"

"I don't know."

"Can you walk? I can't carry you up the hill."

Aillas tried to rise, but fell. He tried again, with Suldrun's arm around his waist, and stood swaying.

"Come now, I'll try to hold you."

Step by step they climbed up through the garden. At the ruins they stopped to rest. Aillas said weakly, "I must tell you that I am Troice. I fell from a ship. If I am captured I will be put in prison—at the very least."

Suldrun laughed. "You are already in a prison. Mine. I am not allowed to leave. Don't worry; I will keep you safe."

She helped him to his feet; at last they reached the chapel.

As best she could Suldrun immobilized Aillas' shoulder with bandages and withes and made him lie upon her couch. Aillas accepted her ministrations and lay watching her: what crimes had this beautiful girl committed that she should be so imprisoned? Suldrun fed him first honey and wine, then porridge. Aillas became warm and comfortable and fell asleep.

By evening Aillas' body burned with fever. Suldrun knew no remedy save damp cloths on the forehead. By midnight the fever cooled, and Aillas slept. Suldrun made herself as comfortable as possible on the floor before the fire.

In the morning Aillas awoke, half-convinced that his circumstances were unreal, that he was living a dream. Gradually he allowed himself to remember the *Smaadra*. Who had thrown him into the sea? Trewan? By reason of sudden madness? Why else? His manner since visiting the Troice cog at Ys had been most peculiar. What could have happened aboard the cog? What possibly could have driven Trewan past the brink of sanity?

On the third day Aillas decided that he had broken no bones and Suldrun eased his bandages. When the sun rose high the two descended into the garden and sat among the fallen columns of the old Roman villa. Through the golden afternoon they told each other of their lives. "This is not our first meeting," said Aillas. "Do you remember visitors from Troicinet about ten years ago? I remember you."

Suldrun reflected. "There have always been dozens of delegations. I seem to remember someone like you. It was so long ago; I can't be sure."

Aillas took her hand, the first time he had touched her in affection. "As soon as I am strong we will escape. It will be a simple affair to climb the stones yonder; then it's over the hill and away."

Suldrun spoke in a half-whisper, husky and fearful. "If we were captured"—she hunched her shoulders together—"the King would show us no pity."

In a subdued voice Aillas said: "We won't be captured! Especially if we plan well, and are all-cautious." He sat up straight, and spoke with great energy. "We will be free and away through the countryside! We'll travel by night and hide by day; we'll be one with the vagabonds, and who will know us?"

Aillas' optimism began to infect Suldrun; the prospect of freedom became exhilarating. "Do you really think we'll escape?"

"Of course! How could it be otherwise?"

Suldrun gazed pensively down the garden and over the sea. "I don't know. I have never expected to be happy. I am happy now—even though I am frightened." She laughed nervously. "It makes for a strange mood."

"Don't be frightened," said Aillas. Her nearness overwhelmed him; he put his arm around her waist. Suldrun jumped to her feet. "I feel as if a thousand eyes are watching us!"

"Insects, birds, a lizard or two." Aillas scanned the cliffs. "I see no one else."

Suldrun looked up and down the garden. "Nor do I. Still..." She seated herself at a demure distance of three feet, and turned him an arch side-glance. "Your health seems to be on the mend."

"Yes. I feel very well, and I cannot bear to look at you without wanting to touch you." He moved close to her; laughing, she slid away.

"Aillas, no! Wait till your arm is better!"

"I'll be careful of my arm."

"Someone might come."

"Who would be so bold?"

"Bagnold. The priest Umphred. My father the King."

Aillas groaned. "Destiny could not be so unkind."

Suldrun said in a soft voice: "Destiny doesn't really care."

Night came to the garden. Sitting before the fire the two supped on bread, onions and mussels which Suldrun had gathered from the tidal rocks. Once again they talked of escape. Suldrun said wistfully, "Perhaps I will feel strange away from this garden. Every tree, every stone, is known to me...But, since you came, everything is different. The garden is going from me." Looking into the fire, she gave a little shiver.

"What is wrong?" asked Aillas.

"I am afraid."

"Of what?"

"I don't know."

"We could leave tonight, but for my arm. Another few days and I'll be strong again. In the meantime we must plan. The woman who brings your food; what of her?"

"At noon she brings a basket and takes back the empty basket from the day before. I never speak to her."

"Could she be bribed?"

"To do what?"

"To bring the food as usual, discard it, and take back the empty basket next day. With a week's start, we could be far away and never fear capture."

"Bagnold would never dare, even if she were so disposed, which she isn't. And we have nothing to bribe her with."

"Have you no jewels, no gold?"

"In my cabinet at the palace I have gold and gems."

"Which is to say, they are inaccessible."

Suldrun considered. "Not necessarily. The East Tower is quiet after sunset. I could go directly up to my chamber, and no one would notice. I could be in, out and away in a trice."

"Is it truly so simple?"

"Yes! I have gone this way hundreds of times, and seldom have I met anyone along the way."

"We cannot bribe Bagnold, so we will have free only a day, from noon till noon, plus whatever time your father needs to organize a search."

"An hour, no more. He moves quickly and with decision."

"So then, we must have a peasant's disguise, and this is easier said than done. Is there no one whom you trust?"

"One only, the nurse who tended me when I was small."

"And where is she?"

"Her name is Ehirme. She lives on a steading south along the road. She would give us clothes, or anything we asked for without stint, if she knew my need."

"With disguise, a day's start and gold for passage to Troicinet, freedom is ours. And once across the Lir you will be simply Suldrun of Watershade. No one will know you for Princess Suldrun of Lyonesse save only me and perhaps my father, who will love you as I do."

Suldrun looked up at him. "Do you truly love me?"

Aillas took her hands and pulled her to her feet; their faces were only inches apart. They kissed each other.

"I love you most dearly," said Aillas. "I never want to be parted from you."

"I love you, Aillas, nor do I wish us to be parted ever."

In a transport of joy the two looked into each other's eyes. Aillas said: "Treachery and tribulation brought me here, but I give thanks for all of it."

"I have been sad too," said Suldrun. "Still, if I had not been sent away from the palace, I could not have salvaged your poor drowned corpse!"

"So then! For murderous Trewan and cruel Casmir: our thanks!" He bent his face to Suldrun's; they kissed again and again; then, sinking to the couch, lay locked in each other's arms, and presently lost themselves in ardor.

Weeks passed, swift and strange: a period of bliss, made the more vivid by its background of high adventure. The pain in Aillas' shoulder subsided, and one day in the early afternoon, he scaled the cliff to the east of the garden and traversed the rocky slope on the seaward side of the Urquial, slowly and gingerly, since his boots were at the bottom of the sea and he went unshod. Beyond the Urquial he pushed through an undergrowth of scrub oak, elderberry and rowan, and so gained the road.

At this time of day, few folk were abroad. Aillas encountered a drover with a flock of sheep and a small boy leading a goat, and neither gave him more than a cursory glance.

A mile along the road he turned into a lane which wound away between hedgerows, and presently arrived at the steading where Ehirme lived with her husband and children.

Aillas halted in the shadow of the hedge. To his left, at the far side of a meadow, Chastain, the husband and his two oldest sons, cut hay. The cottage lay at the back of a kitchen garden, where leeks, carrots, turnips and cabbages grew in neat rows. Smoke rose from the chimney.

Aillas pondered the situation. If he went to the door and someone other than Ehirme showed herself, awkward questions might be asked, for which he had no answers.

The difficulty resolved itself. From the door came a stocky round-faced woman carrying a bucket. She set out toward the pig-sty. Aillas called out: "Ehirme! Dame Ehirme!"

The woman, pausing, examined Aillas with doubt and curiosity, then slowly approached. "What do you want?"

"You are Ehirme?"

"Yes."

"Would you do a service, in secret, for Princess Suldrun?"

Ehirme put down the bucket. "Please explain, and I'll tell you whether such service lies within my power."

"And in any event you'll keep the secret?"

"That I will do. Who are you?"

"I am Aillas, a gentleman of Troicinet. I fell from a ship and Suldrun saved me from drowning. We are resolved to escape the garden and make our way to Troicinet. We need a disguise of old clothes, hats and shoes, and Suldrun has no friend but you. We cannot pay at this time, but if you help us, you will be well rewarded when I return to Troicinet."

Ehirme reflected, the creases in her weather-beaten face twitching to the flux of her thoughts. She said: "I will help you as best I can. I have long suffered for the cruelty done to poor little Suldrun, who never harmed so much as an insect. Do you need only clothes?"

"Nothing more, and our most grateful thanks for these."

"The woman who brings Suldrun food—I know her well; she is Bagnold, an ill-natured creature rancid with gloom. So soon

126

as she notices untouched food she will scuttle to King Casmir and the search will be on."

Aillas gave a fatalistic shrug. "We have no choice, and we will hide well by daylight."

"Do you carry sharp weapons? Wicked things move by night. Often I see them hopping about the meadow, and flying across the clouds."

"I will find a good cudgel; that must suffice."

Ehirme gave a noncommittal grunt. "I will go to market every day. On my way back I will open the postern, empty the basket, and Bagnold will be deceived. I can do this safely for a week, and by then the trail will be cold."

"That will mean great risk for you. If Casmir discovered your doing he would show no mercy!"

"The postern is hidden behind the bush. Who will notice me? I will take care not to be seen."

Aillas made a few more half-hearted protests, to which Ehirme paid no heed. She looked out over the meadow and across the woodland beyond. "In the forest past the village Glymwode live my old father and mother. He is a woodcutter, and their hut is solitary. When we have butter and cheese to spare, I send it to them by my son Collen and the donkey. Tomorrow morning I will bring you smocks, hats, and shoes, on my way to market. Tomorrow night, an hour after sunset, I will meet you here, at this spot, and you will sleep in the hay. At sunrise Collen will be ready, and you will travel to Glymwode. No one will know of your escape, and you may travel by day; who will connect the Princess Suldrun with three peasants and a donkey? My father and mother will keep you safe until danger is past, and then you shall travel to Troicinet, perhaps by way of Dahaut, a longer road but safer."

Aillas said humbly: "I do not know how to thank you. At least, not until I reach Troicinet, and there I will be able to make my gratitude real."

"No need for gratitude! If I can steal poor Suldrun away from the tyrant Casmir, I will have reward enough. Tomorrow night then, an hour after sunset, I will meet you here!"

Aillas returned to the garden and told Suldrun of Ehirme's arrangements. "So we do not need to skulk like thieves through the night after all."

Tears started from Suldrun's eyes. "My dear faithful Ehirme!

I never fully appreciated her kindness!"

"From Troicinet we will reward her loyalty."

"And we still need gold. I must visit my chambers in Haidion."

"The thought frightens me."

"It is no great matter. In a twinkling I can slip into the palace and out again."

Dusk came to darken the garden. "Now," said Suldrun, "I will go to Haidion."

Aillas rose to his feet. "I must go with you, if only to the palace."

"As you like."

Aillas climbed over the wall, unbarred the postern, and Suldrun passed through. For a moment they stood close to the wall. A half-dozen dim lights showed at various levels of the Peinhador. The Urquial was vacant in the dusk.

Suldrun looked down along the arcade. "Come."

Through the arches lights twinkled up from Lyonesse Town. The night was warm; the arcades smelled of stone and occasionally a whiff of ammonia, where someone had eased his bladder. At the orangery the fragrance of flower and fruit overcame all else. Above loomed Haidion, with the glow of candles and lamps outlining its windows.

The door into the East Tower showed as a half-oval of deep shadow. Suldrun whispered: "Best that you wait here."

"But what if someone comes?"

"Go back to the orangery and wait there." Suldrun pressed the latch and pushed at the great iron and timber door. With a groan it swung open. Suldrun peered through the crack into the Octagon. She looked back to Aillas. "I'm going in—" From the top of the arcade came the sound of voices and the clatter of footsteps. Suldrun pulled Aillas into the palace. "Come with me then."

The two crossed the Octagon, which was illuminated by a single rack of heavy candles. To the left an arch opened on the the Long Gallery; stairs ahead rose to the upper levels.

The Long Gallery was vacant for its whole length. From the Respondency came the sound of voices lilting and laughing in gay conversation. Suldrun took Aillas' arm. "Come."

They ran up the stairs and in short order stood outside Suldrun's chambers. A massive lock joined a pair of hasps riveted into stone and wood.

Aillas examined the lock and the door, and gave a few half-hearted twists to the lock. "We can't get in. The door is too strong."

Suldrun took him along the hall to another door, this without a lock. "A bed-chamber, for noble maidens who might be visiting me." She opened the door, listened. No sound. The room smelled of sachet and unguents, with an unpleasant overtone of soiled garments.

Suldrun whispered: "Someone sleeps here, but she is away at her revels."

They crossed the room to the window. Suldrun eased open the casement. "You must wait here. I've come this way many times when I wanted to avoid Dame Boudetta."

Aillas looked dubiously toward the door. "I hope no one comes in."

"If so, you must hide in the clothes-press, or under the bed. I won't be long." She slid out the window, edged along the wide stone coping to her old chamber. She pushed at the casement, forced it open, then jumped down to the floor. The room smelled of dust and long days of emptiness, in sunlight and rain. A trace of perfume still hung in the air, a melancholy recollection of years gone by, and tears came to Suldrun's eyes.

She went to the chest where she had stored her possessions. Nothing had been disturbed. She found the secret drawer and pulled it open; within, so her fingers told her, were those oddments and ornaments, precious gems, gold and silver which had come into her possession: mostly gifts from visiting kindred; neither Casmir nor Sollace had showered gifts upon their daughter.

Suldrun tied the valuables into a scarf. She went to the window and bade farewell to the chamber. Never would she set foot in there again: of this she felt certain.

She returned through the window, pulled tight the casement and returned to Aillas.

They crossed the dark room, opened the door a crack, then stepped out into the dim corridor. Tonight, of all nights, the palace was busy; many notables were on hand, and up from the Octagon came the sound of voices and the two could not effect the quick departure upon which they had planned. They looked at each other with wide eyes and pounding hearts.

Aillas uttered a soft curse. "So now: we're trapped."

"No!" whispered Suldrun. "We'll go down the back stairs.

Don't worry; one way or another we'll escape! Come!" They ran light-footed along the corridor, and so began a thrilling game which dealt them a series of frights and startlements and had been no part of their expectations. Here and there they ran, gliding on soft feet along old corridors, dodging from chamber to chamber, shrinking back into shadows, peering around corners: from the Respondency into the Chamber of Mirrors, up a spiral staircase to the old observatory, across the roof into a high parlor, where young noble-folk held their trysts, then down a service stairs to a long back corridor which gave on a musicians' gallery, overlooking the Hall of Honors.

Candles in the wall sconces were alight; the hall had been made ready for a ceremonial event, perhaps later in the evening; now the hall stood empty.

Stairs led down into a closet which gave on the Mauve Parlor, so-called for the mauve silk upholstery of its chairs and couches: a splendid room with ivory and snuff-colored paneling and a vivid emerald green rug. Aillas and Suldrun ran quietly to the door, where they looked out into the Long Gallery, at this moment empty of human occupancy.

"It's not far now," said Suldrun. "First we'll make for the Hall of Honors, then, if no one appears, we'll make for the Octagon and out the door."

With a last look right and left, the two ran to the arched alcove in which hung the doors into the Hall of Honors. Suldrun looked back the way they had come, and clutched Aillas' arm. "Someone came out of the library. Quick, inside."

They slipped through the doors into the Hall of Honors. They stood wide-eyed, face to face, holding their breaths. "Who was it?" Aillas whispered.

"I think it was the priest Umphred."

"Perhaps he didn't see us."

"Perhaps not . . . If he did he will be sure to investigate. Come; to the back room!"

"I see no back room!"

"Behind the arras. Quick! He's just outside the door!"

They ran the length of the hall and ducked behind the hanging. Peering through the crack, Aillas saw the far door ease open: slowly, slowly. The portly figure of Brother Umphred was a dark stencil against the lights of the Long Gallery.

For a moment Brother Umphred stood motionless, save for quick shakes of the head. He seemed to give a cluck of puzzlement and came forward into the room, looking right and left.

Suldrun went to the back wall. She found the iron rod and pushed it into the lock-holes.

Aillas asked in astonishment: "What are you doing?"

"Umphred may very well know about this back room. He won't know this other."

The door opened, releasing a suffusion of green-purple light. Suldrun whispered: "If he comes any closer we'll hide in here."

Aillas, standing by the crack, said, "No. He's turning back...He's leaving the hall. Suldrun?"

"I'm in here. It's where the king, my father, keeps covert his private magic. Come look!"

Aillas went to the doorway, glanced gingerly right and left.

"Don't be alarmed," said Suldrun. "I've been in here before. The little imp is a skak; he's closed in his bottle. I'm sure he'd prefer freedom, but I fear his spite. The mirror is Persilian; it speaks in season. The cow's horn yields either fresh milk or hydromel, depending upon how one holds it."

Aillas came slowly forward. The skak glared in annoyance. Colored light-motes caught in tubes jerked in excitement. A gargoyle mask hanging high in the shadows turned down a dyspeptic sneer.

Aillas spoke in alarm: "Come! before we fall afoul of these things!"

Suldrun said, "Nothing has ever done me harm. The mirror knows my name and speaks to me!"

"Magic voices are things of bane! Come! We must leave the palace!"

"One moment, Aillas. The mirror has spoken kindly; perhaps it will do so again. Persilian?"

From the mirror came a melancholy voice: "Who calls 'Persilian'?"

"It is Suldrun! You spoke to me before and called me by name. Here is my lover, Aillas!"

Persilian uttered a groan, then sang in a voice deep and plangent, very slowly so that each word was distinct.

> Aillas knew a moonless tide;
> Suldrun saved him death.
> They joined their souls in wedlock strong
> To give their son his breath.

Aillas: choose from many roads;
Each veers through toil and blood.
But still this night you must be wed
To seal your fatherhood.

Long have I served King Casmir;
He asked me questions three.
Yet never will he speak the rote
to break me full and free.

Aillas, you must take me now,
and hide me all alone;
By Suldrun's tree, there shall I dwell
Beneath the sitting-stone.

Aillas, as if moving in a dream, reached his hands to Persilian's frame. He pulled it free of the metal peg which held it to the wall. Aillas held up the mirror and asked in puzzlement: "How, this very night, can we be wed?"

Persilian's voice, richly full, issued from the mirror: "You have stolen me from Casmir; I am yours. This is your first question. You may ask two more. If you ask a fourth, I am free."

"Very well; as you wish it. So how will we be wed?"

"Return to the garden; the way is safe. There your marriage bonds shall be forged; see to it that they are strong and true. Quick, go now; time presses! You must be gone before Haidion is bolted tight for the night!"

With no more ado Suldrun and Aillas departed the secret room, closing tight the door on the seep of green-purple light. Suldrun looked through the crack in the hangings; the Hall of Honors was empty save for the fifty-four chairs whose personalities had loomed so massively over her childhood. They seemed now shrunken and old and some of their magnificence had gone; still Suldrun felt their brooding contemplation as she and Aillas ran down the hall.

The Long Gallery was empty; the two ran to the Octagon and out into the night. They started up the arcade, then made a hurried detour into the orangery while a quartet of palace guards came stamping, clanking and cursing down from the Urquial.

The steps faded into quiet. Moonlight through the arched intervals cast a succession of pale shapes, alternately silver-gray and darkest black, into the arcade. Across Lyonesse Town lamps yet flickered, but no sound reached the palace. Suldrun and

Aillas slipped from the orangery, ran up under the arcade and so through the postern into the old garden. Aillas brought Persilian from under his tunic. "Mirror, I have put a question and I will be sure to put no more until need arises. Now I will not ask how I must hide you, as you directed; still, if you wished to enlarge upon your previous instructions, I will listen."

Persilian spoke: "Hide me now, Aillas, hide me now, down by the old lime tree. Under the sitting-stone is a crevice. Hide as well the gold you carry, quick as quick can be."

The two descended to the chapel. Aillas went on down the path to the old lime tree; he lifted the sitting-stone and found a crevice into which he placed Persilian and the bag of gold and gems.

Suldrun went to the door of the chapel, where she paused to wonder at the candleglow from within.

She pushed open the door. Across the room sat Brother Umphred, dozing at the table. His eyes opened; he looked at Suldrun.

"Suldrun! You have returned at last! Ah, Suldrun, sweet and wanton! You have been up to mischief! What do you do away from your little domain?"

Suldrun stood silent in dismay. Brother Umphred lifted his portly torso and came forward, smiling a winsome smile, eyelids half-closed, so that his eyes seemed a trifle askew. He took Suldrun's limp hands. "Dearest child! Tell me, where have you been?"

Suldrun tried to draw back, but Brother Umphred tightened his grip. "I went to the palace for a cloak and a gown... Let go my hands."

But Brother Umphred only pulled her closer. His breathing came faster and his face showed a rosy-pink flush. "Suldrun, prettiest of all the earth's creatures! Do you know that I saw you dancing along the corridors with one of the palace lads? I asked myself, can this be the pure Suldrun, the chaste Suldrun, so pensive and demure? I told myself: impossible! But perhaps she is ardent after all!"

"No, no," breathed Suldrun. She jerked to pull away. "Please let me go."

Brother Umphred would not release her. "Be kind, Suldrun! I am a man of noble spirit, still I am not indifferent to beauty! Long, dearest Suldrun, have I yearned to taste your sweet nectar, and remember, my passion is invested in the sanctity of the church! So now, my dearest child, whatever tonight's mischief, it will only have warmed your blood. Embrace me, my golden delight, my sweet mischief, my sly mock-purity!" Brother Umphred bore her down to the couch.

Aillas appeared in the doorway. Suldrun saw him and motioned him to stand back, out of sight. She drew up her knees, and squirmed away from Brother Umphred. "Priest, my father shall hear of your acts!"

"He cares nothing what happens to you," said Brother Umphred thickly. "Now be easy! Or else I must enforce our congress by means of pain."

Aillas could constrain himself no longer. He stepped forward and dealt Brother Umphred a blow to the side of his head, to send him tumbling to the floor. Suldrun said in distress: "Better, Aillas, had you remained away."

"And allowed his beastly lust? First I would kill him! In fact, I will kill him now, for his audacity."

Brother Umphred dragged himself back against the wall, eyes glistening in the candlelight.

Suldrun said hesitantly, "No, Aillas, I don't want his death."

"He will report us to the king."

Brother Umphred cried out: "No, never! I hear a thousand secrets; all are sacred to me!"

Suldrun said thoughtfully. "He will witness our wedlock; in fact, he will marry us by the Christian ceremony which is as lawful as any other."

Brother Umphred struggled to his feet, blurting incoherent phrases.

Aillas told him, "Marry us, then, since you are a priest, and do it properly."

Brother Umphred took time to settle his cassock and compose himself. "Marry you? That is not possible."

"Certainly it is possible," said Suldrun. "You have made marriages among the servants."

"In the chapel at Haidion."

"This is a chapel. You sanctified it yourself."

"It has now been profaned. In any case, I can bring the sacraments only to baptized Christians."

"Then baptize us and quickly!"

Brother Umphred smilingly shook his head. "First you must believe truly and become catechumens. And further, King Casmir would be rageful; he would take vengeance on us all!"

Aillas picked up a stout length of driftwood. "Priest, this cudgel supersedes King Casmir. Marry us now, or I will break your head."

Suldrun took his arm. "No, Aillas! We will marry in the manner of the folk, and he shall witness; then there shall be no talk of who is a Christian and who is not."

Brother Umphred again demurred. "I cannot be a party to your pagan rite."

"You must," said Aillas.

The two stood by the table and chanted the peasant litany of wedlock:

"Witness, all, how we two take the vows of marriage! By this morsel, which together we eat."

The two divided a crust of bread and ate together.

"By this water, which together we drink."

The two drank water from the same cup.

"By this fire, which warms us both."

The two passed their hands through the flame of the candle.

"By the blood which we mingle."

With a thin bodkin Aillas pricked Suldrun's finger, then his own, and joined the droplets of blood.

"By the love which binds our hearts together."

The two kissed, smiled.

"So we engage in solemn wedlock, and now declare ourselves man and wife, in accordance with the laws of man and the benevolent grace of Nature."

Aillas took up pen, ink and a sheet of parchment. "Write, priest! 'Tonight on this date I have witnessed the marriage of Suldrun and Aillas,' and sign your name."

With shaking hands Brother Umphred pushed away the pen. "I fear the wrath of King Casmir!"

"Priest, fear me more!"

In anguish Brother Umphred wrote as he was instructed. "Now let me go my way!"

"So that you may hurry to tell all to King Casmir?" Aillas shook his head. "No."

"Fear nothing!" cried Brother Umphred. "I am silent as the grave! I know a thousand secrets!"

"Swear!" said Suldrun. "Down on your knees. Kiss the sacred book you carry in your pouch, and swear that, by your hope of salvation and by your fear of perpetual Hell, that you will reveal nothing of what you have seen and heard and done tonight."

Brother Umphred, now sweating and ashen-faced, looked from one to the other. Slowly he went to his knees, kissed the book of gospels and swore his oath.

He struggled to his feet. "I have witnessed, I have sworn; it is my right to now depart!"

"No," said Aillas somberly. "I do not trust you. I fear that spite may overwhelm your honor, and so destroy us. It is a chance I cannot accept."

Brother Umphred was momentarily speechless with indignation. "But I have sworn by everything holy!"

"And so, as easily, you might forswear them and so be purged of the sin. Should I kill you in cold blood?"

"No!"

"Then I must do something else with you."

The three stood staring at each other, frozen a moment in time. Aillas stirred. "Priest, wait here, and do not try to leave, on pain of good strokes of the cudgel, as we shall be just outside the door."

Aillas and Suldrun went out into the night, to halt a few yards from the chapel door. Aillas spoke in a husky half-whisper, for fear Brother Umphred might have his ear pressed to the door. "The priest cannot be trusted."

"I agree," said Suldrun. "He is quick as an eel."

"Still, I cannot kill him. We can't tie him or immure him, for Ehirme to tend, since then her help would become known. I can think of a single plan. We must part. At this moment I will take him from the garden. We will proceed east. No one will trouble to notice us; we are not fugitives. I will make sure that he neither escapes nor cries out for succor: a vexing and tedious task, but it must be done. In a week or two I will leave him while he sleeps; I will make my way to Glymwode and seek you out, and all will be as we planned."

Suldrun put her arms around Aillas and laid her head on his chest. "Must we be parted?"

"There is no other way to be secure, save killing the man dead, which I cannot do in cold blood. I will take a few pieces of gold; you take the rest, and Persilian as well. Tomorrow, an hour after sunset, go to Ehirme and she will send you to her father's hut, and there shall I seek you out. Go you now to the lime tree, and bring me back a few small trinkets of gold, to trade for food and drink. I'll stay to guard the priest."

Suldrun ran down the path and a moment later returned with

the gold. They went to the chapel. Brother Umphred stood by the table, looking morosely into the fire.

"Priest," said Aillas, "you and I are to make a journey. Turn your back, if you will; I must bind your arms so that you perform no unseasonable antics. Obey me and you will come to no harm."

"What of my convenience?" blurted Brother Umphred.

"You should have considered that before you came here to-night. Turn around, doff your cassock and put your arms behind you."

Instead, Brother Umphred sprang at Aillas and struck him with the cudgel he likewise had taken from the wood-pile.

Aillas stumbled back; Brother Umphred sent Suldrun reeling. He ran from the chapel, up the path, with Aillas after him, through the postern and out onto the Urquial, bellowing at the top of his voice: "Guards to me! Help! Treason! Murder! Help! To me! Seize the traitor!"

Up from the arcade trooped a company of four, the same which Aillas and Suldrun had avoided by stepping into the orangery. They ran forward to seize both Umphred and Aillas. "What goes on here? Why this horrid outcry?"

"Call King Casmir!" bawled Brother Umphred. "Waste not an instant! This vagabond has troubled the Princess Suldrun: a terrible deed! Bring King Casmir, I say! On the run!"

King Casmir was brought to the scene, and Brother Umphred excitedly made an explanation. "I saw them in the palace! I recognized the princess, and I have also seen this man; he is a vagabond of the streets! I followed them here and, imagine the audacity, they wanted me to marry them by the Christian rite! I refused with all spirit and warned them of their crime!"

Suldrun, standing by the postern, came forward. "Sire, be not angry with us. This is Aillas; we are husband and wife. We love each other dearly; please give us leave to live our lives in tranquility. If you so choose, we will go from Haidion and never return."

Brother Umphred, still excited by his role in the affair, would not be still. "They threatened me; I am almost bereft of reason through their malice! They forced me to witness their wedlock! If I had not signed to the ceremony they would have broken my head!"

Casmir spoke icily: "Silence, enough! I will deal with you later." He gave an order: "Bring me Zerling!" He turned to Suldrun. In times of rage or excitement Casmir kept his voice always even and neutral, and he did so now. "You seem to have disobeyed my command. Whatever your reason it is far from sufficient."

Suldrun said softly: "You are my father; have you no concern for my happiness?"

"I am King of Lyonesse. Whatever my one-time feelings, they were dispelled by the disregard for my wishes, of which you know. Now I find you consorting with a nameless bumpkin. So be it! My anger is not diminished. You shall return to the garden, and there abide. Go!"

Shoulders sagging, Suldrun went to the postern, through, and down into the garden. King Casmir turned to appraise Aillas. "Your presumption is amazing. You shall have ample time to reflect upon it. Zerling! Where is Zerling?"

"Sire, I am here." A squat slope-shouldered man, bald, with a brown beard and round staring eyes, came forward: Zerling, King Casmir's Chief Executioner, the most dreaded man of Lyonesse Town next to Casmir himself.

King Casmir spoke a word into his ear.

Zerling put a halter around Aillas' neck and led him across the Urquial, then around and behind the Peinhador. By the light of the half-moon the halter was removed and a rope was tied around Aillas' chest. He was lifted over a stone verge and lowered into a hole: down, down, down. Finally his feet struck the bottom. In a succinct gesture of finality, the rope was dropped in after him.

There was no sound in the darkness. The air smelled of dank stone with a taint of human decay. For five minutes Aillas stood staring up the shaft. Then he groped to one of the walls: a distance of perhaps seven feet. His foot encountered a hard round object. Reaching down he discovered a skull. Moving to the side, Aillas sat down with his back to the wall. After a period, fatigue weighted his eyelids; he became drowsy. He fought off sleep as best he could for fear of awakening...At last he slept.

He awoke, and his fears were justified. Upon recollection he cried out in disbelief and anguish. How could such tragedy be possible? Tears flooded his eyes; he bent his head into his arms and wept.

An hour passed, while he sat hunched in pure misery.

Light seeped down the shaft; he was able to discern the dimensions of his cell. The floor was a circular area about fourteen feet in diameter, flagged with heavy slabs of stone. The stone walls rose vertically six feet, then funneled up to the central shaft, which entered the cell about twelve feet over the floor. Against the far wall bones and skulls had been piled; Aillas counted ten skulls, and others perhaps were hidden under the pile of bones. Near to where he sat lay another skeleton: evidently the last occupant of the cell.

Aillas rose to his feet. He went to the center of the chamber and looked up the shaft. High above he saw a disk of blue sky, so airy, windswept and free that again tears came to his eyes.

He considered the shaft. The diameter was about five feet; it was cased in rough stone and rose sixty or even seventy feet—exact judgment was difficult—above the point where it entered the chamber.

Aillas turned away. On the walls previous occupants had scratched names and sad mottos. The most recent occupant, on the wall above his skeleton, had scratched a schedule of names, to the number of twelve, ranked in a column. Aillas, too dispirited to feel interest in anything but his own woes, turned away.

The cell was unfurnished. The rope lay in a loose heap under the shaft. Near the bone pile he noticed the rotted remains of other ropes, garments, ancient leather buckles and straps.

The skeleton seemed to watch him from the empty eye-sockets of its skull. Aillas dragged it to the bone pile, and turned the skull so that it could see only the wall. Then he sat down. An inscription on the wall opposite caught his attention: "Newcomer! Welcome to our brotherhood!"

Aillas grunted and turned his attention elsewhere. So began the period of his incarceration.

12

KING CASMIR DESPATCHED AN ENVOY to Tintzin Fyral who, in due course returned with an ivory tube, from which the Chief Herald extracted a scroll. He read to King Casmir:

Noble Sir:

As ever my respectful compliments! I am pleased to learn of your impending visit. Be assured that our welcome will be appropriate to your regal person and distinguished retinue which, so I suggest, should number no more than eight, since at Tintzin Fyral we lack the expansive grace of Haidion.

Again, my most cordial salute!

> Faude Carfilhiot,
> Vale Evander, the Duke.

King Casmir immediately rode north with a retinue of twenty knights, ten servants and three camp-wagons.

The first night the company halted at Duke Baldred's castle, Twannic. On the second day they rode north through the Troagh, a chaos of pinnacles and defiles. On the third day they crossed the border into South Ulfland. Halfway through the afternoon, at the Gates of Cerberus, the cliffs closed in to constrict the way, which was blocked by the fortress Kaul Bocach. The garrison consisted of a dozen raggle-taggle soldiers and a commander who found banditry less profitable than exacting tolls from travelers.

At a challenge from the sentry the cavalcade from Lyonesse halted, while the soldiers of the garrison, blinking and scowling under steel caps, slouched out upon the battlements.

The knight Sir Welty rode forward.

"Halt!" called the commander. "Name your names, your origin, destination and purpose, so that we may reckon the lawful toll."

"We are noblemen in the service of King Casmir of Lyonesse. We ride to visit the Duke of Vale Evander, at his invitation, and we are exempt from toll!"

"No one is exempt from toll, save only King Oriante and the great god Mithra. You must pay ten silver florins."

Sir Welty rode back to confer with Casmir, who thoughtfully appraised the fort. "Pay," said King Casmir. "We will deal with these scoundrels on our return."

Sir Welty returned to the fort and contemptuously tossed a pack of coins to the captain.

"Pass, gentlemen."

Two by two the company rode by Kaul Bocach, and that night rested on a meadow beside the south fork of the Evander.

At noon of the following day the troop halted before Tintzin Fyral, where it surmounted a tall crag, as if growing from the substance of the crag itself.

King Casmir and eight of his knights rode forward; the others turned aside and set up a camp beside the Evander.

A herald came out from the castle, and addressed King Casmir. "Sir, I bring Duke Carfilhiot's compliments and his request that you follow me. We ride a crooked road up the side of the crag, but have no concern; the danger is only to enemies. I will lead the way."

As the troop proceeded, the stench of carrion came on the breeze. In the middle distance the Evander flowed across a green meadow where rose an array of twenty poles, half supporting impaled corpses.

"That is hardly a welcoming sight," King Casmir told the herald.

"Sir, it reminds the duke's enemies that his patience is not inexhaustible."

King Casmir shrugged, offended not so much by Carfilhiot's acts as by the odor.

At the base of the crag waited an honor guard of four knights in ceremonial plate armor, and Casmir wondered how Carfilhiot knew so closely the hour of his coming. A signal from Kaul Bocach? Spies at Haidion? Casmir, who had never been able to introduce spies into Tintzin Fyral, frowned at the thought.

The cavalcade mounted the crag by a road cut into the rock, which finally, high in the air, turned under a portcullis into the castle's forecourt.

Duke Carfilhiot came forward; King Casmir dismounted; the two pressed each other in a formal embrace.

"Sir, I am delighted by your visit," said Carfilhiot. "I have arranged no suitable festivities, but not from any lack of good will. In truth, you gave me too short notice."

"I am perfectly suited," said King Casmir. "I am not here for frivolity. Rather, I hope to explore once more matters of mutual advantage."

"Excellent! That is always a topic of interest. This is your first visit to Tintzin Fyral, is it not?"

"I saw it as a young man, but from a distance. It is beyond question a mighty fortress."

"Indeed. We command four important roads: to Lyonesse, to Ys, over the Ulfish moors and the border road north to Dahaut. We are self-sufficient. I have driven a well deep, through solid stone into a flowing aquifer. We maintain supplies for years of siege. Four men could hold the access road against a thousand, or a million. I consider the castle impregnable."

"I am inclined to agree," said Casmir. "Still, what of the saddle? If a force occupied the mountain yonder, conceivably it might bring siege engines to bear."

Carfilhiot turned to inspect the heights to the north, which were connected to the crag by a saddle, as if he had never before noticed this particular vista. "So it would seem."

"But you are not alarmed?"

Carfilhiot laughed, showing perfect white teeth. "My enemies have reflected long and well on Breakback Ridge. As for the saddle, I have my little wiles."

King Casmir nodded. "The view is exceptionally fine."

"True. On a clear day, from my high workroom, I scan the entire vale, from here to Ys. But now you must refresh yourself, and then we can take up our conversation."

Casmir was conducted to a set of high chambers overlooking Vale Evander: a view across twenty miles of soft green landscape to a far glint of sea. Air, fresh save for an occasional cloying taint, blew through the open windows. Casmir thought of Carfilhiot's dead enemies on the meadow below, each silent on his own pole.

An image flickered through his mind: Suldrun pallid and drawn here at Tintzin Fyral, breathing the putrid air. He thrust away the picture. The affair was over and done.

Two bare-chested black Moorish boys, wearing turbans of purple silk, red pantaloons and sandals with spiral toes, helped him with his bath, then dressed him in silk small-clothes and a tawny-buff robe decorated with black rosettes.

Casmir descended to the great hall, past an enormous aviary, where birds of many-colored plumage flew from branch to branch. Carfilhiot awaited him in the great hall; the two men seated themselves on divans and were served frozen fruit sherbet in silver cups.

"Excellent," said Casmir. "Your hospitality is pleasant."

"It is informal and I hope that you will not be supremely bored," murmured Carfilhiot.

Casmir put aside the ice. "I have come here to discuss a matter of importance." He glanced at the servants. Carfilhiot waved them from the room. "Proceed."

Casmir leaned back in his chair. "King Granice recently sent out a diplomatic mission, on one of his new warships. They put into Blaloc, Pomperol, Dahaut, Cluggach in Godelia and Ys. The emissaries decried my ambitions and proposed an alliance to defeat me. They won only lukewarm support, if any, even though"—Casmir smiled a cold smile—"I have made no attempt to disguise my intentions. Each hopes the others will fight the battle; each wishes to be the single kingdom unmolested. Granice, I am sure, expected no more; he wanted to assert both his leadership and his command of the sea. In this he succeeded very well. His ship destroyed a Ska vessel which at once changes our perceptions of the Ska; they can no longer be considered invincible, and Troice sea-power is magnified. They paid a price, losing the commander and one of the two royal princes aboard.

"For me the message is clear. The Troice become stronger; I must strike and cause a dislocation. The obvious place is South Ulfland, from where I can attack the Ska in North Ulfland, before they consolidate their holdings. Once I take the fortress Poëlitetz, Dahaut is at my mercy. Audry cannot fight me from both west and south.

"First then—to take South Ulfland, with maximum facility, which presupposes your cooperation." Casmir paused. Carfilhiot, looking thoughtfully into the fire, made no immediate response.

The silence became uncomfortable. Carfilhiot stirred and said: "You have, as you know, my personal well-wishes, but I am not altogether a free agent, and I must conduct myself with circumspection."

"Indeed," said Casmir. "You apparently do not refer to your nominal liege-lord King Oriante."

"Definitely not."

"Who, may I ask, are the enemies you are so pointedly trying to dissuade?"

Carfilhiot made a motion. "I agree, the stench is appalling. Those are rogues of the moors: petty barons, ten-tuffet lords, little better than bandits, so that an honest man takes his life in his hands to ride out across the fells for a day's hunting. South Ulfland is essentially lawless, save for Vale Evander. Poor Oriante can't dominate his wife, much less a kingdom. Every clan chieftain fancies himself an aristocrat and builds a mountain fortress, from which he raids his neighbors. I have attempted to bring order: a thankless job. I am styled a despot and an ogre. Harshness, however, is the only language these highland brutes understand."

"These are the enemies who cause your circumspection?"

"No." Carfilhiot rose to his feet and went to stand with his back to the fire. He looked down at Casmir with cool dispassion. "In all candor, here are the facts. I am a student of magic. I am taught by the great Tamurello, and I am under obligation, so that I must refer to him matters of policy. That is the situation."

Casmir stared up into Carfilhiot's eyes. "When may I expect your response?"

"Why wait?" asked Carfilhiot. "Let us settle the matter now. Come."

The two climbed to Carfilhiot's workroom, Casmir now quiet, alert and alive with interest.

Carfilhiot's apparatus was almost embarrassingly scant; even Casmir's trifles were impressive by contrast. Perhaps, Casmir speculated, Carfilhiot kept the larger part of his equipment stored in cabinets.

A large map of Hybras, carved in various woods, dominated all else, in both size and evident importance. In a panel at the back of the map had been carved a face: the semblance, so it seemed, of Tamurello, in crude and exaggerated outlines. The craftsman had been at no pains to flatter Tamurello. The forehead bulged over protruding eyes; cheeks and lips were painted a particularly unpleasant red. Carfilhiot pointedly offered no explanations. He pulled at the ear-lobe of the image. "Tamurello! hear the voice of Faude Carfilhiot!" He touched the mouth. "Tamurello, speak!"

In a wooden croak the mouth said: "I hear and speak."

Carfilhiot touched the eyes. "Tamurello! Look upon me and King Casmir of Lyonesse. We are considering the use of his armies in South Ulfland, to quell disorder and to extend King Casmir's wise rule. We understand your policy of detachment; still we ask your advice."

The image spoke: "I advise no alien troops in South Ulfland, most especially the armies of Lyonesse. King Casmir, your goals do you credit, but they would unsettle all Hybras, including Dahaut, to bring inconvenience upon me. I advise that you return to Lyonesse and make peace with Troicinet. Carfilhiot, I advise that you decisively use the might of Tintzin Fyral to bar incursions into South Ulfland."

"Thank you," spoke Carfilhiot. "We will surely take your advice to heart."

Casmir said no word. Together they descended to the parlor, where, for an hour, they spoke courteously of small subjects. Casmir declared himself ready for his bed, and Carfilhiot wished him a comfortable night's sleep.

In the morning King Casmir rose early, expressed gratitude to Carfilhiot for his hospitality, and with no further ado made his departure.

At noon the party approached Kaul Bocach. King Casmir, with half of his knights passed the fort after paying a toll of eight silver florins. A few yards along the road they halted. The rest of the party approached the fortress. The captain of the fortress stepped forward. "Why did you not pass all together? It is now necessary that you pay another eight florins."

Sir Welty dismounted without haste. He seized the captain and held a knife to his throat. "Which will you be: a dead Ulfish cutthroat, or a live soldier in the service of King Casmir of Lyonesse?"

The captain's steel hat fell off, his bald brown pate bobbed as he writhed and struggled. He gasped. "This is treachery! Where is honor?"

"Look yonder; there sits King Casmir. Do you accuse him of dishonor, after mulcting him of his royal money?"

"Naturally not, still—"

Sir Welty pricked him with the knife. "Order your men out for inspection. You will cook over a slow fire if a drop of blood, other than your own, is spilled."

The captain attempted a final defiance. "You expect me to deliver our impregnable Kaul Bocach into your hands without so much as a protest?"

"Protest all you like. In fact, I'll let you go back within. Then you are under siege. We will climb the cliff and drop boulders on the battlements."

"Possible perhaps, but very difficult."

"We will fire logs and thrust them into the passage; they shall blaze and smoulder, you will smoke and bake as the heat spreads. Do you defy the might of Lyonesse?"

The captain heaved a deep breath. "Of course not! As I declared from the very first, I gladly enter the service of the most gracious King Casmir! Ho, guards! Out for inspection!"

Glumly the garrison filed out to stand scowling and disheveled in the sunlight, hair tousled under their steel caps.

Casmir looked them over with contempt. "It might be easier to lop off their heads."

"Have no fear!" cried the captain. "We are the smartest of troops under ordinary circumstances!"

King Casmir shrugged, and turned away. The fortress tolls were loaded into one of the wagons; Sir Welty and fourteen knights remained as a temporary garrison and King Casmir joylessly returned to Lyonesse Town.

In his workroom at Tintzin Fyral Carfilhiot once again engaged the attention of Tamurello.

"Casmir has departed. Our relationship is at best formally polite."

"The very optimum! Kings, like children, tend to be opportunistic. Generosity only spoils them. They equate affability with weakness and hasten to exploit it."

"Casmir's temperament is even less pleasant. He is as singleminded as a fish. I saw him spontaneous only here in my workroom; he is interested in magic, and has ambitions in this direction."

"For Casmir, forever futile. He lacks the patience and here he is much like yourself."

"Possibly true. I am anxious to proceed into the first extensions."

"The situation is as before. The field of analogues must be like a second nature to you. How long can you fix an image in your mind, then change its colors at your will, while holding fixed lineaments?"

"I am not proficient."

"These images should be hard as rocks. Upon conceiving a landscape you must be able to count the leaves on a tree, then recount to the same number."

"That is a difficult exercise. Why can't I merely work the apparatus?"

"Aha! Where will you obtain this apparatus? Despite my love for you, I can part with none of my hard-won operators."

"Still, one can always contrive new apparatus."

"Indeed? I would be glad to learn this hermetic and abstruse secret."

"Still, you agree, it is possible."

"But difficult. Sandestins are no longer innocent nor plentiful nor accommodating . . . Eh! Ha!" This was a sudden exclamation. Tamurello spoke in a changed voice. "A thought occurs to me. It's so beautiful a thought that I hardly dare to think it."

"Tell me this thought."

Tamurello's silence was that of a man engaged in a complex calculation. Finally he said: "It is a dangerous thought. I could neither advocate nor even suggest such a thought!"

"Tell me the thought!"

"Even so much is to join in its implementation!"

"It must be a dangerous thought indeed."

"True. Let us pass on to safer subjects. I might make this mischievous observation: one way to secure magical apparatus is, in blunt language, to rob another magician, who thereupon may become too feeble to avenge the predation—especially if he does not know its perpetrator."

"So far I follow you closely. What then?"

"Suppose one were to rob a magician: who would he choose to victimize? Murgen? Me? Baibalides? Never. The consequences would be certain, swift and awful. One would seek a novice still fresh to his lore, and preferably one with an amplitude of equipment, so that the theft yields a good return. Also, the victim should be one whom he perceives as an enemy of the future. The time to weaken, or even destroy, that person is now! I speak of course in the purest of hypothetical terms."

"For the purposes of illustration and still hypothetically, who might such a person be?"

Tamurello could not bring himself to utter a name. "Even hypothetical contingencies must be explored down several levels, and whole areas of duplicity must be arranged; we will talk more of this later, meanwhile, not a word to anyone else!"

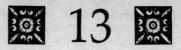

13

SHIMROD, SCION OF MURGEN THE MAGICIAN, early demonstrated an inner impulse of extraordinary strength, and in due course wandered beyond Murgen's control into autonomy.

The two were not obviously similar, save for competence, resource and a certain immoderacy of imagination, which in Shimrod evinced itself as an antic humor and a sometimes painful capacity for sentiment.

In appearance the two were even less alike. Murgen revealed himself as a strong white-haired man of indefinable age. Shimrod appeared as a young man with an almost ingenuous expression. He was spare, long of leg, with sandy-buff hair and hazel-gray eyes. His jaw was long, his cheeks somewhat concave, his mouth wide and twisted as if at some wry reflection.

After a time of loose-footed wandering Shimrod took up residence at Trilda, a manse on Lally Meadow, formerly occupied by Murgen, in the Forest of Tantrevalles, and there settled himself to the serious study of magic, using the books, patterns, apparatus and operators which Murgen had given into his custody.

Trilda was a congenial seat for intensive study. The air smelled fresh of foliage. The sun shone by day, the moon and stars by night. Solitude was near-absolute; ordinary folk seldom ventured so deep into the forest. Trilda had been built by Hilario, a minor magician of many quaint fancies. The rooms were seldom square and overlooked Lally Meadow through bay windows of many sizes and shapes. The steep roof, in addition to six chimneys, disposed itself in innumerable dormers, gables, ridges; and the highest verge supported a black iron weathercock, which served in double stead as a ghost-chaser.

Murgen had dammed the brook to create a pond; the overflow

turned a wheel beside the workroom, where it powered a dozen different machines, including a lathe and a bellows for his hot-fire.

Halflings occasionally came to the edge of the forest to watch Shimrod when he went out on the meadow, but otherwise ignored him for fear of his magic.

The seasons passed; autumn turned to winter. Flakes of snow drifted down from the sky to shroud the meadow in silence. Shimrod kept his fires crackling and began an intensive study of Balberry's *Abstracts and Excerpts*, a vast compendium of exercises, methods, forms and patterns inscribed in antique or even imaginary languages. Using a lens fashioned from a sandestin's eye, Shimrod read these inscriptions as if they were plain tongue.

Shimrod took his meals from a cloth of bounty, which, when spread on a table, produced a toothsome feast. For entertainment he schooled himself in the use of the lute, a skill appreciated by fairies of Tuddifot Shee, at the opposite end of Lally Meadow, who loved music, though no doubt for the wrong reasons. Fairies constructed viols, guitars and grass-pipes of fine quality, but their music at best was a plaintive undisciplined sweetness, like the sound of distant windchimes. At worst they made a clangor of unrelated stridencies, which they could not distinguish from their best. Withal, they were the vainest of the vain. Fairy musicians, discovering that a human passerby had chanced to hear them, invariably inquired how he had enjoyed the music, and woe betide the graceless churl who spoke his mind, for then he was set to dancing for a period comprising a week, a day, an hour, a minute and a second, without pause. However, should the listener declare himself enraptured he might well be rewarded by the vain and gloating halfling. Often, when Shimrod played his lute, he found fairy creatures, large and small,* sitting on the fence, bundled in green coats with red scarves and peaked hats. If he acknowledged their presence, they offered fulsome approbation and asked for more music. On certain occasions fairy horn-players asked to play along with him; each time Shimrod made polite refusal; if he allowed such

---

*Fairies maintain no specific size indefinitely. When dealing with men they often appear the size of children, seldom larger. When caught unawares, they seem on occasion only four inches to a foot tall. The fairies themselves take no heed of size. See Glossary II.

a duet he might find himself playing forever: by day, by night, across the meadow, in the treetops, higgledy-piggledy through thorn and thicket, across the moors, underground in the shees.* The secret, so Shimrod knew, was never to accept the fairies' terms, but always to close the deal on one's own stipulations, otherwise the bargain was sure to turn sour.

One of those who listened as Shimrod played was a beautiful fairy maiden with flowing nut-brown hair. Shimrod tried to lure her into his house with the offer of sweetmeats. One day she approached and stood looking at him, mouth curved, eyes glinting with mischief. "And why would you wish me inside that great house of yours?"

"Shall I be truthful? I would hope to make love to you."

"Ah! But that is sweetness you should never try to taste, for you might become mad, and follow me forever making vain entreaties."

"'Vain', always and always? And you would cruelly deny me?"

"Perhaps."

"What if you discovered that warm human love was more pleasing than your birdlike fairy couplings? Then who would beseech and who would follow whom forever, making the vain entreaties of a love-sick fairy maid?"

The fairy screwed up her face in puzzlement. "That concept has never occurred to me."

"Then come inside and we shall see. First I will pour you wine of pomegranates. Then we will slip from our clothes and warm our skins by firelight."

"And then?"

"Then we will make the test to learn whose love is the warmer."

The fairy maiden pulled her mouth together in a pout of mock-outrage. "I should not flaunt before a stranger."

"But I am no stranger. Even now, when you look at me, you melt with love."

"I am frightened." Quickly she retreated and Shimrod saw her no more.

Spring arrived; the snows melted and flowers bedizened the meadow. One sunny morning Shimrod left his manse and wan-

---

*Fairies share with humans the qualities of malice, spite, treachery, envy and ruthlessness; they lack the equally human traits of clemency kindness, pity. The fairy sense of humor never amuses its victim.

153

dered the meadow rejoicing in the flowers, the bright green foliage, the bird calls. He discovered a track leading north into the forest which he never before had noticed.

Under the oaks, thick-boled with sprawling branches, he followed the trail: back, forth, over a hillock, down into a dark glen, then up and through a clearing, walled with tall silver birches, sprinkled with blue corn-flowers. The way led up over an outcrop of black rocks, and now, through the forest, Shimrod heard laments and outcries, punctuated by a reverberant thudding sound. Shimrod ran light-footed through the woods, to discover among the rocks a tarn of black-green water. To the side a long-bearded troll, with an extravagantly large cudgel, beat a lank furry creature hanging like a rug on a line between a pair of trees. With every blow the creature cried out for mercy: "Stop! No more! You are breaking my bones! Have you no pity? You have mistaken me; this is clear! My name is Grofinet! No more! Use logic and reason!"

Shimrod moved forward. "Stop the blows!"

The troll, five feet tall and burly, jumped around in surprise. He lacked a neck; his head rested directly on the shoulders. He wore a dirty jerkin and trousers; a leather cod-piece encased a set of very large genitals.

Shimrod sauntered forward. "Why must you beat poor Grofinet?"

"Why does one do anything?" growled the troll. "From a sense of purpose! For the sake of a job well done!"

"That is a good response, but it leaves many questions unanswered," said Shimrod.

"Possibly so, but no matter. Be off with you. I wish to thrash this bastard hybrid of two bad dreams."

"It is all a mistake!" bawled Grofinet. "It must be resolved before damage is done! Lower me to the ground, where we can talk calmly, without prejudice."

The troll struck out with his cudgel. "Silence!"

In a frantic spasm Grofinet won free of the bonds. He scrambled about the clearing on long big-footed legs, hopping and dodging, while the troll chased after with his cudgel. Shimrod stepped forward and pushed the troll into the tarn. A few oily bubbles rose to the surface and the tarn was once more smooth.

"Sir, that was a deft act," said Grofinet. "I am in your debt!"

Shimrod spoke modestly: "Truly, no great matter."

"I regret that I must differ with you."

"Quite rightly," said Shimrod. "I spoke without thinking, and now I will bid you good day."

"One moment, sir. May I ask as to whom I am indebted?"

"I am Shimrod; I live at Trilda, a mile or so through the forest."

"Surprising! Few men of the human race visit these parts alone."

"I am a magician of sorts," said Shimrod. "The halflings avoid me." He looked Grofinet up and down. "I must say that I have never seen another like you. What is your sort?"

Grofinet replied in a rather lofty manner. "That is a topic which gentle-folk seldom see fit to discuss."

"My apologies! I intended no vulgarity. Once again, I bid you good day."

"I will conduct you to Trilda," said Grofinet. "These are dangerous parts. It is the least I can do."

"As you wish."

The two returned to Lally Meadow. Shimrod halted. "You need come no farther. Trilda is only a few steps yonder."

"As we walked," said Grofinet, "I pondered. It came to me that I am much in your debt."

"Say nothing more," declared Shimrod. "I am happy to have been of help."

"That is easy for you to say, but the burden weighs on my pride! I am forced to declare myself in your service, until the score is settled. Do not refuse; I am adamant! You need provide only my food and shelter. I will take responsibility for tasks which otherwise might distract you, and even perform minor magics."

"Ah! You are also a magician?"

"An amateur of the art, little more. You may instruct me further, if you like. After all, two trained minds are better than one. And never forget security! When a person intently looks forward, he leaves his backside unguarded!"

Shimrod could not shake Grofinet's resolution, and Grofinet became a member of the household.

At first Grofinet and his activities were a distraction; ten times in the first week Shimrod paused on the very verge of sending Grofinet away, but always drew back in the face of Grofinet's virtues, which were notable. Grofinet caused no irregularities and disturbed none of Shimrod's properties. He was remarkably tidy, and never out of sorts; indeed, Grofinet's high spirits caused the distractions. His mind was fertile and his enthusiasms came one upon the other. For the first few days Grofinet conducted himself with exaggerated diffidence; even so, while Shimrod strained to memorize the interminable lists in The Order of Mutables, Grofinet loped about the house talking to imaginary, or at least invisible, companions.

Presently Shimrod's exasperation became amusement, and he found himself looking forward to Grofinet's next outbreak of foolishness. One day Shimrod waved a fly from his work-table; at once Grofinet became the vigilant enemy of flies, moths, bees, and other winged insects, allowing them no trespass. Unable to catch them, he opened wide the front door, then herded the individual insect to the outdoors. Meanwhile a dozen others entered. Shimrod noticed Grofinet's efforts and worked a small bane upon Trilda, which sent every insect fleeing posthaste from the house. Grofinet was greatly pleased by his success.

At last, bored with boasting of his triumph over the insects, Grofinet developed a new caprice. He spent several days contriving wings of withe and yellow silk, which he strapped to his lank torso. Looking from his window Shimrod watched him running across Lally Meadow, flapping his wings and bounding into the air, hoping to fly like a bird. Shimrod was tempted to lift Grofinet by magic and flit him aloft. He controlled the whimsy lest Grofinet become dangerously elated and bring himself to harm. Later in the afternoon Grofinet attempted a great bound and fell into Lally Water. The fairies of Tuddifot Shee spent themselves in immoderate glee, rolling and tumbling, kicking their legs into the air. Grofinet threw aside the wings in disgust, and limped back to Trilda.

Grofinet next gave himself to the study of the Egyptian pyramids. "They are extraordinarily fine and a credit to the pharaohs!" declared Grofinet.

"Exactly so."

On the next morning Grofinet spoke further on the subject. "These mighty monuments are fascinating in their simplicity."

"True."

"I wonder what might be their scope?"

Shimrod shrugged. "A hundred yards to the side, more or less, or so I suppose."

Later Shimrod observed Grofinet pacing out dimensions along

Lally Meadow. He called out: "What are you doing?"

"Nothing of consequence."

"I hope you are not planning to build a pyramid! It would block the sunlight!"

Grofinet paused in his pacing. "Perhaps you are right." He reluctantly suspended his plans, but quickly discovered a new interest. During the evening Shimrod came into the parlor to light the lamps. Grofinet stepped from the shadows. "Now then, Sir Shimrod, did you see me as you passed?"

Shimrod's mind had been elsewhere, and Grofinet had stood somewhat back past his range of vision. "For a fact," said Shimrod, I utterly failed to see you."

"In that case," said Grofinet, "I have learned the technique of invisibility!"

"Wonderful! What is your secret?"

"I use the force of sheer will to put myself beyond perception!"

"I must learn this method."

"Intellectual thrust, pure and simple, is the key," said Grofinet, and added the warning: "If you fail, don't be disappointed. It is a difficult feat."

"We shall see."

The following day Grofinet experimented with his new sleight. Shimrod would call: "Grofinet! Where are you? Have you gone invisible again?" Whereupon Grofinet would step from a corner of the room in triumph.

One day Grofinet suspended himself from the ceiling beams of the workroom, on a pair of straps, to hang as if in a hammock. Shimrod, upon entering the room, might have noticed nothing, except that Grofinet had neglected to put up his tail, which dangled into the middle of the room, terminating in a tuft of tawny fur.

Grofinet at last decided to put by all his previous ambitions and to become a magician in earnest. To this end he frequented the workroom, to watch Shimrod at his manipulations. He was, however, intensely afraid of fire; whenever Shimrod, for one reason or another, excited a tongue of flame, Grofinet bounded from the room in a panic, and at last put by his plans to become a magician.

Midsummer's Eve drew near. Coincidentally a series of vivid dreams came to disturb Shimrod's sleep. The landscape was always the same: a terrace of white stone overlooking a beach of white sand and a calm blue sea beyond. A marble balustrade enclosed the terrace, and low surf broke into foam along the beach.

In the first dream Shimrod leaned on the balustrade, idly surveying the sea. Along the beach came walking a dark-haired maiden, in a sleeveless smock of a soft gray-brown cloth. As she approached, Shimrod saw that she was slender and an inch or so taller than medium stature. Black hair, caught in a twist of dark red twine, hung almost to her shoulders. Her arms and bare feet were graceful; her skin was a pale olive. Shimrod thought her exquisitely beautiful, with an added quality which included both mystery and a kind of provocation that, rather than overt, was implicit in her very existence. As she passed, she turned Shimrod a somber half-smile, neither inviting nor forbidding, then went along the beach and out of sight. Shimrod stirred in his sleep and awoke.

The second dream was the same, except that Shimrod called to the maiden and invited her to the terrace; she hesitated, smilingly shook her head and passed on.

On the third night, she halted and spoke: "Why do you call me, Shimrod?"

"I want you to stop, and at least talk with me."

The maiden demurred. "I think not. I know very little of men, and I am frightened, for I feel a strange impulse when I pass by."

On the fourth night, the maiden of the dream paused, hesitated, then slowly approached the terrace. Shimrod stepped down to meet her, but she halted and Shimrod found that he could approach her no more closely, which in the context of the dream seemed not unnatural. He asked: "Today will you speak to me?"

"I know of nothing to tell you."

"Why do you walk the beach?"

"Because it pleases me."

"Whence do you come and where do you go?"

"I am a creature of your dreams; I walk in and out of thought."

"Dream-thing or not, come closer and stay with me. Since the dream is mine, you must obey."

"That is not the nature of dreams." As she turned away, she looked over her shoulder, and when at last Shimrod awoke, he remembered the exact quality of her expression. Enchantment! But to what purpose?

Shimrod walked out on the meadow, considering the situation from every conceivable aspect. A sweet enticement was being laid upon him by subtle means, and no doubt to his eventual disadvantage. Who might work such a spell? Shimrod cast among the persons known to him, but none would seem to have reason to beguile him with so strangely beautiful a maiden.

He returned to the workroom and tried to cast a portent, but the necessary detachment failed him and the portent broke into a spatter of discordant colors.

He sat late in the workroom that night while a cool dark wind sighed through the trees at the back of the manse. The prospect of sleep brought him both misgivings and an uneasy tingle of anticipation which he tried to quell, but which persisted nevertheless. "Very well then," Shimrod told himself in a surge of bravado, "let us face up to the matter and discover where it leads."

He took himself to his couch. Sleep was slow in coming; for hours he twitched through a troubled doze, sensitive to every fancy which chose to look into his mind. At last he slept.

The dream came presently. Shimrod stood on the terrace; along the beach came the maiden, bare-armed and bare-footed, her black hair blowing in the sea-wind. She approached without haste. Shimrod waited imperturbably, leaning on the balustrade. To show impatience was poor policy, even in a dream. The maiden drew near; Shimrod descended the wide marble stairs.

The wind died, and also the surf; the dark-haired maiden halted and stood waiting. Shimrod moved closer and a waft of perfume reached him: the odor of violets. The two stood only a yard apart; he might have touched her.

She looked into his face, smiling her pensive half-smile. She spoke. "Shimrod, I may visit you no more."

"What is to stay you?"

"My time is short. I must go to a place behind the star Achernar."

"Is this of your own will where you would go?"

"I am enchanted."

"Tell me how to break the enchantment!"

The maiden seemed to hesitate. "Not here."

"Where then?"

159

"I will go to the Goblins Fair; will you meet me there?"

"Yes! Tell me of the enchantment so that I may fix the counter-spell."

The maiden moved slowly away. "At the Goblins Fair." With a single backward glance she departed.

Shimrod thoughtfully watched her retreating form...From behind him came a roaring sound, as of many voices raised in fury. He felt the thud of heavy footsteps, and stood paralyzed, unable to move or look over his shoulder.

He awoke on his couch at Trilda, heart pumping and throat tight. The time was the darkest hour of the night, long before dawn could even be imagined. The fire had guttered low in the fireplace. All to be seen of Grofinet, softly snoring in his deep cushion was a foot and a lank tail.

Shimrod built up the fire and returned to his couch. He lay listening to sounds of the night. From across the meadow came a sad sweet whistle, of a bird awakened, perhaps by an owl.

Shimrod closed his eyes and so slept the remainder of the night.

The time of the Goblins Fair was close at hand. Shimrod packed all his magical apparatus, books, librams, philtres and operators into a case, upon which he worked a spell of obfuscation, so that the case was first shrunk, then turned in from out seven times to the terms of a secret sequence, so as finally to resemble a heavy black brick which Shimrod hid under the hearth.

Grofinet watched from the doorway in total perplexity. "Why do you do all this?"

"Because I must leave Trilda for a short period, and thieves will not steal what they cannot find."

Grofinet pondered the remark, his tail twitching first this way then that, in synchrony with his thoughts. "This, of course, is a prudent act. Still, while I am on guard, no thief would dare so much as to look in this direction."

"No doubt," said Shimrod, "but with double precautions our property is doubly safe."

Grofinet, had no more to say, and went outside to survey the meadow. Shimrod took occasion to effect a third precaution and installed a House Eye high in the shadows where it might survey household events.

Shimrod packed a small knapsack and went to issue final

instructions to Grofinet, who lay dozing in the sunlight. "Grofinet, a last word!"

Grofinet raised his head. "Speak; I am alert."

"I am going to the Goblins Fair. You are now in charge of security and discipline. No creature wild or otherwise is to be invited inside. Pay no heed to flattery or soft words. Inform one and all that this is the manse Trilda, where no one is allowed."

"I understand, in every detail," declared Grofinet. "My vision is keen; I have the fortitude of a lion. Not so much as a flea shall enter the house."

"Precisely correct. I am on my way."

"Farewell, Shimrod! Trilda is secure!"

Shimrod set off into the forest. Once beyond Grofinet's range of vision, he brought four white feathers from his pouch and fixed them to his boots. He sang out: "Feather boots, be faithful to my needs; take me where I will."

The feathers fluttered to lift Shimrod and slide him away through the forest, under oaks pierced by shafts of sunlight. Celandine, violets, harebells grew in the shade; the clearings were bright with buttercups, cowslips and red poppies.

Miles went by. He passed fairy shees: Black Aster, Catterlein, Feair Foiry and Shadow Thawn, seat of Rhodion, king of all fairies. He passed goblin houses, under the heavy roots of oak trees, and the ruins once occupied by the ogre Fidaugh. When Shimrod paused to drink from a spring, a soft voice called his name from behind a tree. "Shimrod, Shimrod, where are you bound?"

"Along the path and beyond," said Shimrod and started along the way. The soft voice came after him: "Alas, Shimrod, that you did not stay your steps, if only for a moment, perhaps to alter events to come!"

Shimrod made no reply, nor paused, on the theory that anything offered in the Forest of Tantrevalles must command an exorbitant price. The voice faded to a murmur and was gone.

He presently joined the Great North Road, an avenue only a trifle wider than the first, and bounded north at speed.

He paused to drink water where an outcrop of gray rock rose beside the way, and low green bushes laden with dark red riddleberries, from which fairies pressed their wine, were shaded by twisted black cypresses, growing in cracks and crevices. Shimrod reached to pick the berries, but, noting a flutter of filmy garments, he thought better of such boldness and turned back to the way, only to be pelted with a handful of berries. Shimrod ignored the impudence, as well as the trills and titters which followed.

The sun sank low and Shimrod entered a region of low rocks and outcrops, where the trees grew gnarled and contorted and the sunlight seemed the color of dilute blood, while the shadows were smears of dark blue. Nothing moved, no wind stirred the leaves; yet this strange territory was surely perilous and had best be put behind before nightfall; Shimrod ran north at great speed.

The sun dropped past the horizon; mournful colors filled the sky. Shimrod climbed to the top of a stony mound. He placed down a small box, which expanded to the dimensions of a hut. Shimrod entered, closed and barred the door, ate from the larder, then reclined on the couch and slept. He awoke during the night and for half an hour watched processions of small red and blue lights moving across the forest floor, then returned to his couch.

An hour later his rest was disturbed by the cautious scrape of fingers, or claws: first along the wall; then at his door, pushing and prying; then at the panes of the window. Then the hut thudded as the creature leapt to the roof.

Shimrod set the lamp aglow, drew his sword and waited.

A moment passed.

Down the chimney reached a long arm, the color of putty. The fingers, tipped with little pads like the toes of a frog, reached into the room. Shimrod struck with his sword, severing the hand at the wrist. The stump oozed black-green blood; from the roof came a moan of dismal distress. The creature fell to the ground and once again there was silence.

Shimrod examined the severed member. Rings decorated the four fingers; the thumb wore a heavy silver ring with a turquoise cabochon. An inscription mysterious to Shimrod encircled the stone. Magic? Whatever its nature, it had failed to protect the hand.

Shimrod cut loose the rings, washed them well, tucked them into his pouch and returned to sleep.

In the morning Shimrod reduced the hut and proceeded along the trail, which stopped short on the banks of the River Tway; Shimrod crossed at a single bound. The trail continued beside the river, which at intervals widened into placid ponds reflecting weeping willows and reeds. Then the river swerved south and the trail once more north.

Two hours into the afternoon he arrived at the iron post which marked that intersection known as Twitten's Corner. A sign, The Laughing Sun and The Crying Moon hung at the door of a long low inn, constructed of rough-hewn timber. Directly below the sign a heavy door bound with iron clasps opened into the common-room of the inn.

Entering, Shimrod saw tables and benches to the left side, a counter to the right. Here worked a tall narrow-faced youth with white hair and silver eyes, and—so Shimrod surmised—a proportion of halfling blood in his veins.

Shimrod approached the counter. The youth came to serve him. "Sir?"

"I wish accommodation, if such is available."

"I believe that we are full, sir, owing to the fair; but you had best ask of Hockshank the innkeeper. I am the pot-boy and lack all authority."

"Be so good, then, as to summon Hockshank."

A voice spoke: "Who pronounces my name?"

From the kitchen came a man of heavy shoulders, short legs and no perceptible neck. Thick hair with much the look of old thatch covered the dome of his head; golden eyes and pointed ears again indicated halfling blood.

Shimrod responded: "I spoke your name, sir. I wish accommodation, but I understand that you may be full."

"That is more or less true. Usually I can supply all grades of accommodation, at varying prices, but now the choice is limited. What did you have in mind?"

"I would hope for a chamber clean and airy, without insect population, a comfortable bed, good food and low to moderate rates."

Hockshank rubbed his chin. "This morning one of my guests was stung by a brass-horned natrid. He became uneasy and ran off down the West Road without settling his account. I can offer you his chamber, along with good food, at moderate cost. Or you may share a stall with the natrid for a lesser sum."

"I prefer the room," said Shimrod.

"That would be my own choice," said Hockshank. "This way, then." He led Shimrod to a chamber which Shimrod found adequate to his needs.

Hockshank said, "You speak with a good voice and carry yourself like a gentleman; still, I detect about you the odor of magic."

"It emanates, perhaps, from these rings."

"Interesting!" said Hockshank. "For such rings I will trade you a high-spirited black unicorn. Some say that only a virgin may ride this creature, but never believe it. What does a unicorn care about chastity? Even were he so nice, how would he make his findings? Would maidens be apt to display the evidence so readily? I think not. We may dismiss the concept as an engaging fable, but no more."

"In any case, I need no unicorn."

Hockshank, disappointed, took his departure.

Shimrod shortly returned to the common-room, where he took a leisurely supper. Other visitors to the Goblins Fair sat in small groups discussing their wares and transacting business. Little conviviality was evident; there was no hearty tossing back of beer, nor jests called across the room. Rather, the patrons bent low over their tables muttering and whispering, with suspicious glances darted to the side. Heads jerked back in outrage; eyeballs rolled toward the ceiling. There were quivering fists, sudden indrawn breaths, sibilant exclamations at prices considered excessive. These were dealers in amulets, talismans, effectuaries, curios and oddments, of value real or purported. Two wore the blue and white striped robes of Mauretania, another the coarse tunic of Ireland. Several used the flat accents of Armorica and one golden-haired man with blue eyes and blunt features might have been a Lombard or an Eastern Goth. A certain number displayed the signals of halfling blood: pointed ears, eyes of odd color, extra fingers. Few women were present, and none resembled the maiden Shimrod had come to meet.

Shimrod finished his supper, then went to his chamber where he slept undisturbed the night through.

In the morning Shimrod breakfasted upon apricots, bread and bacon, then sauntered without haste to the meadow behind the inn, which was already enclosed within a ring of booths.

For an hour Shimrod strolled here and there, then seated himself on a bench between a cage of beautiful young hobgoblins with green wings, and a vendor of aphrodisiacs.

The day passed without notable event; Shimrod returned to the inn.

The next day also was spent in vain, though the fair had

reached its peak of activity. Shimrod waited without impatience; by the very nature of such affairs, the maiden would delay her appearance until Shimrod's restlessness had eroded his prudence—if indeed she elected to appear at all.

Midway through the afternoon of the third day, the maiden entered the clearing. She wore a long black cloak flared over a pale tan gown. The hood was thrown back to reveal a circlet of white and purple violets around her black hair. She looked about the meadow in a frowning reverie, as if wondering why she had come. Her gaze fell upon Shimrod, passed him by, then dubiously returned.

Shimrod rose to his feet and approached her. He spoke in a gentle voice: "Dream-maiden, I am here."

Sidelong, over her shoulder, she watched him approach, smiling her half-smile. Slowly she turned to face him. She seemed, thought Shimrod, somewhat more self-assured, more certainly a creature of flesh and blood than the maiden of abstract beauty who had walked through his dreams. She said: "I am here too, as I promised."

Shimrod's patience had been tried by the wait. He made a terse observation: "You came in no fury of haste."

The maiden showed only amusement. "I knew you would wait."

"If you came only to laugh at me, I am not gratified."

"One way or the other, I am here."

Shimrod considered her with analytical detachment, which she seemed to find irksome. She asked: "Why do you look at me so?"

"I wonder what you want of me."

She shook her head sadly. "You are wary. You do not trust me."

"You would think me a fool if I did."

She laughed. "Still, a gallant reckless fool."

"I am gallant and reckless to be here at all."

"You were not so distrustful in the dreaming."

"Then you were dreaming too when you walked along the beach?"

"How could I enter your dreams unless you were in mine? But you must ask no questions. You are Shimrod, I am Melancthe; we are together and that defines our world."

Shimrod took her hands and drew her a step closer; the odor of violets suffused the air between then. "Each time you speak

165

you reveal a new paradox. How could you know to call me Shimrod? I named no names in my dreams."

Melancthe laughed. "Be reasonable, Shimrod! Is it likely that I should wander into the dream of someone even whose name I did not know? To do so would violate the precepts of both politeness and propriety."

"That is a marvelous and fresh viewpoint," said Shimrod. "I am surprised that you dared so boldly. You must know that in dreams propriety is often disregarded."

Melancthe tilted her head, grimaced, jerked her shoulders, as might a silly young girl. "I would take care to avoid improper dreams."

Shimrod led her to a bench somewhat apart from the traffic of the fair. The two sat half-facing, knees almost touching.

Shimrod said: "The truth and all the truth must be known!"

"How so, Shimrod?"

"If I may not ask questions, or—more accurately—if you give me no answers, how can I not feel uneasiness and distrust in your company?"

She leaned half an inch toward him and he again noticed the scent of violets. "You came here freely, to meet someone you had known only in your dreams. Was this not an act of commitment?"

"In a certain sense. You beguiled me with your beauty. I gladly succumbed. I yearned then as I do now, to take such fabulous beauty and such intelligence for my own. In coming here I made an implicit pledge, in the realm of love. In meeting me here, you also made the same implicit pledge."

"I spoke neither pledge nor promise."

"Nor did I. Now they must be spoken by both of us, so that all things may be justly weighed."

Melancthe laughed uncomfortably and moved on the bench. "The words will not come to my mouth. I cannot speak them. Somehow I am constrained."

"By your virtue?"

"Yes, if you must have it so."

Shimrod reached and took her hands in his. "If we are to be lovers, then virtue must stand aside."

"It is more than virtue alone. It is dread."

"Of what?"

"I find it too strange to talk about."

"Love need not be dreadful. We must relieve you of this fear."

Melancthe said softly: "You are holding my hands in yours."

"Yes."

"You are the first to hold me."

Shimrod looked into her face. Her mouth, rose-red on the pale olive of her face, was fascinating in its flexibility. He leaned forward and kissed her, though she might have turned her head to avoid him. He thought her mouth trembled under his.

She drew away. "That meant nothing!"

"It meant only that as lovers we kissed each other."

"Nothing truly happened!"

Shimrod shook his head in perplexity. "Who is seducing whom? If we are working to the same ends, there is no need for so many cross-purposes."

Melancthe groped for a reply. Shimrod pulled her close and would have kissed her again, but she pulled away. "First you must serve me."

"In what fashion?"

"It is simple enough. In the forest nearby a door opens into the otherwhere Irerly. One of us must go through this door and bring back thirteen gems of different colors, while the other guards the access."

"That would seem to be dangerous work. At least for whomever enters Irerly."

"That is why I came to you." Melancthe rose to her feet. "Come, I will show you."

"Now?"

"Why not? The door is yonder through the forest."

"Very well, then; lead the way."

Melancthe, hesitating, looked askance at Shimrod. His manner was altogether too easy. She had expected beseechments, protests, stipulations and attempts to force her into commitments which so far she felt she had evaded. "Come then."

She took him away from the meadow and along a faint trail into the forest. The trail led this way and that, through dappled shade, past logs supporting brackets and shelves of archaic fungus, beside clusters of celandines, anemones, monks-hood and harebells. Sounds faded behind them and they were alone.

They came to a small glade shadowed under tall birch, alders and oaks. An outcrop of black gabbro edged up from among dozens of white amaryllis, to become a low crag with a single steep face. Into this face of black rock an iron-bound door had been fitted.

Shimrod looked around the clearing. He listened. He searched sky and trees. Nothing could be seen or heard.

Melancthe went to the door. She pulled at a heavy iron latch, drew it ajar, to display a wall of blank rock.

Shimrod watched from a little distance with a polite if detached interest.

Melancthe looked at him from the corner of her eye. Shimrod's unconcern seemed most peculiar. From her cape Melancthe brought a curious hexagonal pattern, which she touched to the center of the stone, where it clung. After a moment the stone dissolved to become luminous mist. She stood back and turned to Shimrod. "There is the gap into Irerly."

"And a fine gap it is. There are questions I must ask if I am to guard effectively. First, how long will you be gone? I would not care to shiver here all night through."

Melancthe, turning, approached Shimrod and put her hands on his shoulders. The odor of violets came sweetly across the air. "Shimrod, do you love me?"

"I am fascinated and obsessed." Shimrod put his arms around her waist and drew her close. "Today it is too late for Irerly. Come, we will return to the inn. Tonight you will share my chamber, and much else besides."

Melancthe, with her face three inches from his, said softly, "Would you truly wish to learn how much I could love you?"

"That is exactly what I have in mind. Come! Irerly can wait."

"Shimrod, do this for me. Go into Irerly and bring me thirteen spangling jewels, each of a different color, and I will guard the passage."

"And then?"

"You will see."

Shimrod tried to take her to the turf. "Now."

"No, Shimrod! After!"

The two stared eye to eye, Shimrod thought, I dare press her no further; already I have forced her to a statement.

He closed his fingertips against an amulet and spoke between his teeth the syllables of a spell which had lain heavy in his mind, and time separated into seven strands. One strand of the seven lengthened and looped away at right angles, to create a temporal hiatus; along this strand moved Shimrod, while Melancthe, the clearing in the forest and all beyond remained static.

14

MURGEN RESIDED AT SWER SMOD, a stone manse of fifty vast echoing chambers, high in the Teach tac Teach.

At the best speed of the feathered boots Shimrod flew, bounded and leapt along the East-West Road from Twitten's Corner to Oswy Undervale, then by a side trail to Swer Smod. Murgen's dreadful sentries allowed him to pass unchallenged.

The front door opened at Shimrod's approach. He entered to find Murgen awaiting him at a large table laid with a linen cloth and silver utensils.

"Be seated," said Murgen. "You will be both hungry and thirsty."

"I am both."

Servants brought tureens and platters; Shimrod satisfied his hunger while Murgen tasted trifles of this and that, and listened silently while Shimrod told of his dreams, of Melancthe and the opening into Irerly.

"I feel that she came to me under compulsion, otherwise her conduct can't be explained. At one moment she shows an almost childlike cordiality, the next she becomes totally cynical in her calculations. Purportedly she wants thirteen gems from Irerly, but I suspect that her motives are otherwise. She is so sure of my infatuation that she barely troubles to dissemble."

Murgen said: "The affair exudes the odor of Tamurello. If he defeats you he weakens me. Then, since he uses Melancthe, his agency cannot be proved. He toyed with the witch Desmëi, then tired of her. For revenge she contrived two creatures of ideal beauty: Melancthe and Faude Carfilhiot. She intended that Melancthe, aloof and unattainable, should madden Tamurello. Alas for Desmëi! Tamurello preferred Faude Carfilhiot who is far from

169

aloof; together they range the near and far shores of unnatural junction."

"How could Tamurello control Melancthe?"

"I have no inkling of how it might be, if indeed he is involved."

"So then—what should I do?"

"Yours is the passion; you must fulfill it as you choose."

"Well then, what of Irerly?"

"If you go there as you are now, you will never return; that is my guess."

Shimrod spoke sadly: "I find it hard to join such faithlessness with such beauty. She gambles a dangerous game, with her living self for her stake."

"No less do you, with your dead self as yours."

Shimrod, daunted by the thought, sat back in his chair. "Worst of all she intends to win. And yet..."

Murgen waited. "'And yet?'"

"Only that."

"I see." Murgen poured wine into the two glasses. "She must not win, if for no other reason than to thwart Tamurello. Now and perhaps forever hence I am preoccupied with Doom. I saw the portent in the form of a tall sea-green wave. I must address myself to the problem and you may have my power perhaps before you are ready for it. Prepare yourself, Shimrod. But first: purge yourself of the infatuation, and there is but a single means to this end."

Shimrod returned to Twitten's Corner on his feathered feet. He proceeded to the glade where he had left Melancthe; she stood as he had left her. He searched the glade; no one skulked in the shade. He looked into the portal: green striations swam and swirled to blur the passage into Irerly. From his pouch he took a ball of yarn. After knotting the loose end into a crack in the iron of the door, he tossed the ball into the opening. Now he rewove the seven strands of time, and re-entered the ordinary environment. Melancthe's words still hung in the air: "And then you will see."

"You must promise."

Melancthe sighed. "When you come back, you shall have all my love."

Shimrod reflected. "And we shall be lovers, in spirit and body: so you promise?"

Melancthe winced and closed her eyes. "Yes. I will praise you and caress you and you may commit your erotic fornications upon my body. Is that definite enough?"

"I will accept it in lieu of anything better. Tell me something of Irerly and what I must look for."

"You will find yourself in an interesting land of living mountains. They bellow and yell, but for the most part it is all braggadocio. I am told that they are ordinarily benign."

"And should I encounter one of the other sort?"

Melancthe smiled her pensive smile. "Then we shall avoid the qualms and perplexities of your return."

The remark, thought Shimrod, might as happily been left unsaid.

Melancthe went on in an abstracted voice. "Perceptions occur by unusual methods." She gave Shimrod three small transparent disks. "These will expedite your search; in fact, you will go instantly mad without them. As soon as you pass the portal, place these on your cheeks and your forehead; they are sandestin scales and will accommodate your senses to Irerly. What is that pack you carry? I had not noticed it before."

"Personal effects and the like; don't concern yourself. What of the gems?"

"They occur in thirteen colors not known here. Their function, either here or there, I do not know, but you must find them and bring them away."

"Exactly so," said Shimrod. "Now kiss me, to demonstrate good will."

"Shimrod, you are far too frivolous."

"And trusting?"

Melancthe, as Shimrod watched, seemed to flicker, or give a quick jerk of movement. Now she was smiling. "'Trusting'? Not altogether. Now then, even to enter Irerly, you will need this sheath. It is stuff to protect you from emanations. Take these as well." She tendered a pair of iron scorpions crawling at the end of golden chains. "These are named Hither and Thither. One will take you there; the other will bring you here. You need nothing more."

"And you will wait here?"

"Yes, dear Shimrod. Now go."

Shimrod enveloped himself in the sheath, placed the sandestin scales to his forehead and cheeks, took the iron charms. "Thither! Take me to Irerly!" He slipped into the passage, picked up his ball of yarn and went forward. Green fluctuations swarmed and pulsed. A green wind whirled him afar, another force of mingled mauve and blue-green sent him careening in other directions. The yarn spun out between his fingers. The iron scorpion known as Thither gave a great bound and pulled Shimrod to a passing luminosity, and down into Irerly.

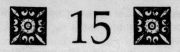

15

IN IRERLY CONDITIONS WERE LESS EASY than Shimrod had hoped. The sheath of sandestin-stuff lacked consistency and allowed sound and two other Irerlish sentiments, *toice* and *gliry,* to chafe against his flesh. The iron insects, both Hither and Thither, at once shriveled into mounds of ash. The fabric of Irerly was viciously malign, or—so Shimrod speculated—the creatures might not have been sandestins after all. Further, the disks intended to assist perception were out of proper adjustment, and Shimrod experienced a startling set of dislocations: a sound that reached him as a jet of ill-smelling liquid; other scents were red cones and yellow triangles which, upon adjustment of the disks, disappeared completely. Vision expressed itself as taut lines striking across space, dripping fire.

He worked at the disks, testing various orientations, quivering to implausible pains and sounds which crawled across his skin on spider-legs, until by accident the incoming percepts made contact with the appropriate areas of his brain. The unpleasant sensations dwindled, at least temporarily, and Shimrod gratefully took stock of Irerly.

He apprehended a landscape of vast extent dotted with isolated mountains of gray-yellow custard, each terminating in a ludicrous semi-human face. All faces were turned toward himself, displaying outrage and censure. Some showed cataclysmic scowls and grimaces, others produced thunderous belches of disdain. The most intemperate extruded a pair of liver-colored tongues, dripping magma which tinkled in falling, like small bells; one or two spat jets of hissing green sound, which Shimrod avoided, so that they struck other mountains, to cause new disturbance.

Shimrod in accordance with Murgen's instructions, called out in an amicable voice: "Gentlemen, gentlemen! Tranquility! After all, I am a guest in your remarkable domain, and I deserve your consideration!"

One great mountain, seventy-five miles distant, roared in a crescendo: "Others named themselves guests, but instead proved to be thieves and predators! They came to plunder us of our thunder-eggs; now we trust no one. I request the mountains Mank and Elfard to concatenate upon your substance."

Shimrod again called for attention. "I am not what you think! The great magicians of the Elder Isles recognize the harms you have endured. They marvel at your stoic patience. Indeed, I have been sent here to make commendations for these qualities and your general excellence. Never have I witnessed magma ejected with such precision! Never before have there been such grotesque gesticulations."

"That is easy to say," grumbled the mountain who previously had spoken.

"Further," declared Shimrod, "I and my fellows vie in our detestation of thieves and predators. We have killed several and now wish to restore the booty. Gentlemen, I have here as many of your thunder-eggs as was possible to recover on short notice." He opened his knapsack and poured out a number of river pebbles. The mountains displayed doubt and bafflement, and several began to produce small jets of magma.

A strip of parchment emerged from Shimrod's sack. He plucked it from the atmosphere and read:

"I, Murgen, write these words. You now know that beauty and faith are not interchangeable qualities! After you deceived the witch Melancthe with a hiatus, she worked a similar trick and plucked you clean of your thunder-eggs, so that the mountains might strike you with jets of magma. I suspected such a trick and stood by, to work a third hiatus, during which I replaced in your pouch the thunder-eggs and all else she had stolen. Proceed as before, but go warily!"

Shimrod called out to the mountains: "And now, the thunder-eggs!" He groped into his pouch and brought forth a sack. With a flourish he spread the contents upon a nearby excrescence. The mountains became at once mollified and gave over their displays. One of the most notable, at a distance of a hundred and twenty miles, projected a meaning: "Well done! Accept our friendly welcome. Do you intend to reside here at length?"

"Urgent business calls me home almost immediately. I merely wished to restore your property and to take note of your splendid achievements."

"Allow me to explain a few aspects of our beloved land. As a basis you must understand that we subscribe to three competing religions: The Doctrine of Arcoid Clincture; the Shrouded Macrolith, which I personally consider a fallacy; and the noble Derelictionary Tocsin. These differ in significant detail." The mountain continued in this wise for a goodly period, propounding analogies and examples and from time to time gently testing Shimrod's understanding of the unfamiliar enlightenments.

Shimrod at last said: "Most interesting! My ideas have been profoundly altered."

"A pity you must depart! Do you intend to return, perhaps, with more thunder-eggs?"

"As soon as possible! In the meantime I would like to take with me a few souvenirs, to keep Irerly fresh in my memory."

"No problem whatever. What strikes your fancy?"

"Well—what about the small glittering objects which show many entrancing colors, thirteen in all? I might well accept a set of those."

"You refer to the florid little pustules which accumulate around certain of our orifices; we think of them as chancres, if you will forgive the word. Take as many as you like."

"In that case, however many will fit into this pouch."

"It will accommodate only a single set. Mank, Idisk! A few of your choicest pustules, if you will! Now, returning to our discussion of teleological anomalies, how do your own savants reconcile the various antic overviews to which we have made reference?"

"Well—in the main, they take the bad with the good."

"Aha! That would be consonant with Original Gnosticism, as I have long suspected. Well, perhaps strong feelings are unwise. You have packed your keepsakes? Good. Incidentally, how will you return? I notice that your sandestins have dissipated into dust."

"I need only follow this line to the portal."

"A clever theory! It implies a whole new and revolutionary logic."

A far mountain ejected high a jet of blue magma, to express displeasure. "As always, Dodar's concepts almost superstitiously range the inconceivable."

"Not so!" declared Dodar stoutly. "A final anecdote to illustrate my point—but no! I see that Shimrod is anxious to depart. A pleasant journey then!"

Shimrod groped his way along the yarn, sometimes in several directions at once, through clouds of bitter music, across the soft bellies of what he whimsically conceived to be dead ideas. Green and blue winds thrust from below and above, with such force that he feared for the strength of the yarn, which seemed to have acquired a curious resilience. Finally the ball of yarn reached its original dimension and Shimrod knew that he must be close upon the aperture. He came upon a sandestin in the form of a fresh-faced boy, sitting on a rock and holding the end of the yarn.

Shimrod halted. The sandestin rose languidly erect. "You are carrying thirteen baubles?"

"So I am, and I am now ready to return."

"Give me the baubles; I must convey them through the whorl."

Shimrod demurred. "Better that I carry them. They are too delicate for the care of a subordinate."

The sandestin tossed aside the loose end of yarn and disappeared into green mist, and Shimrod was left holding a useless ball of yarn. Time passed. Shimrod waited, ever more uncomfortable. His protective mantle had frayed to the verge of collapse and his perceptual disks were presenting sets of unreliable images.

The sandestin returned, with the air of one who had nothing better to do. "I am instructed as before. Give me the baubles."

"Not one. Does your mistress consider me such a mooncalf?"

The sandestin departed into a tangle of green membranes, looking with sardonic finality back over its shoulder.

Shimrod sighed. Faithlessness, utter and absolute, had been proved. From his pouch he brought those articles provided by Murgen: a sandestin of that sort known as a hexamorph, several capsules of gas, and a tile inscribed with the spell of Invincible Thrust.

Shimrod instructed the sandestin: "Lead me back through the whorl, back to the glade by Twitten's Corner."

"The sphincter has been sealed by your enemies. We must

go by way of the five clefts and a perturbation. Wear gas and prepare to use the spell."

Shimrod surrounded himself in gas from one of the bladders; it clung to him like syrup. The sandestin led him a far way, and eventually allowed him to rest. "Be at your ease; we must wait."

Time passed, of a duration Shimrod could not reckon. The sandestin spoke: "Prepare your spell."

Shimrod took the syllables into his mind, and the runes faded from the tile, leaving a blank shard.

"Now. Speak your spell."

Shimrod stood in the glade where he had come with Melancthe. She was nowhere to be seen. The time was late afternoon on a gray chilly day of late autumn, or winter. Clouds hung low over the glade; trees surrounding held up stark branches, marking the sky with black. The face of the bluff no longer showed an iron door.

The Laughing Sun and The Crying Moon on this winter evening was warm and comfortable and almost empty of guests. Hockshank the landlord welcomed Shimrod with a polite smile. "I am happy to see you, sir. I feared that you had suffered a mishap."

"Your fears were by and large accurate."

"It is no novelty. Each year folk strangely disappear from the fair."

Shimrod's garments were torn and the fabric had suffered rot; when he looked in the mirror he saw haggard cheeks, staring eyes and skin stained the curious brown of weathered wood.

After his supper he sat brooding by the fire. Melancthe, he reasoned, had sent him into Irerly for one of several possible purposes: to acquire the thirteen spangled gems, to ensure his death, or both. His death would seem her prime purpose. Otherwise she might have allowed him to bring out the gems. At the cost of her virtue? Shimrod smiled. She would break her promise as easily as she had broken faith.

In the morning Shimrod paid his score, adjusted the feathers to his new boots and departed Twitten's Corner.

In due course he arrived at Trilda. The meadow showed dreary and bleak under the lowering clouds. An additional quality of desolation surrounded the manse. Shimrod approached, step by step, then halted to appraise the manse. The door hung ajar.

He went forward slowly and entered through the broken door, into the parlor, and here he found the corpse of Grofinet, who had been suspended from the ceiling-beams by his lank legs and burned over a fire, presumably that he might be forced to reveal the location of Shimrod's treasures. By the look of affairs, Grofinet's tail had first been roasted away, inch by inch, on a brazier. At the last his head had been lowered into the flames. No doubt, in a hysteria, he had screamed out his knowledge, suffering agonies as much for his own weakness as for the fire he dreaded so much. And then, to silence his raving, someone had split his charred face with a cleaver.

Shimrod looked under the hearth, but the gnarled object which represented his store of magical adjuncts was gone. He had expected nothing else. He knew rudimentary skills, a few charlatan's tricks, a clever spell or two. Never a great magician, Shimrod was now barely a magician of any sort.

Melancthe! She had given him no more faith than he had given her. Still, he would have brought her no great harm, while she had sealed the portal against him, so that he should die in Irerly.

"Melancthe, dire Melancthe! For your crimes you will suffer! I escaped and so I won, but in that absence caused by you I lost my possessions and Grofinet lost his life; you will suffer accordingly!" So raved Shimrod as he stalked about the manse.

The robbers who had seized upon his absence to pillage Trilda, they also must be captured and punished: who might they be?

The House Eye! Established for just such contingencies! But no, first he would bury Grofinet; and this he did, in a bower behind the manse, along with his friend's small possessions. He finished in the fading light of late afternoon. Returning inside the manse he set every lamp aglow, and built a fire in the fireplace. Still Trilda seemed bleak.

Shimrod brought the House Eye down from the ridge-beam, and set it on the carved table in the parlor, where, upon stimulus, it recreated what it had observed during Shimrod's absence.

The first few days passed without incident. Grofinet zealously discharged his duties and all was well. Then, during the middle of a languid summer afternoon the nunciator cried out: "I spy two strangers, of ilk unknown. They approach from the south!"

Grofinet hurriedly donned his dress helmet and took up what he considered a posture of authority in the doorway. He called out: "Strangers, be so good as to halt! This is Trilda, manse of

178

the Master Magician Shimrod, and at the moment under my protection. Since I recognize no business with you, in courtesy go your way."

A voice replied: "We request of you refreshment: a loaf, a bite of cheese, a cup of wine, and we will travel onward."

"Come no further! I will bring you food and drink where you stand, then you must go your way at once. Such are my orders!"

"Sir knight, we shall do as you deem proper."

Grofinet, flattered, turned away, but was instantly seized and trussed tight with leather straps, and so began the dreadful business of the afternoon.

The intruders were two: a tall handsome man with the clothes and manners of a gentleman, and his subordinate. The gentleman was of fine and graceful physique; glossy black hair framed a set of well-shaped features. He wore dark green hunting leathers, with a black cape and carried the long sword of a knight.

The second robber showed two inches less of stature and six inches more of girth. His features were compressed, twisted, crumpled together, as if smeared. A nutmeg-brown mustache drooped over his mouth. His arms were heavy; his legs were thin and seemed to pain him as he walked, so that he used a careful mincing gait. It was he who worked mischief upon Grofinet, while the other leaned against a table drinking wine and offering suggestions.

At last the deed was done. Grofinet hung smoking; the involuted box of valuables had been taken from its hiding place.

"So far so good," declared the black-haired knight, "though Shimrod has snarled his treasures into a riddle. Still, we have each done well."

"It is a happy occasion. I have toiled long and hard. Now I may rest and enjoy my wealth."

The knight laughed indulgently. "I rejoice for you. After a lifetime of lopping heads, winding the rack and twisting noses, you have become a person of substance, perhaps even of social pretension. Will you become a gentleman?"

"Not I. My face tells all. 'Here,' it says, 'stands a thief and a hangman.' So be it: good trades both, and alas for my sore knees that bar me from either."

"A pity! Such skills as yours are rare."

"In all truth, I've lost my taste for gut-cutting by firelight, and as for thieving, my poor sore knees are no longer fit for the trade. They bend both ways and snap aloud. Still, I won't deny myself a bit of purse-slitting and picking of pockets for amusement's sake."

"So where will you go for your new career?"

"I'll be away to Dahaut and there I'll follow the fairs, and perhaps I'll become a Christian. If you need me, leave word in Avallon at the place I mentioned."

Shimrod flew on feathered feet to Swer Smod. A proclamation hung on the door:

> The land is uneasy and the future is uncertain. Murgen must give over his ease that he may solve the problems of Doom. To those who have come as visitors he regrets his absence. Friends and persons in need may take shelter, but my protection is not guaranteed. To those who intend harm I need say nothing. They already know.

Shimrod indited a message, which he left on the table of the main hall:

> There is little to say other than that I have come and gone. On my travels affairs went according to plan, but there were losses at Trilda. I will return, so I hope, within the year, or as soon as justice has been done. I leave in your care the gems of thirteen colors.

He ate from Murgen's larder, and slept on a couch in the hall.

In the morning he dressed in the costume of a wandering musician: a green brimless cap pointed at the front with a panache of owl's feathers, tight trousers of green twill, a blue tunic and a nut-brown cape.

On the great table he found a silver penny, a dagger and a small six-stringed cadensis of unusual shape which, almost of its own accord, produced lively tunes. Shimrod pocketed the coin, tucked the dagger into his girdle, slung the cadensis over his shoulder. Then, departing Swer Smod, he set off across the Forest of Tantrevalles toward Dahaut.

16

IN A BELL-SHAPED CELL fourteen feet in diameter and seventy feet underground, days were differentiated by the most trivial circumstances: the drip of rain, the glimpse of blue sky, an extra crust in the rations. Aillas recorded the passage of days by placing pebbles on a ledge. Each ten pebbles in the "unit" area yielded a single pebble in the "ten" area. On the day after nine "tens" and nine "units," Aillas placed a single pebble in the "hundred" area.

He was fed a loaf of bread, a jug of water and either a bundle of carrots or turnips, or a head of cabbage, every three days, by means of a basket lowered from above.

Aillas often wondered how long he would live. At first he lay inert, in apathy. At last, with vast effort, he forced himself to exercise: pushing, pulling, jumping, tumbling. As his muscular tone returned, so rose his morale. Escape: not impossible. But how? He tried scratching handholds into the stone wall; the proportions and cross section of the cell guaranteed failure for this approach. He tried to lift the stones of the floor, that he might pile them and so reach the shaft, but the joints were too tight and the blocks too heavy: another program he was forced to discard.

The days passed, one by one, and the months. In the garden the days and months also passed and Suldrun swelled with the child conceived by Aillas and herself.

King Casmir had forbidden the garden to all but a deaf-mute kitchen maid.

Brother Umphred however considered himself, a priest of the cloth, exempt from the ban, and visited Suldrun after about three months. Hoping for news Suldrun tolerated his presence, but Brother Umphred could tell her nothing. He suspected that Aillas had felt the full weight of King Casmir's wrath, and since this was also Suldrun's belief, she put no more questions. Brother Umphred attempted a few half-hearted intimacies, at which Suldrun went into the chapel and closed the door. And Brother Umphred departed without noticing that Suldrun already had started to swell.

Three months later he returned and now Suldrun's condition was evident.

Brother Umphred made the sly observation: "Suldrun, my dear, you are becoming stout."

Without words Suldrun once more rose to her feet and went into the chapel.

Brother Umphred sat a few moments in deep reflection, then went to consult his register. He calculated forward from the date of marriage and arrived at a tentative birth-date. Since conception had occurred several weeks before the marriage, his date was just so much in error, a detail which escaped Brother Umphred's attention. The great fact was pregnancy: how best could he profit from this choice item of knowledge which seemed known only to himself?

Further weeks passed by. Brother Umphred contrived a hundred schemes, but none gained him advantage and he held his tongue.

Suldrun well understood Brother Umphred's calculations. Her concern grew as her time approached. Sooner or later Brother Umphred must sidle up to King Casmir and, in that unlikely mingling of humility and impudence, disclose her precious secret.

What then? Her imagination dared not venture so far. Whatever might happen would not be to her liking.

The time grew short. In a sudden panic Suldrun scrambled up the hillside and over the wall. She hid herself where she could watch the peasants on their way to and from the market.

On the second day she intercepted Ehirme, who, after whispered exclamations of astonishment climbed over the stones and into the garden. She wept and hugged Suldrun, and demanded to know what had gone wrong with the plan to escape. All had been in readiness!

Suldrun explained as best she could.

"What of Aillas?"

Suldrun knew nothing. The silence was sinister. Aillas must be considered dead. Together they wept anew and Ehirme cursed the unnatural tyrant who would visit such misery upon his daughter.

Ehirme calculated months and days. She judged time against cycles of the moon, and so determined when Suldrun most likely would give birth. The time was near: perhaps five days, perhaps ten; no more, and all without a vestige of preparation.

"You shall run away again, tonight!" declared Ehirme.

Wistfully Suldrun rejected the idea. "You are the first they would think of, and terrible things would happen."

"What of the child? They will take it away from you."

Once more Suldrun could not restrain tears and Ehirme held her close. "Listen now to a crafty thought! My niece is a half-wit; three times she has come pregnant by the stable-boy, another half-wit. The first two infants died at once, from sheer confusion. She is already cramping and presently will deliver her third brat, which no one, least of all herself, wants. Be of good cheer! Somehow we shall rescue the situation."

Suldrun said sadly: "There is very little now to rescue."

"We shall see!"

Ehirme's niece bore her brat: a girl, according to external evidence. Like its predecessors, it went into convulsions, emitted a few squeaks and died face down in its own discharges.

The corpse was packed into a box, over which—since the niece had been persuaded to Christianity—Brother Umphred intoned a few pious words, and the box was taken off by Ehirme for burial.

At noon of the following day Suldrun went into labor. Close on sunset, haggard, hollow-eyed but relatively cheerful, she gave birth to a son whom she named Dhrun, after a Danaan hero who ruled the worlds of Arcturus.

Ehirme washed Dhrun well and dressed him in clean linens. Late in the evening she returned with a small box. Up under the olive trees she dug a shallow grave into which she unceremoniously slid the dead infant. She broke the box and burnt it in the fireplace. Suldrun lay on her couch watching with big eyes.

Ehirme waited until the flames died low and the baby slept. "Now I must leave. I will not tell you where Dhrun will go, so that, in all cases, he will be safe from Casmir. In a month or two, or three, you will disappear, and go to your baby and live thereafter, so I hope, without sorrow."

Suldrun said softly: "Ehirme, I fear!"

Ehirme hunched up her heavy shoulders. "In truth, I fear too. But whatever happens, we have done our best."

Brother Umphred sat at a small table of ebony and ivory, across from Queen Sollace. With great concentration he studied a set of wooden tablets, each carved with hermetic import understood only by Brother Umphred. To either side of the table burned candles of bayberry wax.

Brother Umphred leaned forward as if in astonishment. "Can it be? Another child born into the royal family?"

Queen Sollace uttered a throaty laugh. "There, Umphred, is either jest or nonsense."

"The signs are clear. A blue star hangs in the grotto of the nymph Merleach. Cambianus ascends to the seventh; here, there—see them now!—are other nascents. No other meaning is plausible. The time is now. My dear queen, you must summon an escort and make inspection. Let your wisdom be the test!"

"'Inspection'? Do you mean..." Sollace's voice trailed off into surmise.

"I know only what the tablets tell me."

Sollace heaved herself to her feet and summoned ladies from the adjoining parlor. "Come! Whim is on me to walk out of doors."

The group, chattering, laughing and complaining of the untoward exercise, marched up the arcade, sidled through the postern and picked their way down through the rocks to the chapel.

Suldrun appeared. Immediately she knew why they had come.

Queen Sollace gave her a critical inspection. "Suldrun, what is all this nonsense?"

"What nonsense, royal mother?"

"That you were pregnant with child. I see that this is not so, for which I give thanks. Priest, your tablets have deceived you!"

"Madame, the tablets are seldom wrong."

"But you can see for yourself!"

Brother Umphred frowned and pulled at his chin. "She is not now pregnant, so it would seem."

Queen Sollace stared at him a moment then swept to the chapel and looked within. "There is no child here."

"Then it would seem to be elsewhere."

Now exasperated, Queen Sollace swung upon Suldrun. "Once and for all, let us have the truth of this!"

Brother Umphred added thoughtfully, "If collusion exists, it can easily be discovered."

Suldrun turned Brother Umphred a glance of contempt. "I gave birth to a daughter. She opened her eyes on the world; she saw the cruelty in which life must be lived, and closed her eyes again. I buried her yonder in great sorrow."

Queen Sollace made a gesture of frustration and signaled a page boy. "Fetch the king; this is a matter for his attention, not mine. I would never have pent the girl here in the first place."

King Casmir arrived, already in a foul humor which he masked behind a face of somber impassivity.

King Casmir stared at Suldrun. "What are the facts?"

"I bore a child. She died."

Desmëi's prediction, in regard to Suldrun's first-born son, jerked to the forefront of Casmir's mind. "Girl? A girl?"

For Suldrun deception was difficult. She nodded. "I buried her on the hillside."

King Casmir looked around the circle of faces and pointed to Umphred. "You, priest, with your dainty marriages and mincing cant: you are the man for this job. Bring hither the corpse."

Boiling with fury he could not express, Brother Umphred humbly bowed his head and went to the grave. In the final rays of afternoon, he pulled aside the black mold with delicate white hands. A foot below the surface he found the linen cloth in which the dead infant had been wrapped. As he dug away the dirt the cloth fell open to reveal the head. Brother Umphred paused in his digging. Through his mind passed a swift set of images and echoes of past confrontations. The images and echoes broke and vanished. He lifted the dead infant in its cloth and carried it to the chapel and placed it before King Casmir.

For an instant Brother Umphred looked toward Suldrun and met her gaze, and in that single glance conveyed to her all the bitter hurt her remarks across the years had done to him.

"Sire," said the priest, "here is the corpse of a female infant. It is not Suldrun's child. I performed final rites over this child three or four days ago. It is the bastard of one Megweth, by the groom Ralf."

King Casmir uttered a terse bark of laughter. "And I was so to be deceived?" He looked toward his entourage and pointed to a sergeant. "Take priest and corpse to the mother and learn the truth of this matter. If the infants have been transferred, bring with you the living child."

The visitors departed the garden, leaving Suldrun alone in the light of a waxing moon.

The sergeant, with Brother Umphred, visited Megweth, who gave quick information that the corpse had been given into the care of Ehirme for burial.

The sergeant returned to Haidion not only with Megweth, but also Ehirme.

Ehirme spoke humbly to King Casmir. "Sire, if I have done wrong, be sure that my reason was only love for your blessed daughter the Princess Suldrun, who does not deserve the woe of her life."

King Casmir lowered his eyelids. "Woman, are you declaring that my judgment in regard to the disobedient Suldrun is incorrect?"

"Sire, I speak not from disrespect, but from faith that you wish to hear truth from your subjects. I do believe that you were far too harsh on the poor bit of a girl. I beg you to let her live a happy life with her own child. She will thank you for the mercy, as will I and all your subjects, for she has in her entire life never done a wrong."

The room was silent. Everyone furtively watched King Casmir, who in his turn pondered... The woman of course was right, thought Casmir. Now to show mercy was equivalent to the admission that he had indeed dealt harshly with his daughter. He could discern no graceful retreat. With mercy impractical, he could only reaffirm his previous position.

"Ehirme, your loyalty is commendable. I can only wish that my daughter had given me a similar service. I will not here and now review her case, not explain the apparent severity of her punishment, save to state that, as a royal princess her first duty is to the kingdom.

"We will discuss this matter no longer. I now refer to that child borne by Princess Suldrun in what seems to have been lawful wedlock, which makes the child legitimate, hence a subject for my dutiful concern. I must now ask the seneschal to send you out with a suitable escort, that we may have the child here at Haidion where it belongs."

Ehirme blinked indecisively. "May I ask, sire, without giving offense: what of Princess Suldrun, since the child is hers?"

Again King Casmir pondered his reply; again he spoke gently. "You are properly steadfast in your concern for the errant princess.

"First, as to the marriage, I now declare it void, null and contrary to the interests of the state, though the child can only be considered legitimate. As for Princess Suldrun, I will go so far: if she submissively declares her wrong-doing, if she will affirm an intent to act henceforth in full obedience to my orders, she may return to Haidion, and assume the condition of mother to her child. But first and immediately we shall fetch the child."

Ehirme licked her lips, wiped her nose with the back of her hand, looked to right, then to left. She said in a tentative voice: "Your Majesty's edict is very good. I beg your leave to bring these words of hope to the Princess Suldrun, and lessen her grief. May I just run now to the garden?"

King Casmir gave a grim nod. "You may do so, as soon as we know where to find the child."

"Your Majesty, I cannot reveal her secret! In your generosity, bring her here and tell her the good news!"

King Casmir's eyelids dropped the sixteenth part of an inch. "Do not put loyalty to the princess above duty to me, your king. I ask you the question once more only. Where is the child?"

Ehirme croaked, "Sire, I beg that you put the question to Suldrun."

King Casmir gave a small jerk of the head and twitch of the hand: signals adequately familiar to those who served him, and Ehirme was led from the hall.

During the night Suldrun's sleep, fitful at the best, was disturbed by a periodic mad howling from the Peinhador. She could not identify the quality of the sound, and tried to ignore it.

Padraig, Ehirme's third son, rushed across the Urquial to the Peinhador and flung himself upon Zerling. "No more! She will not tell you, but I will! Only now have I returned from Glymwode, where I took the cursed brat; there you will find it."

Zerling suspended torment upon the sprawled mound of flesh, and informed King Casmir, who instantly sent a party of four knights and two wet nurses in a carriage to retrieve the child. Then he asked Zerling: "Did the message come through the woman's mouth?"

"No, your Majesty. She will not speak."

"Prepare to cut a hand and a foot each from her husband and sons, unless she passes the words through her mouth."

Ehirme saw the grisly preparations through filmed eyes. Zerling said: "Woman, a party is on its way to bring the child back from Glymwode. The king insists that, in order to obey his command, you respond to the question; otherwise your husband and sons must each lose a hand and foot. I ask you: where is the child?"

Padraig cried out: "Speak, mother! Silence has no more meaning!"

Ehirme said in a heavy croak, "The baby is at Glymwode. There, you have it."

Zerling loosed the men and sent them out into the Urquial. Then he took a pincers, pulled Ehirme's tongue from her head and slit it in two. With red-hot iron he seared the wound to staunch the blood, and such was Casmir's final penalty upon Ehirme.

In the garden the first day went by slowly, instant after hesitant instant, each approaching diffidently, as if on tiptoe, to hurry across the plane of the present and lose itself among the glooms and shadows of the past.

The second day was hazy, less breathless, but the air hung heavy with portent.

The third day, still hazy, seemed sluggish and drained of sensibility, yet somehow innocent and sweet, as if ready for renewal. On this day Suldrun went slowly about the garden, pausing at times to touch the trunk of a tree, or the face of a stone. With head bent she walked the length of her beach, and only once paused to look to sea. Then she climbed the path, to sit among the ruins.

The afternoon passed: a golden dreaming time, and the stone cliffs encompassed the whole of the universe.

The sun sank softly and quietly. Suldrun nodded pensively, as if here were elucidation of an uncertainty, though tears coursed down her cheeks.

The stars appeared. Suldrun descended to the old lime tree and, in the dim light of the stars, she hanged herself. The moon, rising over the ridge, shone on a limp form and a sad sweet face, already preoccupied with her new knowledge.

17

AT THE BOTTOM OF THE OUBLIETTE, Aillas no longer considered himself alone. With great patience he had arranged along one wall twelve skeletons. In days long past, when each of the individuals so represented had walked his term of days as a man, and at the end as a prisoner, each had scratched his name, and often a motto, into the rock wall: twelve names to match twelve skeletons. There had been no rescues, pardons, or escapes; such seemed to be the message of the correspondence. Aillas started to inscribe his own name, using the edge of a buckle; then in a spasm of anger he desisted. Such an act meant resignation, and presaged the thirteenth skeleton.

Aillas confronted his new friends. To each he had assigned one of the names, possibly without accuracy. "Still," Aillas told the group, "a name is a name, and were one of you to address me incorrectly, I would take no offense."

He called his new friends to order: "Gentlemen, we sit in conclave, to share our collective wisdom and to ratify a common policy. There are no rules of order; let spontaneity serve us all, within the limits of decorum.

"Our general topic is 'escape.' It is a subject we all have considered, evidently without enlightenment. Some of you may regard the matter as no longer consequential; still, a victory for one is a victory for all! Let us define the problem. Simply stated, it is the act of ascending the shaft, from here to the surface. I believe that if I were able to gain the bottom of the shaft I could climb crab-wise to the surface.

"To this end, I need to elevate myself twelve feet into the shaft, and this is a formidable problem. I cannot jump so high. I have no ladder. You, my colleagues, while strong of bone, lack sinew and muscle... Might it be that with a resourceful use of

189

these bones and yonder rope something could be contrived? I see before me twelve skulls, twelve pelvises, twenty-four thigh-bones, twenty-four shin-bones, and a like number of upper arms and lower arms, many ribs and a large number of accessory parts.

"Gentlemen, there is work to be done. The time has come for adjournment. Will someone make the appropriate motion?"

A guttural voice said: "I move to dissolve the conference *sine die*."

Aillas stared around the line of skeletons. Which had spoken? Or had it been his own voice? After a pause he asked: "Are there negative votes?"

Silence.

"In that case," said Aillas, "the conclave is dissolved."

He set himself to work at once, disassembling each skeleton, sorting the components, testing them in new combinations to discover optimum linkages. Then he began to build, fitting bone to bone with care and precision, grinding against stone when necessary and securing the joints with rope fiber. He started with four pelvises, which he joined with struts of bound ribs. Upon this foundation he mounted the four largest femurs and surmounted these with four more pelvises, and braced with more ribs. Upon this platform he fixed four more femurs, and four final pelvises, bracing and cross-bracing to insure rigidity. He had now achieved a ladder of two stages, which when he tested it bore his weight with no complaint. Then up another stage and another. He worked without haste, while days became weeks, determined that the ladder should not fail at the critical moment. To control sidewise sway, he worked bone splinters into the floor and set up rope guys; the solidity of the structure gave him a ferocious satisfaction. The ladder was now his whole life, a thing of beauty in itself, so that escape began to be of less consequence than the magnificent ladder. He reveled in the spare white struts, the neat joints, the noble upward thrust.

The ladder was finished. The top level, contrived of ulnas and radii, stood only two feet under the opening of the shaft, and Aillas, with vast caution, practiced inserting himself into the shaft. There was nothing to delay his departure, except to await the next basket of bread and water, so that he might avoid meeting Zerling on his way to feed him. At the next feeding, when Zerling pulled up the untouched food, he would nod sagely and thereafter bring no more baskets.

The bread and water arrived at noon. Aillas took them from the basket, which was then drawn empty up the shaft.

The afternoon waned; never had time passed so slowly. The top of the shaft darkened; evening had come. Aillas mounted the ladder. He placed his shoulders against one side of the shaft, his feet against the other, to wedge himself in place. Then six inches at a time he thrust himself up the shaft: at first awkwardly, with fear lest he slip, then with increasing ease. He paused once to rest, and again, when he had approached to three feet from the top, to listen.

Silence.

He continued, now gritting his teeth and grimacing in tension. He thrust his shoulders over the edge of the low wall and rolled to the side. He put his feet to solid ground, stood erect.

The night was quiet around him. To one side the mass of the Peinhador blotted out the sky. Aillas ran crouching to the old wall which enclosed the Urquial. Like a great black rat he skulked through the shadows and around to the old postern.

The door stood ajar, sagging on a broken hinge. Aillas looked uncertainly down the trail. He slipped through the aperture, crouching uneasily. No challenge came from the dark. Aillas sensed that the garden was untenanted.

He descended the path to the chapel. As he expected, no candle glimmered; the hearth was dead. He proceeded down the path. The moon, rising over the hills, shone on the wan marble of the ruins. Aillas paused, to look and listen, then descended to the lime tree.

"Aillas."

He halted. Again he heard the voice, speaking in a dreary half-whisper. "Aillas."

He approached the lime tree. "Suldrun? I am here."

Beside the tree stood a shape of wisps and mist.

"Aillas, Aillas, you are too late; they have taken our son."

Aillas spoke in astonishment. "'Our son'?"

"He is named Dhrun, and now he is forever gone from me...Oh Aillas, it is not pleasant to be dead."

Tears started from Aillas' eyes. "Poor Suldrun. How could they treat you so?"

"Life was not kind to me. Now it is gone."

"Suldrun, come back to me!"

The pale shape moved and seemed to smile. "No. I am cold and dank. Are you not afraid?"

"I will never be afraid again. Take my hands, I will give you warmth."

Again the shape shifted in the moonlight. "I am Suldrun, yet I am not Suldrun. I ache with a chill all your warmth could never melt...I am tired; I must go."

"Suldrun! Stay with me, I beg you!"

"Dear Aillas, you would find me bad company."

"Who betrayed us? The priest?"

"The priest indeed. Dhrun, our dear little boy: find him, give him care and love. Say that you will!"

"I will do so, as best I can."

"Dear Aillas, I must go."

Aillas stood alone, his heart too full even for the flowing of tears. The garden was empty except for himself. The moon rose into the sky. Aillas finally bestirred himself. He dug under the roots of the lime tree and brought out Persilian the mirror and the pouch with the coins and gems from Suldrun's chamber.

He spent the rest of the night in the grass under the olive trees. At dawn he scaled the rocks and hid in the undergrowth beside the road.

A band of beggars and pilgrims came from the direction of Kercelot, east along the coast. Aillas joined them and so came down into Lyonesse Town. Recognition? He feared it not at all. Who could know this haggard gray-faced wretch for Prince Aillas of Troicinet?

Where the Sfer Arct met the Chale a cluster of inns displayed their boards. At the Four Mallows, Aillas took lodging, and, finally heeding the reproaches of his stomach, made a slow meal of cabbage soup, bread and wine, eating with great caution lest the unaccustomed food work mischief on his shrunken stomach. The food made him drowsy; he went to his cubicle and shaking out the straw pallet, slept into the afternoon.

Awakening, he stared around the walls in alarm close to consternation. He lay back, body trembling and at last eased his racing pulse...For a period he sat cross-legged on the pallet, sweltering in terror. How had he held his sanity so dark and deep below the ground? Urgencies now thronged upon him; truly he needed time to think, to plan, to recover his poise.

He rose to his feet and went down to the area at the front of the inn, where an arbor of vines and climbing roses shielded benches and tables from the hot afternoon sunlight.

Aillas seated himself at a bench beside the road, and a serving boy brought him beer and fried oat-cakes. Two urgencies pulled him in opposite directions: a near-unbearable homesickness for Watershade, and a longing, reinforced by the charge laid upon him, to find his son.

A dock-side barber shaved him and cut his hair. He bought garments at a booth, washed at a public bath, dressed in his new clothes, and felt immeasurably better. Now he might be taken for a seaman or a tradesman's apprentice.

He returned to the arbor in front of the Four Mallows, which had become busy with late afternoon trade. Aillas drank from a mug of beer and listened to such scraps of conversation as he could overhear, hoping for news. An old man with a flat florid face, silky-clean white hair and a mild blue gaze settled himself across the table. He gave Aillas an amiable greeting, ordered beer and fish-cakes and wasted no time engaging Aillas in conversation. Aillas, wary of Casmir's notorious corps of informers, responded with simple-minded innocence. The old man's name, so Aillas gathered from the salute of a passerby, was Byssante. He needed no encouragement and provided Aillas information of all kinds. He touched upon the war and Aillas learned that conditions were generally as before. The Troice still immobilized the ports of Lyonesse. A fleet of Troice warships had won a notable victory over the Ska, effectively sealing the Lir from their depredations.

Aillas spoke only: "Exactly so!" and "So I understand!" and "Such things happen, alas!" But this was enough, especially when Aillas ordered more beer and so provided Byssante a second wind.

"What King Casmir plans for Lyonesse, I fear is not succeeding of its own weight, though if Casmir heard my opinion, he'd have me crotch to stock in a trice. Still, the conditions may go even worse, depending upon the Troice succession."

"How so?"

"Well, King Granice is old and fierce but he can't live forever. Should Granice die today, the crown goes to Ospero, who lacks all ferocity. When Ospero dies, Prince Trewan takes the crown, since Ospero's son was lost at sea. If Ospero dies before Granice, Trewan takes the crown directly. Trewan is said to be a fire-breathing warrior; Lyonesse can expect the worst. Were I King Casmir, I would sue for peace on the best terms to be had, and put my grand ambitions aside."

"That might well be the best of it," Aillas agreed. "But what of Prince Arbamet? Did he not hold first claim to the throne after Granice?"

"Arbamet died of injuries when he fell from a horse, something more than a year ago. Still, it's all the same. One is as savage as the next, so that now even the Ska won't come near. Ah my throat! So much talking is dry work. What of it, lad? Can you oblige an old pensioner a stoup of beer?"

Without enthusiasm Aillas called the serving boy. "A measure of beer for this gentleman. Nothing more for me."

Byssante spoke on, while Aillas brooded over what he had heard. Prince Arbamet, Trewan's father, had been alive when he had departed Domreis aboard the *Smaadra*. The line of succession had been straight: Granice through Arbamet to Trewan, and thereafter Trewan's male progeny. At Ys, Trewan had visited the Troice cog, and apparently had learned of his father's death. The line of descent then became painful from his point of view: Granice through Ospero to Aillas, bypassing Trewan altogether. No wonder Trewan had returned from the Troice cog in a glum mood! And no mystery whatever why Aillas must be murdered!

Swift return to Troicinet was imperative—but what of Dhrun, his son?

Almost as if in response Byssante rapped him with a pink knuckle. "Look you yonder! The ruling house of Lyonesse drives forth for an afternoon airing!"

Preceded by a pair of mounted heralds and followed by twelve soldiers in dress uniform, a splendid carriage drawn by six white unicorns rolled down the Sfer Arct. Facing forward, King Casmir and Prince Cassander, a slender big-eyed youth fourteen years old, rode in the back seat. On the seat across sat Queen Sollace in a gown of green silk and Fareult, Duchess of Relsimore, who carried in her lap, or more accurately, tried to control, an auburn-haired infant in a white gown. The child wanted to climb up on the back of the seat despite Lady Fareult's admonitions and King Casmir's scowling. Queen Sollace merely averted her gaze.

"There you have the royal family," said Byssante with an indulgent wave of the hand. "King Casmir, Prince Cassander and Queen Sollace and a lady whom I don't know. Beside her stands the Princess Madouc, daughter to Princess Suldrun, now dead by her own hand."

"Princess Madouc? A girl?"

"Aye, an odd little creature she's said to be." Byssante finished his beer. "You are a lucky fellow to witness royal pomp so close at hand! And now I'm off to my nap."

Aillas went to his chamber. Sitting on the chair, he unwrapped Persilian and set it on the night-stand. The mirror, in one of its flippant moods, reflected the wall first upside-down, then reversed left to right, then showed a window giving on the stable-yard, then with King Casmir peering balefully in through the window.

Aillas said: "Persilian."

"I am here."

Aillas spoke with great caution, lest inadvertently he phrase a casual remark in the form of a question. "I may ask you three questions, then no more."

"You may ask a fourth question. I will answer, but then I will be free. You have already asked one question."

Aillas spoke carefully: "I want to find my son Dhrun, take him into my custody, then return with him quickly and safely to Troicinet. Tell me how best to do this."

"You must put your requirements in the form of a question."

"How can I do as I described?"

"That is essentially three questions."

"Very well," said Aillas. "Tell me how to find my son."

"Ask Ehirme."

"Only that?" cried Aillas. "Two words and no more?"

"The reply is adequate," said Persilian and would say no more. Aillas wrapped the mirror in a cloth and tucked it under the straw pallet.

The time was late afternoon. Aillas strolled out along the Chale, brooding upon what he had learned. At the shop of a Moorish goldsmith he offered for sale a pair of Suldrun's emeralds, each the size of a pea.

The Moor examined the gems in turn, using a magnifying lens of a sort strange and new. Completing his appraisal he spoke in a studiously flat voice. "These are excellent gems. I will pay one hundred silver florins for each—approximately half their worth. That is my first, last and only offer."

"Done," said Aillas. The Moor laid out gold and silver coins, which Aillas swept into his pouch, then departed the shop.

At sunset Aillas returned to the Four Mallows where he supped upon fried fish, bread and wine. He slept soundly and when he awoke the oubliette seemed a bad dream. He took breakfast, paid his account, slung the parcel containing Persilian over his shoulder and set out along the shore-road south.

By a route remembered from what seemed a previous existence he tramped to the farmstead where Ehirme made her home. As before he halted by the hedge and took stock of the surroundings. As before men and boys worked hay. In the kitchen garden a stocky old crone hobbled among the cabbages, cutting weeds with a hoe. As Aillas watched, three small pigs escaped from the sty and trotted briskly into the turnip patch. The crone gave a peculiar warbling scream and a small girl ran from the cottage to chase the pigs who darted everywhere except toward the sty.

The girl ran panting past the gate. Aillas stopped her. "Would you tell Ehirme that someone at the gate wishes to speak to her?"

The girl looked him up and down in hostility and distrust. She called out to the old woman who weeded the cabbages, then resumed her pursuit of the pigs, in which she now was joined by a small black dog.

The old woman hobbled toward the gate. A shawl thrown over her head, and projecting a little past her face, shaded her features.

Aillas stared in consternation. This crooked old creature: was it Ehirme? She drew close: first a step of the right leg, then a lurch of the hip, and a swing around of the left leg. She halted. Her face showed odd distortions and creases; her eyes seemed to have sunk in their sockets.

Aillas stammered: "Ehirme! What has happened to you?"

Ehirme opened her mouth and produced a set of warbling vocables, none intelligible to Aillas. She made a sign of frustration and called the girl, who came to stand beside her. The girl told Aillas: "King Casmir cut her tongue and hurt her everywhere."

Ehirme spoke; the girl listened carefully, then, turning to Aillas, translated. "She wants to know what happened to you."

"They put me in an underground dungeon. I escaped, and now I want to find my son."

Ehirme spoke; the girl just shook her head. Aillas asked: "What did she say?"

"Things about King Casmir."

196

"Ehirme, where is my son Dhrun?"

A moment of incomprehensible warbling, which the girl translated: "She doesn't know what has happened. She sent the baby to her mother, out by the great forest. Casmir sent out a party but they brought back a girl. So the baby boy must still be there."

"And how will I find this place?"

"Go up to the Old Street, then east to Little Saffield. Here take the side road north to Tawn Timble, and thence to the village Glymwode. There you must ask for Graithe the wood-cutter and Wynes, his wife."

Aillas looked into his pouch and brought out a necklace of pink pearls. He gave it to Ehirme, who accepted it without enthusiasm. "This was Suldrun's necklace. When I reach Troicinet I will send for you, and you will live out your years in comfort and as much content as may be possible."

Ehirme produced a low quacking sound.

"She says that it is kind of you to make the offer, but that she does not know if the men would wish to leave their land."

"We will settle such affairs later. Here I am only Aillas the vagabond, and I have nothing to give except my gratitude."

"So it may be."

Late in the day Aillas arrived at Little Saffield, a market town beside the River Timble, built all of ocher-gray country stone. At the center of town Aillas found the Black Ox Inn, where he took lodging for the night.

In the morning he set off along a lane which followed the River Timble north, in the shade of poplar trees along the riverbank. Crows soared over the fields, notifying all who would listen of his presence.

Sunlight burnt through the early mist and warmed his face; already he was losing the haunted pallor of his captivity. As he walked an odd thought passed through his mind: "Some day I must return and visit my twelve good friends..." He uttered a grim sound. What an idea! Return into the dark hole? Never...He calculated. Today Zerling would drop the bucket with his rations. The bread and water would remain in the basket and the poor underground wight would be deemed dead. Zerling might perhaps report as much to King Casmir. How would the king react to the news? An indifferent shrug? A twitch of curiosity as to the father of his daughter's child? Aillas smiled a thin hard smile and for a space amused himself with possible directions of the future.

The landscape to the north ended at a dark loom across the northern horizon: the Forest of Tantrevalles. As Aillas approached, the countryside altered, to become ever more thoroughly steeped in time. Colors seemed richer and heavier; shadows were more emphatic and showed curious colors of their own. The River Timble, shaded under willows and poplars, wandered away in stately meanders; the road turned and entered the town Tawn Timble.

At the inn Aillas ate a dish of broad beans and drank an earthenware mug of beer.

The way to Glymwode led across the meadows, ever closer to the gloom of the forest, sometimes skirting the verge, sometimes passing under outlying copses.

Halfway through the afternoon Aillas trudged into Glymwode. The landlord at the Yellow Man Inn directed him to the cottage of Graithe the woodcutter. He asked in puzzlement: "What brings so many fine folk to visit Graithe? He's but a common man and no more than a woodcutter."

"The explanation is simple enough," said Aillas. "Certain grand folk at Lyonesse Town wanted a child brought up quietly, if you get my meaning, and then they changed their minds."

"Ah!" The landlord laid a sly finger alongside his nose. "Now it's clear. Still, a far way just to veil an indiscretion."

"Bah! One cannot judge the high-born by sensible standards!"

"That is a basic truth!" declared the landlord. "They live with their heads above the clouds! Well then, you know the way. Don't stray into the woods, especially after nightfall; you might find things you weren't seeking."

"In all likelihood I'll be back here before sunset. Will you have a bed for me?"

"Aye. If nothing better, you'll have a pallet in the loft."

Aillas departed the inn, and in due course found the cottage of Graithe and Wynes: a small two-room hut built of stone and timber, with a thatched roof, at the very edge of the forest. A spare old man with a white beard worked to split a log with maul and wedges. A stocky woman in a homespun smock and shawl tilled the garden. At Aillas' approach both drew erect and in silence watched him come.

Aillas halted in the dooryard and waited while the man and woman slowly approached.

"You are Graithe and Wynes?" asked Aillas.

The man gave his head a terse nod. "Who are you? What do you want?"

"Your daughter Ehirme sent me here."

The two stood, watching him, still as statues. Aillas sensed the psychic reek of fear. He said: "I haven't come to trouble you; quite the contrary. I am Suldrun's husband and the father of our child. It was a boy named Dhrun. Ehirme sent him here; King Casmir's soldiers brought back a girl named Madouc. So then, where is my son Dhrun?"

Wynes began to wail. Graithe held up his hand. "Quiet, woman, we have done no wrong. Fellow, whatever your name, the affair is one we are done with. Our daughter suffered a great anguish. We despise with all our hatred those persons who brought her pain. King Casmir took the child; there is no more to say."

"Only this. Casmir locked me in a deep dungeon, from which I have only just escaped. He is my enemy no less than yours, as someday he will learn. I ask for what is my right. Give me my boy, or tell me where to find him."

"This is nothing to us!" cried Wynes. "We are old; we survive from day to day. When our horse dies, how will we take our wood to the village? Some winter soon we shall starve."

Aillas reached into his pouch and brought out another of Suldrun's possessions: a wrist-band of gold set with garnets and rubies. To this he added a pair of gold crowns. "Now I can help you only this much, but at least you need not fear starvation. Now tell me of my son."

Wynes hesitantly took the gold. "Very well, I shall tell you of your son. Graithe went into the forest to cut faggots. I carried the baby in a basket, and set it on the ground while I gathered mushrooms. Alas! we were close by Madling Meadow, and the fairies of Thripsey Shee worked a mischief. They took the boy and left a fairy-child in the basket. I noticed nothing till I reached to take the baby and it bit me. Then I looked and saw the red-haired girl-brat and I knew that the fairies had been at work."

Graithe spoke. "Then the king's soldiery arrived. They asked for the baby on pain of death, and we gave them the changeling, and bad cess to it."

Aillas looked from face to face in bafflement. Then he turned to gaze into the forest. At last he said: "Can you take me to Thripsey Shee?"

"Oh yes, we can take you there, and should you make awkwardness, they'll give you a toad's head, like they did poor Wilclaw the drover; or give you dancing feet, so that you'll dance the roads and byways forever and that was the fate of a lad named Dingle, when they caught him eating their honey."

"Never bother the fairies," Wynes told him. "Be grateful when they leave you in peace."

"But my son, Dhrun! How does he fare?"

18

WITHIN AND ABOUT THE Forest of Tantrevalles existed a hundred or more fairy shees, each the castle of a fairy tribe. Thripsey Shee on Madling Meadow, little more than a mile within the precincts of the forest, was ruled by King Throbius and his spouse Queen Bossum. His realm included Madling Meadow and as much of the forest surrounding as was consistent with his dignity. The fairies at Thripsey numbered eighty-six. Among them were:

BOAB: who used the semblance of a pale green youth with grasshopper wings and antennae. He carried a black quill pen plucked from the tail of a raven and recorded all the events and transactions of the tribe on sheets pressed from lily petals.

TUTTERWIT: an imp who liked to visit human houses and tease the cats. He also liked to peer through windows, moaning and grimacing until someone's attention was engaged, then jerk quickly from sight.

GUNDELINE: a slender maiden of enchanting charm, with flowing lavender hair and green fingernails. She mimed, preened, cut capers, but never spoke, and no one knew her well. She licked saffron from poppy pistils with quick darts of her pointed green tongue.

WONE: she liked to rise early, before dawn, and flavor dew drops with assorted flower nectars.

MURDOCK: a fat brown goblin who tanned mouseskins and wove the down of baby owls into soft gray blankets for fairy children.

FLINK: who forged fairy swords, using techniques of antique force. He was a great braggart and often sang the ballad celebrating the famous duel he had fought with the goblin Dangott.

SHIMMIR: audaciously she had mocked Queen Bossum and capered silently behind her, mimicking the queen's flouncing gait, while all the fairies sat hunched, hands pressed to mouths, to stop their laughter. In punishment Queen Bossum turned her feet backward and put a carbuncle on her nose.

FALAEL: who manifested himself as a pale brown imp, with the body of a boy and the face of a girl. Falael was incessantly mischievous, and when villagers came to the forest to gather berries and nuts, it was usually Falael who caused their nuts to explode and transformed their strawberries to toads and beetles.

And then there was Twisk, who usually appeared as an orange-haired maiden wearing a gown of gray gauze. One day while wading in the shallows of Tilhilvelly Pond, she was surprised by the troll Mangeon. He seized her about the waist, carried her to the bank, ripped away the gray gauze gown and prepared to make an erotic junction. At the sight of his priapic instrument, which was grotesquely large and covered with warts, Twisk became frantic with fear. By dint of jerks, twists and contortions she foiled the best efforts of the sweating Mangeon. But her strength waned and Mangeon's weight began to grow oppressive. She tried to protect herself with magic, but in her excitement she could remember only a spell used to relieve dropsy in farm animals, which, lacking better, she uttered, and it proved efficacious. Mangeon's massive organ shriveled to the size of a small acorn and became lost in the folds of his great gray belly.

Mangeon uttered a scream of dismay, but Twisk showed no remorse. Mangeon cried out in fury: "Vixen, you have done me a double mischief, and you shall do appropriate penance."

He took her to a road which skirted the forest. At a crossroads he fashioned a kind of pillory and affixed her to this construction. Over her head he posted a sign: DO WHAT YOU WILL WITH ME and stood back. "Here you stay until three passersby, be they dolts, lickpennies or great earls, have their way with you, and that is the spell I invoke upon you, so that in the future you may choose to be more accommodating to those who accost you beside Tilhilvelly Pond."

Mangeon sauntered away, and Twisk was left alone.

The first to pass was the knight Sir Jaucinet of Castle Cloud in Dahaut. He halted his horse and appraised the situation with a wondering glance. "'DO WHAT YOU WILL WITH ME,'" he read. "Lady, why do you suffer this indignity?"

"Sir knight, I do not suffer so by choice," said Twisk. "I did not attach myself to the pillory in this position and I did not display the sign."

"Who then is responsible?"

"The troll Mangeon, for his revenge."

"Then, surely, I will help you escape, in any way possible."

Sir Jaucinet dismounted, removed his helmet, showing himself as a flaxen-haired gentleman with long mustaches and of good aspect. He attempted to loosen the bonds which confined Twisk, but to no avail. He said at last: "Lady, these bonds are proof against my efforts."

"In that case," sighed Twisk, "please obey the instruction implicit in the sign. Only after three such encounters will the bonds loosen."

"It is not a gallant act," said Sir Jaucinet. "Still, I will abide by my promise." So saying, he did what he could to assist in her release.

Sir Jaucinet would have stayed to share her vigil and assist her further if need be, but she begged him to leave. "Other travelers might be discouraged from stopping if they saw you here. So you must go, and at once! For the day is waning and I would hope to be home before night."

"This is a lonely road," said Sir Jaucinet. "Still, it is occasionally used by vagabonds and lepers, and good luck may attend you. Lady, I bid you good-day."

Sir Jaucinet adjusted his helm, mounted his horse and departed.

An hour passed while the sun sank into the west. At this time Twisk heard a whistling and presently saw a peasant boy on his way home after a day's work in the fields. Like Sir Jaucinet, he stopped short in amazement, then slowly approached. Twisk smiled at him ruefully. "As you see, sir, I am bound here. I cannot leave and I cannot resist you, no matter what might be your impulse."

"My impulse is simple enough," said the ploughboy. "But I wasn't born yesterday and I want to know how the sign reads."

"It says: *Do what you will . . .*"

"Ah then, that's all right. I was fearing it might be either a price or a quarantine."

With no more ado he raised his smock and conjoined to Twisk with rude zest. "And now, madam, if you will excuse me, I must hurry home, as there'll be bacon tonight with the turnips, and you've given me a hunger."

The ploughboy disappeared into the evening, while Twisk in disquiet contemplated the coming of night.

With darkness a chill crept through the air, and an overcast blotted out the stars so that the night was black. Twisk huddled, shivering and miserable, and listened to the sounds of the night with fearful attention.

The hours passed slowly. At midnight Twisk heard a soft sound: the pad of slow footsteps along the road. The footsteps halted, and something which could see through the dark paused to inspect her.

It approached, and even with her fairy vision Twisk could see only a tall outline.

It stood before her and touched her with cold fingers. Twisk spoke in a trembling voice: "Sir? Who are you? May I know your identity?"

The creature made no response. In tremulous terror Twisk held out her hand and felt a garment, like a cloak, which when disturbed wafted forth an unsettling odor.

The creature came close and subjected Twisk to a cold embrace, which left her only half-conscious.

The creature departed along the road and Twisk fell to the ground, soiled but free.

She ran through the dark toward Thripsey Shee. The clouds broke; starlight helped her on her way, and so she arrived home. She cleansed herself as best she could then went to her green velvet chamber to rest.

Fairies, though they never forget an injury, are resilient to misfortune, and Twisk quickly put the experience out of mind, and was only reminded of the event when she found herself large with child.

In her term she gave birth to a red-haired girl which even in its willow basket, under its owl's-down quilt, surveyed the world with a precocious wisdom.

Who—or what—was the father? The uncertainty caused Twisk a nagging vexation, and she took no pleasure in her child. One day Wynes, the woodcutter's wife, brought a baby boy into the forest. Without a second thought Twisk took the blond baby and left in its place the strangely wise girl.

In such fashion did Dhrun, son of Aillas and Suldrun, come

to Thripsey Shee, and so, in due course did Madouc, of uncertain parentage, enter the palace Haidion.

Fairy babies are often guilty of peevishness, tantrums and malice. Dhrun, a merry baby with a dozen endearing traits, charmed the fairies with his amiability, as well as his glossy blond curls, dark blue eyes, and a mouth always pursed and crooked as if on the verge of a grin. He was named Tippit, showered with kisses and fed nuts, flower nectar and grass-seed bread.

Fairies are impatient with awkwardness; Dhrun's education proceeded quickly. He learned flower-lore and the sentiments of herbs; he climbed trees and explored all of Madling Meadow, from Grassy Knoll to Twankbow Water. He learned the language of the land as well as the secret language of the fairies, which so often is mistaken for bird-calls.

Time in a fairy fort moves at a rapid rate, and a sidereal year was eight years in the life of Dhrun. The first half of this time was happy and uncomplicated. When he might be said to have reached the age of five (such determinations being rather indefinite), he put the question to Twisk, toward whom he felt as he might toward an indulgent, if flighty, sister. "Why can't I have wings like Digby, and fly? It's something, if you please, that I would like to do."

Twisk, sitting in the grass with a plait of cowslips, made a large gesture. "Flying is for fairy children. You are not quite a fairy, though you're my adorable Tippit, and I shall weave these cowslips into your hair and you will seem ever so handsome, far more than Digby, with his sly fox-face."

Dhrun persisted. "Still, if I am not quite a fairy, what am I?"

"Well, you are something very grand, that is sure: perhaps a prince of the royal court; and your name is really Dhrun." She had learned this fact in a strange fashion. Curious as to the condition of her red-haired daughter, Twisk had visited the cottage of Graithe and Wynes, and had witnessed the coming of King Casmir's deputation. Afterwards she lay hidden in the thatch, listening to the lamentations of Wynes for the lost baby Dhrun.

Dhrun was not entirely pleased with the information. "I think that I would rather be a fairy."

"We shall have to see about that," said Twisk, jumping to her feet. "For now, you are Prince Tippit, Lord of all cowslips."

For a period all was as before, and Dhrun put the unwelcome knowledge to the back of his mind. King Throbius, after all, wielded marvelous magic; in due course, if asked nicely, King Throbius would make him a fairy.

A single individual of the shee showed him animosity: this was Falael, with the girl's face and the boy's body, whose mind seethed with ingenious mischief. He marshaled two armies of mice and dressed them in splendid uniforms. The first army wore red and gold; the second wore blue and white with silver helmets. They marched bravely upon each other from opposite sides of the meadow and fought a great battle, while the fairies of Thripsey Shee applauded deeds of valor and wept for dead heroes.

Falael also had a gift for music. He assembled an orchestra of hedgehogs, weasels, crows and lizards and trained them in the use of musical instruments. So skillfully did they play and so melodious were their tunes that King Throbius allowed them to play at the Great Pavanne of the Vernal Equinox. Falael thereupon tired of the orchestra. The crows took flight; two weasel bassoonists attacked a hedgehog who had been beating his drum with too much zeal, and the orchestra dissolved.

Falael, from boredom, next transformed Dhrun's nose into a long green eel which, by swinging about, was able to transfix Dhrun with a quizzical stare. Dhrun ran to Twisk for succor; she indignantly complained to King Throbius, who set matters right and for punishment condemned Falael to utter silence for a week and a day: a sad penalty for the verbose Falael.

Upon conclusion of his punishment Falael remained silent three more days for sheer perversity. On the fourth day he approached Dhrun. "Through your spite I incurred humiliation: I, Falael of the many excellences! Are you now puzzled by my displeasure?"

Dhrun spoke with dignity: "I attached no eel to your nose; remember that!"

"I acted only in fun, and why should you wish to blight my beautiful face? In contrast, your face is like a handful of dough with two prunes for eyes. It is a coarse face, an arena for stupid thoughts. Who could expect better of a mortal?" In triumph Falael leapt in the air, turned a triple somersault and striking a pose drifted away across the meadow.

Dhrun sought out Twisk. "Am I truly a mortal? Can I never be a fairy?"

Twisk inspected him a moment. "You are a mortal, yes. You never will be a fairy."

Thereafter Dhrun's life insensibly altered. The easy innocence of the old ways became strained; the fairies looked at him side-long; every day he felt more isolated.

Summer came to Madling Meadow. One morning Twisk approached Dhrun, and, in a voice like the tinkle of silver bells, said, "The time has come; you must leave the shee and make your own way in the world."

Dhrun stood heartbroken, with tears running down his cheeks. Twisk said: "Your name now is Dhrun. You are the son of a prince and a princess. Your mother is disappeared from the living, and of your father I know nothing, but it will serve no purpose to seek him out."

"But where shall I go?"

"Follow the wind! Go where fortune leads you!"

Dhrun turned away and with tears blinding his eyes started to leave.

"Wait!" called Twisk. "All are gathered to bid you farewell. You shall not go without our gifts."

The fairies of Thripsey Shee, unwontedly subdued, bade Dhrun farewell. King Throbius spoke: "Tippit, or Dhrun, as you must now be known, the time has come. Now you grieve at the parting, because we are real and true and dear, but soon you will forget us, and we will become like flickers in the fire. When you are old you will wonder at the strange dreams of your childhood."

The fairies of the shee came crowding around Dhrun, crying and laughing together. They dressed him in fine clothes: a dark green doublet with silver buttons, blue breeches of stout linen twill, green stockings, black shoes, a black cap with a rolled brim, pointed bill and scarlet plume.

The blacksmith Flink gave Dhrun a fairy sword. "The name of this sword is Dassenach. It will grow as you grow, and always match your stature. Its edge will never fail and it will come to your hand whenever you call its name!"

Boab placed a locket around his neck. "This is a talisman against fear. Wear this black stone always and you will never lack courage."

Nismus brought him a set of pipes. "Here is music. When

you play, heels will fly and you will never lack jolly companionship."

King Throbius and Queen Bossum both kissed Dhrun on the forehead. The queen gave him a small purse containing a gold crown, a silver florin and a copper penny. "This is a magic purse," she told him. "It will never go empty, and better, if you ever give a coin and want it back, you need only tap the purse and the coin will fly back to you."

"Now step bravely forth," said King Throbius. "Go your way and do not look back, on pain of seven years bad luck, for such is the manner one must leave a fairy shee."

Dhrun turned away and marched across Madling Meadow, eyes steadfastly fixed on the way he must go. Falael, sitting somewhat aside, had taken no part in the farewells. Now he sent after Dhrun a bubble of sound, which no one could hear. It wafted across the meadow and burst upon Dhrun's ear, to startle him. "Dhrun! Dhrun! One moment!"

Dhrun halted and looked back, only to discover an empty meadow echoing with Falael's taunting laughter. Where was the shee, where the pavilions, the proud standards with the billowing gonfalons? All to be seen was a low mound in the center of the meadow, with a stunted oak tree growing from the top.

Troubled, Dhrun turned away from the meadow. Would King Throbius truly visit seven years bad luck upon him when the fault lay with Falael? Fairy law was often inflexible.

A flotilla of summer clouds covered the sun and the forest became gloomy. Dhrun lost his sense of direction and instead of traveling south to the edge of the forest, he wandered first west, then gradually around to the north and ever deeper into the woods: under ancient oaks with gnarled boles and great outflung branches, across mossy outcrops of stone, beside quiet streams fringed by ferns, and so the day passed. Toward sunset he made a bed of fern and bracken, and when darkness came he bedded himself under the ferns. For a long while he lay awake listening to the sounds of the forest. Of animals he felt no fear; they would sense the presence of fairy-stuff and give him a wide berth. Other creatures wandered the woods, and if one should scent him, what then? Dhrun refused to consider the possibilities. He touched the talisman which hung around his neck. "A great relief to be protected from fear," he told himself. "Otherwise I might not be able to sleep for anxiety."

At last his eyes grew heavy, and he slept.

The clouds broke; a half-moon sailed the sky and moonlight filtered through the leaves to the forest floor, and so passed the night.

At dawn Dhrun stirred and sat up in his nest of fronds. He stared here and there, then remembered his banishment from the shee. He sat disconsolate, arms around knees, feeling lonely and lost... Far off through the forest he heard a bird call, and listened attentively... It was a bird only, not fairy speech. Dhrun took himself from his couch and brushed himself clean. Nearby he found a ledge growing thick with strawberries and he made a good breakfast, and presently his spirits rose. Perhaps it was all for the best. Since he was not a fairy, it was high time that he should be making his way in the world of men. Was he not, after all, the son of a prince and princess? He need only discover his parents, and all would be well.

He pondered the forest. Yesterday he undoubtedly had taken the wrong turning; which direction then was correct? Dhrun knew little of the lands surrounding the forest, nor had he learned to read directions by the sun. He set off at a slant and presently came to a stream with the semblance of a path along its bank.

Dhrun halted, to look and listen. Paths meant traffic; in the forest such traffic might well be baleful. It might be the better part of wisdom to cross the stream, and continue through the untraveled forest. On the other hand, a path must lead somewhere, and if he conducted himself with caution, he could surely avoid danger. And, after all, where was the danger which he could not face down and conquer, with the aid of his talisman and his good sword Dassenach?

Dhrun threw back his shoulders, set off along the path, which, slanting into the northeast, took him ever deeper into the forest.

He walked two hours, discovering along the way a clearing planted with plum and apricot trees, which had long gone wild.

Dhrun inspected the clearing. It seemed deserted and quiet. Bees flew among buttercups, red clover and purslane; nowhere was there a sign of habitation. Still Dhrun stood back, deterred by a whole host of subconscious warnings. He called out: "Whoever owns this fruit, please listen to me. I am hungry; I would like to pick ten apricots and ten plums. Please, may I do so?"

Silence.

Dhrun called: "If you do not forbid me, I will consider the fruit to be a gift, for which my thanks."

From behind a tree not thirty feet away hopped a troll, with a narrow forehead and a great red nose from which sprouted a mustache of nose-hairs. He carried a net and a wooden pitchfork.

"Thief! I forbid you my fruit! Had you plucked a single apricot your life would have been mine! I would have captured you and fattened you on apricots and sold you to the ogre Arbogast! For ten apricots and ten plums I demand a copper penny."

"A good price, for fruit otherwise going to waste," said Dhrun. "Will you not be paid with my thanks?"

"Thanks put no turnips in the pot. A copper coin or dine on grass."

"Very well," said Dhrun. He took the copper coin from his purse and tossed it to the troll, who gave a grunt of satisfaction.

"Ten apricots, ten plums: no more; and it would be an act of greed to select only the choicest."

Dhrun picked ten good apricots and ten plums while the troll counted the score. When he plucked the last plum, the troll shouted: "No more; be off with you!"

Dhrun sauntered along the trail eating the fruit. When he had finished, he drank water from the stream and continued along the way. After half a mile he stopped, tapped the purse. When he looked inside the penny had returned.

The stream widened to become a pond, shaded under four majestic oaks.

Dhrun pulled some young rushes, washed their crisp white roots. He found cress and wild lettuce, and made a meal of the fresh sharp salad, then continued along the path.

The stream joined a river; Dhrun could proceed no further without crossing one or the other. He noticed a neat wooden bridge spanning the stream, but again, impelled by caution, he halted before setting foot on the structure.

No one could be seen, nor could he discover any evidence that passage might be restricted. "If not, well and good," Dhrun told himself. "Still, it is better that first I ask permission."

He called out: "Bridge-keeper, ho! I want to use the bridge!"

There was no response. Dhrun, however, thought he heard rustling sounds from under the bridge.

"Bridge-keeper! If you forbid my passage, make yourself known! Otherwise I will cross the bridge and pay you with my thanks."

From the deep shade under the bridge hopped a furious troll, wearing purple fustian. He was even more ugly than the previous troll, with warts and wens protruding from his forehead, which hung like a crag over a little red nose with the nostrils turned forward. "What is all this yammer? Why do you disturb my rest?"

"I want to cross the bridge."

"Set a single foot upon my valuable bridge and I will put you in my basket. To cross this bridge you must pay a silver florin."

"That is a very dear toll."

"No matter. Pay as do all decent folk, or turn back the way you have come."

"If I must, I must." Dhrun opened his purse, took out the silver florin and tossed it to the troll, who bit at it and thrust it into his pouch. "Go your way, and in the future make less noise about it."

Dhrun crossed the bridge and continued along the path. For a space the trees thinned and sunlight warmed his shoulders, to cheerful effect. It was not so bad after all, being footloose and independent! Especially with a purse which retrieved money spent unwillingly. Dhrun now tapped the purse, and the coin returned, marked by the troll's teeth. Dhrun went on his way, whistling a tune.

Trees again shrouded the path; to one side a knoll rose steeply above the path from a thicket of flowering myrtle and white dimble-flower.

A sudden startling outcry; out on the path behind him sprang two great black dogs, slavering and snarling. Chains constrained them; they lunged against the chains, jerking, rearing, gnashing their teeth. Appalled, Dhrun jumped around, Dassenach in hand, ready to defend himself. Cautiously he backed away, but with a great roar two more dogs, as savage as the first pair, lunged at his back and Dhrun had to jump for his life.

He found himself trapped between two pairs of raving beasts, each more anxious than his fellows to snap the chain and hurl himself at Dhrun's throat.

Dhrun bethought himself of his talisman. "Remarkable that I am not terrified!" he told himself in a quavering voice. "Well, then, I must prove my mettle and kill these horrid creatures!"

He flourished his sword Dassenach. "Dogs beware! I am ready to end your evil lives!"

From above came a peremptory call. The dogs fell silent and stood rigid in ferocious attitudes. Dhrun looked up to see a small house built of timbers on a ledge ten feet above the road. On the porch stood a troll who seemed to combine all the repulsive aspects of the first two. He wore snuff-brown garments, black boots with iron buckles and an odd conical hat tilted to one side. He called out furiously: "Harm my dogs at your peril! So much as a scratch and I will truss you in ropes and deliver you to Arbogast!"

"Order the dogs from the path!" cried Dhrun. "I will gladly go my way in peace!"

"It is not so easy! You disturbed their rest and mine as well with your whistling and chirrups; you should have passed more quietly! Now you must pay a stern penalty: a gold crown, at the very least!"

"It is far too much," said Dhrun, "but my time is valuable, and I am forced to pay." He extracted the gold crown from his purse and tossed it up to the troll who hefted it in his hand to test its weight. "Well then, I suppose I must relent. Dogs, away!"

The dogs slunk into the shrubbery and Dhrun slipped past with a tingling skin. He ran at full speed down the trail for as long as he was able, then halted, tapped the purse and went his way.

A mile passed and the path joined a road paved with brown bricks. Odd to find such a fine road in the depths of the forest, thought Dhrun. With one direction as good as the other, Dhrun turned left.

For an hour Dhrun marched along the road, while rays of sunlight slanted through the foliage at an ever lower angle . . . He stopped short. A vibration in the air: thud, thud, thud. Dhrun jumped from the road and hid behind a tree. Along the road came an ogre, rocking from side to side on heavy bowed legs. He stood fifteen feet tall; his arms and torso, like his legs, were knotted with wads of muscle! His belly thrust forward in a paunch. A great crush hat sheltered a gray face of surpassing ugliness. On his back he carried a wicker basket containing a pair of children.

Away down the road marched the ogre, and the thud-thud-thud of his footsteps became muffled in the distance.

Dhrun returned to the road beset by a dozen emotions, the strongest a strange sentiment which caused him a loose feeling in the bowels and a drooping of the jaw. Fear? Certainly not! His talisman protected him from so unmanly an emotion. What then? Rage, evidently, that Arbogast the ogre should so persecute human children.

Dhrun set out after the ogre. There was not far to go. The road rose over a little hill, then dipped down into a meadow. At the center stood Arbogast's hall, a great grim structure of gray stone, with a roof of green copper plates.

Before the hall the ground had been tilled and planted with cabbage, leeks, turnips, and onions, with currant bushes growing to the side. A dozen children, aged from six to twelve, worked in the garden under the vigilant eye of an overseer boy, perhaps fourteen years old. He was black-haired and thick-bodied, with an odd face: heavy and square above, then slanting in to a foxy mouth and a small sharp chin. He carried a rude whip, fashioned from a willow switch, with a cord tied to the end. From time to time he cracked the whip to urge greater zeal upon his charges. As he stalked around the garden, he issued orders and threats: "Now then, Arvil, get your hands dirty; don't be shy! Every weed must be pulled today. Bertrude, do you have problems? Do the weeds evade you? Quick now! The task must be done!... Not so hard on that cabbage, Pode! Cultivate the soil, don't destroy the plant!"

He pretended to notice Arbogast, and saluted. "Good day, your honor; all goes well here, no fear as to that when Nerulf is on the job."

Arbogast turned up the basket, to tumble a pair of girls out on the turf. One was blonde, the other dark; and each about twelve years old.

Arbogast pinched an iron ring around each girl's neck. He spoke in a rumbling bellow: "Now! Run away as you like, and learn what the others learned!"

"Quite right, sir, quite right!" called Nerulf from the garden. "No one dares to leave you, sir! And if they did, trust me to catch them!"

Arbogast paid him no heed. "To work!" he bellowed at the girls. "I like fine cabbages; see to it!" He lumbered across the meadow to his hall. The great portal opened; he entered and the portal remained open behind him.

The sun sank low; the children worked more slowly; even Nerulf's threats and whip-snappings took on a listless quality. Presently the children stopped work altogether and stood in a huddle, darting furtive looks toward the hall. Nerulf raised his whip on high. "Formation now, neat and orderly! March!"

The children formed themselves into a straggling double line and marched into the hall. The portal closed behind them with a fateful *clang!* that echoed across the meadow.

Twilight blurred the landscape. From windows high at the side of the hall came the yellow light of lamps.

Dhrun cautiously approached the hall, and, after touching his talisman, climbed the rough stone wall to one of the windows, using cracks and crevices as a ladder. He drew himself up to the broad stone sill. The shutters stood ajar; inching forward, Dhrun looked across the entire main hall, which was illuminated by six lamps in wall brackets and flames in the great fireplace.

Arbogast sat at a table, drinking wine from a pewter stoup. At the far end of the room the children sat against the wall, watching Arbogast with horrified fascination. At the hearth the carcass of a child, stuffed with onions, trussed and spitted, roasted over the fire. Nerulf turned the spit and from time to time basted the meat with oil and drippings. Cabbages and turnips boiled in a great black cauldron.

Arbogast drank wine and belched. Then, taking up a diabolo, he spread his massive legs, and rolled the spindle back and forth, chortling at the motion. The children sat huddled, watching with wide eyes and lax mouths. One of the small boys began to whimper. Arbogast turned him a cold glance. Nerulf called out in a voice pointedly soft and melodious: "Silence, Daffin!"

In due course Arbogast made his meal, throwing bones into the fire, while the children dined on cabbage soup.

For a few minutes Arbogast drank wine, dozed and belched. Then he swung around in his chair and regarded the children who at once pressed closer together. Again Daffin whimpered and again he was chided by Nerulf, who nevertheless seemed as uneasy as any of the others.

Arbogast reached into a high cabinet and brought two bottles down to the table, the first tall and green, the second squat and black-purple. Next, he set out two mugs, one green, the other purple, and into each he poured a dollop of wine. To the green mug he carefully added a drop from the green bottle, and into the purple mug, a drop from the black-purple bottle.

Arbogast now rose to his feet; wheezing and grunting he hunched across the room. He kicked Nerulf into the corner, then stood inspecting the group. He pointed a finger. "You two, step forward!"

Trembling, the two girls he had captured that day moved

away from the wall. Dhrun, watching from the window, thought them both very pretty, especially the blonde girl, though the dark-haired girl was perhaps half a year closer to womanhood.

Arbogast spoke in a voice now foolishly arch and jovial. "So here: a pair of fine young pullets, choice and tasty. How do you call yourselves? You!" He pointed at the blonde girl. "Your name?"

"Glyneth."

"And you?"

"Farence."

"Lovely, lovely. Both charming! Who is to be the lucky one? Tonight it shall be Farence."

He seized the dark-haired girl, hoisted her up to his great twenty-foot bed. "Off with your clothes!"

Farence started to cry and beg for mercy. Arbogast gave a ferocious snort of mingled annoyance and pleasure. "Hurry! Or I'll tear them from your back and then you'll have no clothes to wear!"

Stifling her sobs, Farence stepped from her smock. Arbogast chattered in delight. "A pretty sight! What is so toothsome as a nude maiden, shy and delicate?" He went to the table and drank the contents of the purple cup. At once he dwindled in stature to become a squat powerful troll, no taller than Nerulf. Without delay, he hopped up on the bed, discarded his own garments, and busied himself with erotic activities.

Dhrun watched all from the window, his knees limp, the blood pulsing in his throat. Disgust? Horror? Naturally not fear, and he touched the talisman gratefully. Nonetheless the emotion, whatever its nature, had a curiously debilitating effect.

Arbogast was indefatigable. Long after Farence became limp he continued his activity. Finally he collapsed upon the couch with a groan of satisfaction, and instantly fell asleep.

Dhrun was visited by an amusing notion, and, insulated from fear, was not thereby deterred. He lowered himself to the top of Arbogast's high-backed chair, and jumped down to the table. He poured the contents of the green cup out on the floor, added new wine and two drops from the purple bottle. He then climbed back to the window and hid behind the curtain.

The night passed and the fire burned low. Arbogast snored; the children were silent save for an occasional whimper.

The gray light of morning seeped through the windows. Arbogast awoke. He lay for a minute, then hopped to the floor. He visited the privy, voided, and returning, went to the hearth, where he blew up the fire and piled on fresh fuel. When the flames roared and crackled, he went to his table and climbing upon the chair, took up the green mug and swallowed its contents. Instantly, by virtue of the drops which Dhrun had mixed into the wine, he shrank in size until he was only a foot tall. Dhrun at once leapt down from the window, to chair, to table, to floor. He drew his sword and cut the scurrying squawking creature into pieces. These pieces squirmed and struggled and sought to join themselves, and Dhrun could not relax from his work. Glyneth ran forward and seizing the fresh cut pieces threw them into the fire, where they burnt to ash and so were destroyed. Meanwhile Dhrun placed the head into a pot and clapped on the cover, whereupon the head tried to pull itself out by means of tongue and teeth.

The remaining children came forward. Dhrun, wiping his sword on Arbogast's greasy crush hat said: "You need fear no more harm; Arbogast is helpless."

Nerulf licked his lips and stalked forward. "And who, may I ask, are you?"

"My name is Dhrun; I am a chance passerby."

"I see." Nerulf drew a deep breath and squared his meaty shoulders. He was, thought Dhrun, a person not at all prepossessing, with his coarse features, thick mouth, pointed chin and narrow black eyes. "Well then," said Nerulf, "please accept our compliments. It was exactly the plan I was about to carry out myself, as a matter of fact; still, you made quite a decent job of it. Now, let me think. We've got to reorganize; how shall we proceed? First, this mess must be cleaned. Pode and Hloude: mops and buckets. A good job now; I don't want to see a single smear when you're done. Dhrun, you can help them. Gretina, Zoel, Glyneth, Bertrude: explore the larder, bring out the best and prepare us all a fine breakfast. Lossamy and Fulp: carry all of Arbogast's clothes outside, also the blankets, and perhaps the place will smell better."

While Nerulf issued further orders, Dhrun climbed to the table top. He poured an ounce of wine into both green and purple mugs, and added to each a drop from the appropriate bottle. He swallowed the green potion, and at once became twelve feet tall. He jumped to the floor and seized the astonished

216

Nerulf by the iron ring around his neck. From the table Dhrun brought the purple potion and thrust it into Nerulf's mouth. "Drink!"

Nerulf attempted to protest, but was allowed no choice. "Drink!"

Nerulf gulped the potion and shrank to become a burly imp about two feet tall. Dhrun prepared to resume his ordinary size but Glyneth stopped him. "First remove the iron rings from about our necks."

One by one the children filed past Dhrun. He nicked the metal with his blade Dassenach, then twisted once, twice, and broke the rings apart. When all had been liberated, Dhrun reduced to his normal height. With great care he wrapped the two bottles and tucked them into his pouch. The other children meanwhile had found sticks and were beating Nerulf with intense satisfaction. Nerulf howled, danced and begged for mercy, but found none and was beaten until he was black and blue. For a few moments Nerulf was allowed surcease, until one of the children was reminded anew of some past cruelty and Nerulf was beaten again.

The girls declared themselves willing to prepare a bountiful feast, of ham and sausages, candied currants, partridge pie, fine bread and butter and gallons of Arbogast's best wine, but they refused to start until the fireplace was cleared of ash and bones: all too vivid mementos of their servitude. Everyone worked with a will, and soon the hall was comparatively clean.

At noon a great banquet was served. By some means Arbogast's head had managed to raise itself to the rim of the pot, to which it hooked its teeth and pressed up the lid with its forehead, and with its two eyes watched from the darkness inside the pot as the children reveled in the best the castle's larder could afford. When they had finished their meal, Dhrun noticed that the lid had fallen from the pot, which now was empty. He set up a shout and all ran looking for the missing head. Pode and Daffin discovered it halfway across the meadow, pulling itself forward by snapping at the ground with its teeth. They knocked it back toward the hall, and in the front yard built a kind of gallows, from which they suspended the head by an iron wire tied to the mud-colored hair. At the insistence of all, the better that they could regard their erstwhile captor, Dhrun forced a drop of green potion into the red mouth, and the head resumed its natural size, and even issued a set of rasping orders, which were joyfully ignored.

While the head watched aghast, the children piled faggots below and brought fire from the hearth to set the faggots ablaze. Dhrun brought out his pipes and played while the children danced in a circle. The head roared and supplicated but was allowed no mercy. At last the head was reduced to ash, and Arbogast the ogre was no more.

Fatigued by the day's events, the children trooped back into the hall. They supped on porridge and soup of cabbage, with good crusty bread and more of Arbogast's wine; then they prepared to sleep. A few of the more hardy climbed up on Arbogast's bed, desipite the rancid stench; the others sprawled before the fire.

Dhrun, weary in every bone from his vigil of the night before, not to mention his deeds of the day, nonetheless found himself unable to sleep. He lay before the fire, head propped on his hands and considered his adventures. He had not fared too badly. Perhaps seven years of bad luck had not been inflicted upon him after all.

The fire burned low. Dhrun went to the wood-box for logs. He dropped them upon the coals, to send showers of red sparks veering up the chimney. The flames flared high, and glinted back from the eyes of Glyneth, who also sat awake. She joined Dhrun in front of the fireplace. The two sat clasping their knees and looking into the flames. Glyneth spoke in a husky half-whisper: "No one has troubled to thank you for saving our lives. I do so now. Thank you, dear Dhrun; you are gallant and kind and remarkably brave."

Dhrun said in a wistful voice: "I would hope to be gallant and kind, since I am the son of a prince and a princess, but as for bravery, I can honorably claim none."

"Sheer nonsense! Only a person of great bravery would have done as you did."

Dhrun gave a bitter laugh. He touched his talisman. "The fairies knew my fearfulness and gave me this amulet of courage; without it I could have dared nothing."

"I'm not at all certain of that," said Glyneth. "Amulet or none, I consider you very brave."

"That is good to hear," said Dhrun mournfully. "I wish it were so."

"All this to the side, why would the fairies give you such a gift, or any gift whatever? They are not ordinarily so generous."

"I lived with the fairies all my days at Thripsey Shee, on Madling Meadow. Three days ago they cast me out, though many of them loved me and gave me gifts. There were one or two who wished me ill and tricked me so that when I looked back I incurred seven years of bad luck."

Glyneth took Dhrun's hand and held it against her cheek. "How could they be so cruel?"

"It was strictly the fault of Falael, who lives for such mischief. And what of you? Why are you here?"

Glyneth smiled sadly into the fire. "It's a dreary tale. Are you sure you want to hear it?"

"If you want to tell it."

"I'll leave out the worst parts. I lived in North Ulfland, at the town Throckshaw. My father was a squire. We lived in a fine house with glass windows and feather-beds and a rug on the parlor floor. There were eggs and porridge for breakfast, sausages and roasted pullets at noon dinner and a good soup for supper, with a salad of garden greens.

"Count Julk ruled the land from Castle Sfeg; he was at war with the Ska, who already had settled the Foreshore. To the south of Throckshaw is Poëlitetz: a pass through the Teach tac Teach into Dahaut and a place coveted by the Ska. Always the Ska put pressure on us; always Count Julk drove them back. One day a hundred Ska knights on black horses raided Throckshaw. The men of the town took up arms and drove them away. A week later an army of five hundred Ska riding black horses drove up from the Foreshore and reduced Throckshaw. They killed my father and mother, and burnt our house. I hid under the hay with my cat Pettis, and watched while they rode back and forth screaming like demons. Count Julk appeared with his knights, but the Ska killed him, conquered the countryside, and perhaps Poëlitetz as well.

"When the Ska left Throckshaw, I took a few silver coins and ran away with Pettis. Twice I was almost captured by vagabonds. One night I ventured into an old barn. A great dog came roaring at me. Rather than running, my brave Pettis attacked the beast and was killed. The farmer came to investigate and discovered me. He and his wife were kind folk and gave me a home. I was almost content, though I worked hard in the buttery, and also during the threshing. But one of the sons began to molest me, and to suggest careless behavior. I dared no longer walk alone to the barn for fear he would find me. One day a procession came by. They called themselves *Relicts of Old Gomar** and were on pilgrimage to a celebration at Godwyne Foiry, the ruins of Old Gomar's capitol, at the edge of the Great Forest, over the Teach tac Teach and into Dahaut. I joined them and so left the farmhouse.

"We crossed the mountains in safety, and came to Godwyne Foiry. We camped at the edge of the ruins and all was well, until the day before Midsummer's Eve when I learned of the celebrations and what would be expected of me. The men wear the horns of goats and elk, nothing more. They paint their faces blue and their legs brown. The women plait the leaves of ash trees into their hair and wear cinctures of twenty-four rowan berries about their waists. Each time a woman consorts with a man, he breaks one of her berries; and whichever woman first breaks all her berries is declared the incarnation of the love goddess Sobh. I was told that at least six of the men were planning to lay hands on me at once, even though I am not yet truly a woman. I left the camp that very night and hid in the forest.

"I had a dozen frights and a dozen close escapes, and finally a witch trapped me under her hat and sold me to Arbogast, and you know the rest."

The two sat silently, looking into the fire. Dhrun said: "I wish I could travel with you and protect you, but I am burdened with seven years bad luck, or so I fear, which I would not share with you."

Glyneth leaned her head on Dhrun's shoulder. "I would gladly take the chance."

They sat talking long into the night, while the fire once again lapsed to coals. There was quiet inside and outside the hall, disturbed only by a pitter-patter from above, caused, according to Glyneth, by the ghosts of dead children running along the roof.

In the morning the children breakfasted, then broke into Arbogast's strong-room, where they found a chest of jewels, five baskets full of gold crowns, a set of precious silver punchbowls, intricately carved to depict events of the mythical ages, and dozens of other treasures.

---

*Gomar: ancient kingdom comprising all of North Hybras and the Hesperian Islands.

For a time the children frolicked and played with the riches, imagining themselves lords of vast estates, and even Farence took a wan pleasure in the game.

Throughout the afternoon the wealth was shared out equally among the children, all save Nerulf, who was allowed nothing.

After a supper of leeks, preserved goose, white bread and butter and a rich plum-duff with wine sauce, the children gathered around the fireplace to crack nuts and sip cordials. Daffin, Pode, Fulp, Arvil, Hloude, Lossamy and Dhrun were the boys, along with the morose imp Nerulf. The girls were Gretina, Zoel, Bertrude, Farence, Wiedelin and Glyneth. The youngest were Arvil and Zoel; the oldest, aside from Nerulf, were Lossamy and Farence.

For hours they discussed their circumstances, and the best route through the Forest of Tantrevalles into civilized countryside. Pode and Hloude seemed best acquainted with the terrain. Optimally, so they declared, the group should follow the brick road north to the first river which would necessarily join the Murmeil. They should follow the Murmeil out into the open lands of Dahaut, or perhaps by some stroke of luck they might find or purchase a boat, or even build a raft. "Indeed, with our wealth we can easily obtain a boat and float in ease and comfort downstream to Gehadion Towers, or, should we choose, all the way to Avallon." Such was Pode's opinion.

Finally, an hour before midnight, all stretched out and slept: all except Nerulf, who sat another two hours scowling into the dying embers.

19

IN PREPARATION FOR THEIR journey the children brought the ogre's cart around to the front door of the hall, greased the axles well with tallow and loaded their treasures aboard. Across the shafts they tied poles, so that nine of them could pull and another three push from behind. Only Nerulf was unable to assist, but no one thought that he would help in any case, since the cart carried no property of his own. The children bade farewell to Arbogast Hall and set off along the brown brick road. The day was fresh; the wind herded a hundred clouds from the Atlantic high across the forest. The children pulled and pushed with a will and the cart trundled along the brick road at a good rate, while Nerulf ran at best speed behind in the dust. At noon the party stopped to dine on bread, meat and heavy brown beer, then continued north and east.

During the late afternoon the road entered a clearing, grown over with rank grass and a half-dozen crippled apple trees. To one side stood a small ruined abbey, built by Christian missionaries of the first fervent wave. Though the roof had fallen in, the structure offered at least the semblance of shelter. The children built a fire and made a meal of withered apples, bread and cheese, with cress and water from a nearby stream. They made beds of grass and rested gratefully after the labors of the day. All were happy and confident; luck seemed to have turned their way.

The night passed without incident. In the morning the group prepared to set off along the road. Nerulf approached Dhrun, head bowed and hands clasped across his chest. "Sir Dhrun, let me say that the punishment you have visited upon me was well-deserved. I never realized my arrogance until I was forced to do so. But now my faults have been revealed to me in sharpest detail. I believe that I have learned my lesson and that I am a new person, decent and honorable. Therefore, I ask that you restore me to my natural condition, so that I may push the cart. I want none of the treasure; I deserve none, but I want to help the others arrive to safety with their valuables. If you see fit not to grant my request, I shall understand and harbor no ill feelings. After all, the fault was mine alone. Still, I am heartily tired of running full speed all day in the dust, tripping over pebbles, fearful of drowning in puddles. What will you tell me, Sir Dhrun?"

Dhrun listened without sympathy. "Wait until we reach civilized safety; then I'll restore you to size."

"Ah, Sir Dhrun, do you not trust me?" cried Nerulf. "In that case, let us part company here and now, since I cannot survive another day of running and bounding behind the cart. Proceed along the road to the great Murmeil and follow its banks to Gehadion Towers. The best of luck to all of you! I will follow at my own pace." Nerulf wiped his eyes with a dirty knuckle. "Sometime you may be sauntering through a carnival in your fine clothes and chance to notice a manikin beating a drum or performing ludicrous antics; if so, please spare the poor fellow a penny as it might be your old companion Nerulf—if of course I survive the beasts of Tantrevalles."

Dhrun considered a long moment. "You have truly repented of your past conduct?"

"I despise myself!" cried Nerulf. "I look back upon the old Nerulf with disdain!"

"In that case there is no point in prolonging your punishment." Dhrun poured a drop from the green bottle into a cup of water. "Drink this, resume your proper condition, become a true comrade to the rest of us, and perhaps you will profit in the end."

"Thank you, Sir Dhrun!" Nerulf drank the potion, and expanded to become his old burly self. Quick as a wink he leapt upon Dhrun, threw him to the ground, tore away his sword Dassenach and buckled it around his own thick waist. Then he took the green bottle and the purple bottle and flung them against a stone, so that they shattered and all their contents were lost. "There will be no more of that foolishness," declared Nerulf. "I am the largest and strongest, and once again I am in power." He kicked Dhrun. "To your feet!"

"You told me that you had repented your old ways!" cried Dhrun indignantly.

"True! I was not severe enough. I allowed too much ease. Things will now be different. Out to the cart, everyone!"

The frightened children gathered at the cart and waited while Nerulf cut an alder switch and tied three cords to the end, to make a crude but serviceable whip.

"Line up!" barked Nerulf. "Quick then! Pode, Daffin, do you taunt me? Would you care to taste the whip? Silence! All attend my words with great care; they will not be repeated.

"First, I am your master, and you live by my command.

"Second, the treasure is mine. Every gem, every coin, every last tittle and scrap.

"Third, our destination is Cluggach in Godelia. The Celts ask far fewer questions than the Dauts, and interfere not at all in anyone's business.

"Fourth"—here Nerulf paused and smiled unpleasantly—"when I was helpless you took up sticks and beat me. I recall each and every blow, and if those who struck me now find their skins tingling, the premonition is sound. Bare bottoms will turn to the sky! Switches will whistle and welts will appear!

"That is all I wish to say, but I will gladly answer questions."

No one spoke, though a morose thought passed through Dhrun's mind: seven years had barely started, but already bad luck had struck with vindictive force.

"Then take your places at the cart!"

"Today we move fast; our style is brisk! Not like yesterday when you eased and ambled." Nerulf climbed aboard the cart and made himself comfortable. "Be away! Smartly! Heads back, heels in the air!" He cracked the whip. "Pode! Less pumping of the elbows. Daffin! Open your eyes; you'll have us all in the ditch! Dhrun, more gracefully, show us a fine smart stride! And off we go through the beautiful morning, and it's a happy time for all!...Here now! Why the slackening? You girls especially, you're running like hens!"

"We're tired," gasped Glyneth.

"So soon? Well, perhaps I overestimated your strength, as it seems so easy from here. And you in particular; I don't want you too limp, as tonight I shall put you to another kind of exertion. Ha ha! Pleasure for him who holds the whip! Forward once more, at half-speed."

Dhrun took occasion to whisper to Glyneth: "Don't worry; he won't harm you. Mine is a magic sword and comes to my command. At the proper time I will call it to my hand and hold him helpless."

Glyneth nodded despondently.

During the middle afternoon the road rose into a line of low hills and the children failed against the weight of cart, treasure and Nerulf. First using his whip, then dismounting, and finally helping to push, Nerulf assisted in bringing the cart to the high ridge. A short but steep stretch of road intervened between the cart and the shores of Lake Lingolen. Nerulf cut down a forty-foot pine tree with Dhrun's sword and tied it as a drag to the rear of the cart and the slope was negotiated safely.

They found themselves on a marshy margin between lake and the dark hills, upon which the sun was declining.

Up from the marsh thrust a number of islands; one of them served as refuge for a gang of bandits. Their lookouts had already taken note of the cart; now they sprang from ambush. The children, for an instant paralyzed, fled in all directions. As soon as the bandits discovered the nature of their booty they gave up all thought of pursuit.

Dhrun and Glyneth fled together, along the road to the east. They ran until their chests hurt and cramps bound their legs; then they threw themselves into the tall grass beside the road to rest.

An instant later another fugitive flung himself down beside them: Nerulf.

Dhrun sighed. "Seven years bad luck: will it always be this bad?"

"Stop that insolence!" hissed Nerulf. "I am still in command, in case you are uncertain. Now stand up!"

"What for? I'm tired."

"No matter. My great treasure has been lost; still, it's just possible that a few gems are hidden about your person. On your feet! You too, Glyneth!"

Dhrun and Glyneth rose slowly. In Dhrun's pouch Nerulf discovered the old purse and turned it out into his hand. He grunted in disgust. "A crown, a florin, a penny: just barely better than nothing." He cast the old purse to the ground. With quiet dignity Dhrun picked it up and restored it to his pouch.

Nerulf searched Glyneth's person, his hands lingering along the contours of her fresh young body, but he found no objects of value. "Well, let's go on for a bit; perhaps we'll find shelter for the night."

The three walked along the road, watching over their shoulders for signs of pursuit, but none appeared. The woodland became extremely heavy and dark; the three, despite fatigue, moved along the road at good speed, and presently emerged once again on open lands beside the marsh.

The setting sun shone from beyond the hills along the underside of clouds sailing across the lake; they cast an unreal dark golden light over the marsh.

Nerulf noticed a small promontory, almost an island, protruding fifty yards into the marsh, with a weeping-willow tree at its highest point. Nerulf turned upon Dhrun a look of lowering menace. "Glyneth and I will spend the night here," he announced. "You go elsewhere, starting now, and never come back. And consider yourself lucky, since I have you to thank for my beatings. Go!" With that he went to the edge of the marsh and using Dhrun's sword began to cut rushes for a bed.

Dhrun went off a few yards, and stopped to think. He could recover Dassenach at any time, but to no great effect. Nerulf could run away until he found a weapon: large stones, a long cudgel, or he could merely step behind a tree and challenge Dhrun to come at him. In all cases Nerulf, with his size and strength could overpower Dhrun and kill him if so he chose.

Nerulf, looking up, saw Dhrun and cried out: "Did I not order you to go?" He made a run at Dhrun, who quickly retreated into the dense woods. Here he found a dead branch and broke it to make a stout cudgel four feet long. Then he returned to the marsh.

Nerulf had waded out to where the reeds grew thick and soft. Dhrun signaled to Glyneth. She ran to join him and Dhrun gave her quick instructions.

Nerulf looked up and saw the two standing together. He called out to Dhrun: "What are you doing here? I told you to leave and never return! You disobeyed me and I now sentence you to death."

Glyneth saw something rise from the marsh behind Nerulf. She shrieked and pointed her finger.

Nerulf uttered a scornful laugh. "Do you think you can fool

me with that old trick? I am somewhat more—" He felt a soft touch on his arm and looking down saw a long-fingered gray hand with knobby knuckles and a clammy skin. Nerulf stood rigid; then, as if forced against his will, he looked around, to discover himself face to face with a heceptor. He uttered a strangled yell and staggering backward flourished the sword Dassenach, with which he had been cutting reeds.

Dhrun and Glyneth fled away from the lakeshore to the road, where they halted and looked back.

Out on the marsh Nerulf backed slowly away from the advancing heceptor who menaced him with arms on high, hands and fingers angled downwards. Nerulf tried to make play with the sword and pierced the heceptor's shoulder, to elicit a hiss of sad reproach.

The time had come. Dhrun called: "Dassenach! To me!"

The sword jerked from Nerulf's fingers and flew across the marsh to Dhrun's hand. Somberly he tucked it into its scabbard. The heceptor lurched forward, enfolded Nerulf and bore him screaming down into the muck.

With darkness upon them and the stars appearing in profusion, Dhrun and Glyneth climbed to the top of a grassy knoll a few yards from the road. They gathered armfuls of grass, made a pleasant bed and stretched out their weary bodies. For half an hour they watched the stars, big and softly white. Presently they became drowsy and, huddled together, slept soundly until morning.

After two comparatively uneventful days of travel, Dhrun and Glyneth arrived at a broad river, which Glyneth felt must surely be the Murmeil itself. A massive stone bridge spanned the river and here the ancient brick road came to an end.

Before setting foot on the bridge Dhrun called out three times for the toll-taker, but none showed himself and they crossed the bridge unchallenged.

Now there were three roads from which to choose. One led east along the river bank; another proceeded upstream beside the river; a third wandered away to the north, as if it had no particular destination in mind.

Dhrun and Glyneth set off to the east, and for two days followed the river through landscapes and riverscapes of wonderful beauty. Glyneth rejoiced at the fine weather. "Think,

Dhrun! If you were truly cursed with bad luck, the rain would drench our skins and there would be snow to freeze our bones!"

"I wish I could believe so."

"There's no doubt at all. And look yonder at the beautiful berries! Just in time for our lunch! Isn't that good luck?"

Dhrun was willing to be convinced. "It would seem so."

"Of course! We'll talk no more of curses." Glyneth ran to the thicket which bordered a small stream near where it tumbled down a declivity into the Murmeil.

"Wait!" cried Dhrun, "or we'll know bad luck for sure!" He called out: "Does anyone forbid us these berries?"

There was no response and the two ate their fill of ripe black-berries.

For a space they lay resting in the shade. "Now that we're almost out of the forest, it's time to make plans," said Glyneth. "Have you thought of what we should do?"

"Yes indeed. We will travel here and there and try to discover my father and mother. If I am truly a prince, then we will live in a castle and I shall insist that you be made a princess as well. You shall have fine clothes, a carriage and also another cat like Pettis."

Glyneth, laughing, kissed Dhrun's cheek. "I'd like to live in a castle. We're sure to find your father and mother, since there are not all that many princes and princesses!"

Glyneth became drowsy. Her eyelids drooped and she dozed. Dhrun, becoming restless, went to explore a path which bordered the stream. He walked a hundred feet and looked back. Glyneth still lay asleep. He walked another hundred feet, and another. The forest seemed very still; the trees rose majestically high, taller than any Dhrun had seen before, to create a luminous green canopy far overhead.

The path crossed a rocky little hummock. Dhrun, climbing up to the top, found himself overlooking a tarn shaded beneath the great trees. Five nude dryads waded in the shallows of the tarn: slender creatures with rose-pink mouths and long brown hair, small breasts, slim thighs and unutterably lovely faces. Like fairies they showed no pubic hair; like fairies they seemed made of stuff less gross than blood and meat and bone.

For a minute Dhrun stared entranced; then he took sudden fright and slowly backed away.

He was seen. Tinkling little outcries of dismay reached his

ears. Carelessly strewn along the bank, almost at Dhrun's feet, were the fillets which bound their brown hair; a mortal seizing such a fillet held the dryad in power, to serve his caprice forever, but Dhrun knew nothing of this.

One of the dryads splashed water toward Dhrun. He saw the drops rise into the air and sparkle in the sunlight, whereupon they became small golden bees, which darted into Dhrun's eyes and buzzed in circles, blotting out his sight.

Dhrun screamed in shock and fell to his knees. "Fairies, you have blinded me! I only chanced on you by mistake! Do you hear me?"

Silence. Only the sound of leaves stirring in the afternoon airs.

"Fairies!" cried Dhrun, tears running down his cheeks. "Would you blind me for so small an offense?"

Silence, definite and final.

Dhrun groped back along the trail, guided by the sound of the little stream. Halfway along the trail he met Glyneth, who, awakening and seeing no Dhrun, had come to find him. Instantly she recognized his distress and ran forward. "Dhrun! What is the trouble?"

Dhrun took a deep breath, and tried to speak in a courageous voice, which despite his efforts quavered and cracked. "I went along the trail; I saw five dryads bathing in a pool; they splashed bees into my eyes and now I can't see!" In spite of his talisman, Dhrun could barely restrain his grief.

"Oh Dhrun!" Glyneth came close. "Open your eyes wide; let me look."

Dhrun stared toward her face. "What do you see?"

Glyneth said haltingly: "Very strange! I see circles of golden light, one around the other, with brown in between."

"It's the bees! They've filled my eyes with buzzing and dark honey!"

"Dhrun, dearest Dhrun!" Glyneth hugged him and kissed him, and used every endearment she knew. "How could they be so wicked!"

"I know why," he said bleakly. "Seven years bad luck. I wonder what will happen next. You had better go away and leave me—"

"Dhrun! How can you say such a thing?"

"—so that if I fall in a hole, you need not fall in too."

230

"Never would I leave you!"

"That is foolishness. This is a terrible world, so I am discovering. It is all you can do to care for yourself, let alone me."

"But you are the one I love most in all the world! Somehow we'll survive! When the seven years is over there'll be nothing left but good luck forever!"

"But I'll be blind!" cried Dhrun, again with a quaver in his voice.

"Well, that's not sure either. Magic blinded you; magic will cure you. What do you think of that?"

"I hope that you're right." Dhrun clutched his talisman. "How grateful I am for my bravery, even though I can't be proud of it. I suspect that I am a fearful coward at heart."

"Amulet or none, you are the brave Dhrun, and one way or another, we shall get on in the world."

Dhrun reflected a moment, then brought out his magic purse. "Best that you carry this; with my luck a crow will swoop down and carry it away."

Glyneth looked into the purse and cried out in amazement. "Nerulf emptied it; now I see gold and silver and copper!"

"It is a magic purse, and we never need fear poverty, so long as the purse is safe."

Glyneth tucked the purse into her bodice. "I'll be as careful as careful can be." She looked up the trail. "Perhaps I should go to the pool and tell the dryads what a terrible mistake they made..."

"You'd never find them. They are as heartless as fairies, or worse. They might even do mischief on you. Let's leave this place."

Late in the afternoon they came upon the ruins of a Christian chapel, constructed by a missionary now long forgotten. To the side grew a plum tree and a quince tree, both heavy with fruit. The plums were ripe; the quince, though of a fine color, tasted acrid and bitter. Glyneth picked a gallon of plums, upon which they made a somewhat meager supper. Glyneth piled up grass for a soft bed among the toppled stones, while Dhrun sat staring out across the river.

"I think the forest is thinning," Glyneth told Dhrun. "It won't be long before we're safe among civilized folk. Then we'll have bread and meat to eat, milk to drink, and beds to sleep in."

231

Sunset flared over the Forest of Tantrevalles, then faded to dusk. Dhrun and Glyneth went to their bed; they became drowsy and slept.

Somewhat before midnight the half-moon rose, cast a reflection on the river, and shone in Glyneth's face, awakening her. She lay warm and drowsy, listening to the crickets and frogs... A far drumming sound caught her ear. It grew louder, and with it the jingle of chain and the squeak of saddle-leather. Glyneth raised up on her elbow, to see a dozen horsemen come pounding along the river road. They crouched low in their saddles with cloaks flapping behind; moonlight illuminated their antique gear and black leather helmets with flaring ear-pieces. One of the riders, head almost into his horse's mane, turned to look toward Glyneth. Moonlight shone into his pallid face; then the ghostly cavalcade was away. The drumming died into the distance and was gone.

Glyneth sank back into the grass and at last slept.

At dawn Glyneth roused herself quietly and tried to strike a hot spark from a piece of flint she had found, and so to blow up a fire, but met no success.

Dhrun awoke. He gave a startled cry, which he quickly stifled. Then after a moment he said: "It's not a dream after all."

Glyneth looked in Dhrun's eyes. "I still see the golden circles." She kissed Dhrun. "But don't brood, we'll find some way to cure you. Remember what I said yesterday? Magic gives, magic takes."

"I'm sure that you are right." Dhrun's voice was hollow. "In any case, there's no help for it." He rose to his feet and almost immediately tripped on a root and fell. Throwing out his arms, he caught the chain where hung his amulet and sent both chain and amulet flying.

Glyneth came on the run. "Are you hurt? Oh, your poor knee, it's all bleeding from the sharp stone!"

"Never mind the knee," croaked Dhrun. "I've lost my talisman; I broke the chain and now it's gone!"

"It won't run away," said Glyneth in a practical voice. "First I'll bandage your knee and then I'll find your talisman."

She tore a strip from her petticoat and washed the scratch with water from a little spring. "We'll just let that dry, then I'll wrap it nicely in a bandage and you'll be as frisky as ever."

232

"Glyneth, find my talisman, please! It's something which must not be put off. Suppose a mouse drags it away?"

"It would become the bravest of mice! The cats and owls would turn tail and flee." She patted Dhrun's cheek. "But I'll find it now . . . It must have gone in this direction." She dropped to her hands and knees, and looked here and there. Almost at once she saw the amulet. As luck would have it, the cabochon had fallen hard against a stone and had shattered into a dozen pieces.

"Do you see it?" asked Dhrun anxiously.

"I think it's in this clump of grass." Glyneth found a small smooth pebble and pressed it into the setting. With the edge of a larger stone, she pushed down the flange, so as to secure the pebble in place. "Here it is in the grass! Let me fix the chain." She bent the twisted link back into alignment and hung the amulet around Dhrun's neck, to his great relief. "There you are, as good as new."

The two breakfasted on plums and continued along beside the river. The forest straggled out to become a parkland of copses separated by meadows of long grasses waving in the wind. They came upon a deserted hut, shelter for those herdsmen who dared forage their flocks so close to the wolves, griswolds and bears of the forest.

Another mile, and another, and they came to a pleasant two-story stone cottage, with flower boxes under the upper windows. A stone fence surrounded a garden of forget-me-not wallflower, pansies and angel's pincushion. A pair of chimneys at either gable supported chimney pots high above the fresh clean thatch. Further along the road could be seen a village of gray stone cottages huddled in a swale. A crone in black gown and white apron weeded the garden. She paused to watch Dhrun and Glyneth approach, then gave her head a shake and returned to work.

As Glyneth and Dhrun neared the gate a plump and pretty woman of mature years stepped out upon the little porch. "Well then, children, what are you doing so far from home?"

Glyneth answered: "I'm afraid, mistress, that we're vagabonds. We have neither home nor family."

In surprise the woman looked back up the way the two had come. "But this road leads nowhere!"

"We've just come through the Forest of Tantrevalles."

"Then you bear charmed lives! What are your names? You may call me Dame Melissa."

"I am Glyneth and this is Dhrun. The fairies sent bees into his eyes and now he can't see."

"Ah! A pity! They are often cruel! Come here, Dhrun, let me see your eyes."

Dhrun stepped forward and Dame Melissa studied the concentric rings of gold and amber. "I know one or two trifles of magic, but not so much as a true witch, and I can do nothing for you."

"Perhaps you would sell us a bite of bread and cheese," Glyneth suggested. "We've eaten only plums today and yesterday."

"Of course, and you need not think of payment. Didas? Where are you? We have a pair of hungry children here! Bring milk and butter and cheese from the dairy. Come in, dears. Go back to the kitchen and I think we can find something nice."

When Dhrun and Glyneth had seated themselves at the scrubbed wooden table, Dame Melissa served them first bread and a rich soup of mutton and barley, then a tasty dish of chicken cooked with saffron and walnuts, and finally cheese and juicy green grapes.

Dame Melissa sat to the side sipping a tea brewed from the leaves of lemon verbena and smiled to watch them eat. "I see that you are both healthy young persons," she said. "Are you brother and sister?"

"It amounts to that," said Glyneth. "But in truth we're not related. We've both suffered troubles and we think ourselves lucky to be together, since neither of us has anyone else."

Dame Melissa said soothingly: "You're now in Far Dahaut, out of the dreadful forest, and I'm sure things will go better for you."

"I hope so. We can't thank you enough for the wonderful dinner, but we mustn't intrude upon you. If you'll excuse us, we'll be on our way."

"Whyever so soon? It's afternoon. I'm sure you're tired. There's a nice room for Glyneth just above, and a good bed in the garret for Dhrun. You shall have a supper of bread and milk and a sweet-cake or two, then you may eat apples before the fire and tell me your adventures. Then tomorrow, when you're well rested, you'll be on your way."

Glyneth hesitated and looked at Dhrun.

"Do stay," pleaded Dame Melissa. "Sometimes it's lonely here with no one but crotchety old Didas."

"I don't mind," said Dhrun. "Perhaps you can tell us where to find a powerful magician, to draw the bees from my eyes."

"I'll give the matter thought, and I'll ask Didas as well; she knows a bit of everything."

Glyneth sighed. "I'm afraid you'll spoil us. Vagabonds are not supposed to trouble over good food and soft beds."

"Just one night, then a good breakfast, and you can be on your way."

"Then we thank you again for your kindness."

"Not at all. It gives me pleasure to see such pretty children enjoying my house. I ask only that you do not molest Dame Didas. She is very old, and a trifle crabbed—even, I am sorry to say, a bit eery. But if you leave her be, she will not trouble you."

"Naturally, we will treat her with all politeness."

"Thank you, my dear. Now, why do you not go outside and enjoy the flower garden until supper time?"

"Thank you, Dame Melissa."

The two went out into the garden, where Glyneth led Dhrun from flower to flower, that he might find pleasure in the fragrance.

After an hour of going from plant to plant, sniffing and smelling, Dhrun became bored and stretched out on a patch of lawn, to doze in the sunshine, while Glyneth went to puzzle out the mystery of a sun dial.

Someone gestured from the side of the cottage; looking around, Glyneth saw Dame Didas, who instantly signaled her first to caution and silence, then beckoned her to come.

Glyneth slowly approached. Dame Didas, in a fever of impatience, signaled her to haste. Glyneth moved forward more quickly.

Dame Didas asked, "What did Dame Melissa tell you about me?"

Glyneth hesitated, then spoke out bravely. "She said not to bother you; that you were very old and often irritable, or even a little, well, unpredictable."

Dame Didas gave a dry chuckle. "As for that, you'll have a chance to judge for yourself. In the meanwhile—now heed me, girl, heed me!—drink no milk with your supper. I will call to

235

Dame Melissa; while she is distracted pour the milk into the sink, then pretend to have finished. After supper say that you are very tired and would like to go to bed. Do you understand?"

"Yes, Dame Didas."

"Disregard me to your peril! Tonight, when the house is quiet, and Dame Melissa has gone to her workroom, I'll explain. Will you heed me?"

"Yes, Dame Didas. If I may say so, you seem neither crabbed nor eery."

"That's a good girl. Until tonight then. Now I must hurry back to the weeds; they grow as fast as I'm able to pull them."

The afternoon passed. At sunset Dame Melissa called them in to supper. On the kitchen table she placed a fresh crusty loaf, butter and a dish of pickled mushrooms. She had already poured mugs of milk for both Glyneth and Dhrun; there was also a milk jug if they wanted more.

"Sit down, children," said Dame Melissa. "Are your hands clean? Good. Eat as much as you wish; and drink your milk. It is fresh and good."

"Thank you, Dame Melissa."

From the drawing room came the voice of Dame Didas. "Melissa, come at once! I want a word with you!"

"Later, Didas, later!" But Melissa rose to her feet and walked to the doorway; instantly Glyneth poured out the milk from both mugs. She whispered to Dhrun: "Pretend to drink from the empty mug."

When Dame Melissa returned, both Glyneth and Dhrun were apparently in the act of draining the milk in their mugs.

Dame Melissa said nothing, but turned away and paid no more heed to them.

Glyneth and Dhrun ate a slice of crusty bread with butter; then Glyneth simulated a yawn. "We're both tired, Dame Melissa. If you'll excuse us, we'd like to go to bed."

"Of course! Glyneth, you may help Dhrun to his bed and you know your own room."

Glyneth, carrying a candle, took Dhrun up to the garret. Dhrun asked dubiously: "Aren't you afraid to be alone?"

"A little, but not too much."

"I'm no longer a fighter," said Dhrun wistfully. "Still, if I hear you cry out I'll be there."

Glyneth descended to her room and lay on the bed fully clothed. A few minutes later Didas appeared. "She's in her workroom now; we have a few moments to talk. To start, let me say that Dame Melissa, as she calls herself, is a dire witch. When I was fifteen years old, she gave me drugged milk to drink, then transferred herself into my body—that which she wears today. I, a fifteen-year-old girl, was housed in the body Melissa had been using: a woman about forty years old. That was twenty-five years ago. Tonight she will change my forty-year-old body for yours. You will be Dame Melissa and she will be Glyneth, only she will wield power and you will end your days as a serving woman like me. Dhrun will be put to work carrying water from the river to her orchard. She is in her workroom now preparing the magic."

"How can we stop her?" asked Glyneth in a shaking voice.

"I want to do more than stop her!" spat Didas. "I want to destroy her!"

"So do I—but how?"

"Come with me; quick now!"

Didas and Glyneth ran out to the pig-sty. A young pig lay on a sheet. "I've washed it and drugged it," said Didas. "Help me carry it upstairs."

Once in Glyneth's room they dressed the pig in a nightgown and a mob-cap, and lay it in the bed, face to the wall.

"Quick now!" whispered Didas. "She'll be on her way. Into the closet!"

They had barely shut themselves in when they heard footsteps on the stairs. Dame Melissa, wearing a pink gown and carrying a red candle in each hand, entered the room.

Above the bed a pair of censers hung from hooks; Melissa touched fire to them and, smouldering, they gave off an acrid smoke.

Melissa lay down on the bed beside the pig. She placed a black bar across her neck and the neck of the pig, then spoke an incantation:

> I into thee!
> Thou into me!
> Straitly and swiftly, let the change be!
> *Bezadiah!*

There was a sudden startled squealing as the pig discovered itself in the undrugged body of Melissa. Didas sprang from the closet, dragged the pig to the floor, and pushing the erstwhile

Melissa to the wall lay beside her. She arranged the black bar from across her neck to that of Melissa. She inhaled the smoke from the censers and uttered the incantation:

> I into thee!
> Thou into me!
> Straitly and swiftly, let the change be!
> *Bezadiah!*

At once the pig's frightened squealing came from the body of the crone Didas. Melissa arose from the bed and spoke to Glyneth: "Be calm, child. All is done. I am once more in my own body. I have been cheated of my youth and all my young years, and who can make restitution? But help me now. First we'll take the old Didas down to the sty, where at least it will feel secure. It is a sick old body and soon will die."

"Poor pig," muttered Glyneth.

They led the creature once known as Didas down to the sty and tied her to a post. Then, returning to the bedroom, they carried out the body of the pig which was beginning to stir. Melissa tied it securely to a tree beside the cottage then drenched it with a pan of cold water.

At once the pig regained consciousness. It tried to speak, but its tongue and oral cavity made the sounds incomprehensible. It began to wail, in terror and grief.

"So there you are, witch," said the new Dame Melissa. "I don't know how I look to you through a pig's eyes, or how much you can hear through a pig's ear, but your witching days are at an end."

Next morning Glyneth awoke Dhrun with a report of the previous night's events. Dhrun felt somewhat aggrieved because of his exclusion from the affair, but held his tongue.

The legitimate Dame Melissa prepared a breakfast of fried perch fresh from the river. While Dhrun and Glyneth ate, the butcher's apprentice came to the door. "Dame Melissa, you have stock to sell?"

"True, quite true! A fine yearling sow, for which I have no need. You'll find her tied to a tree at the back. Ignore the strange sounds it makes. I'll settle accounts with your master on my next visit into town."

"Exactly so, Dame Melissa. I noticed the animal as I arrived and it seems in prime condition. With your permission, I'll be away and about my duties." The butcher's boy departed and presently could be seen through the window, leading the squealing pig down the road.

Almost immediately after, Glyneth said politely: "I think that we also had better be on our way, as we have far to go today."

"You must do as you think best," said Dame Melissa. "There is much work to be done, otherwise I would urge you to visit with me somewhat longer. One moment." She left the room and presently returned with a gold piece for Dhrun and another for Glyneth. "Please do not thank me; I am overcome with joy to know once more my own body, which has been so misused."

For fear of disturbing the magic force resident in the old purse, they tucked the gold coins into the waistband of Dhrun's trousers, then, bidding Dame Melissa farewell they set off along the road.

"Now that we're safely out of the forest, we can start to make plans," said Glyneth. "First, we'll find a wise man, who'll direct us to one even wiser, who'll take us to the First Sage of the Kingdom, and he will chase the bees from your eyes. And then..."

"And then what?"

"We shall learn what we can of princes and princesses, and which might have a son named Dhrun."

"If I can survive seven years bad luck, that will be enough."

"Well then, one thing at a time. March now! Forward, step, step, step! Ahead is the village and if we can believe the signpost, its name is Wookin."

On a bench before the village inn an old man sat whittling long yellow-white curls from a length of green alder.

Glyneth approached him somewhat diffidently. "Sir, who is considered the wisest man in Wookin?"

The old man ruminated for the space required to shave two exquisitely curled shavings of alder-wood. "I will vouchsafe an honest response. Mind you now, Wookin appears placid and easy, but the Forest of Tantrevalles looms nearby. A dire witch lives a mile up the road and casts her shadow across Wookin. The next village along the way is Lumarth, at a distance of six miles. Each of these miles is dedicated to the memory of the robber who only a week ago made that mile his own, under the leadership of Janton Throatcut. Last week the six gathered to celebrate Janton's name day, and they were captured by Numinante the Thief-taker. At Three-mile Crossroad you will still discover our famous and most curious landmark, old Six-at-a-Gulp. Directly north, barely outside the village, stands a set of dolmens, arranged to form the In-and-Out Maze, whose origin is unknown. In Wookin reside a vampire, a poison-eater, and a woman who converses with snakes. Wookin must be the most diverse village of Dahaut. I have survived here eighty years. Do I then need to do more than declare myself the wisest man of Wookin?"

"Sir, you would seem to be the man we seek. This boy is Prince Dhrun. Fairies sent golden bees to buzz circles in his eyes, and he is blind. Tell us who might cure him, or failing that, whom we might ask?"

"I can recommend no one near at hand. This is fairy magic and must be lifted by a fairy spell. Seek out Rhodion, king of all fairies, who wears a green hat with a red feather. Take his hat and he must do your bidding."

"How can we find King Rhodion? Truly, it is most important."

"Even the wisest man of Wookin cannot rive that riddle. He often visits the great fairs where he buys ribands and teazles and other such kickshaws. I saw him once at Tinkwood Fair, a merry old gentleman riding a goat."

Glyneth asked: "Does he always ride a goat?"

"Seldom."

"Then how does one know him? At fairs one finds merry gentlemen by the hundreds."

The old man shaved a curl from his alder switch. "There, admittedly, is the weak link in the plan," he said. "Perhaps you might better be served by a sorcerer. There is Tamurello at Faroli and Quatz by Lullwater. Tamurello will demand a toilsome service, which might require a visit to the ends of the earth: once more a flaw in the scheme. As for Quatz, he is dead. If you could by some means offer to resuscitate him, I daresay he would commit himself to almost anything."

"Perhaps so," said Glyneth in a subdued voice. "But how—"

"Tut tut! You have noticed the flaw. Still, it well may yield to clever planning. So say I, the wisest man of Wookin."

From the inn came a stern-faced matron. "Come, grandfather! It is time for your nap. Then you may sit up tonight for an hour or two, because the moon rises late."

"Good, good! We are old enemies, the moon and I," he explained to Glyneth. "The wicked moon sends rays of ice to freeze my marrow, and I take pains to avoid them. On yonder hill I plan a great moon-trap, and when the moon comes walking and spying and peeping for to find my window, I'll pull the latch and then there'll be no more of my milk curdled on moony nights!"

"And high time too, eh, grandfather? Well, bid your friends goodby and come along to your nice neat's-foot soup."

In silence Dhrun and Glyneth trudged away from Wookin. At last Dhrun spoke: "Much of what he said made remarkably good sense."

"So it seemed to me," said Glyneth.

Just beyond Wookin, the Murmeil River swung to the south, and the road went through a land partly wooded, partly tilled to barley, oats and cattle fodder. At intervals placid farmsteads drowsed in the shade of oaks and elms, all built of the local gray trap and thatched with straw.

Dhrun and Glyneth walked a mile, then another, meeting in all three wayfarers: a boy leading a team of horses; a drover with a herd of goats and a wandering tinker. Upon the fresh country air crept a taint, which grew stronger: first in breaths and whiffs, then in sudden and violent power, so heavy and rich that Glyneth and Dhrun stopped short in the road.

Glyneth took Dhrun's hand. "Come, we'll move quickly and so be past the sooner."

The two trotted along the road, holding their breaths against the stench. A hundred yards further they came to a crossroad, with a gallows to the side. A signboard, pointing east-west, north-south read:

BLANDWALLOW: 3 — TUMBY: 2
WOOKIN: 3 — LUMARTH: 3

From the gallows, gaunt across the sky, dangled six dead men.

Glyneth and Dhrun hurried past, to stop short once more. On a low stump sat a tall thin man with a long thin face. He wore somber garments but went hatless; his hair, dead black and straight, clung to his narrow scalp.

Glyneth thought both the circumstances and the man somewhat sinister and would have passed along the road with no more than a polite greeting, but the man lifted a long arm to stay them.

"Please, my dears, what is the news from Wookin? My vigil is now three days old and these gentlemen died with uncommonly stiff necks."

"We heard no news, sir, save that regarding the death of six bandits, which you must know."

"Why are you waiting?" asked Dhrun, with disarming simplicity.

"Ha hwee!" The thin man contrived a thin high-pitched chuckle. "A theory propounded by the savants asserts that every niche in the social structure, no matter how constricted, finds someone to fill it. I admit to a specialized occupation, which in fact has not so much as acquired a name. Not to put too keen an edge on it, I wait under gallows until the corpse drops, whereupon I assume possession of the clothes and valuables. I find little competition in the field; the work is dull, and I will never become wealthy, but at least it is honest, and I have time to daydream."

"Interesting," said Glyneth. "Good-day, sir."

"One moment." He appraised the still shapes above him. "I thought to have number two today for sure." He took up an implement which leaned against the gallows: a long pole with a forked end. He pressed the rope immediately above the knot and gave a vigorous shake. The cadaver hung as before. "My name, should you choose to know it, is Nahabod, and sometimes I am known as Nab the Narrow."

"Thank you, sir. And now if you don't mind, we'll be going."

"Wait! I have an observation to make which you may find interesting. Yonder, number two in order, hangs old Tonker the carpenter, who drove two nails into his mother's head: stiff-necked to the end. Notice"—he pointed with his pole, and his voice became somewhat didactic—"the purple bruise. This is usual and ordinary for the first four days. Then a crimson flush sets in, followed by this chalky pallor, and which indicates that the object is about to descend. By these signals I judged Tonker ripe. Well, enough for today. Tonker will fall tomorrow and after him Pilbane the Dancer, who robbed along the highway for thirteen years, and would have been robbing today had not Numinante the Thief-taker discovered him asleep and Pilbane danced one last jig. Next is Kam the farmer. A leper walked in front of his six fine milch-cows, at this very crossroads, and all six went dry. Since it is unlawful to shed a leper's blood, Kam drenched him with oil and set him ablaze. It is said the leper bounded from here to Lumarth using only fourteen strides. Numinante read the law over-rigorously and now Kam dangles in mid-air. Number six on the end, is Bosco, a chef of good repute. For many years he suffered the foibles of old Lord Tremoy. One day, in a spirit of mischief, he urinated into his lordship's soup. Alas! the deed was witnessed by three pot-boys and the pastry chef. Alas! there hangs Bosco!"

Glyneth, interested in spite of herself, asked: "And the next?"

Nab the Narrow rapped the dangling feet with his pole. "This is Pirriclaw, a robber with an extraordinary set of perceptions. He could stare at a likely prospect—like this"—here Nab shot his head forward and fixed his eyes upon Dhrun—"and like this!" He turned the same penetrating glance upon Glyneth. "In that instant he was able to divine the place where his prospect carried his or her valuables, and a useful sleight it was!" Nab gave his head a shake of regretful nostalgia for the passing of so marvelous a talent.

Dhrun's hand crept to his neck, to ensure the safety of his amulet; almost without thinking Glyneth touched her bodice where she had hidden the magic purse.

Nab the Narrow, still contemplating the cadaver, seemed not to notice. "Poor Pirriclaw! Numinante took him in his prime, and now I wait for his garments—with anticipation, I may add. Pirriclaw dressed in only the best and demanded triple-stitching. He is of my general proportion, and perhaps I will wear the garments myself!"

"And what of the last corpse?"

"Him? He amounts to little. Cloth buskins, clothes thrice mended and lacking all style. This gallows is known as Six-at-a-Gulp. Both law and custom forbid the hanging of five or four or three or two or one from the ancient beam. A fleering ne'er-do-well named Yoder Gray Ears stole eggs from under Widow Hod's black hen, and Numinante decided to make an example of him, and also make a sixth for old Six-at-a-Gulp; and for the first time in his life Yoder Gray Ears served a useful purpose. He went to his death, if not a happy man, at least a person whose life has yielded a final fulfillment, and not all of us can make this claim."

Glyneth nodded dubiously. Nab's remarks were becoming a

trifle too rhapsodic and she wondered if he might be amusing himself at their expense. She took Dhrun's arm. "Come along; it's still three miles to Lumarth."

"A safe three miles now that Numinante has swept so clean," said Nab the Narrow.

"One last question. Can you direct us to a fair where wise men and magicians gather?"

"Yes indeed. Thirty miles past Lumarth is the town Hazelwood, where they mark the Druid festivals with a fair. Be there in two weeks for Lugrasad of the Druids!"

Glyneth and Dhrun proceeded along the road. A half-mile they walked, then out from behind a blackberry thicket sprang a tall thin robber. He wore a long black cloak, a black cloth over all his face, save his eyes, and a flat-crowned black hat, with an extremely broad brim. In his left hand he brandished a dagger on high.

"Stand and deliver!" he cried harshly. "Else I slit your throats from ear to ear!"

He advanced on Glyneth, plunged his hand into her bodice and seized the purse from its snug place between her breasts. Next he turned to Dhrun and flourished the dagger. "Your valuables, and with a will!"

"My valuables are no concern of yours."

"But they are! I declare that I own the world and all its fruits. Whoever without leave uses my goods incurs my most furious wrath; is this not justice?"

Dhrun, bewildered, had no response; meanwhile the robber deftly lifted the amulet from his neck. "Pshaw! What is this? Well, we'll sort it out later. Go your ways now, in humility and be more careful in the future!"

Glyneth, grimly silent, and Dhrun, sobbing with rage, continued along the road. Behind them came a fleeing laugh. "Ha hwee!" Then the robber disappeared into the underbrush.

An hour later Glyneth and Dhrun arrived at the village Lumarth. They went at once to the inn marked by the sign of the Blue Goose, where Glyneth asked where she might find Numinante the Thief-taker.

"By the whims of Fortunatus, you'll find Numinante himself in the common-room, drinking ale from a pot the size of his head."

"Thank you, sir." Glyneth entered the common-room with

caution. At other inns she had been subjected to indignities: drunken kisses, over-familiar pats on the haunch, leers and tickles. At the counter sat a man of medium size, with a look of prim sobriety, belied by the stoup from which he drank his ale.

Glyneth approached him confidently; here was no man to take liberties.

"Sir Numinante?"

"Well, lass?"

"I have a criminal act to report."

"Say on; this is my business."

"At the crossroads we met a Nahabod, or Nab the Narrow, who waited for the cadavers to drop that he might take their clothes. We talked a bit, then went our way. Not half a mile along, out from the woods jumped a robber who took all we owned."

Numinante said: "My dear, you were robbed by the great Janton Throatcut himself. Only last week I hanged high his six henchmen. He was in the act of taking their shoes for his collection; he does not care a fig for clothes."

"But he told us of Tonker the carpenter, Bosco the chef, the two robbers Pirriclaw and I forget the other—"

"Possibly so. They ranged the countryside with Janton like a pack of wild dogs. But Janton is leaving these parts and will take his business elsewhere. Someday I will hang him as well, but— we must take these pleasures as they come."

"Can't you send out to search for him?" asked Dhrun. "He took my amulet and our purse of money."

"I could send out," said Numinante, "but to what profit? He has bolt-holes everywhere. All I can do at the moment is feed you at the king's expense. Enric! Feed these children on your best. One of those fat pullets from the spit, a good slice of beef and another of suet pudding, with cider to wash it down."

"At once, Sir Numinante."

Glyneth said, "One thing more, sir. As you see, Dhrun here has been blinded by the forest fairies. We have been advised to seek a magician who will set matters straight. Can you suggest someone who might help us?"

Numinante swallowed a good pint of ale. After reflection he said: "I know of such persons, but by reputation only. In this case I cannot help you, since I have no magic, and only magicians know other magicians."

"Janton suggested that we visit the fair at Hazelwood, and press our inquiries there."

"That would seem sound advice—unless he proposes to meet you along the way and rob you yet again. I see that Enric has laid you a good meal; eat with appetite."

With sagging shoulders Dhrun and Glyneth followed Enric to the table he had set and though he had provided his best, the food lacked savor. A dozen times Glyneth opened her mouth to tell Dhrun that he had lost only an ordinary pebble, that his fairy stone had been broken to bits; as many times she closed her mouth, ashamed to admit her deception.

Enric showed them the road to Hazelwood, "It's up hill and down dale for fifteen miles, then through Wheary Woods, then across the Lanklands, up and over the Far Hills, then follow the Sham River into Hazelwood. You'll be a good four days in the going. I take it you carry no great sum of money?"

"We have two gold crowns, sir."

"Let me change one into florins and pennies and you'll have an easier time of it."

With eight silver florins and twenty copper pennies chinking in a small cloth sack, and with a single gold crown secure in the waistband of Dhrun's trousers, the two set out along the road to Hazelwood.

Four days later, hungry and footsore, Dhrun and Glyneth arrived at Hazelwood. The journey had been uneventful save for an episode late one afternoon near the village Maude. A scant half-mile short of town they heard moans emanating from the ditch at the side of the road. Running to look, they discovered a crippled old man who had wandered from the road and had fallen into a growth of burdock.

With vast effort Dhrun and Glyneth brought him to the road and assisted him into the village, where he collapsed on a bench. "Thank you, my dears," he said. "If dying must be done, better here than in a ditch."

"But why should you die?" asked Glyneth. "I have seen living folk in far worse case than you."

"Perhaps so, but they were surrounded by loved ones or were able to work. I have not a copper to my name and no one will hire me, and so I will die."

Glyneth took Dhrun aside. "We can't abandon him here."

Dhrun spoke in a hollow voice. "We certainly can't take him with us."

"I know. Even less could I walk away and leave him sitting here in despair."

"What do you want to do?"

"I know we can't help everyone we meet, but we can help this particular person."

"The gold crown?"

"Yes."

Wordlessly Dhrun worked the coin from his waistband and gave it to Glyneth. She took it to the old man. "This is all we can spare, but it will help you for a while."

"My blessings on you both!"

Dhrun and Glyneth continued to the inn, only to discover that all the chambers were occupied. "The loft over the stable is full of fresh hay, and you may sleep there for a penny, and if you'll help me in the kitchen for an hour or so, I'll serve you your supper."

In the kitchen Dhrun shelled peas and Glyneth scoured pots until the innkeeper rushed forward. "No more, no more! I can see my face in them now! Come, you've earned your supper."

He took them to a table in the corner of the kitchen and served them first a soup of leeks and lentils, then slices of pork roasted with apples, bread and gravy and a fresh peach apiece for dessert.

They left the kitchen by way of the common-room, where a great festivity seemed in progress. Three musicians, with drums, a flageolet and a double lute, played merry quicksteps. Looking through ranked onlookers Glyneth discovered the old cripple to whom they had given the gold coin now drunk and dancing a boisterous hornpipe with both legs flying through the air. Then he seized the serving wench and the two danced an extravagant prancing cakewalk up and down the length of the common-room, the old man with one arm around the serving wench and the other holding high a great pot of ale. Glyneth spoke to one of the bystanders: "Who is that old man? When I saw him last he appeared to be crippled."

"He is Ludolf the knave and no more crippled than you or I. He'll saunter out of town, make himself comfortable beside the road. When a traveler passes he starts to moan in a pitiful fashion, and as like as not the traveler helps him into town. Then

Ludolf blithers and sniffs and the traveler usually gives him a coin or two. Today he must have encountered a bashaw from the Indies."

Sadly Glyneth led Dhrun to the stable, and up a ladder into the loft. Here she told Dhrun of what she had seen in the common-room. Dhrun became furious. He gritted his teeth and drew back the corners of his mouth. "I despise liars and cheaters!"

Glyneth laughed mournfully. "Dhrun, we mustn't trouble ourselves. I won't say we've learned a lesson, because we might do the same thing again tomorrow."

"With many more precautions."

"True. But at least we need not feel ashamed of ourselves."

From Maude to Hazelwood the road took them through a varied landscape of forest and field, mountain and valley, but they encountered neither harms nor alarms, and arrived in Hazelwood at noon on the fifth day out of Lumarth. The festival had not yet commenced, but already booths, pavilions, platforms and other furniture of the fair were in the process of construction.

Glyneth, holding tight to Dhrun's hand, appraised the activity.

"It looks as if there will be more merchants than ordinary folk. Perhaps they'll all sell to each other. It's truly gay, with all the hammering and new bunting."

"What is that delightful smell?" asked Dhrun. "It reminds me of how hungry I am."

"About twenty yards to windward a man in a white hat is frying sausages. I agree that the smell is tantalizing—but we have only seven florins and a few odd pennies to our name, which I hope will keep us until somehow we can earn more money."

"Is the sausage-seller doing a brisk business?"

"Not really."

"Then let's try to win him some trade."

"All very well, but how?"

"With these." Dhrun brought out his pipes.

"Very good idea." Glyneth led Dhrun close to the sausage-seller's booth. "Now play," she whispered. "Brave tunes, happy tunes, hungry tunes!"

Dhrun began to play, at first slowly and carefully, then his fingers seemed to move of themselves and fairly flew over the stops, and from the instrument came a set of lovely skirling melodies. Folk stopped to listen; they gathered around the sausage-seller's stand, and many bought sausages, so that the vendor became very busy.

After a period Glyneth approached the sausage-seller. "Please, sir, may we too have sausages, since we are very hungry. After we eat, we'll play again."

"That is a good bargain from my standpoint." The sausage-seller fed them a meal of bread and fried sausages, then Dhrun played once more: jigs and jump-ups, merry wind-arounds, reels and hornpipes, to set the heels to twitching and the nose to trembling along the aroma of frying sausages, until, inside the hour, the sausage-seller had sold all his wares, whereupon Glyneth and Dhrun sidled inconspicuously away from the stand.

In the shadow of a nearby van stood a tall young man with strong wide shoulders, long legs, a long nose and clear gray eyes. Lank sand-colored hair hung to his ears, but he wore neither beard nor mustache. As Glyneth and Dhrun passed by he stepped forward and accosted them.

"I have enjoyed your music," he told Dhrun. "Where did you learn such sleight?"

"It's a gift, sir, from the fairies of Thripsey Shee. They gave me the pipes, a purse of money, an amulet of bravery and seven years' bad luck. We've lost purse and amulet, but I still keep the pipes and the bad luck, which hangs on me like a bad smell."

"Thripsey Shee is far away, in Lyonesse. How did you arrive here?"

"We traveled through the great forest," said Glyneth. "Dhrun discovered some forest fairies; they were bathing and quite naked. They sent magic bees into his eyes and now he can't see, until we drive the bees away."

"And how do you propose to do that?"

"We have been advised to seek out Rhodion, king of the fairies, and seize his hat, which will force him to do our bidding."

"That is sound advice as far as it goes. But first you must find King Rhodion, which is not at all simple."

"He is said to frequent fairs: a merry gentleman in a green hat," said Glyneth. "That is something to start on."

"Yes indeed... Look! There goes one now! And here comes another!"

Glyneth said dubiously: "I don't think either of them is King

Rhodion, certainly not the drunken man, even though he is the merrier of the two. In any case, we have other advice: to ask the aid of an arch-magician."

"Again the advice is easier spoken than acted upon. The magicians take pains to isolate themselves from what otherwise would be an endless stream of supplicants." Looking from one somber face to the other, he said: "Still, there may be a way to avoid these difficulties. Let me introduce myself. I am Doctor Fidelius. I travel Dahaut in this van which is drawn by two miraculous horses. The placard on the side explains my business."

Glyneth read:

DOCTOR FIDELIUS
Grand gnostic, seer, magician.
HEALER OF SORE KNEES

...Mysteries analyzed and resolved: incantations uttered in known and unknown languages.
...Dealer in analgesics, salves, roborants and despumatics.
...Tinctures to relieve nausea, itch, ache, gripe, scurf, buboes, canker.

SORE KNEES A SPECIALTY

Glyneth, looking back to Doctor Fidelius, asked tentatively: "Are you truly a magician?"

"Indeed I am," said Doctor Fidelius. "Watch this coin! I hold it in my hand, then presto and hey-nonny-no! Where does the coin go?"

"Into your other hand."

"No. It is here on your shoulder. And look! Here is another on your other shoulder! What do you say to that!"

"Marvelous! Can you cure Dhrun's eyes?"

Doctor Fidelius shook his head. "But I know a magician who can and who, so I believe, will."

"Wonderful! Will you take us to him?"

Doctor Fidelius again shook his head. "Not now. I have urgent business in Dahaut which must be done. Then I will visit Murgen the magician."

Dhrun asked: "Could we find this magician without your help?"

250

"Never. The road is long and dangerous and he guards his privacy well."

Glyneth asked diffidently: "Is your business in Dahaut likely to take a very long time?"

"That is hard to say. Sooner or later a certain man will visit my van, and then..."

"'And then'?"

"I expect that we will visit Murgen the magician. Meanwhile you shall join my company. Dhrun shall play the pipes to attract custom, Glyneth will sell salves, powders and lucky charms, and I will watch the crowds."

"That is very generous of you," said Glyneth, "but neither Dhrun nor I have skill in medicine."

"No matter! I am a mountebank! My medicines are useless, but I sell them cheap and usually they work as well as if prescribed by Hyrcomus Galienus himself. Dismiss your qualms, if you have any. The profits are not large but always we will eat good food and drink good wine, and when the rain falls we shall be snug inside the van."

Dhrun said glumly, "I carry a fairy's curse of seven years' bad luck. It may well infect you and your undertakings."

Glyneth explained: "Dhrun lived most of his life in a fairy castle until they cast him out with the curse on his head."

Dhrun said: "It was the imp Falael, who brought it down on me, just as I departed the shee. I would reflect it back on him if only I could."

"The curse must be lifted," declared Doctor Fidelius. "Perhaps we should watch for King Rhodion after all. If you are playing the fairy pipes he'll be sure to step up close to listen!"

"Then what?" asked Glyneth.

"You must seize his hat. He will roar and bluster, but in the end he will do your bidding."

Glyneth frowningly considered the program. "It seems rather rude to steal the hat of an utter stranger," she said. "If I made a mistake, the gentleman will no doubt roar and bluster, and then chase me and catch me and give me a fine beating."

Doctor Fidelius agreed. "Of course that is possible. As I pointed out, many merry gentlemen wear green hats. Still, King Rhodion can be known by three signs. First, his ears show no lobes and are pointed at the top. Second, his feet are long and narrow, with long fairy toes. Third, his fingers are webbed like frog's feet and show green fingernails. Also, so it is said, when you

251

stand close beside him, he gives off a waft, not of sweat and garlic, but of saffron and willow-catkins. So, Glyneth, you must be ever on the alert. I will also be watching, and between us we may well capture Rhodion's hat."

Glyneth hugged Dhrun and kissed his cheek. "Do you hear that? You must play your best and sooner or later King Rhodion will wander by. Then it's off and away with seven years bad luck."

"Only good luck will bring him past. So I have seven years to wait. By then I'll be old and crippled."

"Dhrun, you are ridiculous! Good music always defeats bad luck, and never forget it!"

"I endorse that view!" said Doctor Fidelius. "Come with me now, both of you. We have a few changes to make."

Doctor Fidelius took the two children to a merchant dealing in fine shoes and garments. At the sight of Dhrun and Glyneth he threw his hands into the air. "Into the back room with you."

Servants set out tubs of warm water and sweet-scented Byzantine soap. Dhrun and Glyneth disrobed and washed away the grime and grit of travel. The servants brought them towels and chemises of linen, then they were dressed in handsome new garments: blue trousers, a white shirt and a nutmeg-buff tunic for Dhrun; a frock of pale green lawn for Glyneth and a dark green ribbon for her hair. Other garments were packed into a case and sent back to the van.

Doctor Fidelius surveyed the two with approval. "Where are the two ragamuffins? We have here a gallant prince and a beautiful princess!"

Glyneth laughed. "My father was only a squire of town Throckshaw in Ulfland, but Dhrun's father is a prince and his mother a princess."

Doctor Fidelius' interest was aroused. "Who told you this?" he asked Dhrun.

"The fairies."

Doctor Fidelius spoke slowly: "If this is true, as well it may be, you are a very important person. Your mother may have been Suldrun, Princess of Lyonesse. I am sorry to say that she is dead."

"And my father?"

"I know nothing of him. He is rather a mysterious figure."

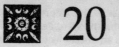 **20**

EARLY IN THE MORNING, with the sun low behind the trees and dew still wet on the grass, Graithe the woodcutter took Aillas to Madling Meadow. He indicated a low mound on which grew a small gnarled oak. "That is Thripsey Shee. To mortal eyes it looks like very little, but long ago, when I was young and rash, I stole here through the woods of a Midsummer's Eve, when the fairies do not trouble to dissemble; and where you now see hummocks of turf and an old tree, I saw pavilions of silk and a million fairy lamps and towers rising one on the other. The fairies ordered musicians for a pavanne, and the music began. I felt that I must run out and join them, but I knew that if I danced so much as one step on fairy sward, I must dance without surcease the rest of my life, so I put my hands over my ears and went staggering away like a man bereft."

Aillas searched Madling Meadow. He heard bird-calls and tinkles which might have been laughter. He walked three steps out into the meadow. "Fairies, I pray you, listen to me! I am Aillas, and the boy Dhrun is my son. Will someone please come to talk to me?"

Silence fell across Madling Meadow, except for what might have been another bird call. Near the mound lupines and larkspur jerked and bobbed, though the morning air was calm.

Graithe pulled at his sleeve. "Come away. They are preparing mischief. If they wished to talk to you they would have done so at once. Now they are plotting harm. Come away, before you suffer their tricks."

The two returned through the woods. Graithe said, "They are a strange folk. They think no more of us than we do of a fish."

Aillas took his leave of Graithe. On the way back to the village

Glymwode he turned aside and approached a half-decayed stump. From the wrapping he took Persilian and propped it upright on the stump. For an instant he saw himself in the glass, comely despite the harsh structure of jaw, chin and cheekbone, with eyes bright as blue lights. Then Persilian, from perversity, altered the image, and Aillas found himself looking into the face of a hedgehog.

Aillas spoke: "Persilian, I need your help."

"Do you wish to put a question?"

"Yes."

"It will be your third."

"I know. Therefore, I want to describe the sense of my question, so that you will not return a glib evasion. I am seeking my son Dhrun, who was taken by the fairies of Thripsey Shee. I will ask you: 'How may I bring my son alive and well into my own custody?' I want to know exactly how to locate my son, release him from Thripsey Shee in possession of his health, youth and mental faculties, without incurring penalty. I want to locate and free my son now and not in a program involving weeks, months or years, nor do I want to be fooled or frustrated in some way I haven't considered. Therefore, Persilian—"

"Has it occurred to you," asked Persilian, "that your manner is most arrogant? That you demand my help as if it were a duty I owed you, and you, like all the others, jealously refuse to free me by asking a fourth question? Do you wonder that I regard your problems with detachment? Have you reflected an instant upon my yearnings? No, you exploit me and my power as you might use a horse to draw a load; you chide and dominer as if by some heroic deed you had earned the right to command me, when in fact, you stole me in the most furtive manner from King Casmir; do you still choose to hector me?"

After a confused moment Aillas spoke in a subdued voice: "Your complaints for the most part are fair. Still, at this moment, I am driven to find my son to the exclusion of all else.

"Therefore, Persilian, I must repeat my charge: give me in full detail a response to this question: "How may I bring my son into my care and custody?"

Persilian spoke in a heavy voice: "Ask Murgen."

Aillas jumped back from the stump in a fury. With great effort he kept his voice even: "That is not a proper response."

"It is good enough," said Persilian airily. "Our urgencies drive us in different directions. Should you choose to ask another question, by all means, do so."

Aillas turned the mirror around, to face across the meadow. He pointed. "Look! In the field yonder is an old well. Time may have little meaning to you, but if I drop you into the well, you will sink into the mud. Soon the well will cave in and you will lie buried, perhaps forever, and that is a duration which must have meaning for you."

"It is a subject which you do not understand," said Persilian, still using a lofty tone. "I remind you that brevity is the essence of wisdom. Since you seem dissatisfied, I will expand upon my instructions. The fairies will give you nothing unless they receive a gift in payment. You have nothing to offer them. Murgen is a Master Magician. He lives at Swer Smod under Mount Gaboon in the Teach tac Teach. Along the way are dangers. At Binkings Gap you must pass under a boulder balanced on a pin. You must kill the guardian raven, or he will drop a feather to topple the boulder on your head. At the River Siss an old woman with a fox's head and a chicken's legs will ask you to carry her across the river. You must act on the instant: cut her in half with your sword and carry each piece over separately. Where the road strikes up Mount Gaboon you will encounter a pair of bearded gryphs. Give each a comb of honey coming and going, which you have brought for the purpose. In front of Swer Smod, call out three times in this fashion: 'Murgen! It is I, Prince Aillas of Troicinet!' When you meet Murgen be not awed; he is a man like yourself—not genial, but not without justice. Listen to his instructions; obey them exactly. I include a final advice, that I may be spared any more reproaches. Will you ride a horse?"

"That is my plan."

"Stable your horse at the village Oswy Undervale before you arrive at the River Siss; otherwise it will eat a maddening herb and throw you into the rocks."

"That is valuable advice." Aillas looked longingly back toward Madling Meadow. "It would seem altogether preferable to deal with the fairies now, rather than first visiting Murgen by dangerous ways."

"So it might seem. There are reasons why any advantage lies in visiting Murgen first."

With this, Persilian allowed Aillas' image to reflect once more from the glass. As Aillas watched, his face displayed a set of ludicrous leers and grimaces, then disappeared and the mirror was blank.

At Tawn Timble Aillas traded a golden brooch set with garnets for a strong roan gelding, furnished with bridle, saddle and saddle bags. At an armorer's shop he bought a sword of decent quality, a dagger in the heavy-bladed Lyonesse style, an old bow, brittle and cantankerous but serviceable, so Aillas estimated, if oiled and drawn with a sensitive touch, along with twelve arrows and a quiver. At a haberdashery he bought a black cloak, a black forester's cap. The town cobbler fitted him with comfortable black boots. Astride his horse he once more felt himself a gentleman.

Leaving Tawn Timble, Aillas rode south to Little Saffield, then west along Old Street, with the Forest of Tantrevalles a dark margin across the north landscape. The Forest retreated and ahead the blue shadows of the great Teach tac Teach loomed into the air.

At Frogmarsh, Aillas turned north along Bittershaw Road and in due course arrived at Oswy Undervale: a lethargic settlement of two hundred inhabitants. Aillas took lodging at the Peacock Inn and spent the afternoon honing his sword and testing the flight of his arrows against a straw butt in a field behind the inn. The bow seemed to be sound but in need of work; the arrows flew adequately true out to forty yards and somewhat beyond. Aillas took a melancholy pleasure from sending arrow after arrow into a six-inch target; his skills had not deserted him.

Early in the morning, with his horse stabled behind the inn, he set off afoot along the trail to the west. He climbed a long rise of sandy waste strewn with stones and boulders, where grew only thistle and bitter-grass. At the top of the rise he overlooked a broad valley. To the west and away to the north, ever higher, crag on crag, rose the mighty Teach tac Teach, blocking passage into the Ulflands. Directly below, the trail dropped by traverses to the floor of the valley, and here flowed the River Siss, down from the Troaghs back of Cape Farewell, and away to join the Sweet Yellow. Across the valley he thought to make out Swer Smod, high on the flanks of Mount Gaboon, but the shapes and shadows made for deception and he could not be sure of what he saw.

He started down the way, running light-footed, sliding and jumping, and so in short order reached the valley. He found himself in an orchard of apple trees laden with red fruit, but he marched resolutely past and so arrived at the riverbank. On a stump sat a woman with the mask of a red fox and the legs of a chicken.

Aillas gave her a thoughtful inspection. Finally she cried out: "Man, why do you stare so?"

"Madame Fox-face, you are most unusual."

"That is no reason to embarrass me."

"I intended no discourtesy, madame. You are as you are."

"Notice that I sit here in all dignity. It was not I who came cavorting and romping like a mad-cap down the hillside. I could never deign such frolics; folk would think me a hoyden."

"I was perhaps a trifle boisterous," Aillas admitted. "Would you allow me a question, out of sheer curiosity?"

"Provided that it is not impertinent."

"You must judge and let it be understood that in asking the question I incur no obligation."

"Ask on."

"Your face is that of a red fox, your torso that of a woman, your limbs those of a fowl. Which influence guides you as you live your life?"

"The question is noncupatory. Now it is my turn to request a boon."

"But I specifically renounced all obligation."

"I appeal to your chivalrous training. Would you see a poor frightened creature swept away before your eyes? Carry me across the river, if you please."

"That is a request no gentleman could ignore," said Aillas. "Step this way, down to the water's edge and point out the easiest crossing."

"Gladly." The woman strutted down the path toward the river. Aillas drew his sword and with a single great stroke across the waist, cut the woman in twain.

The pieces would not rest. The pelvis and legs ran hither and yon; the upper torso dealt furious blows to the ground, while the head called objurgations to chill Aillas' blood. At last he said: "Quiet, woman! Where is your vaunted dignity?"

"Go your way!" she screeched. "My retribution will not be long in coming!"

Aillas thoughtfully caught the back of her tunic, dragged her to the water and across the ford. "With legs on one side and arms on the other, you will be less tempted to do wicked deeds!"

The woman responded with a new spate of curses, and Aillas went his way. The path led up a hillside; he paused to look back. The woman had raised her head to whistle; the legs bounded across the river; the two parts fitted themselves together and the creature once again was whole. Aillas went somberly on his way: up Mount Gaboon, where all the lands to the east lay spread below, for the most part dark green forest, then across a wasteland where lived not so much as a blade of grass. A cliff rose sheer above the area, and the trail apparently had reached its end. Two steps further and Aillas saw Binkings Gap, a narrow crevice into the cliff. At the mouth of the gap a pedestal ten feet high terminated in a point on which, in precise balance, rested an enormous boulder.

With utmost caution Aillas approached. Nearby, on the branch of a dead tree, perched a raven, with one red eye attentively fixed upon Aillas. Aillas turned his back, nocked arrow to bow, swung about, drew and let fly. The raven toppled and fell in a flapping heap to the ground. As it did so it brushed the balanced boulder with its wing. The boulder swayed, leaned, and crashed into the passage.

Aillas retrieved his arrow, cut the wings and tail from the bird and tucked the articles into his pack; someday he would fletch his twelve arrows in black.

The trail led up through Binkings Gap to a terrace above the cliff. A mile away, under the jut of Mount Gaboon, Swer Smod overlooked the panorama: a castle of no great size, fortified only by a high wall and a pair of bartizans overlooking the portal.

Beside the trail, in the shade of eight black cypress trees, a pair of bearded gryphs eight feet tall played chess at a stone table. As Aillas approached, they put aside the chess and picked up knives. "Step this way," said one, "to save us the trouble of rising."

Aillas took two combs of honey from his pack and placed them on the stone table. "Sirs, here is your honey."

The gryphs emitted dismal groans. "Again honey," said one. "And surely insipid," gloomed the other.

Aillas said: "One should rejoice upon what one has, rather then lament for that which one has not."

The gryphs looked up in displeasure. The first uttered a sinister hiss. The other said: "One becomes sated with platitudes no less than with honey, so that one often breaks another's bones in one's vexation."

"Enjoy your meal in leisure and good health," said Aillas; and continued to the main portal. Here a tall woman of advanced years, wearing a white robe, watched Aillas' approach. He bowed in full courtesy. "Madame, I am here to confer with Murgen, upon a matter of importance. Will you please notify him that Aillas, Prince of Troicinet, awaits his pleasure?"

The woman, speaking no word, made a gesture and turned away. Aillas followed her across a court, along a hall, and into a parlor furnished with a carpet, a table and a pair of heavy chairs. Cases along the back wall displayed hundreds of books and the room smelled pleasantly of the old leather bindings.

The woman pointed to a chair. "Sit." She went from the room, to return with a tray of nutcakes and a cup of tawny wine which she placed before Aillas; then once again she left the room.

Into the hall came Murgen, wearing a gray peasant smock. Aillas had expected an older man, or at least a man of sage appearance. Murgen wore no beard. His hair was white from natural tendency rather than age; his blue eyes were as bright as Aillas' own.

Murgen spoke: "You are here to consult me?"

"Sir, I am Aillas. My father is Prince Ospero of Troicinet; I am Prince in direct line to the throne. Something less than two years ago I met the Princess Suldrun of Lyonesse. We loved each other and were married. King Casmir immured me in a deep dungeon. I finally escaped to find that Suldrun had killed herself in despair and that our son Dhrun had been taken as a changeling by the fairies of Thripsey Shee. I went to Thripsey Shee, but they remained invisible. I beg that you help me rescue my son."

Murgen poured a small quantity of wine into two goblets. "You come to me empty-handed?"

"I carry nothing of value, save a few bits of jewelery which were once Suldrun's. I am sure you care nothing for these. I can offer you only the mirror Persilian, which I stole from King Casmir. Persilian will answer three questions, to your advantage if you phrase the questions correctly. If you ask a fourth question, Persilian goes free. I offer him to you on the condition that you will ask the fourth question, and so liberate him."

Murgen held out his hand. "Give me Persilian. I accept your conditions."

Aillas relinquished the mirror. Murgen twitched his finger and spoke a quiet syllable. A white porcelain box floated across

259

the room, and settled on the table. Murgen threw back the lid and turned the contents out upon the table: thirteen gems, cut, so it seemed, from gray quartz. Murgen watched him with a small smile. "You find these uninteresting?"

"I would judge them so."

Murgen touched them lovingly with his finger, moving them into patterns. He heaved a sigh. "Thirteen nonpareils, each encompassing a mental universe. Well, I must avoid avarice. There are more where these came from. So be it. Take this one; it is gay and enthralling by the light of sunrise. Go to Thripsey Shee just as the first rays of sunlight sweep down across the meadow. Do not go by moonlight, or you will suffer a death of weird invention. Show the crystal to the sunrise, let it glint in the rays. Do not let it from your grasp until a bargain has been made. The fairies will honor their word precisely; they are, despite popular belief, a most exact-minded race. They will fulfill their terms: no less, and certainly not an iota more, so bargain with care!" Murgen rose to his feet. "I bid you farewell."

"A moment, sir. The gryphs are truculent. They are not happy with their honey. I think they would prefer to suck the marrow from my bones."

"They are easily diverted," said Murgen. "Offer two combs to one and none to the other."

"What of the boulder at Binkings Gap? Will that be poised as before?"

"At this very moment the raven balances the stone in place— no mean feat for a bird lacking both wings and tail. It is vengeful, so I suspect." Murgen held out a coil of pale blue rope. "Near the head of the defile a tree overhangs the cliff. Pass the rope around the tree, make a loop to sit in and lower yourself down the cliff."

"What of the fox-faced woman at the River Siss?"

Murgen shrugged. "You must find some way to trick her. Otherwise she will claw your eyes out with a single kick of her leg. The scratch of her fingernail paralyzes; do not allow her approach."

Aillas rose to his feet. "I thank you for your help; still, I wonder why you make the way so dangerous. Many who visit you must consider themselves your friends."

"Yes, no doubt." The subject clearly failed to interest Murgen. "As a matter of fact, the hazards have been established by my enemies, not by me."

"With the gryphs so close to Swer Smod? That is insolence."

Murgen dismissed the matter with a gesture. "It is beneath my dignity to notice. And now, Prince Aillas, I wish you a safe journey."

Murgen departed the room; the woman in the white robes led Aillas along the dim halls to the portal. She looked up to the sky where the sun had already passed the zenith. "If you hurry," she said, "you will reach Oswy Undervale before dusk turns to dark."

Aillas went briskly back down the trail. He approached the grotto where sat the two gryphs. They turned to observe Aillas' coming. "Will you dare once again to offer us insipid honey? We crave more savory stuff!"

"Apparently you are both famished with hunger," said Aillas. "That is the way of it. Now then—"

Aillas brought out two combs of honey. "Ordinarily I would offer one comb to each of you, but one must be more hungry than the other, and he should have both. I leave them here, and the decision shall be yours."

Aillas backed away from the instant altercation and before he was fifty yards along the trail the gryphs were pulling each other's beards. Though Aillas hurried, sounds of the dispute reached his ears for many minutes.

He came to Binkings Gap, and warily peered over the edge of the cliff. The great boulder, as before, swayed in precarious balance. The raven stood nearby, still lacking wings and tail, with head cocked and one round red eye staring up the gorge. Its feathers were bedraggled; it half-sat, half-stood on its bent yellow legs.

Fifty yards to the east, a twisted old cedar tree extended its crooked trunk over the lip of the cliff. Aillas threw the rope over the trunk where a crotch would hold it away from the cliff's face. In one end he tied a loop, arranged it under his haunches, pulled the line taut, swung out over the void, and lowered himself to the base of the cliff. He pulled the tail of the line over the tree-trunk, made a coil and slung it over his shoulder.

The raven stood as before, head cocked, ready to thrust at the boulder. Aillas silently approached from the opposite side and prodded the boulder with the tip of his sword. It toppled and crashed, while the raven uttered cries of dismay.

Aillas continued along the trail, down the slopes of Mount Gaboon.

Ahead a line of trees marked the course of the River Siss. Aillas halted. Somewhere, so he surmised, the fox-woman lay in ambush. The most likely spot would seem to be a thicket of stunted hazel only a hundred yards along the trail. He could make a detour either upstream or down, and swim the river rather than crossing by the ford.

Aillas drew back and, keeping to cover as much as possible, made a wide half-circle in a downstream direction to the river-bank. A fringe of willows barred him from the water, and he was forced to turn upstream. Nothing stirred, at the thicket or elsewhere. Aillas began to feel taut. The silence was unnerving. He stopped to listen again, but heard only the gurgle of the water. Sword in hand, he proceeded upstream, step by step... Approaching the ford, he came to a clump of heavy reed-grass, swaying in the wind... In the wind? He turned quickly to look down into the red mask of the fox-woman, sitting hunched like a frog. He swung his sword as she thrust herself high, and cut off her head at the neck. The torso and legs tumbled into a heap; the head fell at the water's edge. Aillas nudged it out into the stream with his sword. It bobbed and rolled downstream. The torso clawed itself erect and began to run aimlessly here and there, waving its arms, darting and jumping, finally to disappear over the rise toward Mount Gaboon.

Aillas washed his sword, crossed the ford and returned to Oswy Undervale, arriving just as dusk became dark. He dined on bread and ham, drank a pint of wine and went immediately to his chamber.

In the dark he brought out the gray gem which Murgen had allowed him. It showed a pale shine, the color of a misty day. Quite dull, reflected Aillas. But when he looked away he thought he sensed a peculiar flash at the corner of his vision, a perception to which he could put no name.

He tried several times, but failed to reproduce the sensation, and presently he fell asleep.

21

FOUR UNEVENTFUL DAYS brought Aillas to Tawn Timble. Here he bought two plump chickens, a ham, a flitch of bacon and four jugs of red wine. He packed some of the goods in his saddle-bags, tied the rest to his saddle and rode north through Glym-wode, to the cottage of Graithe and Wynes.

Graithe came to meet him. At the sight of the provisions he called back into the cottage: "Woman, start the fire under the spit! Tonight we dine like lords."

"We will dine and drink well," said Aillas. "Still I must arrive at Madling Meadow before tomorrow's daybreak."

The three supped on chickens stuffed with barley and onions and roasted to a turn, hearth-cake set to catch the drippings, a pot of fieldgreens simmered with bacon, a salad of cress.

"If I ate so much every night, I would no longer care to chop logs in the morning," declared Graithe.

"Pray the day will arrive!" exclaimed Wynes.

"Who knows? Perhaps even before you expect it," said Aillas. "But I am tired and I must arise before sun-up."

Half an hour before sunrise Aillas stood by Madling Meadow. He waited in the gloom under the trees until the first glint of rising sun showed in the east, then slowly started across the dew-wet grass, the gem in his hand. As he neared the hummock he began to hear small twitters and warblings in a register almost too high for his ear to perceive. Something slapped at the hand which carried the gem; Aillas only clenched his hand the tighter. Invisible fingertips tweaked his ears and pulled his hair; his hat was whisked away and flung high in the air.

Aillas spoke in a gentle voice: "Fairies, kind fairies: do not treat me so! I am Aillas, father to my son Dhrun, whom you loved."

There was a moment of breathless silence. Aillas continued toward the hummock, to halt twenty yards short.

The hummock suddenly became misty, and underwent changes, as of images gathering and going, shifting in and out of focus.

From the hummock came a red carpet, unrolling almost to where Aillas stood. Along the carpet came a fairy five feet tall, pale brown of skin, with an over-sheen of olive-green. He wore a scarlet robe trimmed with white weasel-heads, a fragile crown of gold strands and green velvet slippers. To right and left other fairies showed on the margin of visibility, never totally substantial.

"I am King Throbius," stated the fairy. "You are indeed the father of our beloved Dhrun?"

"Yes, your Majesty."

"In that case, our love transfers in part to you, and you will find no harm at Thripsey Shee."

"I give you my thanks, your Majesty."

"No thanks are needed; we are honored by your presence. What is that which you hold in your hand?"

Another fairy spoke softly: "Oh, the thrilling dazzle!"

"Your Majesty, this is a magic gem, of enormous value!"

Fairy voices murmured: "True, true. A fervent gem, of magic hue."

"Allow me to hold it," said King Throbius, in a peremptory voice.

"Your Majesty, ordinarily your wishes would command me, but I have been most solemnly instructed. I want my son Dhrun returned to me alive and well; then and only then may I relinquish the gem."

From the fairies came murmurs of surprise and disapproval: "A naughty fellow!" "Just so, the mortals!" "One can never trust their gentility." "Pale and coarse as rats!"

King Throbius spoke: "I regret to state that Dhrun is no longer resident among us. He grew into boyhood and we were forced to send him away."

Aillas gaped in astonishment. "He is barely a year old!"

"In the shee time jerks and skips like a may-fly. We never

264

trouble to reckon it out. When Dhrun left, he was, in your terms, perhaps nine years old."

Aillas stood silent.

"Please give me the pretty bauble," coaxed King Throbius, in the voice he might use upon a skittish cow whose milk he hoped to steal.

"My position remains the same. Only when you give me my son."

"That is next to impossible. He departed some time ago. Now then"—King Throbius' voice became harsh—"do as I command or never will you see your son again!"

Aillas uttered a wild laugh. "I have never seen him yet! What have I to lose?"

"We can transform you into a badger," piped a voice.

"Or a milkweed fluff."

"Or a sparrow with the horns of an elk."

Aillas asked King Throbius: "You promised me your love and protection; now I am threatened. Is this fairy honor?"

"Our honor is bright," declared King Throbius in a ringing voice. He nodded crisply right and left in satisfaction, as his subjects called out endorsement.

"In that case, I return to my offer: this fabulous gem for my son."

A shrill voice cried out: "That may not be, since it would bring good luck to Dhrun! I hate him, most severely! I brought a mordet* on him."

King Throbius spoke in the silkiest of voices: "And what was the mordet?"

"Aha, harrumf. Seven years."

"Indeed. I find myself vexed. For seven years you shall taste not nectar but tooth-twisting vinegar. For seven years you will smell bad smells and never find the source. For seven years your wings will fail you and your legs will weigh heavy as lead and sink you four inches deep into all but the hardest ground. For seven years you will carry all slops and slimes from the shee. For seven years you will know an itch on your belly that no scratching will relieve. And for seven years you will not be allowed to look upon the pretty new bauble."

Falael seemed most distressed by the final injunction. "Oh,

---

*A unit of acrimony and malice, as expressed in the terms of a curse.

the bauble? Good King Throbius, do not taunt me so! I crave that color! It is my most cherished thing!"

"So it must be! Away with you!"

Aillas asked: "Then you will bring back Dhrun?"

"Would you take me into a fairy war with Trelawny Shee, or Zady Shee, or Misty Valley Shee? Or any other shee which guards the forest? You must ask a reasonable price for your bit of stone. Flink!"

"Here, sir."

"What can we offer Prince Aillas to fulfill his needs?"

"Sir, I might suggest the Never-fail, as carried by Sir Chil the fairy knight."

"A happy thought! Flink, you are most ingenious! Go, prepare the implement, on this instant!"

"On this instant it shall be, sir!"

Aillas ostentatiously put his hand, with the gem, into his pouch. "What is a 'Never-fail'?"

Flink's voice, breathless and shrill, sounded beside King Throbius. "I have it here, sir, after great and diligent toil at your order."

"When I require haste, Flink hurries," King Throbius told Aillas. "When I use the word 'instant,' he understands the word to mean 'now.'"

"Just so," panted Flink. "Ah, how I have toiled to please Prince Aillas! If he deigns me only one word of praise, I am more than repaid!"

"That is the true Flink speaking!" King Throbius told Aillas. "Honest and fine is Flink!"

"I am interested less in Flink than in my son Dhrun. You were about to bring him to me."

"Better! The Never-fail will serve you all your life long, always to indicate where Lord Dhrun may be found. Notice!" King Throbius displayed an irregular object three inches in diameter, carved from a walnut burl and suspended from a chain. A protuberance to the side terminated in a point tipped with a sharp tooth.

King Throbius dangled the Never-fail on its chain. "You will note the direction indicated by the white fairy-tooth? Along that slant you will find your son Dhrun. The Never-fail is failure-proof and warranted forever. Take it! The instrument will guide you infallibly to your son!"

Aillas indignantly shook his head. "It points north, into the forest, where only fools and fairies go. This Never-fail points the direction of my own death—or it may take me without fail to Dhrun's corpse."

King Throbius studied the instrument. "He is alive, otherwise the tooth would not snap to direction with such vigor. As for your own safety, I can only say that danger exists everywhere, for you and for me. Would you feel secure walking the streets of Lyonesse Town? I suspect not. Or even Domreis, where Prince Trewan hopes to make himself king? Danger is like the air we breathe. Why cavil at the club of an ogre or the maw of an ossip? Death comes to all mortals."

"Bah!" muttered Aillas. "Flink is fast on his feet; let him run out into the forest with the Never-fail and bring back my son."

From all sides came titters, quickly stilled when King Throbius, not amused, thrust his arm upward. "The sun stands hot and high; the dew is going and the bees are first at our flower-cups. I am losing my zest for transactions. What are your final terms?"

"As before I want my son, sound and safe. That means no mordets of bad luck and Dhrun my son in my safe possession. For this, the gem."

"One can only do the reasonable and convenient," said King Throbius. "Falael shall lift the mordet. As for Dhrun: here is the Never-fail and with it our warranty: it shall lead you to Dhrun in life's full vigor. Take it now." He pressed the Never-fail into Aillas' hands, who thereupon released his grip on the gem. King Throbius snatched it and held it high. "It is ours!"

From all sides came a suspiration of awe and joy: "Ah!" "Ah, see it glow!" "A lump, a lummox!" "Look what he gave for a trifle!" "For such a treasure he might have claimed a wind-boat, or a palanquin carried by racing griffins, with fairy maids in attendance!" "Or a castle of twenty towers on Misty Meadow!" "Oh the fool, the fool!"

The illusions flickered; King Throbius began to lose his definition. "Wait!" cried Aillas. He caught hold of the scarlet cloak. "What of the mordet? It must be lifted!"

Flink spoke aghast: "Mortal, you have touched the royal garment! That is an irredemptible offense!"

"Your promises protect me," said Aillas. "The mordet of bad luck must be lifted!"

"Tiresome," sighed King Throbius. "I suppose I must see to it. Falael! You, yonder, so industriously scratching your belly—remove your curse and I will remove the itch."

"Honor is at stake!" cried Falael. "Would you have me seem a weathercock?"

"No one will take the slightest notice."

"Let him apologize for his evil side-glances."

Aillas said: "As his father, I will act as surrogate and tender his profound regrets for those deeds which disturbed you."

"After all, it was not kind to treat me so."

"Of course not! You are sensitive and just."

"In that case I will remind King Throbius that the mordet was his own; I merely tricked Dhrun into looking back."

"Is that the way of it?" demanded King Throbius.

Flink said: "Just so, your Majesty."

"Then I can do nothing. The royal curse is indelible."

"Give me back the gem!" cried Aillas. "You have not held to your bargain."

"I promised to do all reasonable and convenient. This I have done; anything more is not convenient. Flink! Aillas becomes tiresome. On which hem did he seize my robe—north, east, south or west?"

"On the west, sire."

"The west, eh? Well, we cannot harm him, but we can move him. Take him west, since that seems to be his preference, as far as possible."

Aillas was whirled up and away through the sky. Windy draughts howled in his ears; sun, clouds and earth tumbled across his vision. He lofted high in trajectory, then dropped toward glittering sunlit water, and alighted on sand at the edge of the surf. "Here is west as west may be," said a voice choking with merriment. "Think kindly of us! Were we rude, west might have been another half-mile."

The voice was gone. Aillas, rising shakily to his feet, stood alone on a bleak promontory not far from a town. The Never-fail had been tossed on the wet sand at his feet; he picked it up before the surf could carry it away.

Aillas organized his thoughts. Apparently he stood at Cape Farewell, at the far western edge of Lyonesse. The town would be Pargetta.

Aillas held the Never-fail suspended. The tooth jerked about to point toward the the northeast.

Aillas heaved a deep sigh of frustration, then trudged up the beach to Pargetta, hard under the Castle Malisse. He ate bread and fried fish at the inn, then, after an hour's wrangling with the hostler, he bought a hammer-headed gray stallion of mature years, with a willful disposition and no grace whatever, but still capable of good service if not used too hard, and—no small consideration—of a price relatively low.

Never-fail pointed to the northeast; with half the day still ahead, Aillas set off along Old Street,* up the valley of the River Syrinx and into the fastnesses of the Troagh, the southern culmination of the Teach tac Teach. He passed the night at a lonely mountain inn and late the next day he arrived at Nolsby Sevan, market town and junction of three important roads: The Sfer Arct leading south to Lyonesse Town, Old Street, and the Ulf Passway winding north into the Ulflands, by way of Kaul Bocach.

Aillas took lodging at the White Horse Inn and next day set off to the north along the Ulf Passway, at the best speed his obstinate mount would allow. His plans were not elaborate nor, by the nature of things, fully detailed. He would ride up the Passway, enter South Ulfland at Kaul Bocach, and proceed into Dahaut along the Trompada, somehow giving Tintzin Fyral a wide berth. At Camperdilly Corners he would leave the Trompada for the East-West Road: a route which according to the Never-Fail should take him more or less directly to Dhrun, if so much were allowed by the seven-year mordet.

A few miles along the way Aillas overtook a band of itinerant peddlers bound for Ys and towns along the South Ulf coast. Aillas joined the group to avoid passing Kaul Bocach alone, so perhaps to be an object of suspicion.

At Kaul Bocach there was unsettling news, brought by refugees from the north. The Ska had once more erupted across both North and South Ulfland, almost isolating the city Oäldes, with King Oriante and his paltry court, and the puzzle remained

---

*Old Street, running from the Atlantic to the Gulf of Cantabria, had been laid by the Magdals two thousand years before the coming of the Danaans. According to popular lore every step along Old Street overlooked a battlefield. When the full moon shone at Beltane, ghosts of the slain came out to stand along Old Street and stare at their adversaries across the way.

why the Ska used such forbearance toward the powerless Oriante.

In another operation the Ska had driven east to the Dahaut border and beyond, to seize the great fortress Poëlitetz overlooking the Plain of Shadows.

Ska strategy presented no mysteries to the day sergeant at Kaul Bocach. "They intend to take the Ulflands, North and South, as a pike takes a perch. Can there be any doubt? A bite at a time: a nip here, a gnaw there, and soon the black flag flies from Tawzy Head to Cape Tay, and someday they may be bold enough to try for Ys and Vale Evander, if ever they could take Tintzin Fyral." He held up his hand. "No, don't tell me! That's not the way of a pike with a perch; he takes all at a gulp. But it's all one in the end!"

Somewhat daunted the peddlers took counsel in a grove of aspen trees, and finally decided to proceed with caution, at least as far as Ys.

Five miles along the road the peddlers met a straggle of peasant folk, some with horses or donkeys, others driving farm carts loaded with household possessions, others going afoot, with infants and children: refugees, so they identified themselves, driven from their steadings by the Ska. One great black army, so they stated, had already stormed across South Ulfland, obliterating resistance, enslaving able men and women, burning the keeps and castles of the Ulfish barons.

Again the peddlers, now in distress, took counsel, and once again decided to proceed at least as far as Tintzin Fyral. "But no farther until safety is assured!" declared the most sagacious of the group. "Remember: one step into the Vale and we must pay the Duke's tolls!"

"On then!" said another. "To Tintzin Fyral, and we shall see how the land lies."

The group continued along the road, only in short order to meet another band of refugees, who brought news of the most startling sort: the Ska army had reached Tintzin Fyral and even now had placed it under attack.

There was no more question of going forward; the peddlers turned in their tracks and returned south far more briskly than they had come.

Aillas remained alone on the road. Tintzin Fyral lay yet another five miles ahead. He had no choice but to attempt to discover a route to detour Tintzin Fyral: one which climbed into the mountains, over, then descended once more to the Trompada.

At a small steep ravine choked with scrub-oak and stunted cedar, Aillas dismounted and led his horse up the faintest of trails toward the skyline. Harsh vegetation blocked the way; loose rocks rolled underfoot and the hammer-headed gray horse had no taste for mountain climbing. During the first hour Aillas progressed only a mile. After another hour he arrived at the ridge of a spur which splayed out from the central crag. The route became easier and led in a direction parallel to the road below, but always climbing, up toward that flat-topped mountain known as Tac Tor: the highest point within range of vision.

Tintzin Fyral could not be far away. Stopping to catch his breath, Aillas thought to hear far faint shouts. Thoughtfully he continued, keeping as much to cover as possible. Tintzin Fyral, he calculated, stood across Vale Evander, immediately beyond Tac Tor. He was approaching the scene of siege far closer than he had intended.

Sunset found him a hundred yards below the summit, in a little dell beside a covert of mountain larches. Aillas cut himself a bed of boughs, tied his horse on a long tether near a rivulet seeping from a spring. Forgoing the comfort of a fire, he ate bread and cheese from his saddle-bag. From his pouch he brought Never-fail and watched as the tooth swung to the northeast, with perhaps a trifle more easting than before.

He tucked Never-fail into his pouch, shoved pouch and saddle-bags deep under a laurel bush and went out on the ridge to look around the landscape. Afterglow had not yet left the sky and a full moon of enormous dimensions rose from the black loom of Forest Tantrevalles. Nowhere could be seen gleam of candle or lamp, nor the flicker of fire.

Aillas considered the flat summit, only a hundred yards above. In the half-light he noticed a trail; others had fared this way before, though not by the route he had come.

Aillas followed the path to the summit to find a flat area of three or four acres, with a stone altar and five dolmens at the center, standing stark and quiet in the moonlight.

Giving wide berth to the altar Aillas crossed the flat summit, to where the opposite brink dropped away in a cliff. Tintzin Fyral seemed so close that he might have flung a stone across and down to the roof of the highest tower. The castle was illuminated as if for a gala, windows aglow with golden light. Along the ridge behind the castle hundreds of small fires flickered red and orange; among them moved a company of tall somber warriors, to a number Aillas could not estimate. At their back, dim in the firelight, stood the gaunt frames of four large siege engines. Clearly here was no chance or capricious escapade.

The chasm at Aillas' feet dropped sheer to the floor of Vale Evander. Below the castle torches lit a parade-ground, now unoccupied; other torches, in parallel rows, marked the parapets of a wall across the narrow neck of the Vale: like the parade-ground devoid of defenders.

A mile to the west, along the ridge, another spatter of camp-fires indicated a second encampment, presumably Ska.

The scene was one of weird grandeur which affected Aillas with awe. He watched for a period, then turned away and descended through the moonlight to his own camp.

The night was unseasonably cool. Aillas lay on his bed of boughs, shivering under cloak and saddle-blanket. Presently he slept, but only fitfully, waking from time to time to watch the progress of the moon across the sky. Once, with the moon halfway down in the west he heard a far contralto cry of misery: something between a howl and a moan, which brought up the hairs at the the back of his neck. He huddled deep into his bed. Minutes passed; the call was not repeated. At last he fell into a torpor which kept him asleep somewhat longer than he had intended, and he awoke only when rays from the rising sun shone into his face.

He rose lethargically, washed his face in the stream and considered how best to proceed. The trail to the summit might well lead down to join the Trompada: a convenient route, if it avoided the Ska. He decided to return to the summit the better to spy out the lay of the land. Taking a crust of bread and a knob of cheese to eat along the way, he climbed to the top. The mountains below and behind fell away in humping spurs, gulches and wallowing folds almost to the verge of the forest. As best he could determine the trail descended to the Trompada and so would serve him well.

On this clear sunny morning the air smelled sweet of mountain herbs: heather, gorse, rosemary, cedar. Aillas crossed the summit to see how went the siege of Tintzin Fyral. It was, he reflected, an episode of great significance; if the Ska commanded both Poëlitetz and Tintzin Fyral, they effectively controlled the Ulflands.

Approaching the brink he dropped to his hands and knees to avoid impinging his silhouette on the skyline; nearing the brink he went flat and crawled, and at last peered out across the gorge. Almost below Tintzin Fyral reared high on its tall crag: close, but not so close as it had seemed the night before, when he thought he could fling a stone across the chasm to the roof. Now it was clear that the castle lay beyond all but the strongest arrow-flight. The uppermost tower culminated in a terrace guarded by parapets. A swayback saddle, or ridge joined the castle to the heights beyond, where the closest vantage area, reinforced from below by a retaining wall of stone blocks, overlooked the castle well within bowshot range. Remarkable, thought Aillas, the foolish arrogance of Faude Carfilhiot, to allow so convenient a platform to remain unguarded. The area now swarmed with Ska troops. They wore steel caps, and long-sleeved black surcoats; they moved with a grim and agile purpose, which suggested an army of black killer-ants. If King Casmir had hoped to create an alliance, or at the very least a truce with the Ska, his hopes now were blasted, since by the attack the Ska had declared themselves his adversaries.

Both the castle and Vale Evander seemed lethargic this bright morning. No peasant tilled his field nor walked the road, nor were Carfilhiot's troops anywhere visible. By dint of great exertion the Ska had transported four large catapults across the moors, up the mountainside and along the ridge which commanded Tintzin Fyral. As Aillas watched they dragged the engines forward. They were, so he saw, heavily built devices capable of tossing a hundred-pound boulder the distance to Tintzin Fyral, to knock down a merlon, break open an embrasure, rupture a wall, and eventually, after repeated blows, to demolish the high tower itself. Worked by competent engineers, and with uniform missiles, their accuracy could be almost exact.

As Aillas watched, they worked the catapults forward to the edge of that vantage overlooking Tintzin Fyral.

Carfilhiot himself strolled out upon the terrace, wearing a pale blue morning gown: apparently he had just risen from bed. Ska archers immediately ran forward and sent a flight of arrows singing across the gorge. Carfilhiot stepped behind a merlon with a frown of annoyance for the interruption of his promenade. Three of his retainers appeared on the roof and quickly erected sections of metal mesh along the parapets so as to ward away Ska arrows, and Carfilhiot was again able to take the morning air. The Ska watched him with perplexity and exchanged ironic comments, meanwhile proceeding to ballast their catapults.

Aillas knew that he must depart, but could not bring himself to leave. The stage was set, the curtains drawn, the actors had appeared: the drama was about to begin. The Ska manned the windlasses. The massive propulsion beams bent backward, groaning and creaking; stone missiles were placed into the projection chutes. The master archers turned screws, perfecting their aim. All was ready for the first volley.

Carfilhiot suddenly seemed to take cognizance of the threat to his tower. He made an annoyed gesture and spoke a word over his shoulder. Underneath the catapults the stone abutments supporting the vantage collapsed. Down toppled catapults, missiles, rubble, archers, engineers and ordinary troops. They fell a long way, with hallucinatory slowness: down, down, twisting, wheeling, bounding and sliding the last hundred feet, to stop in an unpleasant tangle of stone, timbers and broken bodies.

Carfilhiot took a final turn around the terrace, and went into the castle.

The Ska assessed the situation, stern rather than angry. Aillas drew back, beyond the Ska range of vision. High time for him to be on his way, as far and as fast as possible. He looked toward the stone altar in a new spirit of speculation. Carfilhiot was clearly a man of wily tricks. Would he leave so tempting a lookout point for presumptive enemies unprotected? Aillas, suddenly nervous, took a final look toward Tintzin Fyral. Ska workgangs, evidently slaves, were dragging timbers along the ridge. The Ska, though bereft of their catapults, were not yet abandoning the siege. Aillas watched for a minute, two minutes. He turned away from the edge of the cliff and found confronting him a patrol of seven men wearing Ska black: a corporal and six warriors, two standing with bows drawn.

Aillas held up his hands. "I am a traveler only; let me go my way."

The corporal, a tall man with a strange wild face, gave a guttural croak of derision. "Up here on the mountain? You are a spy!"

"A spy? For what purpose? What could I tell anyone? That

the Ska are attacking Tintzin Fyral? I came up here to find a safe route around the battle."

"You are quite safe now. Come along; even two-legs* have their uses."

The Ska took Aillas' sword and tied a rope around his neck. He was led down from Tac Tor, across the gorge and up to the Ska encampment. He was stripped of his garments, shorn bald, forced to wash using yellow soap and water, then he was given new garments of gray linsey-woolsey, and finally a smith riveted an iron collar around his neck, with a ring to which a chain might be attached.

Aillas was seized by four men in gray tunics and bent face down over a log. His trousers were dropped; the smith brought a red-hot iron and branded his right buttock. He heard the sizzle of burning flesh and smelled the subsequent odor, which prompted him to droop his head and vomit, inducing those who held him to curse and jump aside, but they continued to hold him while a bandage was slapped down over the burn. Then he was hoisted to his feet.

A Ska sergeant called to him. "Pull up your trousers and come over here."

Aillas obeyed.

"Name?"

"Aillas."

The sergeant wrote in a ledger. "Place of birth?"

"I don't know."

Again the sergeant wrote, then he looked up. "Today luck is your friend; you now may call yourself Skaling, inferior only to a natural Ska. Acts of violence against Ska or Skaling; sexual perversion; lack of cleanliness; insubordination; sullen, insolent, truculent or disorderly behavior are not tolerated. Forget your past; it is a dream! You are now Skaling, and the Ska way is your way. You are assigned to Group Leader Taussig. Obey him, work faithfully: you shall have no cause for complaint.

---

*Two-leg: a semi-contemptuous term applied by the Ska to all other men than themselves: a contraction of "two-legged animal," to designate a middle category between "Ska" and "four-leg." Another common pejorative, *nyel*: "horse-smell" made reference to the difference in body odor between Ska and other races, the Ska seeming to smell, not unpleasantly, of camphor, turpentine, a trace of musk.

Yonder is Taussig; report to him immediately."

Taussig, a short grizzled Skaling, half-walked and half-hopped on one straight and one crooked leg, making tense gestures and squinting through narrow pale blue eyes as if in a state of chronic anger. He gave Aillas a brief inspection and clipped a long light chain to Aillas' collar. "I am Taussig. Whatever your name, forget it. You are now Taussig Six. When I yell 'Six' I mean you. I run a tight squad. I compete in production. To please me, you must compete and try to outdo all the other squads. Do you understand?"

"I understand your words," said Aillas.

"That is not proper! Say 'Yes sir!'"

"Yes, sir."

"Already I feel resentment and resistance in you. Be wary! I am fair but not forgiving! Work your best, or better than your best, so that we all make grade. Slack and shirk, and I suffer as well as you, and this must not be! Come now, to work!"

Taussig's platoon, with the addition of Aillas, was now at its full complement of six. Taussig took them down into a stony sun-baked gully and put them to work dragging timbers up to the ridge and downslope to where Ska and Skaling worked together to build a timber tunnel along the saddle toward Tintzin Fyral, through which a battering ram might then be swung against the castle gate. On the parapets Carfilhiot's archers watched for targets: Ska or Skaling alike. Whenever one such exposed himself an arrow instantly darted down from above.

When the timber passage reached halfway across the saddle, Carfilhiot raised an onager to the turret, and began to launch hundred-pound stones at the timber structure: to no avail; the timbers were elastic and cunningly joined. The stones, striking the timbers, crushed bark, splintered the surface, then tumbled away down into the gulch.

Aillas quickly discovered that his fellows in Taussig's platoon were no more anxious to elevate Taussig's grade than himself. Taussig, hence, ran bobbing and limping back and forth in a state of frenzy, calling exhortations, threats and abuse. "Shoulders into it, Five!" "Pull, pull!" "Are you all sick?" "Three, you corpse! Pull now!" "Six, I'm watching you! I know your kind! You're dogging it already!" So far as Aillas could determine Taussig's squad achieved as much as the other, and he heard Taussig's outcries with indifference. The morning's calamity had left him numb; the full scope was only just beginning to make itself felt.

At noon the Skalings were fed bread and soup. Aillas sat on his left buttock, in a state of numb reverie. During the morning Aillas had been teamed with Yane, a taciturn North Ulf, perhaps forty years old. Yane was of no great stature, sinewy and long-armed, with dark coarse hair and a pinched leathery face. Yane watched Aillas a few minutes, then said gruffly: "Eat, lad; keep up your strength. No good comes of brooding."

"I have affairs which I can't neglect."

"Forget them; your new life has started."

Aillas shook his head. "Not for me."

Yane grunted. "If you try to escape everyone in your squad is flogged and drops in grade, including Taussig. So everyone watches everyone else."

"No one escapes?"

"Seldom."

"What of yourself? Have you never attempted escape?"

"Escape is more difficult than you might think. It is a subject no one discusses."

"And no one is freed?"

"After your stint you are pensioned. They don't care what you do then."

"How long is a 'stint'?"

"Thirty years."

Aillas groaned. "Who here is chief among the Ska?"

"He is Duke Mertaz; there he stands yonder... Where are you going?"

"I must speak to him." Aillas rose painfully to his feet and crossed to where a tall Ska stood brooding down upon Tintzin Fyral. Aillas halted in front of him. "Sir, you are Duke Mertaz?"

"I am he." The Ska surveyed Aillas with gray-green eyes.

Aillas spoke in a reasonable voice. "Sir, this morning your soldiers captured me and clamped this collar around my neck."

"Indeed."

"In my own country I am a nobleman. I see no reason why I should be treated this way. Our countries are not at war."

"The Ska are at war with all the world. We expect no mercy from our enemies; we give none."

"Then I ask that you abide by the rules of warfare and allow me to ransom my freedom."

"We are not a numerous people; our need is labor, not gold. Today you were branded with a date-mark. Thirty years you must serve, then you will be freed with a generous pension. If you attempt to escape, you will be maimed or killed. We expect such attempts and are alert. Our laws are simple and admit of no ambiguity. Obey them. Go back to your work."

Aillas returned to where Yane sat watching. "Well?"

"He told me I must work thirty years."

Yane chuckled and rose to his feet. "Taussig summons us."

Across the downs convoys of bullock-carts brought timbers from the mountains. Skaling squads dragged the timbers up the ridge; foot by foot the timber tunnel thrust across the saddle toward Tintzin Fyral.

The construction approached the castle walls. Carfilhiot's warriors on the parapets dropped bladders of oil upon the timbers and sent down fire-arrows. Orange flames roared high; at the same time drops of blazing oil seeped through cracks. Those who worked below were forced to retreat.

Special contrivances fabricated of sheet copper were brought forward by a trained squad, and fitted over the timbers, to form a protective roof; flaming oil thereupon flowed off to burn harmlessly on the ground.

Foot by foot the tunnel approached the castle walls. The defenders displayed a rather sinister lassitude.

The tunnel reached the castle walls. A heavy battering ram, shod with iron, was carried forward; Ska warriors crowded the tunnel, ready to surge through the ruptured portal. From somewhere high on the tower, a massive ball of iron swung down and around at the end of a chain, to strike the timber construction fairly, at a spot thirty feet from the tower wall, to sweep timbers, ram and warriors over the edge of the saddle and down into the gully: another tangle of timbers and crushed bodies on top of the tangle already there.

From the ridge the Ska commanders stood in the light of sunset, contemplating the destruction of their works. There was a pause in the business of the siege. The Skalings gathered in a hollow to evade the steady wind from the west. Aillas like the others crouched in the wan light, back to the wind, watching sidelong the Ska silhouettes along the skyline.

There would be no further action against Tintzin Fyral on this night. The Skalings trooped down-hill to the camp, where they were fed porridge boiled with dried cod. The corporals marched

on command; he spoke to no one save an occasional mutter to Yane who hunched along beside him.

The column passed only half a mile inland from the fortified town Oäldes, where King Oriante had long held court, uttering sonorous commands which were seldom obeyed and spending much time in the palace garden among his tame white rabbits. At the sight of Ska troops, the portcullis dropped with a clang and archers mounted the walls. The Ska paid no heed and continued along the coast road, with Atlantic swells crashing into surf along the shore.

A Ska patrol rode up with news which quickly filtered down to the Skalings: King Oriante had died in a convulsion and feeble-minded Quilcy had succeeded to the throne of South Ulfland. He shared his father's interest in white rabbits and was said to eat nothing but custard, honey buns and trifle.

Yane explained to Aillas why the Ska allowed Oriante and now Quilcy to reign unmolested. "They cause the Ska no inconvenience. From the Ska point of view Quilcy can reign forever, so long as he keeps to his doll houses."

The column entered North Ulfland, the boundary marked only by a cairn beside the road. Fishing villages along the way were deserted except for old men and women, the able-bodied having fled to avoid indenture.

On a dreary morning, with the wind carrying salt spume a hundred yards inshore, the column passed under an ancient Firbolg beacon-tower, built to raise the clans against Danaan raiders, and so entered the Foreshore, in effect Ska territory. The villages now were totally deserted, with the former inhabitants killed, enslaved, or driven away. At Vax, the column broke into several components. A few took ship for Skaghane; a few continued along the coastal road toward the granite quarries, where certain intractable Skalings would spend the rest of their lives chipping granite. Another contingent, including Taussig and his platoon, swung inland toward Castle Sank, the seat of Duke* Luhalcx and a staging station for Skaling convoys en route to Poëlitetz.

---

*Memorandum: 'King,' 'prince,' 'duke,' 'lord,' 'baron,' 'ordinary,' are used arbitrarily and inexactly to indicate somewhat similar levels of status among the Ska. Functionally, the differences in rank are peculiar to the Ska, in that only 'king,' 'prince,' and 'duke,' are hereditary, and all save 'king' may be earned by valor or other notable achievement. Thus, an 'ordinary,' having killed or captured five armed enemies becomes a 'knight.' By other exactly codified achievements he becomes a 'baron,' then 'lord,' 'duke,' then finally 'grand duke' or 'prince.' The king is elected by vote of the dukes; his dynasty persists along its direct male lineage, until the line becomes extinct or is voted out of power at a conclave of dukes.

For a brief discussion of Ska history see Glossary III.

22

AT CASTLE SANK TAUSSIG'S GANG was assigned to the saw-mill. A ponderous water-wheel, moving a linkage of iron levers, raised and lowered a straight-bladed saw of forged steel nine feet long and worth its weight in gold. The saw squared timbers and cut planks with a speed and accuracy Aillas found remarkable. Skalings with long experience controlled the mechanism, lovingly sharpened the teeth, and apparently worked without coercion or supervision. Taussig's gang was assigned to the seasoning shed, where they stacked and restacked planks.

Over the weeks Aillas gradually, a trifle at at a time, incurred Taussig's disfavor and dislike. Taussig despised Aillas' fastidious habits and his disinclination to work any more energetically than was absolutely necessary. Yane shared Taussig's disfavor because he managed to achieve his share of the work without perceptible effort, which caused Taussig to suspect him of shirking, though he could never demonstrate as much.

At first Taussig tried to reason with Aillas. "Look you now! I've been watching and you don't deceive me an instant! Why do you give yourself such airs, as if you were a former lord? You will never better yourself by such means. Do you know what happens to shirkers and fiddity-didjets? They are put to work in the lead mines, and if they short their stint they are sent to the sword factory and their bodies' blood hardens the steel. I advise you to show me somewhat more zeal."

Aillas responded as politely as possible. "The Ska took me against my will; they broke apart my life; they have done me great harm; why should I exert myself for their benefit?"

"Your life has changed; true!" argued Taussig. "Make the best of it, like the rest of us! Think! Thirty years is not so long a time! They will either send you away a free man with ten gold coins, or they will give you a farmstead with a hut, a woman, animals; and your children are free from indenture. Is that not generous?"

"For the best part of my life?" Aillas sneered and turned away. Taussig angrily called him back. "Perhaps you scorn the future! Not I! When my gang performs poorly, I take demerits. I want none on your account!" Taussig hopped away, his face mottled with fury.

Two days later Taussig led Aillas and Yane to the yard at the rear of Castle Sank. He spoke no word, but the jerk of his elbows, the bob of his head were freighted with portent.

Where the gate opened into the yard, he swung about and at last gave vent to his rage. "They were wanting a pair of house-servants and I spoke up with my heart full! Now I am free of you both and Imboden the steward is your master. Try him with your provocations and learn what boon it brings you!"

Aillas studied the congested face thrust toward his own, then shrugged and turned away. Yane stood in despondent boredom. There was nothing more to be said.

Taussig called across the yard to a scullion. "Summon Imboden; bring him here!" He turned a darkling leer over his shoulder. "Neither of you will like Imboden. He has the vanity of a peacock and the soul of a stoat. Your easy days of loitering in the sunshine are over."

Imboden came out on a porch overlooking the yard: a man of late maturity, narrow-shouldered with thin arms, long thin shanks, a swag of a belly. Dank locks clung to his scalp; he seemed to have no face, only a cluster of large features: long ears, a long lumpy nose, round black eyes encircled by arsenical rings, a drooping gray mouth. He made an imperious gesture toward Taussig, who roared: "Over here! I will not set foot in the castle yard!"

Imboden uttered an impatient oath, descended the steps and crossed the yard, using a peculiar strutting gait, which aroused Taussig's levity. "Come along now, you peculiar old goat! I haven't all day to waste!" To Aillas and Yane he said: "He's half-Ska, a bastard by a Celt woman: the worst of all worlds for a Skaling and he makes everyone know it."

Imboden halted at the gate. "Well, what now?"

"Here's a pair of house-monkeys for you. This one is finicky and washes overmuch; this one thinks himself wiser than the rest of us, principally me. Take them in good health."

Imboden looked the two up and down. He jerked his thumb

at Aillas. "This one has a strange wild look for one so young. He is not sick?"

"Sound as a hero in limb and lung!"

Imboden inspected Yane. "This one has the cast of a villain. I suppose he is sweet as honey?"

"He is deft and quick and walks as quiet as the ghost of a dead cat."

"Very well; they will do." Imboden made the smallest of signs.

In great glee Taussig told Aillas and Yane: "That means: 'Come along.' Oho, but you'll enjoy his signals, since he is too shy to speak!"

Imboden raked Taussig with a look of withering scorn, then turned and strutted across the yard with Aillas and Yane following. Where the stone steps rose to the porch Imboden made another small gesture, no more than a twitch of the finger. From the gate Taussig bawled: "That means he wants you to wait there!" With a chortling hoot of laughter Taussig went his way.

Minutes passed. Aillas became restless. Urgencies began to work upon him. He looked toward the gate and the open country beyond. "Perhaps now is the time," he muttered to Yane. "There may never be a better!"

"There may never be a worse," observed Yane. "Taussig waits just yonder. He'd like nothing better than to see us run for it, since now he'd evade the flogging."

"The gate, the fields so close—they are tantalizing."

"Inside of five minutes they'd have the dogs on us."

Out on the porch came a slight sad-faced man in gray and yellow livery: short yellow trousers buckled below the knee on black stockings, a gray vest over a yellow shirt. A black bowl-shaped cap concealed his hair, which was evidently clipped short. "I am Cyprian; I have no title; call me slave-master, foreman, intercessor, chief Skaling—whatever you like. You will take orders from me, but only because I alone am privileged to speak with Imboden; he converses with the seneschal, who is Ska and is named Sir Kel. He receives those orders from Duke Luhalcx which ultimately are transferred through me to you. Presumably if you had a message for Duke Luhalcx you would utter it first to me. What are your names?"

"I am Yane."

"That would seem Ulfish. And you?"

"Aillas."

"'Aillas'? That would be a name from the south. Lyonesse?"

"Troicinet."

"Well, no matter. Origins at Sank, like the kinds of meat in a sausage, are of no interest to anyone. Come with me; I'll find your dress and explain the rules of conduct, which as intelligent men, you already know. In simple terms they are—" Cyprian raised four fingers. "First, obey orders exactly. Second, be clean. Third, be as invisible as air. Never intrude upon the Ska attention. I believe that they will not, cannot, see a Skaling unless he does something remarkable or noisy. Fourth, and obviously: attempt no escape. It distresses everyone except the dogs which enjoy snarling men to bits. They can follow scent a month old, and you will be tracked down."

Aillas asked: "What then?"

Cyprian laughed a gentle sad laugh. "Suppose you owned a horse, and it persisted in running away. What would you do with it?"

"Much would depend on the horse."

"Precisely. If it were old, lame and vicious, you would kill it. If it were young and strong, you would do nothing to limit its ability but you would send it to where an expert might break its spirit. If it were fit only for the treadmill, you might blind it."

"I would not do such things."

"In any case, that is the principle. A skilled clerk might lose a foot. The best to be said of the Ska is that they seldom, if ever, torture. The more useful you make yourself, the easier it goes when the dogs chase you down. Come now, to the dormitory. The barber will cut your hair."

Aillas and Yane followed Cyprian through a cool back passage to the Skaling dormitory. The barber pressed a shallow bowl over the head of each in turn and cut their hair off square halfway across the forehead, and so around to the back. In a lavatory they stood under a flow of water and washed with soft-soap mixed with fine sand, then shaved their faces.

Cyprian brought them gray and yellow livery. "Remember, the inconspicuous Skaling finds the least blame. Never address yourself to Imboden; he is more haughty than Duke Luhalcx himself. Lady Chraio is a kind woman of even disposition and insists that the Skaling be fed well. Lord Alvicx, the oldest son, is erratic and somewhat unpredictable. The Lady Tatzel, the daughter, is pleasant to look at but is easily vexed. Still, she is not mordant and causes no great difficulties. So long as you move quietly and never turn your head to watch, you will be invisible to them. For a period you must clean floors; this is how we all begin."

Aillas had known many fine palaces and rich manor houses; there was, however, at Castle Sank an austere magnificence which impressed him, and which he could not totally comprehend. He discovered neither galleries nor promenades; the chambers communicated by short, often crooked passages. High ceilings tended to be lost in the shadows, thus to give an impression of mysterious space. Windows, narrow and small, perforated the walls at irregular intervals, the glass panes tinting incoming light misty amber or pale blue. Not all the rooms served functions obvious to Aillas, nor, indeed, did Duke Luhalcx, nor his lady Chraio, nor their children Alvicx and Tatzel, act according to tenets he comprehended. Each moved about the somber castle as if it were a stage where only this single person acted. All spoke in quiet voices, as often as not using Skalrad, a language far older than human history. They seldom laughed; their only humor seemed to be quiet irony or terse understatement. Each personality was like a citadel; each often seemed in a state of deep reverie, or caught in a flow of inner ideas more absorbing than conversation. Occasionally one or the other would exhibit sudden flair or extravagance, to be damped as suddenly as it appeared. Aillas, though never far from his own concerns, could not avoid an ever-growing fascination with the folk who inhabited Castle Sank. As a slave he was as inconspicuous as a door. Covertly Aillas watched the denizens of Castle Sank as they went about the business of their lives.

At all times Duke Luhalcx, his family and their associates wore formal costumes of great sophistication, which were changed several times daily, according to occasion. The costumes and their appurtenances carried large symbolic freight of an import known only to themselves. On many occasions Aillas heard fascinating references he found incomprehensible. The family in public or in private demonstrated the formal manners they might have used with strangers. If affection between family members were present, it showed itself in signals too subtle for Aillas' perceptions.

Duke Luhalcx, tall, gaunt, hard of feature, with sea-green eyes, carried himself with decisive and unthinking dignity, at once easy and exact, which Aillas never saw disturbed: as if

Luhalcx, for every contingency, had ready an appropriate response. He was the 127th of his line; in the "Chamber of Ancient Honors"* he displayed ceremonial masks carved in Norway long before the coming of the Ur-Goths. Lady Chraio, tall and slender, seemed almost unnaturally remote. Even when the ladies of visiting dignitaries were on hand, Aillas often noticed her alone at her loom or carving pear-wood bowls. She wore her straight black hair in orthodox style, cut at the level of her jaw bones on the sides and back of the head, higher across the forehead.

Lady Tatzel, about sixteen years old, was slender and taut, with small high breasts, narrow flanks like those of a boy, a peculiar zest and energy which seemed to carry her off the ground as she walked. She had a rather charming mannerism of walking, at times with head tilted to the side, a smile trembling on her mouth, at some private amusement known to no one but herself. She wore her hair like her mother and most Ska women, square across the forehead and below the ears. Her features were engagingly irregular; her personality vivid and direct. Her brother, Lord Alvicx, was about Aillas' own age, and of all the family, the most restless and uneasy. He carried himself with a swagger and spoke with more emphasis than any of the others. According to Cyprian he had fought a dozen battles with distinction and could claim knighthood in his own right for the foe-men he had killed.

The duties assigned to Aillas were menial. He was required to clean fireplaces, scrub flagstones, polish bronze lamps and fill them with oil. The work allowed him access to most of the castle except the sleeping chambers; he worked well enough to satisfy Cyprian and remained sufficiently inconspicuous that Imboden paid him no heed, and during all his waking moments he pondered methods of escape.

Cyprian seemed to read his mind. "The dogs, the dogs, the terrible dogs! They are a breed known only to the Ska; once they are put on a scent they never relent. To be sure, Skalings have been known to escape, sometimes with the aid of magical devices. But sometimes the Ska also use magic and the Skaling is caught up!"

"I thought the Ska were ignorant of magic."

"Who knows?" asked Cyprian, extending his arms and

---

*Obviously the expression "Chamber of Ancient Honors" is no more than an approximate translation.

spreading his fingers. "Magic is quite beyond my understanding. Perhaps the Ska remember their magic from the far past. There surely are not many Ska magicians: at least not to my knowledge."

"I can't believe they'd waste their time capturing escaped slaves."

"You may well be right. Why should they bother? For every slave to escape, a hundred are recaptured. Not by magicians, but by dogs."

"Don't any runaways steal horses?"

"It's been tried, but seldom with success. Ska horses obey Ska commands. When a simple Daut or an Ulf tries to ride, the horse makes no move, or backs and squats, or it runs in circles, or it throws the rider. Do you think to ride a Ska horse for your swift escape. Is that what you had in mind?"

"I have nothing in mind," said Aillas rather curtly.

Cyprian smiled his melancholy smile. "It was for me an obsession—at first. Then the years went by, and the yearning became dim, and now I know that never will I be other than what I am until my thirty years are up."

"What of Imboden? Has he not been slave thirty years?"

"Ten years ago they were up. For us Imboden poses as a free man and a Ska; the Ska consider him a high-caste Skaling. He is a bitter and lonely man; his problems have made him strange and queer."

One evening as Aillas and Yane supped on bread and soup, Aillas spoke of Cyprian's preoccupation with escape. "Whenever I talk to him the subject seems to come up."

Yane responded with a grunt of sour amusement. "That habit has been noticed elsewhere."

"Perhaps it is only wistful daydreaming, or the like."

"Possibly so. Still, if I planned to depart Castle Sank in haste, I would not first notify Cyprian."

"To do so would seem a pointless courtesy. Especially since now I know how to escape Castle Sank, despite horses, dogs and Cyprian."

Yane looked at him sidelong. "That is valuable information. Do you plan to share it?"

"In due course. What rivers flow nearby?"

"There is only one of consequence: River Malkish, about three miles south. Escapers always make for this river, but it traps them. If they try to float down to the sea, they are drowned in

289

the cataracts. If they wade upstream, dogs search each bank of the river and in due course pick up the trail. The river is a false ally; the Ska know it better than we do."

Aillas nodded and said no more. Thereafter, in his conversations with Cyprian he spoke of escape only in terms of theory, and Cyprian presently lost interest in the subject.

Up to the age of eleven or twelve Ska girls looked and acted like boys. Thereafter they altered, inevitably and properly. Young men and maidens mingled freely, controlled by the formality which regulated all Ska conduct at least as effectively as vigilant chaperonage.

At Castle Sank on sunny afternoons the young folk resorted to the garden terrace at the south side of the castle, where, according to their mood they played chess or backgammon, ate pomegranates, bantered with each other in the careful manner which other races thought dull, or watched as one among them challenged that perverse engine known as the hurlo-thrumbo. This device, intended for the training of swordsmen, that they might learn deftness and accuracy, dealt the clumsy challenger a mighty buffet if he failed to thrust into a small swinging target.

Lord Alvicx, who was vain in his swordsmanship, considered himself expert in the game of outwitting the hurlo-thrumbo, and was always ready to demonstrate his skill, especially when Lady Tatzel brought her friends out upon the terrace.

To dramatize his grace and artistry he had developed a reckless foot-stamping style of attack which he embellished with flourishes of the sword and ancient Ska war cries.

On one such afternoon two of Alvicx's friends had already been discomfited by the machine, with nothing to show for their exercise save sore heads. Shaking his own head in mock-commiseration, Lord Alvicx took a sword from the table and set upon the machine, uttering guttural cries, leaping forward and back, ducking and thrusting, reviling the machine. "Ah, you whirling devil! Strike out at me, would you? Then what about this? And this? Oh, the treachery! Once again! In and out!" As he sprang backward he toppled a marble urn which broke into shards on the flagstones.

Tatzel called out: "Well struck, Alvicx! With your awful rump you have destroyed your victim!"

Her friends looked away and into the sky with that faint smile which served Ska in the place of laughter.

Sir Kel, the seneschal, observing the damage, notified Imboden, who instructed Cyprian. In due course Aillas was sent to remove the broken urn. He rolled a small barrow out upon the terrace, loaded aboard the marble shards, then swept up the dirt with a broom and a pan.

Alvicx once again engaged the hurlo-thrumbo with more energy than ever, and so tripped over the barrow, to fall among the shards and dirt. Aillas had gone down upon his knees to sweep up the last of the dirt. Alvicx jumped erect and kicked Aillas on the buttocks.

For a second Aillas remained rigid, then restraint dissolved. Rising to his feet he shoved Alvicx into the hurlo-thrumbo, which caused the padded arm to swing about and deal its usual blow upon the side of Alvicx's face.

Alvicx flourished his sword in a circle. "Villain!" He thrust at Aillas, who ducked back and seized a sword from the table. He fended off Alvicx's second thrust, then countered with such ferocity that Alvicx was forced back across the terrace. The situation was unprecedented; how could a Skaling outmatch the superb and skillful Alvicx? Across the terrace they moved, Alvicx trying to attack but constantly put on the defensive by his opponent's skill. He lunged; Aillas flicked aside his blade and backed Alvicx over the balustrade with the point of his sword pressing against Alvicx's throat.

"If this were the battlefield I could have killed you—easily," spoke Aillas in a voice tense with passion. "Be grateful that now I only trifle with you."

Aillas drew back the sword, replaced it on the table. He looked around the group and his eyes met those of the Lady Tatzel. For a moment their gazes remained in contact, then Aillas turned away and, righting the barrow, once again began to load it with pieces of the marble.

Alvicx watched brooding from across the terrace. He made his decision and signaled to a Ska guard. "Take this cur out behind the stable and kill him."

From a balcony overlooking the terrace Duke Luhalcx spoke. "That command, Lord Alvicx, does you no credit, and shames both the honor of our house and the justice of our race. I suggest that you rescind it."

Alvicx stared up at his father. Slowly he turned and spoke in a wooden voice: "Guards, ignore my order."

He bowed to his sister and their various guests, who had

stood by in frozen-faced fascination; then he marched from the terrace. Aillas returned to the barrow, finished loading the shards, while Lady Tatzel and her friends conducted a muted conversation, watching him from the corner of their eyes. Aillas paid them no heed. He swept the last of the soil from the flagstones, then wheeled the barrow away.

Cyprian communicated his opinion of the affair with a single sad-eyed grimace of reproach, and at supper sat pointedly alone, with his face turned to the door.

Yane spoke to Aillas in low tones. "Is it true that you stabbed Alvicx with his own sword?"

"Not at all! I fenced with him a moment or two; I touched him with my point. It was no great affair."

"Not for you. For Alvicx it is shame, and so you will suffer."

"In what way?"

Yane laughed. "He hasn't yet made up his mind."

23

THE MAIN HALL AT CASTLE SANK extended from a formal parlor at the western end to a retiring room for visiting ladies at the east. Along the way tall narrow portals opened into various halls and chambers, including the Repository, in which were collected curios, clan honors, trophies of battle and engagements at sea, sacred objects. On shelves stood books bound in leather, or sheets of beechwood. One wide wall displayed ancestral portraits, burned into panels of bleached birch by the strokes of a red-hot needle. The technique had never altered; the face of a post-glacial chieftain showed lineaments as keen as the portrait of Duke Luhalcx, limned five years before.

In niches beside the entrance stood a pair of sphinxes carved from blocks of black diorite: the Tronen, or fetishes of the house. Once each week Aillas washed the Tronen, using warm water, mixed with milkweed sap.

Midway through the morning Aillas washed the Tronen and wiped them dry with a soft cloth. Looking along the hall, he saw approaching the Lady Tatzel, slender as a wand in a dark green gown. Black hair bounced beside her intent pale face. She passed Aillas unheeding, leaving in her wake a breath of vaguely floral scent, suggesting the damp herbs of primeval Norway.

A few moments later she returned from her errand. Passing Aillas she halted, then came back, stopped and studied him, detail by detail.

Aillas looked up briefly, scowled and continued with his work.

Tatzel satisfied her curiosity and turned to go her way. First she spoke in the most limpid of voices: "With your brown hair I would take you for a Celt. Still, you look somewhat less coarse."

Again Aillas glanced at her. "I am Troice."

Tatzel hesitated on her going. "Troice, Celt, whatever you

may be: have done with wildness: intractable slaves are gelded."

Aillas stopped his work, limp with outrage. Slowly he rose to his feet, and drawing a deep breath managed to speak in a controlled voice. "I am no slave. I am a nobleman of Troicinet held captive by a tribe of bandits."

Tatzel's mouth drooped and she turned as if to leave. But she paused. "The world has taught us fury; otherwise we would yet be in Norway. If you were Ska, you too would take all others either for enemy or slave; there is no one else. So it must be, and so you must submit."

"Look at me," said Aillas. "Do you take me for one to submit?"

"Already you have submitted."

"I submit now so that later I may bring a Troice army to take down Castle Sank stone by stone, and then you will think with a different logic."

Tatzel laughed, tossed her head and proceeded down the hall.

In a storage chamber Aillas encountered Yane. "Castle Sank is becoming oppressive," said Aillas. "I will be gelded unless I mend my ways."

"Alvicx is already selecting a knife."

"In that case, it is time to leave."

Yane looked over his shoulder; they were alone. "Any time is a good time, were it not for the dogs."

"The dogs can be fooled. The problem is how to evade Cyprian long enough to reach the river."

"The dogs won't be fooled by the river."

"If I can escape the castle, I can escape the dogs."

Yane pulled at his chin. "Let me consider the problem."

Over their supper Yane said: "There is a way to leave the castle. But we must take another man with us."

"Who is that?"

"His name is Cargus. He works as under-cook in the kitchen."

"Can he be trusted?"

"No more and no less than you or I. What about the dogs?"

"We will need half an hour in the carpenter's shed."

"The shed is empty at noon. Here is Cyprian. Nose to the soup."

Cargus stood only an inch taller than Yane but where Yane was built half-askew from sinew and twisted bone, Cargus bulked thick with muscle. The girth of his neck exceeded that of his massive arms. His black hair was cropped short; small black eyes glittered under heavy black brows. In the kitchen-yard he told Yane and Aillas: "I have gathered a quart measure of the fungus known as wolf-bane; it poisons but seldom kills. Tonight it goes into the soup, and spices the pot-pies for the great table. Guts will gurgle tonight everywhere in Castle Sank. Tainted meat will be blamed."

Yane grumbled. "If you could poison dogs as well, we'd walk away at our ease."

"A nice thought, but I have no access to the kennels."

For their supper Yane and Aillas ate only bread and cabbage, and watched with gratification as Cyprian consumed two bowls of soup.

In the morning, as Cargus had predicted, the entire population of the castle suffered cramps of the stomach, together with chills, nausea, fever, hallucinations and a ringing of the ears.

Cargus went to where Cyprian crouched head down over the commissary table, shivering uncontrollably. Cargus cried out in a harsh voice: "You must take action! The scullions refuse to stir and my bins overflow with garbage!"

"Empty them yourself," groaned Cyprian. "I cannot put my mind to such trifles. Doom is upon me!"

"I am cook, not scullion. Here, you two!" He called out to Yane and Aillas. "You can at least walk! Empty my bins and be quick about it!"

"Never!" growled Yane. "Do it yourself."

Cargus turned on Cyprian. "My bins must be cleared! Give orders or I will make a complaint to startle Imboden off his chamber-pot!"

Cyprian waved a feeble hand to Yane and Aillas. "Go, you two, empty this devil his bins, even if you must crawl."

Aillas, Yane and Cargus carried bags of garbage to the rubbish heap and took up the parcels which they had left previously. They set off at a trot across the countryside, keeping to the cover of underbrush and trees.

A half-mile east of the castle they passed over the brow of a hill and thereafter without fear of visual detection, made good speed to the southeast, giving a wide berth to the lumber mill. They ran until winded, then walked, then ran again, and within the hour arrived at the river Malkish.

At this point the water flowed broad and shallow, though

above it roared down from the mountain through steep ravines, and downstream raced in sullen fury through a set of narrow gorges where many runaway Skalings had been battered and broken on the rocks. Without hesitation Aillas, Yane and Cargus plunged into the stream and waded across, through water often as deep as their chests, with parcels held above their heads. As they neared the opposite bank they halted to inspect the shore.

Nothing immediately suited their purpose, and they waded upstream until they came upon a small beach covered with packed gravel, with a low slope grown over with grass at the back. From their parcels they took the articles which Aillas and Yane had built in the carpenter's shed: stilts, with straw pads tied securely over the ends.

Still in the water, they mounted the stilts and the three waded ashore, disturbing the beach as little as possible. Up the slope they stepped and the padded stilt-ends left neither marks nor odor to excite the hounds.

For an hour the three walked on the stilts. At a rivulet, they waded into the steam and dismounted to rest. Then once more they took to the stilts, lest their pursuers, failing to pick up a spoor at the river, might cast about in concentric sweeps of ever greater radius.

Another hour they stalked on the stilts, up a gradual slope through a sparse forest of stunted pines where the thin red soil lay in pockets. The land had no utility for cultivation; the few peasants who at one time had collected resin for turpentine, or grazed pigs, had fled the Ska; the fugitives traveled an uninhabited wasteland, which suited them well.

At another stream they dismounted from the stilts and sat to rest on a ledge of rock. They drank water and ate bread and cheese from their packs. Listening, they heard no far-off belling of the hounds, but they had come a good distance and expected to hear nothing; probably their absence had not yet been noticed. The three congratulated themselves that they had possibly a full day's headstart over any pursuit.

They discarded the stilts and waded upstream in an easterly direction, and presently entered an upland of curious aspect, where ancient pinnacles and crags of decaying black rock rose above valleys once tilled but now deserted. For a space they followed an old road which led at last to the ruins of an ancient fort.

A few miles beyond the land once again became wild and rose to a region of rolling moors. Rejoicing in the freedom of the high skies, the three set off into the hazy east.

They were not alone on the moor. Up from a swale a half-mile south, under four flapping black flags, rode a troop of Ska warriors. Galloping forward, they surrounded the fugitives.

The leader, a stern-faced baron in black armor, spared them only a single glance and no words whatever. Ropes were attached to the iron collars; the three Skalings were led away to the north.

Late in the day the troop met a wagon-train loaded with victual of various sorts. At the rear marched forty men linked neck to neck by ropes. To this column were joined Aillas, Yane and Cargus, and so, willy-nilly, forced to follow the wagon train north. In due course they entered the kingdom of Dahaut and arrived at Poëlitetz, that immense fortress guarding the central buttress of the Teach tac Teach and overlooking the Plain of Shadows.

24

WHERE DAHAUT BORDERED ON NORTH ULFLAND a scarp eighty miles long, the front face of the Teach tac Teach, overlooked the Plain of Shadows. At a place named Poëlitetz, the river Tamsour, flowing down from the snows of Mount Agon, cut a chasm which allowed relatively easy access from Dahaut to the moors of North Ulfland. Poëlitetz had been fortified as long as men had made war across the Elder Isles; whoever held Poëlitetz controlled the peace of Far Dahaut. The Ska, upon seizing Poëlitetz, began an enormous work, to guard the fortress from the west as well as the east, so that it might be totally impregnable. They had closed the defile with masonry walls thirty feet thick, leaving a passage twelve feet wide and ten feet high, controlled by three iron gates, one behind the other. Fortress and scarp showed a single impervious face to the Plain of Shadows.

The better to reconnoiter the Plain of Shadows, the Ska had started to drive a tunnel out under the plain toward a hillock overgrown with scrub oak at a distance of a quarter-mile from the base of the scarp. The tunnel was a project executed with the utmost secrecy, concealed from all but a few Ska of high rank and those who dug the tunnel, Skalings of Category Six: Intractables.

Upon arrival at Poëlitetz, Aillas, Yane and Cargus were subjected to a perfunctory inquisition. Then, instead of the maiming or mutilation which they had expected, they were taken to a special barracks, where a company of forty Skalings were held in isolation: the tunnel gang. They worked ten-and-a-half-hour shifts, with three half-hour rest periods. In the barracks they were guarded by an elite platoon of Ska soldiers and allowed contact with no other persons of Poëlitetz. All realized that they worked as components of a death-squad. Upon completion of the tunnel they would be killed.

With death clear and large before them, none of the Skalings worked in haste: a situation which the Ska found easier to accept than to alter. So long as reasonable progress was made, the work was allowed to go its own pace. The routine each day was identical. Each Skaling had his assigned duty. The tunnel, fifteen feet below the surface of the plain, ran through shale and compressed silt. Four men dug at the front face with picks and mattocks. Three men scooped the detritus into baskets which were loaded upon barrows and wheeled back down the tunnel to the entrance. The barrows were dumped into hoppers which were hoisted aloft by a crane, swung over a wagon, emptied, and returned below. A bellows powered by oxen walking around a windlass blew air into a leather tube, which led to the tunnel face. As the tunnel advanced, cribbing was set into place so that the overhead and the sides were lined with tarred cedar timbers.

Every two or three days Ska engineers extended a pair of cords by which the direction of the tunnel was guided and with a waterlevel* measured horizontal deflection.

A Ska overseer directed the Skalings with a pair of soldiers to enforce discipline, should such control be needed. The overseer and the guards tended to remain at the open end of the tunnel, where the air was cool and fresh. By noting the rate at which the wagons were filled, the overseer could estimate the vigor at which the Skalings performed their duties. If work went well, the Skalings ate well, and drank wine with their meals. If they slacked or loitered, their rations dwindled in proportion.

Two shifts worked the tunnel: noon to midnight and midnight to noon. Neither could be said to be preferable since the Skalings never saw the sun and knew that they were never to see it again.

Aillas, Cargus and Yane were assigned to the noon-midnight shift. Immediately they began to consider escape. The prospects were even more discouraging than those at Castle Sank. Barred

---

*The water-level comes in several forms. The Ska used a pair of wooden troughs twenty feet long with a section four inches square. Water in the troughs lay perfectly horizontal; floats at each end allowed the troughs themselves to be adjusted to the horizontal. By shifting the troughs in succession, the desired horizontal could be extended indefinitely, with an accuracy limited only by the patience of the engineer.

doors and suspicious guards confined them off-duty; they worked in a tube similarly sealed against exit.

After only two days of work, Aillas told Yane and Cargus: "We can escape. It is possible."

"You are more perceptive than I," said Yane.

"Or I," said Cargus.

"There is one single difficulty. We shall need the cooperation of the entire shift. The question becomes: are any so broken that they might betray us?"

"Where would be the motive? Everyone sees his own ghost dancing ahead of him."

"Some persons are traitors by nature; they take pleasure in treachery."

The three, squatting by the wall of the chamber in which they spent the off-hours, considered their fellows, one by one. Cargus said at last: "If we share together the prospect of escape, there will be no betrayal."

"We have to assume as much," said Yane. "We have no better choice."

Fourteen men worked the shift, with another six whose duties never took them into the tunnel. Fourteen men bound themselves in a desperate compact and at once the operation began.

The tunnel now reached about two hundred yards in an easterly direction under the plain. Another two hundred yards remained, through shale, with occasionally an inexplicable ball of iron-hard blue sandstone sometimes three feet in diameter. Except for the sandstone, the ground yielded to the pick; the face moved forward ten to fifteen feet a day. A pair of carpenters installed cribbing as the tunnel advanced. They left several posts loose, so that they might be pulled to the side. In the gap thus cleared certain members of the gang dug a side-tunnel, slanting toward the surface. The dirt was shoveled into baskets, loaded aboard barrows and transported back precisely like dirt taken from the face of the tunnel. By partially closing two men into the side-tunnel, and with the rest of the men working somewhat harder, there seemed no lessening of progress. Always someone with a loaded barrow waited thirty yards from the start of the tunnel, should the overseer decide to make an inspection, in which case, the lookout jumped on the ventilation tube to warn his fellows. If necessary he was prepared to turn over his barrow, ostensibly by accident, so as to delay the overseer. Then when the overseer passed, the barrow was rolled so as to flatten the ventilation tube. The far end became so stifling that the overseer spent as little time as possible in the tunnel.

The side-tunnel, dug five feet high and three feet wide, and slanting sharply upward, went swiftly, and the diggers probed continually with cautious strokes, lest, in their zeal, they strike a great hole into the surface which might be visible from the fortress. At last they found roots, of grasses and shrubs, then dark topsoil and they knew the surface was close above.

At sunset the tunnel-Skalings took their supper in a chamber at the head of the tunnel, then returned to work.

Ten minutes later Aillas went to summon Kildred the overseer, a tall Ska of middle-age, with a scarred face, a bald head and a manner remote even for a Ska. As usual Kildred sat gaming with the guards. He looked over his shoulder at the approach of Aillas. "What now?"

"The diggers have struck a dike of blue rock. They want rock-splitters and drills."

"'Rock-splitters'? What tools are these?"

"I don't know. I just carry messages."

Kildred muttered a curse and rose to his feet. "Come; let us look at this blue dike."

He stalked into the tunnel, followed by Aillas, through the murky orange flicker of oil lamps, to the tunnel face. When he bent to look for the blue dike, Cargus struck him with an iron bar, killing him at once.

The time was now twilight. The crew gathered by the side-tunnel where the diggers were now striking up at the soft topsoil.

Aillas wheeled a barrow of dirt to the end chamber. "There will be no more dirt for a time," he told the winch-tender, in a voice loud enough for the guards to hear. "We have hit a lode of rock." The guards looked over their shoulders, then returned to their dice. The winch-tender followed Aillas back into the tunnel.

The escape tunnel was open. The Skalings climbed out into late twilight, including the winch-tender who knew nothing of the plot but was happy to escape. All lay flat in the sedge and saw-grass. Aillas and Yane, the last men to depart the tunnel, pulled the supporting posts back in place, leaving no clue as to their function. Once on the surface they wedged the escape hole tight with bracken, pounded dirt into the choked hole and transplanted grass. "Let them think magic," said Aillas. "All the better if they do!"

The erstwhile Skalings ran crouching across the Plain of Shadows, through the gathering dark, eastward and ever deeper into the kingdom of Dahaut. Poëlitetz, the great Ska fortress, loomed black on the sky behind them. The group paused to look back. "Ska," said Aillas, "you strange dark-souled folk from the past! Next time we meet I will carry a sword. You owe me dear for the pain you put on me and the labor you took from me!"

An hour of running, trotting, and walking brought the band to the Gloden River, whose headwaters included the Tamsour.

The moon, almost full, rose above the river, laying a trail of moonlight on the water. Beside the moon-silvered veils of an enormous weeping willow, the band paused to rest and discuss their situation. Aillas told them: "We are fifteen: a strong band. Some of you want to go home; others may have no homes to go to. I can offer prospects if you will join me in what I must do. I have a quest. First it takes me south to Tac Tor, then I can't say where: perhaps Dahaut, to find my son. Then we will go to Troicinet, where I control both wealth, honor and estate. Those of you who follow me as my comrades, to join my quest and, so I hope, to return with me to Troicinet, will profit well; I swear it! I will grant them good lands, and they shall bear the title Knight-Companion. Be warned! The way is dangerous! First to Tac Tor beside Tintzin Fyral, then who knows where? So choose. Go your own way or come with me, for here is where we part company. I will cross the river and travel south with my companions. The rest would do well to travel east across the plain and into the settled parts of Dahaut. Who will come with me?"

"I am with you," said Cargus. "I have nowhere else to go."

"And I," said Yane.

"We joined ourselves during dark days," said one called Qualls. "Why separate now? Especially since I crave land and knighthood."

In the end five others went with Aillas. They crossed the Gloden by a bridge and followed a road which struck off to the south. The others, mostly Daut, chose to go their own ways and continued east beside the Gloden.

The seven who had joined Aillas were first Yane and Cargus, then Garstang, Qualls, Bode, Scharis and Faurfisk: a disparate group. Yane and Cargus were short; Qualls and Bode were tall.

Garstang, who spoke little of himself, displayed the manners of a gentleman, while Faurfisk, massive, fair and blue-eyed, declared himself the bastard of a Gothic pirate upon a Celtic fisherwoman. Scharis, who was not so old as Aillas, was distinguished by a handsome face and a pleasant disposition. Faurfisk, on the other hand, was as ugly as pox, burns and scars could make him. He had been racked by a petty baron of South Ulfland; his hair had whitened and rage was never far from his face. Qualls, a runaway Irish monk, was irresponsibly jovial and declared himself as good a wencher as any bully-bishop of Ireland.

Though the band now stood well inside Dahaut, the proximity of Poëlitetz cast an oppression across the night, and the entire company set off together down the road.

As they walked Garstang spoke to Aillas. "It is necessary that we have an understanding. I am a knight of Lyonesse, from Twanbow Hall, in the Duchy of Ellesmere. Since you are Troice, we are nominally at war. That of course is nonsense, and I earnestly cast my lot with yours, until we enter Lyonesse, when we must go our separate ways."

"So it shall be. But see us now: in slave clothes and iron collars, slinking through the night like scavenger dogs. Two gentlemen indeed! And lacking money, we must steal to eat, like any other band of vagabonds."

"Other hungry gentlemen have made similar compromises. We shall steal side by side, so that neither may scorn the other. And I suggest, that if at all possible we steal from the rich, though the poor are somewhat easier prey."

"Circumstances must guide us...Dogs are barking. There is a village ahead, and almost certainly a smithy."

"At this hour of the night he will be soundly asleep."

"A kindhearted smith might rouse himself to help a desperate group such as ours."

"Or we might rouse him ourselves."

Ahead the houses of a village showed gray in the moonlight. The streets were empty; no light showed save from the tavern, from which came the sounds of boisterous revelry.

"Tomorrow must be a holiday," said Garstang. "Notice in the square, where the cauldron is ready to boil an ox."

"A prodigious cauldron indeed, but where is the smithy?"

"It must be yonder, along the road, if it exists."

The group passed through town and near the outskirts discovered the smithy, at the front of a stone dwelling, in which showed a light.

Aillas went to the door and rapped politely. After a long pause, the door was slowly opened by a youth of seventeen or eighteen. He seemed depressed, even haggard, and when he spoke his voice cracked with strain. "Sir, who are you? What do you want here?"

"Friend, we need the help of a smith. This very day we escaped the Ska and we cannot abide these detestable collars another instant."

The young man stood irresolutely. "My father is smith to Vervold, this village. I am Elric, his son. But since he will never again work his trade, I am now smith. Come along to the shop." He brought a lamp and led the way to the smithy.

"I fear that your work must be an act of charity," said Aillas. "We can pay only the iron of the collars, since we have nothing else."

"No matter." The young smith's voice was listless. One by one the eight fugitives knelt beside the anvil. The smith plied hammer and chisel to cut the rivets; one by one the men arose to their feet free of the collars.

Aillas asked: "What happened to your father? Did he die?"

"Not yet. Tomorrow morning is his time. He will be boiled in a cauldron and fed to the dogs."

"That is bad news. What was his crime?"

"He committed an outrage." Elric's voice was somber. "When Lord Halies stepped from his carriage, my father struck him in the face, and kicked his body and caused Lord Halies pain."

"Insolence, at the very least. What provoked him so?"

"The work of nature. My sister is fifteen years old. She is very beautiful. It was natural that Lord Halies should want to bring her to Fair Aprillion to warm his bed, and who would deny him had she assented to his proposal? But she would not go, and Lord Halies sent his servants to bring her. My father, though a smith, is impractical and thought to set things right by beating and kicking Lord Halies. He now, for his mistake, must boil in a cauldron."

"Lord Halies—is he rich?"

"He lives at Fair Aprillion, in a mansion of sixty chambers. He keeps a stable of fine horses. He eats larks, oysters, and meats roasted with cloves and saffron, with white bread and honey. He drinks of both white and red wines. There are rugs

305

on his floors and silks on his back. He dresses twenty cutthroats in gaudy uniforms and calls them 'paladins.' They enforce all his edicts and many of their own."

"There is good reason to believe that Lord Halies is rich," said Aillas.

"I resent Lord Halies," said Sir Garstang. "Wealth and noble birth are excellent circumstances, coveted by all. Still, the rich nobleman should enjoy his distinction with propriety and never bring shame to his estate as Lord Halies has done. In my opinion he must be chastised, fined, humiliated, and deprived of eight or ten of his fine horses."

"Those are exactly my views," said Aillas. He turned back to Elric. "Lord Halies commands only twenty soldiers?"

"Yes. And also Chief Archer Hunolt, the executioner."

"And tomorrow morning all will come to Vervold to witness the ceremony and Fair Aprillion will be deserted."

Elric uttered a yelp of near-hysterical laughter. "So, while my father boils, you rob the mansion?"

Aillas asked: "How can he boil if the cauldron leaks water?"

"The cauldron is sound. My father mended it himself."

"What is done can be undone. Bring hammer and chisels; and we will punch some holes."

Elric slowly took up the tools. "It will cause delay, but what then?"

"At the very least your father will not boil so soon."

The group left the smithy and returned to the square. As before all houses were dark, save for the yellow flicker of candlelight from the tavern, from which issued a voice raised in song.

Through the moonlight the group approached the cauldron. Aillas motioned to Elric. "Strike!"

Elric set his chisel against the cauldron and struck hard with his hammer, to create a dull clanging sound, like a muffled gong-stroke.

"Again!"

Once more Elric struck; the chisel cut the iron and the cauldron no longer was whole.

Elric cut three more holes and a fourth for good measure, then stood back in mournful exaltation.

"Though they boil me as well, I can never regret this night's work!"

"You shall not be boiled, nor your father either. Where is Fair Aprillion?"

"The lane leads yonder, between the trees."

The door to the tavern opened. Outlined against the rectangle of yellow candlelight, four men staggered out upon the square, where they engaged in raucous repartee.

"Those are Halies' soldiers?" Aillas asked.

"Quite so, and each a brute in his own right."

"Quick then, behind the trees yonder. We will do some summary justice, and also reduce the twenty to sixteen."

Elric made a dubious protest. "We have no weapons."

"What? Are you folk of Vervold all cowards? We outnumber them nine to four!"

Elric had nothing to say.

"Come, quick now!" said Aillas. "Since we have become thieves and assassins, let us act the part!"

The group ran across the square, and hid in the shrubbery beside the lane. Two great elms to either side filtered the moon light to lay a silver filigree across the road.

The nine men found sticks and sto...

...e cauldron needs mending."

...hat we may do what must be

...g and belching.

...oddess of the night, that she ...ht hold the firmament more steady; another cursed him for his loose legs and urged him to crawl on hands and knees. The third could not control an idiotic chortle for a humorous episode known only to himself, or possibly to no one whatever; the fourth tried to hiccup in time with his steps. The four approached. There was a sudden thudding of feet, the sound of hammer breaking into bone, gasps of terror; in seconds four drunken paladins became four corpses.

"Take their weapons," said Aillas. "Drag them behind the hedge."

The group returned to the smithy and bedded down as best they might.

In the morning they rose early, ate porridge and bacon, then armed themselves with what weapons Elric could provide: an old sword, a pair of daggers, iron bars, a bow with a dozen arrows, which Yane at once took into custody. They disguised their gray Skaling smocks in such old torn or discarded garments as the smith's household could provide. In this style, they went to the square, where they found a few dozen folk standing aloof to the sides, scowling toward the cauldron and muttering together.

Elric discovered a pair of cousins and an uncle. They went home, armed themselves with bows and joined the group.

Chief Archer Hunolt came first down the lane from Fair Aprillion, followed by four guards and a wagon carrying a beehive-shaped cage, in which sat the condemned man. He kept his eyes fixed on the floor of the cage, and looked up only once, across the square to the cauldron. Behind marched two more soldiers, these armed with swords and bows.

Hunolt, halting his horse, noticed the damage done to the cauldron. "Here's treachery!" he cried. "Breakage upon his Lordship's property! Who has done this deed?" His voice rang around the square. Heads turned, but no one answered.

He turned to one of his soldiers: "Go you, fetch the smith."

"The smith is in the cage, sir."

"Then fetch the new smith! It is all one."

"There he stands, sir."

"Smith! Come here at once! Th■■■■■■■■■■■■

"So I see."

"Repair it on the quick, so t■■■■■■■■■■■ done."

Elric replied in a surly voice: "I am a smith. That is tinker's work."

"Smith, tinker, call yourself what you like, only fix that pot with good iron, and quickly!"

"Would you have me mend the pot in which to boil my father!"

Hunolt chuckled. "There is irony here, agreed, but it only illustrates the impartial majesty of his Lordship's justice. So then, unless you care to join your father in the pot, to bubble face to face—as you can see there is adequate room—mend the pot."

"I must fetch tools and rivets."

"Be quick!"

Elric went to the smithy for tools. Aillas and his troop had already slipped away up the lane toward Fair Aprillion, to prepare an ambush.

Half an hour passed. The gates opened; Lord Halies rode forth in his carriage with a guard of eight soldiers.

Yane and Elric's uncle and cousins stepped out into the lane behind the column. They bent their bows, loosed arrows: once, twice. The others, who had remained concealed, rushed out and in fifteen seconds the killing was done. Lord Halies was disarmed and, ashen-faced, pulled from the carriage.

Now well-armed, the troop returned to the square. Hunolt stood over Elric, ensuring that he repaired the cauldron at best speed. At near range Bode, Qualls, Yane and all the others who carried bows, loosed a flight of arrows and six more of Halies' paladins died.

Elric struck Hunolt's foot with his hammer; Hunolt screamed and sagged on the broken foot. Elric struck at the other foot with even greater force, to crush it flat, and Hunolt fell writhing upon his back.

Elric released his father from the cage. "Fill the cauldron!" cried Elric. "Bring the faggots!" He dragged Halies to the cauldron. "You ordained a boiling; you shall have one!"

Halies staggered and stared aghast at the cauldron. He babbled entreaties, then screamed threats, to no effect. He was trussed up, knees high and seated in the cauldron, and Hunolt was placed beside him. Water filled the cauldron to cover their chests and fire was given to the faggots. Around the cauldron the folk of Vervold leapt and capered in a delirium of excitement. Presently they joined hands and danced around the cauldron in three concentric circles.

Two days later Aillas and his troop departed Vervold. They wore good clothes, boots of soft leather and carried corselets of the finest chain mail. Their horses were the best the stable at Fair Aprillion could provide, and in their saddle-bags they carried gold and silver.

Their number was now seven. At a banquet Aillas had advised the village elders to select one from among their number to serve as their new lord. "Otherwise another lord of the neighborhood will arrive with his troops, and declare himself lord of the domain."

"The prospect has troubled us," said the smith. "Still, we at the village are too close; we know all each other's secrets and none could command a proper respect. We prefer a strong and honest stranger for the office: one of good heart and generous spirit, one who will mete fair justice, levy light rents and abuse

abuse his privileges no more than absolutely necessary. In short, we ask that you yourself, Sir Aillas, become the new lord of Fair Aprillion and its domains."

"Not I," said Aillas. "I have urgent deeds to do, and already I am late. Choose someone else to serve you."

"Sir Garstang then would be our choice!"

"Well chosen," said Aillas. "He is of noble blood; he is brave and generous."

"Not I," said Sir Garstang. "I have domains of my own elsewhere, which I am anxious to see once more."

"Well then, what of you others?"

"Not I," said Bode. "I am a restless man. What I seek is to be found in the far places."

"Not I," said Yane. "I am one for the tavern, not the hall. I would shame you with my wenching and revelry."

"Not I," said Cargus. "You would not wish a philosopher for your lord."

"Nor a bastard Goth," said Faurfisk.

Qualls spoke in a thoughtful voice: "It would seem that I am the only qualified possibility. I am noble, like all Irishmen; I am just, forbearing, honorable; I also play the lute and sing, and so I can enliven the village festivals with frolics and antics. I am generous but not grandiose. At marriages and hangings I am sober and reverent; ordinarily I am easy, gay and lightsome. Further—"

"Enough, enough!" cried Aillas. "Plainly, you are the man for the job. Lord Qualls, give us leave to depart your domain!"

"Sir, the permission is yours, and my good wishes go with you. I will often wonder as to how you are faring, and my Irish wildness will give me a twinge, but on winter nights, when rain spits at the windows, I will hold my feet to the fire, drink red wine, and be happy that I am Lord Qualls of Fair Aprillion."

The seven rode south along an old road which, according to folk at Vervold, swung southwest around the Forest of Tantrevalles, then turned south eventually to become the Trompada. No one at Vervold had ventured far in this direction—nor any other direction in most cases—and no one could offer sensible information as to what might be encountered.

For a space the road went by haphazard curves and swoops; left, right, up hill, down dale, following a placid river for a time, then angling away through the dim forest. Peasants tilled the meadows and herded cattle. Ten miles from Vervold the peasants had become a different sort: dark of hair and eye, slight of physique, wary to the point of hostility.

As the day progressed the land became harsh, the hills abrupt, the meadows stony, the tillages were less frequent. Late in the afternoon they came to a hamlet, no more than a group of farmhouses built close together for mutual protection and simple conviviality. Aillas paid over a gold piece to the patriarch of one household; in return the troop was provided a great supper of pork grilled over vine cuttings, broad beans and onions, oatbread and wine. The horses were fed hay and stabled in a barn. The patriarch sat for a time with the group to make sure that all ate well and relaxed his taciturnity, so much that he put questions to Aillas: "What sort of folk might you be?"

Aillas pointed around the group: "A Goth. A Celt. Ulfish yonder. There a Galician"—this was Cargus—"and a knight of Lyonesse. I am Troice. We are a mixed group, assembled, if the truth be known, against our will by the Ska."

"I have heard speak of the Ska," said the old man. "They will never dare set foot in these parts. We are not many, but we are furious when aroused."

"We wish you long life," said Aillas, "and many happy feasts like that you have set before us tonight."

"Bah, that was but a hasty collation arranged for unexpected guests. Next time give us notice of your coming."

"Nothing would suit us better," said Aillas. "Still, it is a long hard way, and we are not home yet. What lies along the road to the south?"

"We hear conflicting reports. Some speak of ghosts, others of ogres. Some have been harassed by bandits, others complain of imps riding like knights on armored herons. It is hard to separate fact from hysteria; I can only recommend caution."

The road became no more than a wide trail, winding south into hazy distance. The Forest of Tantrevalles could be seen to the left and the stone cliffs of the Teach tac Teach rose sheer to the right. The farmsteads finally disappeared, though occasional huts and a ruined castle used as a shelter for sheep testified to a sparse population. In one of the old huts the seven stopped to take shelter for the night.

The great forest here loomed close at hand. At intervals Aillas heard strange sounds from the forest which sent tingles along his skin. Scharis stood listening in fascination, and Aillas asked what he heard.

"Can you not hear it?" asked Scharis, his eyes glowing. "It is music; I have never heard its like before."

Aillas listened for a moment. "I hear nothing."

"It comes and goes. Now it has stopped."

"Are you sure it isn't the wind?"

"What wind? The night is calm."

"If it is music, you should not listen. In these parts magic is always close, to the peril of ordinary men."

With a trace of impatience Scharis asked: "How can I not listen to what I want to hear? When it tells me things I want to know?"

"This goes beyond me," said Aillas. He rose to his feet. "I am for bed. Tomorrow we ride long and far."

Aillas set watches, marking off two-hour periods by the sweep of the stars. Bode took the first watch alone, then Garstang and Faurfisk, then Yane and Cargus and finally Aillas and Scharis; and the troop made themselves as comfortable as possible. Almost reluctantly Scharis settled himself, but quickly fell asleep and Aillas gratefully did the same.

When Arcturus reached its appointed place, Aillas and Scharis were aroused and began their sentry duty. Aillas noticed that Scharis no longer gave his attention to sounds from the night. Aillas asked softly: "What of the music? Do you hear it still?"

"No. It moved away even before I slept."

"I wish I might have heard it."

"That might not serve you well."

"How so?"

"You might become as I am, to your sorrow."

Aillas laughed, if somewhat uneasily. "You are not the worst of men. How could I so damage myself?"

Scharis stared into the fire. At last he spoke, half-musing. "For a fact, I am ordinary enough—if anything, much too ordinary. My fault is this: I am easily distracted by quirks and fancies. As you know, I hear inaudible music. Sometimes when I look across the landscape, I glimpse a flicker of motion; when I look in earnest it moves just past the edge of vision. If you were like me, your quest might be delayed or lost and so your question is answered."

Aillas stirred the fire. "I sometimes have sensations—whims, fancies, whatever you call them—of the same kind. I don't give

312

them much thought. They are not so insistent as to cause me concern."

Scharis laughed humorlessly. "Sometimes I think I am mad. Sometimes I am afraid. There are beauties too large to be borne, unless one is eternal." He stared into the fire and gave a sudden nod. "Yes, that is the message of the music."

Aillas spoke uncomfortably. "Scharis, my dear fellow, I think you are having hallucinations. You are over-imaginative; it is as simple as that!"

"How could I imagine so grandly? I heard it, you did not. There are three possibilities. Either my mind is playing me tricks, as you suggest; or, secondly, my perceptions are more acute than yours; or, thirdly—and this is the frightening thought— the music is meant for me alone."

Aillas made a skeptical sound. "Truly, you would do best to put these strange sounds from your mind. If men were intended to probe such mysteries, or if such mysteries actually exist, surely we would know more about them."

"Possibly so."

"Tell me when next these perceptions come on you."

"If you wish."

Dawn came slowly, from gray through pearl to peach. By the time the sun had appeared the seven were on their way, through a pleasant if deserted landscape. At noon they came to a river which Aillas thought must be the Siss on its way to join the Gloden, and the rest of the day they followed the riverbank south. Halfway through the afternoon heavy clouds drifted across the sky. A damp cold wind began to blow, carrying the sound of distant thunder.

Close on sunset the road arrived at a stone bridge of five arches and a crossroads, where the East-West Road, emerging from Forest Tantrevalles, crossed the Trompada and continued through a cleft in the mountains to end at Oäldes in South Ulfland. Beside the crossroads, with the rain starting to fall in earnest, the seven came upon an inn, the Star and Unicorn. They took their horses to the stable and entered the inn, to find a cheerful fire burning in a massive fireplace. Behind a counter stood a tall thin man, bald of pate with a long black beard overhanging his chest, a long nose overhanging his beard, and a pair of wide black eyes half-overhung by eyelids. Beside the fire three men crouched like conspirators over their beer, the brims of low-crowned black hats shading their faces. At another table a man with a thin high-bridged nose and a fine auburn mustache, wearing handsome garments of dark blue and umber, sat alone.

Aillas spoke to the innkeeper. "We will want lodging for the night and the best you can provide in the way of supper. Also, if you please, send someone to care for our horses."

The innkeeper bowed politely, but without warmth. "We shall do our best to fulfill your desires."

The seven went to sit before the fire and the innkeeper brought wine. The three men hunching over their table inspected them covertly and muttered among themselves. The gentleman in dark blue and umber, after a single glance, returned to his private reflections. The seven, relaxing by the fire, drank wine with easy throats. Presently Yane called the service girl to his side. "Now, poppet, how many pitchers of wine have you served us?"

"Three, sir."

"Correct! Now each time you bring a pitcher to the table you must come to me and pronounce its number. Is that clear?"

"Yes, sir."

The landlord strode on jackstraw legs across the room. "What is the trouble, sir?"

"No trouble whatever. The girl tallies the wine as we drink it, and there can be no mistakes in the score."

"Bah! You must not addle the creature's mind with such calculations! I keep score yonder!"

"And I do the same here, and the girl keeps a running balance between us."

The landlord threw his arms in the air and stalked off to his kitchen, from which he presently served the supper. The two service girls, standing somber and watchful in the shadows, came forward deftly to refill goblets and bring fresh pitchers, each time chanting its number to Yane, while the landlord, again leaning sourly behind his counter, kept a parallel score and wondered if he dared water the wine.

Aillas, who drank as much as any, leaned back in his chair and contemplated his comrades as they sat at ease. Garstang, no matter what the circumstances, might never disguise his gentility. Bode, liberated by the wine, forgot his fearsome countenance to become unexpectedly droll. Scharis, like Aillas, sat back in his chair enjoying the comfort. Faurfisk told coarse anecdotes with great gusto and teased the serving girls. Yane spoke little but seemed to take a sardonic pleasure in the high spirits of his friends. Cargus, on the other hand, stared morosely into the fire. Aillas, sitting beside him, finally asked: "What troubles you that your thoughts bring gloom upon you?"

"I think a mixture of thoughts," said Cargus. "They come at me in a medley. I remember old Galicia, and my father and mother, and how I wandered away from their old age when I might have stayed and sweetened their days. I reflect on the Ska and their harsh habits. I think of my immediate condition with food in my belly, gold in my pouch, and my good companions around me, which gives me to ponder the fluxes of life and the brevity of such moments as these; and now you know the cause for my melancholy."

"That is clear enough," said Aillas. "For my part I am happy that we sit here rather than out in the rain; but I am never free of the rage which smoulders in my bones: perhaps it will never leave me despite all revenge."

"You are still young," said Cargus. "Tranquility will come in time."

"As to that I can't say. Vindictiveness may be a graceless emotion, but I will never rest until I redress certain deeds done upon me."

"I much prefer you as a friend than an enemy," said Cargus.

The two men fell silent. The gentleman in umber and dark blue who had been sitting quietly to the side, rose to his feet and approached Aillas. "Sir, I notice that you and your companions conduct yourselves in the manner of gentlemen, tempering your enjoyment with dignity. Allow me, if you will, to utter a probably unnecessary warning."

"Speak, by all means."

"The two girls yonder are patiently waiting. They are less demure than they seem. When you rise to retire, the older will solicit you to intimacy. While she entertains you with her meager equipment, the other rifles your purse. They share the gleanings with the landlord."

"Incredible! They are so small and thin!"

The gentleman smiled ruefully. "This was my own view when last I drank here to excess. Good night, sir."

The gentleman went off to his chamber. Aillas conveyed the intelligence to his companions; the two girls faded away into the shadows, and the landlord brought no more fuel to the fire. Presently the seven staggered off to the straw pallets which had been laid down for them, and so, with the rain hissing and thudding on the thatch overhead, all slept soundly.

In the morning the seven awoke to find that the storm had passed, allowing sunlight of blinding brilliance to illuminate the land. They were served a breakfast of black bread, curds and onions. While Aillas settled accounts with the innkeeper, the others went to prepare the horses for the road.

Aillas was startled by the score. "What? So much? For seven men of modest tastes?"

"You drank a veritable flood of wine. Here is an exact tally: nineteen pitchers of my best Carhaunge Red."

"One moment," said Aillas. He called in Yane. "We are in doubt as to the tally of last night. Can you assist us in any way?"

"Indeed I can. We were served twelve pitchers of wine. I wrote the number on paper and gave it to the girl. The wine was not Carhaunge; it was drawn from that cask yonder marked 'Corriente': two pennies per pitcher."

"Ah!" exclaimed the landlord. "I see my mistake. This is a tally from the night before, when we served a party of ten noblemen."

Aillas scrutinized the score again. "Now then: what is this sum?"

"Miscellaneous services."

"I see. The gentleman who sat at the table yonder: who is he?"

"That would be Sir Descandol, younger son to Lord Maudelet of Gray Fosfre, over the bridge and into Ulfland."

"Sir Descandol was kind enough to warn us of your maids and their predatory mischief. There were no 'miscellaneous services.'"

"Really? In that case, I must delete this item."

"And here: 'Horses—stabling, fodder and drink.' Could seven horses occupy such luxurious expanses, eat so much hay and swill down so much valuable water as to justify the sum of thirteen florins?"

"Aha! You misread the figure, as did I in my grand total. The figure should be two florins."

"I see." Aillas returned to the account. "Your eels are very dear."

"They are out of season."

316

Aillas finally paid the amended account. He asked: "What lies along the road?"

"Wild country. The forest closes in and all is gloom."

"How far to the next inn?"

"Quite some distance."

"You have traveled the road yourself?"

"Through Tantrevalles Forest? Never."

"What of bandits, footpads and the like?"

"You should have put the question to Sir Descandol; he seems to be the authority on such offenses."

"Possibly so, but he was gone before the thought occurred to me. Well, no doubt we shall manage."

The seven set off along the road. The river swung away and the forest closed in from both sides. Yane, riding in the lead, caught a flicker of movement among the leaves. He cried out: "Down, all! Down in the saddle!" He dropped to the ground, snapped arrow to bow and launched a shaft into the gloom, arousing a wail of pain. Meanwhile, a volley of arrows had darted from the forest. The riders, ducking to Yane's cry, were unscathed except for the ponderous Faurfisk, who took an arrow in the chest and died instantly. Dodging, crouching low, his fellows charged into the forest flourishing steel. Yane relied on his bow. He shot three more arrows, striking into a neck, a chest and a leg. Within the forest there were groans, the crashing of bodies, cries of sudden fear. One man tried to flee; Bode sprang upon his back, bore him to the ground, and there disarmed him.

Silence, save for panting and groans. Yane's arrows had killed two and disabled two more. These two and two others lay draining their blood into the forest mold. The three rough-clad men who the night before had sat in the inn over wine were among them.

Aillas turned to Bode's captive, and performed a slight bow, as a knightly courtesy. "Sir Descandol, the landlord declared you an authority upon the region's footpads, and now I understand his reason. Cargus, be good enough to throw a rope over the stout bough yonder. Sir Descandol, last night I knew gratitude for your sage advice, but today I wonder if your motives might not have been simple avarice, that our gold might be reserved for your own use."

Sir Descandol demurred. "Not altogether! I intended first to spare you the humiliation of robbery by a pair of twitterlings."

"Then that was an act of gentility. A pity that we cannot spend an hour or two in an exchange of civilities."

"I am nothing loath," said Sir Descandol.

"Time presses. Bode, bind Sir Descandol's arms and legs, so that he need not perform all manner of graceless postures. We respect his dignity no less than he does ours."

"That is very good of you," said Sir Descandol.

"Now then! Bode, Cargus, Garstang! Heave away hard; hoist Sir Descandol high!"

Faurfisk was buried in the forest under a filigree of sun and shadow. Yane wandered among the corpses and recovered his arrows. Sir Descandol was lowered, the rope reclaimed, coiled and hung on the saddle of Faurfisk's tall black horse. Without a backward glance, the company of six rode away through the forest.

Silence, emphasized rather than broken by far sweet bird-calls, closed in on them. As the day wore on the sunlight passing through foliage became charged with a tawny suffusion, creating shadows dark, deep and tinged with maroon, or mauve, or dark blue. No one spoke; hooves made only muffled sounds.

At sundown the six halted beside a small pond. At midnight, while Aillas and Scharis were on watch, a company of pale blue lights twinkled and flickered through the forest. An hour later a voice in the distance spoke three distinct words. They were unintelligible to Aillas but Scharis rose to his feet and raised his head almost as if to reply.

In wonder Aillas asked: "Did you understand the voice?"

"No."

"Then why did you start to answer?"

"It was almost as if he were talking to me."

"Why should he do that?"

"I don't know...Such things frighten me."

Aillas asked no more questions.

The sun rose; the six ate bread and cheese and continued on their way. The landscape opened to glades and meadows; out-crops of crumbling gray rock lay across the road; trees grew gnarled and twisted.

During the afternoon the sky turned hazy; the sunlight became golden and wan, like the light of autumn. Clouds drifted from the west, ever heavier and more menacing.

Not far from where the road crossed the head of a long

meadow, at the back of a formal garden, stood a palace of gracious if fanciful architecture. A portal of carved marble guarded the entry, which was carefully raked with gravel. In the doorway of the gatehouse stood a gatekeeper in a livery of dark red and blue diaper.

The six halted to inspect the palace, which offered the prospect of shelter for the night, if ordinary standards of hospitality were in force.

Aillas dismounted and approached the gatehouse. The gatekeeper bowed politely. He wore a wide hat of black felt low down his forehead and a small black domino across the top of his face. Beside him leaned a ceremonial halberd; he carried no other weapons.

Aillas spoke: "Who is lord of the palace yonder?"

"This is Villa Meroë, sir, a simple country retreat, where my lord Daldace takes pleasure in the company of his friends."

"This is a lonely region for such a villa."

"That is the case, sir."

"We do not wish to trouble Lord Daldace, but perhaps he might allow us shelter for the night."

"Why not proceed directly to the villa? Lord Daldace is generous and hospitable."

Aillas turned to appraise the villa. "In all candor, I am uneasy. This is the Forest Tantrevalles, and there is a shimmer of enchantment to this place, and we would prefer to avoid events beyond our understanding."

The gatekeeper laughed. "Sir, your caution is in some degree well-founded. Still, you may safely take shelter in the villa and no one will offer you harm. Those enchantments which affect revelers at Villa Meroë will pass you by. Eat only your own victual; drink only the wine now in your possession. In short, take none of the food or drink which is sure to be offered, and the enchantments will serve only to amuse you."

"And if we were to accept food and drink?"

"You might be delayed in your mission, sir."

Aillas turned to his companions, who had gathered at his back. "You heard this man's remarks; he seems truthful and speaks, so it seems, without duplicity. Shall we risk enchantment, or a night riding through the storm?"

"So long as we use only our own provisions and take nothing served within, we would seem to be secure," said Garstang. "Is that right, friend gatekeeper?"

"Sir, that is quite correct."

"Then I for one would prefer bread and cheese in the comfort of the villa, to the same bread and cheese in the wind and rain of the night."

"That is a reasonable analysis," said Aillas. "What of you others? Bode?"

"I would ask this good gatekeeper why he wears the domino."

"Sir, that is the custom here, which in all courtesy you should obey. If you choose to visit Villa Meroë, you must wear the domino I will give you."

"It is most odd," murmured Scharis. "And most intriguing."

"Cargus? Yane?"

"The place reeks of magic," growled Yane.

"It frightens me none," said Cargus. "I know a cantrip against enchantments; I will eat bread and cheese and turn my face away from the marvels."

"So be it," said Aillas. "Gatekeeper, please announce us to Lord Daldace. This is Sir Garstang, a knight of Lyonesse; these are the gentlemen Yane, Scharis, Bode and Cargus, of various parts, and I am Aillas, a gentleman of Troicinet."

"Lord Daldace, through his magic, already expects you," said the gatekeeper. "Be good enough to wear these dominoes. You may leave your horses here and I will have them ready for you in the morning. Naturally, take with you your meat and drink."

The six walked the graveled path, through the garden and across a terrace to Villa Meroë. The setting sun, shining for an instant under the lowering clouds, cast a shaft of light at the doorway, where stood a tall man in a splendid costume of dark red velvet. Black hair, clipped short, curled close to his head. A short beard shrouded jaws and chin; a black domino masked his eyes.

"Gentlemen, I am Lord Daldace, and you are welcome to Villa Meroë, where I hope you will be comfortable for as long as you care to stay."

"Our thanks, your Lordship. We will trouble you a single night only, as important business compels us to the road."

"In that case, sirs, be advised that we are somewhat sybaritic in our tastes, and our entertainments are often beguiling. Eat nothing and drink nothing but your own stuffs, and you will find no difficulties. I hope you will not think the worse of me for the warning."

"Not at all, sir. Our concern is not revelry but only for shelter against the storm."

Lord Daldace made an expansive gesture. "When you have refreshed yourselves, we will talk further."

A footman led the group to a chamber furnished with six couches. An adjacent bathroom offered a flowing fall of warm water, soap of palm and aloes, towels of crushed linen. After bathing they ate the food and drink which they had brought from their saddle-bags.

"Eat well," said Aillas. "Let us not leave this room hungry."

"Better that we did not leave this room at all," observed Yane.

"Impossible!" declared Scharis. "Have you no curiosity?"

"In matters of this sort, very little. I am going directly to that couch."

Cargus said, "I am a great reveler, when the mood comes on me. To watch the revels of other folk sours my disposition. I too will take to the couch, and dream my own dreams."

Bode said: "I will stay; I need no persuasion."

Aillas turned to Garstang. "What of you?"

"If you stay, I will stay. If you go, I will stand by your side, to guard you from greed and intemperance."

"Scharis?"

"I could not contain myself in here. I will go, at least to wander and stare through the holes of my mask."

"Then I will follow, and ward you as Garstang guards me, and we both shall guard Garstang, so we will be reasonably secure."

Scharis shrugged. "As you say."

"Who knows what might occur? We will wander and stare together."

The three masked their faces and left the chamber.

Tall archways overlooked the terrace, where flowering jasmine, orange, elethea and cleanotis perfumed the air. On a settee padded with cushions of dark green velvet the three sat to rest. The clouds which had threatened a great storm had moved to the side; the night air was soft and mild.

A tall man in a dark red costume, with black curly hair and a small black beard, paused to survey them. "Well then, what do you think of my villa?"

Garstang shook his head. "I am beyond speech."

Aillas said: "There is too much to comprehend."

Scharis' face was pale and his eyes shone, but, like Garstang, he had nothing to say.

Aillas gestured to the couch. "Sit awhile with us, Lord Daldace."

"With pleasure."

"We are curious," said Aillas. "There is such overwhelming beauty here; it has almost the unreal quality of a dream."

Lord Daldace looked about as if seeing the villa for the first time. "What are dreams? Ordinary experience is a dream. The eyes, the ears, the nose: they present pictures on the brain, and these pictures are called 'reality.' At night, when we dream, other pictures, of source unknown, are impinged. Sometimes the dream-images are more real than 'reality.' Which is solid, which illusion? Why trouble to make the distinction? When tasting a delicious wine, only a pedant analyzes every component of the flavor. When we admire a beautiful maiden, do we evaluate the particular bones of her skull? I am sure we do not. Accept beauty on its own terms: this is the creed of Villa Meroë."

"What of satiation?"

Lord Daldace smiled. "Have you ever known satiation in a dream?"

"Never," said Garstang. "A dream is always most vivid."

Scharis said: "Both life and dreams are things of exquisite fragility. A thrust, a cut—they are gone: away, like a sweet scent on the wind."

Garstang said: "Perhaps you will answer this: why is everyone masked?"

"A whim, a crotchet, a fancy, a fad! I might counter your question with another. Consider your face: is it not a mask of skin? You three, Aillas, Garstang and Scharis, each is a person favored by nature; your skin-mask commends you to the world. Your comrade Bode is not so fortunate; he would rejoice to go forever with a mask before his face."

"None of your company appears ill-favored," said Garstang. "The gentlemen are noble and the ladies are beautiful. So much is evident despite the masks."

"Perhaps so. Still, late of night, when lovers become intimate and disrobe together, the last article to be removed is the mask."

Scharis asked: "And who plays the music?"

Aillas listened, as did Garstang. "I hear no music."

"Nor I," said Garstang.

"It is very soft," said Lord Daldace. "In fact, perhaps it is unheard." He rose to his feet. "I hope I have satisfied your wonder?"

"Only a churl would require more of you," said Aillas. "You have been more than courteous."

"You are pleasant guests, and I am sorry that you must go on the morrow. But now, a lady awaits me. She is new to Villa Meroë and I am anxious to enjoy her pleasure."

"A last question," said Aillas. "If new guests come, the old ones must leave, or they would congest every hall and chamber of Meroë. When they leave, where do they go?"

Lord Daldace laughed softly. "Where go the folk who live in your dreams when at last you wake?" He bowed and departed.

Three maidens stopped before them. One spoke with mischievous boldness. "Why do you sit so quietly? Do we lack charm?"

The three men rose to their feet. Aillas found himself facing a slender girl with pale blonde hair and features of flower-like delicacy. Eyes of violet-blue looked at him from behind the black domino. Aillas' heart gave a startled jerk, of both pain and joy. He started to speak, then checked himself. "Excuse me," he muttered. "I am not feeling well." He turned away, to find that Garstang had done the same. Garstang said: "It is impossible. She resembles someone who was once very dear to me."

"They are dreams," said Aillas. "They are very hard to resist. Is Lord Daldace so ingenuous, after all?"

"Let us return to our couches. I don't care for dreams quite so real... Where is Scharis?"

The maidens and Scharis were not to be seen. "We must find him," said Aillas. "His temperament will betray him."

They walked the chambers of Meroë, ignoring the soft lights, the fascinations, the tables laden with delicacies. At last they found Scharis, in a small courtyard opening on the terrace. He sat in the company of four others, blowing soft tones from the pipes of a syrinx. The others played various different instruments, to produce music of a haunting sweetness. Close beside Scharis sat a slim dark-haired maiden; she leaned so closely to him that her hair spread across his shoulder. In one hand she held a goblet of purple wine, which she sipped, and then, when the music stopped, she offered to Scharis.

323

Scharis, in rapt abstraction, took it in his hand, but Aillas leaned low over the balustrade and snatched it away. "Scharis, what has come over you? Come along, we must sleep! Tomorrow we will put this dream-castle behind us; it is more dangerous than all the werewolves of Tantrevalles!"

Scharis slowly rose to his feet. He looked down at the girl. "I must go."

The three men returned silently to the sleeping chamber, where Aillas said: "You almost drank from the goblet."

"I know."

"Did you drink before?"

"No." Scharis hesitated. "I kissed the girl, who is much like someone I once loved. She had been drinking wine and a drop hung on her lips. I tasted it."

Aillas groaned. "Then I must discover the antidote from Lord Daldace!"

Again Garstang joined him; the two roamed Meroë but nowhere could they find Lord Daldace.

The lights began to be extinguished; the two at last returned to their chamber. Scharis either slept or feigned sleep.

Morning light entered through high windows. The six men arose and somewhat glumly considered each other. Aillas said heavily: "The day has started. Let us be on our way; we will make our breakfast along the road."

At the gate the horses awaited them though the gatekeeper was nowhere to be seen. Not knowing what he might discover if he looked back, Aillas resolutely kept his head turned away from Villa Meroë. His comrades did likewise, so he noticed.

"Away, then, along the road, and let us forget the palace of dreams!"

The six galloped away with cloaks flapping behind. A mile down the road they halted to take breakfast. Scharis sat by himself to the side. His mood was abstracted and he showed no appetite.

Strange, thought Aillas, how loosely the trousers hung about his legs. And why did his jacket sag so oddly?

Aillas sprang to his feet but not before Scharis slid to the ground, where his clothes lay empty. Aillas dropped to his knees. Scharis' hat fell away; his face, a mask of a substance like pale parchment, slipped askew, and looked—somewhere.

Aillas slowly rose to his feet. He turned to ponder the way

they had come. Bode came up beside him. "Let us ride on," said Bode gruffly. "Nothing can be gained by returning."

The road veered somewhat to the right, and, as the day progressed, began to lead up and down, to follow the contours of swells and swales. The soil grew thin; outcrops of rock appeared; the forest dwindled to sparse straggles of stunted yew and oak, then drew away to the east.

The day was full of wind; clouds raced overhead and the five rode through alternate spaces of sun and shade.

Sunset found them on a desolate fell among hundreds of weathered granite boulders as tall as a man or taller. Garstang and Cargus both declared them to be sarsens, though they stood without perceptible order or regularity.

Beside a rivulet the five halted for the night. They made beds of bracken and passed the night in no great comfort but disturbed only by the whistling of the wind.

At sunrise the five once more took to the saddle and proceeded south along the Trompada, here little more than a path wandering among the sarsen-stones.

At noon the road swung down from the fells to rejoin the River Siss, then followed the riverbank south.

Halfway through the afternoon the road arrived at a fork. By deciphering an age-worn sign-post, they learned that Bittershaw Road angled away to the southeast while the Trompada crossed a bridge and followed the Siss in a southerly direction.

The travelers crossed the bridge and half a mile along the road encountered a peasant leading a donkey loaded with faggots.

Aillas held up his hand; the peasant drew back in alarm. "What now? If you be robbers, I carry no gold, and the same is true even if you not be robbers."

"Enough of your foolishness," growled Cargus. "Where is the best and nearest inn?"

The peasant blinked in perplexity. "The 'best' and the 'nearest,' eh? Is it two inns you want?"

"One is enough," said Aillas.

"In these parts inns are rare. The Old Tower down the way might serve your needs, if you are not over-nice."

"We are nice," said Yane, "but not over-nice. Where is this inn?"

"Fare forward two miles until the road turns to rise for the mountain. A bit of a track leads to the Old Tower."

Aillas tossed him a penny. "Many thanks to you."

Two miles the five followed the river-road. The sun dropped behind the mountains; the four rode in shadow, under pines and cedars.

A bluff overlooked the Siss; here the road turned sharply up the hillside. A trail continued along the side of the bluff, back and forth under heavy foliage, until the outline of a tall round tower stood dark against the sky.

The five rode around the tower under a mouldering wall, to come out upon a flat area overlooking the river a hundred feet below. Of the ancient castle only a corner tower and a wing stood intact. A boy came and took their horses to what had once been the great hall and which now served as a stable.

The five entered the old tower, and found themselves in a place of gloom and a grandeur impregnable to present indignities. A fire in the fireplace sent flickering light across a great round room. Slabs of stone flagged the floor; the walls were unrelieved by hangings. Fifteen feet overhead a balcony circled the room; with another above in the shadows; and above still a third, almost invisible by reason of the gloom.

Rough tables and benches had been placed near the fire. To the other side a fire burned in a second fireplace; here, behind a counter, an old man with a thin face and wispy white hair worked energetically over pots and pans. He seemed to have six hands, all reaching, shaking and stirring. He basted a lamb where it turned on a spit, shook up a pan of pigeons and quails, swung other pots this way and that on their pot-hooks, so that they might receive the proper heat.

For a moment Aillas watched in respectful attention, marveling at the old man's dexterity. At last, taking advantage of a pause in the work, he asked: "Sir, you are the landlord?"

"Correct, my lord. I claim that role, if these makeshift premises deserve such a dignity."

"Dignity is the least of our concerns if you can provide us lodging for the night. From the evidence of my eyes I feel assured of a proper supper."

"Lodging here is of the simplest; you sleep in hay above the stable. My premises offer nothing better and I am too old to make changes."

"How is your ale?" asked Bode. "Serve us cool clear bitter and you will hear no complaints."

"You relieve all my anxieties, since I brew good ale. Be seated, if you will."

The five took seats by the fire and congratulated themselves that they need not spend another windy night in the bracken. A portly woman served them ale in beechwood cups, which by some means accentuated the quality of the brew, and Bode declared: "The landlord is just! He will hear no complaints from me."

Aillas surveyed the other guests where they sat at their tables. There were seven: an elderly peasant and his wife, a pair of peddlers and three young men who might have been woodsmen. Into the room now came a bent old woman, cloaked heavily in gray, with a cowl gathered over her head so that her face was concealed in shadow.

She paused to look about the room. Aillas felt her gaze hesitate as it reached him. Then, crouching and hobbling, she crossed the room to sit at a far table among the shadows.

The portly woman brought their supper: quail, pigeons and partridge on slabs of bread soaked in the grease of the frying; cuts of roasted lamb which exhaled a fragrance of garlic and rosemary, in the Galician style, with a salad of cress and young greens: a meal far better than any they had expected.

As Aillas supped he watched the cloaked woman at the far table, where she took her own supper. Her manners were unsettling; leaning forward, she gobbled up her food at a snap. Aillas watched in covert fascination, and noticed that the woman seemed also to peer toward him from time to time behind the shadow cast by her cowl. She bent her head low to snap up a morsel of meat and her cloak slipped away from her foot.

Aillas spoke to his comrades. "The old woman yonder: notice her and tell me what you see."

Garstang muttered in amazement: "She has a chicken's foot!"

Aillas said, "She is a witch, with a fox mask and the legs of a great fowl. Twice she has attacked me; twice I cut her into two sections; each time she repaired herself."

The witch, turning to stare, noticed their gazes and hastily drew back her foot and darted another look to see if anyone had noticed the lapse. Aillas and his companions pretended indifference. She turned once more to her food, snapping and gulping.

"She forgets nothing," said Aillas, "and certainly she will try to kill me, if not here, then from ambush along the trail."

"In that case," said Bode, "let us kill her first, at this very moment."

Aillas grimaced. "So it must be, even though all will blame us for killing a helpless old woman."

"Not when they see her feet," said Cargus.

"Let us be to it, and have done," said Bode. "I am ready."

"A moment," said Aillas. "I will do the deed. Make your swords ready. One scratch of her claws means death; allow her no scope to spring."

The witch seemed to divine the quality of their conversation. Before they could move she arose and hobbled quickly away into the shadows, and disappeared through a low archway.

Aillas drew his sword and went to the landlord. "You have been entertaining an evil witch; she must be killed."

While the landlord looked on in bewilderment Aillas ran back to the archway and looked through but could see nothing in the dark and dared not proceed. He turned back to the landlord. "Where leads the archway?"

"To the old wing, and the chambers overhead: all ruins."

"Give me a candle."

At a slight sound Bode looked up, to discover the fox-masked woman on the first balcony. With a scream she leapt down at Aillas; Bode thrust out with a stool and struck her aside. She hissed and screamed again, then leapt at Bode with legs outstretched and clawed the length of his face, before Aillas once more hacked her head from her body, which, as before started a mad canter back and forth, buffeting itself against the walls. Cargus forced it down with a bench and Yane hacked away the legs.

Bode lay on his back, clawing at the stone with clenched fingers. His tongue protruded; his face turned black and he died.

Aillas cried in a guttural voice: "This time the fire! Cut this vile thing to bits! Landlord, bring logs and faggots! The fire must burn hot and long!"

The fox-faced head set up a horrid wailing. "No fire! Give me not to the fire!"

The grisly task was complete. Under roaring flames the witch's flesh burned to ashes and the bones crumbled to dust. The guests, pale and dispirited, had gone to their beds in the hay; the landlord and his spouse worked with mops and buckets to clean their soiled floor.

With morning only hours away Aillas, Garstang, Cargus and Yane sat wearily at a table and watched the fire become embers.

The landlord brought them ale. "This is a terrible event! I assure you it is not the policy of the house."

"Sir, do not in any way blame yourself. Be happy that we have made an end to the creature. You and your wife have given noble assistance and you shall not suffer for it."

With the first glimmer of dawn the four buried Bode in a quiet shaded area, at one time a rose garden. They left Bode's horse with the landlord as well as five gold crowns from Bode's pouch, and rode sadly down the hill to the Trompada.

The four toiled up a steep stony valley by a road which twisted and sidled back and forth, up and around bluffs and boulders, and eventually gained to wind-haunted Glayrider Gap. A side road led off across the moors toward Oäldes; the Trompada swung south and slanted down a long declivity, past a series of ancient tin mines to the town Market Flading. At the Tin Man Inn the four travelers, weary after the work of the night before and the toilsome ride of the day, gratefully supped on mutton and barley, and slept on straw pallets in an upper chamber.

In the morning they set out once more along the Trompada, which now followed the North Evander along a wide shallow valley toward the far purple bulk of Tac Tor.

At noon, with Tintzin Fyral only five miles to the south, the land began to rise and close in beside the gorge of the North Evander. Three miles farther along, with the nearness of Tintzin Fyral impressing a sense of menace upon the air, Aillas discovered a dim trail leading away and up a gulley, which he thought might be that trail by which, so long ago, he had hoped to descend from Tac Tor.

The track climbed a long spur which trailed down from Tac Tor like the splayed root of a tree, then followed the rounded ridge by a relatively easy route. Aillas led the way up the trail to the hollow where he had camped, only yards below the flat summit of Tac Tor.

He found the Never-fail where he had left it. As before the tooth pointed something north of east. "In that direction," said Aillas, "is my son, and this is where I must go."

"You can choose from two routes," said Garstang. "Back the way we came, then east; or through Lyonesse by Old Street, then north into Dahaut. The first may be shorter, but the second avoids the forest, and in the end is probably faster."

"The second, by all means," said Aillas.

The four passed by Kaul Bocach and entered Lyonesse without incident. At Nolsby Sevan they swung to the east along Old Street, and after four days of hard riding arrived at the town Audelart. Here Garstang took leave of his comrades. "Twanbow Hall is only twenty miles south. I shall be home for supper and my adventures will be the marvel of all." He embraced his three comrades. "Needless to say, you will always be welcome guests at Twanbow! We have come a long way together; we have known much hardship. Never shall I forget!"

"Nor I."

"Nor I."

"Nor I."

Aillas, Cargus and Yane watched Garstang ride south until he disappeared. Aillas heaved a sigh. "Now we are three."

"One by one we dwindle," said Cargus.

"Come," said Yane. "Let us be off. I lack patience for sentiment."

The three departed Audelart by Old Street and three days later they arrived at Tatwillow, where Old Street crossed Icnield Way. The Never-fail pointed north, in the direction of Avallon: a good sign, or so it would seem, since the direction avoided the forest.

They set off up Icnield Way toward Avallon in Dahaut.

25

GLYNETH AND DHRUN had joined Dr. Fidelius at the Glassblowers Fair in Hazelwood. For the first few days the association was tentative and wary. Glyneth and Dhrun conducted themselves as if walking on eggs, meanwhile watching Dr. Fidelius sidelong that they might anticipate any sudden irrationalities or quick fits of fury. But Dr. Fidelius, after assuring their comfort, showed such even and impersonal politeness that Glyneth began to worry that Dr. Fidelius did not like them.

Shimrod, watching the two from his disguise with the same surreptitious interest they gave him, was impressed by their composure and charmed by their desire to please him. They were, he thought, an extraordinary pair: clean, neat, intelligent and loving. Glyneth's native cheerfulness at times broke free into bursts of exuberance which she quickly controlled lest she annoy Dr. Fidelius. Dhrun tended to long periods of silence, while he sat gazing blankly into the sunlight, thinking his private thoughts.

Upon leaving the Glassblowers Fair, Shimrod turned his wagon north toward the market-town Porroigh and the yearly Sheep-sellers Fair. Late in the afternoon Shimrod drove the wagon off the road and halted in a little glen beside a stream. Glyneth gathered sticks and set a fire; Shimrod erected a tripod, hung a kettle and cooked a stew of chicken, onions, turnips, meadow-greens and parsley, with mustard-seed and garlic for seasoning. Glyneth gathered cress for a salad, and found a clump of morels which Shimrod added to the stew. Dhrun sat quietly by, listening to the wind in the trees and the crackle of the fire.

The three dined well, and sat back to enjoy the dusk. Shimrod looked from one to the other. "I must make a report to you. I have traveled Dahaut now for months, plying from fair to fair, and I never realized my loneliness until these last few days that you two have been with me."

Glyneth heaved a small sigh of relief. "That is good news for us, since we like traveling with you. I don't dare say it's good luck; I might start up the curse."

"Tell me about this curse."

Dhrun and Glyneth told their separate tales and together reported the events they had shared. "So now we are anxious to find Rhodion, the king of all fairies, so that he may remove the curse and give Dhrun back his eyes."

"He'll never pass the skirl of fairy pipes," said Shimrod. "Sooner or later he'll stop to listen, and, rest assured, I too will keep lookout."

Dhrun asked wistfully: "Have you ever yet seen him?"

"Truth to tell, I have been watching for someone else."

Glyneth said: "I know who he is: a man with sore knees, which clack and creak as he walks."

"And how have you come by that knowledge?"

"Because you cry out often about sore knees. When someone comes forward, you look into his face rather than his legs, and you are always disappointed. You give him a jar of salve and send him away still limping."

Shimrod showed a wry smile to the fire. "Am I so transparent?"

"Not really," said Glyneth modestly. "In fact, I think you are quite mysterious."

Shimrod now laughed aloud. "Why do you say that?"

"Oh, for instance, how did you learn to mix so many medicines?"

"No mystery whatever. A few are common remedies, known everywhere. The rest are pulverized bone mixed with lard or neat's-foot oil, with different flavors. They never harm and sometimes they heal. But more than sell medicines I want to find the man with the sore knees. Like Rhodion he comes to fairs and sooner or later I will find him."

Dhrun asked: "Then what will happen?"

"He will tell me where to find someone else."

From south to north across the land went the wagon of Dr. Fidelius and his two young colleagues, pausing at fairs and festivals from Dafnes on the River Lull to Duddlebatz under the stone barrens of Godelia. There were long days of traveling by shaded country lanes, up hill and down dale, through dark woods and old villages. There were nights by firelight while the full moon rode through clouds, and other nights under a sky full of stars. One afternoon, as they crossed a desolate heath, Glyneth heard plaintive sounds from the ditch beside the road. Jumping from the wagon and peering among the thistles she discovered a pair of spotted kittens which had been abandoned and left to die. Glyneth called and the kittens ran anxiously to her. She took them to the wagon, in tears over their plight. When Shimrod gave her leave to keep them, she threw her arms around his neck and kissed him, and Shimrod knew he was her slave forever, even had it not been the case before.

Glyneth named the kittens Smirrish and Sneezer, and at once set about training them to tricks.

From the north they fared into the west, through Ammarsdale and Scarhead, to Tins in the Ulfland March, thirty miles north of the awesome Ska fortress at Poëlitetz. This was a grim land and they were happy to turn east once more, along the Murmeil River.

The summer was long; the days were bittersweet times for each of the three. Strange small misfortunes regularly troubled Dhrun: hot water scalded his hand; rain soaked his bed; as he went to relieve himself behind the hedge he fell into the nettles. Never did he complain, and so earned Shimrod's respect, and Shimrod, from initial skepticism, began to accept the reality of the curse. One day Dhrun stepped on a thorn, driving it deep into his heel. Shimrod removed it while Dhrun sat silent, biting his lip; and Shimrod was moved to hug him and pat his head. "You're a brave lad. One way or another we'll end this curse. At the very worst it can last only seven years."

As always, Dhrun thought a moment before speaking. Then he said: "A thorn is only a trifle. Do you know the bad luck I fear? That you should tire of us and put us off the wagon."

Shimrod laughed and felt his eyes grow moist. He gave Dhrun another hug. "It would not be by my choice: I promise you that. I could not manage without you."

"Still, bad luck is bad luck."

"True. No one knows what the future holds."

Almost immediately after a spark flew from the fire and landed on Dhrun's ankle.

"Ouch," said Dhrun. "More luck."

Each day brought new experiences. At Playmont Fair, Duke

Jocelyn of Castle Foire sponsored a magnificent tournament-at-arms, where armored knights played at combat, and competed in a new sport known as jousting. Mounted on strong horses and wearing full regalia, they charged each other with padded poles, each trying to dislodge his adversary.

From Playmont they traveled to Long Danns, skirting close by the forest of Tantrevalles, arriving at noon and finding the fair in full swing. Shimrod unhitched his marvelous two-headed horses, gave them fodder, lowered the side panel of the wagon, to serve as a platform, raised on high a sign:

DR. FIDELIUS

THAUMATURGE, PAN-SOPHIST, MOUNTEBANK

Relief for Cankers, Gripes and Spasms

SPECIAL TREATMENT OF SORE KNEES
Expert Advice: Free

He then retired into the wagon to don his black robes and necromancer's hat.

On each side of the platform Dhrun and Glyneth beat drums. They were dressed alike, as page-boys, with low white shoes, tight blue hose and pantaloons, doublets striped vertically in blue and black, with white hearts stitched to the black stripes, and low crush-caps of black velvet.

Dr. Fidelius stepped out on the platform. He called to the onlookers: "Sirs and ladies!" Here Dr. Fidelius pointed to his sign. "You will observe that I style myself 'mountebank.' My reason is simple. Who calls a butterfly frivolous? Who insults a cow with the word 'bovine'? Who will call a self-admitted mountebank a fraud?

"Then, am I for a fact mountebank, fraud and charlatan?" Glyneth jumped up to stand beside him. "You must judge for yourselves. Notice here my pretty associate—if you have not already noticed her. Glyneth, open wide your mouth. Sirs and ladies, observe this aperture! These are teeth, this is a tongue, beyond is the oral cavity, in its natural state. Watch now, as I insert into this mouth an orange, neither large, nor yet small, but of exact and proper size. Glyneth, close your mouth, if you will, and if you can...Excellent. Now, sirs and ladies, observe the girl with the distended cheeks. I tap her on the right and on the left, and hey presto! The cheeks are as before! Glyneth, what have you done with the orange? This is most extraordinary! Open your mouth; we are bewildered!"

Glyneth obediently opened her mouth and Dr. Fidelius peered within. He exclaimed in surprise. "What is this?" He reached with thumb and forefinger. "It is not an orange; it is a beautiful red rose! What more is here? Look, sirs and ladies! Three fine ripe cherries! What else? What are these? Horseshoe nails! One, two, three, four, five, six! And what is this! The horseshoe itself! Glyneth, how is this possible? Have you any more surprises? Open wide your mouth... By the moon and sun, a mouse! Glyneth, how can you consume such stuff?"

Glyneth answered in her bright clear voice: "Sir! I have been taking your digestive pastilles!"

Dr. Fidelius threw his hands in the air. "Enough! You defeat me at my own trade!" And Glyneth jumped down from the platform.

"Now then, as to my potions and lotions, my powders, pills and purges; my analepts and anodynes: are they the alleviants I claim them to be? Sirs and ladies, I will make this guarantee: if, upon taking my remedies, you mortify and die, you return the unused medicine for a partial refund. Where else will you hear such a guarantee?

"I am particularly expert in the treatment of sore knees, especially those which creak, clack, or otherwise complain. If you or someone you know is afflicted with sore knees, then I want to see the sufferer.

"Now let me present my other associate: the noble and talented Sir Dhrun. He will play you tunes on the fairy-pipes, to make you laugh, to make you cry, to set your heels to twitching. Meanwhile, Glyneth will dispense the medicines while I prescribe. Sirs and ladies, a final word! You are hereby notified that my embrocations burn and tingle as if distilled from liquid flame. My medicines taste vilely, of cimiter, dogbane and gall: the body quickly returns to robust health so that it need assimilate no more of my foul concoctions! That is the secret of my success. Music, Sir Dhrun!"

As she circulated through the crowd Glyneth watched carefully for a person in a nut-brown suit and a scarlet feather in his green cap, especially one who heard the music with pleasure; but on this sunny forenoon at Long Danns, hard by the Forest of Tantrevalles, no such person showed himself, nor did any obvious scoundrel, of dark visage and long nose, come to Dr. Fidelius for treatment of his sore knees.

In the afternoon a breeze began to blow from the west, to set the banners fluttering. Glyneth brought out a table with high legs and a tall stool for Dhrun. From the wagon she carried a basket. As Dhrun played a jig on the pipes, Glyneth brought out her black and white cats. She tapped the table with a baton and the cats raised on their hind legs and danced in time to the music, hopping and skipping back and forth across the table, and a crowd quickly gathered. At the back a fox-faced young man, small and dapper, seemed to be especially enthusiastic. He snapped his fingers to the music, and presently began to dance, kicking this way and that with great agility. He wore, so Glyneth noted, a green cap with a long red feather. Hurriedly she put her cats in the basket and sidling up behind the dancing man, snatched off his cap, and ran to the back of the wagon. In astonishment the young man chased after her. "What are you up to? Give me my hat!"

"No," said Glyneth. "Not till you grant my wishes."

"Are you mad? What foolishness is this? I can't grant wishes for myself, let alone you. Now give me my cap, or I'll have to take it from you, and beat you well in the bargain."

"Never," declared Glyneth bravely. "You are Rhodion. I have your hat, and I will never let it go until you obey me."

"We'll see about that!" The young man seized Glyneth, and they struggled until the horses snorted, reared and showing long white teeth lunged at the young man, who drew back in fear.

Shimrod jumped down from the wagon and the young man cried out in fury: "This girl of yours is mad! She seizes my cap and runs off with it, and when I ask for it, most civilly, she says no, and names me Rhodion or something similar. My name is Tibbalt; I am chandler at the village Witherwood and I have come to the fair to buy wax. Almost instantly I am snatched hatless by a mad hoyden, who then insists that I obey her! Have you ever heard the like?"

Shimrod gave his head a grave shake. "She is not a bad girl, just a bit impetuous and full of pranks." He stepped forward. "Sir, allow me." He brushed aside Tibbalt's brown hair. "Glyneth, observe! This gentleman's ear-lobes are well developed."

Glyneth looked and nodded. "That is so."

Tibbalt demanded: "What is this to do with my hat?"

"Allow me one more favor," said Shimrod. "Show me your hand... Glyneth, notice the fingernails; there is no trace of web and the fingernails are not filmy."

Glyneth nodded. "I see. So I may give him his hat?"

"Yes indeed, especially since the gentleman exudes the odor of bayberry and bees-wax."

Glyneth returned the hat. "Please, sir, forgive me my prank."

Shimrod gave Tibbalt a pottery jar: "With our compliments, please accept this half-gill of hair pomade, which will cause eyebrows, beard and mustache to grow silky and fine."

Tibbalt departed in good spirits. Glyneth went back to her table in front of the wagon and reported her mistake to Dhrun, who merely shrugged, and once again began to play the pipes. Glyneth again produced her cats, which hopped and danced with zeal, to the great wonder of those who halted to watch. "Wonderful, wonderful!" declared a portly little gentleman with spindle-shanks, thin ankles, long thin feet in green leather shoes with preposterous rolled-up toes. "My lad, where did you learn to play the pipes?"

"Sir, it is a gift from the fairies."

"What a marvel! A true gift of magic!"

The wind blew a sudden gust; the gentleman's green hat whisked from his head and fell at Glyneth's feet. She picked it up and noticed the scarlet feather. Dubiously she looked at the man who smilingly held out his hand. "Thank you, my pretty dear. I will reward you with a kiss."

Glyneth looked at the outstretched hand which was pale and plump, with small delicate fingers. The nails were carefully tended and polished milky-pink. Was this film? The flaps of skin between the fingers: was this web? Glyneth slowly looked up and met the gentleman's eyes. They were fawn-brown. Sparse sandy-red hair curled past his ears. Wind lifted the hair; in fascination Glyneth saw the lobes. They were small: no more than little dimples of pink tissue. She could not see the top of the ears.

The gentleman stamped his foot. "My hat, if you please!"

"One moment, sir, while I brush off the dust." Sneezer and Smirrish once more were popped into the basket, and Glyneth ran off with the hat.

With notable agility the gentleman bounded after her, and so maneuvered to press her back against the front of the wagon where they could not be seen from the common. "Now, miss, my hat, and then you shall have your kiss."

"You may not have your hat until you grant my wishes."

"Eh? What nonsense is this? Why should I grant your wishes?"

"Because, your Majesty, I hold your hat."

The gentleman looked at her sidewise. "Who do you think I am?"

"You are Rhodion, King of the Fairies."

"Ha ha hah! And what do you wish me to do?"

"It is not a great deal. Lift the curse which hangs upon Dhrun and give him back his eyes."

"All for my hat?" The portly gentleman advanced upòn Glyneth with his arms wide. "Now then, my downy little duckling, I will embrace you; what a sweet little armful you are! Now for the kiss, and perhaps something more..."

Glyneth ducked under his arms, jumped cleverly backward and forward, and ran behind the wagon. The gentleman chased after her, calling out endearments and imploring the return of his hat.

One of the horses thrust out its left head to snap viciously at the gentleman's buttocks. He only bounded the faster around the wagon, where Glyneth had halted, grinning in mingled mischief and distaste to see the portly little gentleman in such a state. "Now my little kitten! My adorable little comfit, come for your kiss! Remember, I am King Rat-a-tat-tat, or whatever his name, and I will grant your fondest desires! But first, let us explore beneath that brave doublet!"

Glyneth danced back and threw the hat at the gentleman's feet. "You are not King Rhodion; you are the town barber and a saucy lecher to boot. Take your hat and welcome!"

The gentleman uttered a hoot of exultant laughter. He clapped the hat to his head, and jumped high into the air, clicking his heels to both sides. In great glee he cried: "I tricked you! Oho! What joy to befuddle the mortals! You had my hat, you might have commanded me to your service! But now—"

Shimrod stepped from the shadows behind him and snatched away the hat. "But now"—he tossed the hat to Glyneth—"she has the hat once more, and you must do her bidding!"

King Rhodion stood crestfallen; his eyes round and woeful. "Take pity! Never force a poor old halfling to your will; it wearies me and causes a tumult of grief!"

"I am without pity," said Glyneth. She called Dhrun from his stool and brought him behind the wagon.

"This is Dhrun, who lived his youth at Thripsey Shee."

"Yes, the domain of Throbius, a merry shee, and notable for its pageant!"

"Dhrun was cast out and sent away with a mordet of bad luck on his head and now he is blind, because he watched the dryads as they bathed. You must remove the curse and give him the sight of his eyes!"

Rhodion blew into a little golden pipe and made a sign into the air. A minute passed. From over the wagon came the sounds of the fair, muted as if the fair stood at some far distance. With a small *pop!* King Throbius of Thripsey Shee stood beside them. He dropped to one knee before King Rhodion, who, with a benign gesture, allowed him to stand. "Throbius, here is Dhrun, whom once you nurtured at Thripsey Shee."

"In truth it is Dhrun; I remember him well. He was amiable and gave us all pleasure."

"Then why have you sent him off with a mordet?"

"Exalted! This was the work of a jealous imp, one Falael, who has been roundly punished for his spite."

"Why was not the mordet removed?"

"Exalted, that is bad policy, which induces irreverence among the mortals, to think that they need only sneeze or suffer a bit to gainsay our mordets."

"In this case it must be removed."

King Throbius approached Dhrun and touched his shoulder. "Dhrun, I bless you with the bounties of fortune! I dissolve the fluxes which have worked to your suffering; let the skites of malice who implemented these evils go twittering back to Thinsmole."

Dhrun's face was white and pinched. He listened, showing no quiver of muscle. In a thin voice he asked: "And what of my eyes?"

Throbius said courteously: "Good Sir Dhrun, you were blinded by the dryads. That was bad luck at its most extreme, but it was bad luck by ill chance and not by the malice of the mordet; and so the blinding is not our doing. It is work of the dryad Feodosia, and we cannot melt it."

Shimrod spoke: "Then go now to deal with the dryad Feodosia and offer her fairy favors if she will undo her magic."

"Ah, we captured Feodosia and another named Lauris as they slept; we took them and used them at our pageant for enter-

339

tainment. They became deranged with fury and fled to Arcady, where we cannot go and in any case she has lost all her fairy force."

"So: how will Dhrun's eyes be cured?"

"Not by fairy lore," said King Rhodion. "It lies beyond our craft."

"Then you must concede another boon."

"I want nothing," said Dhrun, in a stony voice. "They can give me only what they took."

Shimrod turned to Glyneth. "You hold the hat, and you may ask a boon."

"What?" cried King Rhodion. "This is the sheerest extortion! Did I not waft King Throbius here and dissolve the mordet?"

"You mended a harm of your own making. That is no boon; that is mere justice and where are the amends for his suffering?"

"He wants none, and we never give what is not wanted."

"Glyneth holds the hat; you must gratify her wishes."

Everyone turned to look at Glyneth. Shimrod asked her: "What do you wish most?"

"I want only to travel with you and Dhrun in this wagon forever."

Shimrod said, "But remember, all things change and we will not ride the wagon forever."

"Then I want to be with you and Dhrun forever."

"That is the future," said Rhodion. "It lies beyond my control, unless you wish me to kill the three of you at this instant and bury you together under the wagon."

Glyneth shook her head. "But you can help me. My cats often disobey and ignore my instructions. If I could talk with them, they could not pretend to misunderstand. I'd also like to talk with horses and birds and all other living things: even the trees and flowers, and the insects!"

King Rhodion grunted. "Trees and flowers neither talk nor listen. They only sigh among themselves. The insects would terrify you, if you heard their speech, and cause you nightmares."

"Then I can speak with birds and animals?"

"Take the lead amulet from my hat, wear it around your neck, and you will have your wish. Do not expect profound insights; birds and animals are usually foolish."

"Sneezer and Smirrish are clever enough," said Glyneth. "I will probably enjoy our conversations."

"Very well then," said portly King Rhodion. He took the hat from Glyneth's loose fingers, and, with wary attention for Shimrod, clapped it on his head. "The game is done; once again I have been outwitted by the mortals, though this time it has been almost a pleasure. Throbius, return as you will to Thripsey and I am away to Shadow Thawn."

King Throbius held up his hand. "One last matter. Perhaps I can make amends for the mordet. Dhrun, listen to me. Many months ago a young knight came to Thripsey Shee and demanded to know all knowledge concerning his son Dhrun. We exchanged gifts: for me a jewel of the color *smaudre*; for him a Never-fail pointing steadfast toward yourself. Has he not found you? Then he has been thwarted, or even killed, since his resolution was clear."

Dhrun spoke huskily: "What was his name?"

"He was Sir Aillas, a prince of Troicinet. I go." His form became tenuous, then disappeared. His voice came as if from far away: "I am gone."

King Rhodion paused on his spindle shanks, walked back around the front of the wagon. "And another small matter, for Glyneth's attention. The amulet is my seal; wearing it you need fear no harm from halflings: neither fairy nor imp, nor troll, nor double-troll. Beware ghosts and horse-heads, gray and white ogres, and things which live under the mire."

King Rhodion passed around the front of the wagon. When the three followed he was nowhere to be seen.

Glyneth went for her cat-basket, which she had stowed on the wagon's front seat, to find that Smirrish had pried the cover ajar and had almost gained his liberty.

Glyneth cried out: "Smirrish, this is sheer wickedness; you know that you are supposed to stay in the basket."

Smirrish said: "It is hot and stuffy inside. I prefer the open air, and I plan to explore the roof of the wagon."

"All very well, but now you must dance and entertain the folk who watch you in admiration."

"If they admire me so much, let them do their own dancing. Sneezer is equally earnest in this regard. We only dance to please you."

"That is sensible, since I feed you the finest milk and fish. Surly cats must make do with bread and water."

Sneezer, listening from within the basket, called out quickly, "Have no fear! If dance we must, then dance we will, though for the life of me, I can't understand why. I care not a fig for those who stop to watch."

The sun died on a couch of sultry clouds; outriders slid overhead to cover the evening sky and darkness came quickly to Long Danns' common. Dozens of small fires flickered and guttered in the cool damp breeze, and the peddlers, merchants and booth-tenders huddled over their suppers, eyes askance at the dismal sky, dreading the prospect of a rain which would drench them and their wares.

At the fire behind their wagon sat Shimrod, Glyneth and Dhrun, waiting for the soup to cook. The three sat absorbed in private thoughts: a silence finally broken by Shimrod. "The day has certainly been of interest."

"It could have been worse and it could have been better," said Glyneth. She looked at Dhrun, who sat, arms clenching knees, staring sightlessly into the fire; but he had nothing to say. "We've removed the curse, so at least we'll have no more bad luck. It won't be good luck, of course, until Dhrun can see again."

Shimrod fed the fire with fresh fuel. "I've searched across Dahaut for the man with the sore knees—this you know. If I don't find him at Avallon Fair we'll travel to Swer Smod in Lyonesse. If anyone can help it will be Murgen."

"Dhrun!" whispered Glyneth. "You mustn't cry!"

"I'm not crying."

"Yes, you are. Tears are running down your cheeks."

Dhrun blinked and put his wrist to his face. "Without you two to help me I'd starve, or the dogs would eat me."

"We wouldn't let you starve." Glyneth put her arm around his shoulders. "You're an important boy, and the son of a prince. Someday you'll be a prince as well."

"I hope so."

"So then, eat your soup, and you'll feel better. I notice also a nice slice of melon waiting for you."

26

CARFILHIOT'S CHAMBERS, at the top of Tintzin Fyral, were of modest dimension, with white plaster walls, scrubbed wooden floors and a bare sufficiency of furnishing. Carfilhiot wanted nothing more elaborate; that spare environment soothed his sometimes over-fervent nature.

Carfilhiot's routines were even. He tended to rise early, often at sun-up, then take a breakfast of fruit, sweet-cakes, raisins and perhaps a few pickled oysters. Always he breakfasted alone. At this time of day the sight and sound of other human beings offended him, and adversely affected the rest of the day.

Summer was changing to autumn; haze blurred the airy spaces over Vale Evander. Carfilhiot felt restless and uneasy, for reasons he could not define. Tintzin Fyral served many of his purposes very well; still it was a place remote: something of a backwater, and he had no command over that motility which other magicians, perhaps of higher order—Carfilhiot thought of himself as a magician—used daily as a matter of course. His fancies, escapades, novelties and caprices—perhaps they were no more than illusions. Time passed and despite his apparent activity, he had proceeded not a whit along the way to his goals. Had his enemies—or his friends—arranged to keep him isolated and ineffectual? Carfilhiot gave a petulant grunt. It could not be, but if so, such folk played dangerous games.

A year previously Tamurello had conveyed him to Faroli, that odd structure of wood and colored glass, deep within the forest. After three days of erotic play the two sat listening to the rain and watching the fire on the hearth. The time was midnight. Carfilhiot, whose mercurial mind never went quiet, said: "Truly, it is time that you taught me magical arts. Do I not deserve at least this from you?"

Tamurello spoke with a sigh. "What a strange and unfamiliar world if everyone were treated according to his deserts!"

Carfilhiot found the remark over-flippant. "So you mock me," he said sadly. "You think me too clumsy and foolish for the sleight."

Tamurello, a massive man whose veins were charged with the dark rank blood of a bull, laughed indulgently. He had heard the plaint before, and he made the same answer he had made before. "To become a sorcerer you must undergo many trials, and work at many dismal exercises. A number of these are profoundly uncomfortable, and perhaps calculated to dissuade those of small motivation."

"That philosophy is narrow and mean," said Carfilhiot.

"If and when you become a master sorcerer, you will guard the prerogatives as jealously as any," said Tamurello.

"Well, instruct me! I am ready to learn! I am strong of will!"

Once more Tamurello laughed. "My dear friend, you are too volatile. Your will may be like iron, but your patience is something less than invincible."

Carfilhiot made an extravagant gesture. "Are there no short-cuts? Certainly I can use magical apparatus without so many tiresome exercises."

"You already have apparatus."

"Shimrod's stuff? It is useless to me."

Tamurello was becoming bored with the discussion. "Most such apparatus is specialized and specific."

"My needs are specific," said Carfilhiot. "My enemies are like wild bees, which can never be conquered. They know where I am; when I set out in pursuit, they dissolve into shadows along the moor."

"Here I may be able to assist you," said Tamurello, "though without, I admit, any great enthusiasm."

On the following day he displayed a large map of the Elder Isles. "Here, as you will notice, is Vale Evander, here Ys, here Tintzin Fyral." He produced a number of manikins carved from blackthorn roots. "Name these little homologues with names, and place them on the map, and they will scuttle to position. Watch!" He took up one of the manikins and spat in its face. "I name you Casmir. Go to Casmir's place!" He put the manikin on the map; it seemed to scamper across the map to Lyonesse Town.

Carfilhiot counted the manikins. "Only twenty?" he cried. "I could use a hundred! I am at war with every petty baron of South Ulfland!"

"Name their names," said Tamurello. "We shall see how many you need."

Grudgingly Carfilhiot named names and Tamurello put the names to the manikins and placed them on the board.

"Still there are more!" protested Carfilhiot. "Is it not understandable that I would wish to know where and when you fare from Faroli? And Melancthe? Her movements are of importance! And what of the magicians: Murgen, Faloury, Myolander and Baibalides? I am interested in their activities."

"You may not learn of the magicians," said Tamurello. "That is not appropriate. Granice, Audry? Well, why not? Melancthe?"

"Melancthe in especial!"

"Very well. Melancthe."

"Then there are Ska chieftains and the notables of Dahaut!"

"Moderation, in the name of Fafhadiste and his three-legged blue goat! The manikins will crowd each other from the map!"

In the end Carfilhiot came away with the map and fifty-nine homologues.

One late summer morning a year later, Carfilhiot went up to his workroom and there inspected the map. Casmir kept to his summer palace at Sarris. At Domreis in Troicinet a glowing white ball on the manikin's head indicated that King Granice had died; his ailing brother Ospero would now be king. At Ys Melancthe wandered the echoing halls of her seaside palace. At Oäldes, north along the coast, Quilcy, the idiot child-king of South Ulfland, played daily at sand-castles on the beach . . . Carfilhiot looked once more to Ys. Melancthe, haughty Melancthe! He saw her seldom; she held herself aloof.

Carfilhiot's gaze ranged the map. With a quickening of the spirit he noticed a displacement: Sir Cadwal of Kaber Keep, had ventured six miles southwest across Dunton Fells. He would seem to be proceeding toward Dravenshaw Forest.

Carfilhiot stood rapt in reflection. Sir Cadwal was one of his most arrogant enemies, despite poverty and an absence of powerful connections. Kaber Keep, a dour fortress above the dreariest sweep of the moors, lacked all cheer, save only security. With only a dozen clansmen at his command Sir Cadwal had long defied Carfilhiot. Ordinarily he hunted in the hills above his keep, where Carfilhiot could not easily attack; today he had ventured down upon the moors: reckless indeed, thought Carfilhiot, most unwise! The keep could not be left undefended, so it would seem that Sir Cadwal rode with only five or six men at his back, and two of these might be his stripling sons.

Malaise forgotten, Carfilhiot sent urgent orders down to the wardroom. Half an hour later, wearing light armor, he descended to the parade ground below his castle. Twenty mounted warriors, his elite of elites, awaited him.

Carfilhiot inspected the troop and could find no fault. They wore polished iron helmets with tall crests, chain cuirasses and jupons of violet velvet embroidered in black. Each carried a lance from which fluttered a lavender and black banneret. From each saddle hung an axe, a bow and arrows to the side; each carried sword and dagger.

Carfilhiot mounted his horse and gave the signal to ride. Two abreast, the troop galloped west, past the reeking poles of penance, beside the drowning-cages along the riverbank and their accessory derricks and down the road toward the village Bloddywen. For reasons of policy Carfilhiot never made demands upon the folk of Bloddywen, nor in any way molested them; still, at his approach children were snatched within, doors and windows were slammed shut, and Carfilhiot rode through empty streets, to his cold amusement.

Above, on the ridge, a watcher noted the cavalcade. He retreated over the brow of the hill and flourished a white flag. A moment later, from the highest portion of a fell a mile to the north a flutter of white acknowledged his signal. Half an hour later, had Carfilhiot been able to observe his magic map, he might have seen the blackthorn manikins designating his most hated adversaries departing their keeps and mountain forts to move down the moors toward the Dravenshaw.

Carfilhiot and his troop clattered through Bloddywen, then turned away from the river and rode up to the moors. Gaining the ridge, Carfilhiot halted his troop, ranged them in a line and addressed them: "Today we hunt Cadwal of Kaber Keep; he is our quarry. We will meet him by the Dravenshaw. So as not to startle his vigilance, we will approach him around the side of Dinkin Tor. Listen now! Take Sir Cadwal alive, and any of his blood who may ride with him. Sir Cadwal must repent the harms

346

he has done me in full measure. Later we will take Kaber Keep; we will drink his wine, bed his women and make free of his bounty. But today we ride to take Sir Cadwal!"

He swung his horse up and around in a fine caracole and galloped away across the moors.

On Hackberry Tor an observer, noting Carfilhiot's movements, ducked behind a crag and there signaled with a white flag until, from two quarters, his signals were acknowledged.

Carfilhiot and his troop rode confidently into the northwest. At Dinkin Tor they halted. One of the number dismounted and climbed to the top of a rock. He called down to Carfilhiot: "Riders, perhaps five or six, at most seven! They approach the Dravenshaw!"

"Quick then," called Carfilhiot, "we'll take them at the forest's edge!"

The column rode west, keeping to the cover of Dewny Swale; at an old road they swung to the north and galloped at full speed for the Dravenshaw.

The road skirted the tumbled stones of a prehistoric fane, then turned directly down toward the Dravenshaw. Across the moor the roan horses ridden by Sir Cadwal's troop glimmered like raw copper in the sunlight. Carfilhiot signaled his men. "Quietly now! A volley of arrows, if necessary, but take Cadwal alive!"

The troop rode beside a stream fringed with willow. Clicks and snaps! A sibilant whir! Arrows across space at flat trajectory! Needle points thrust through chain-mail. There were groans of surprise, cries of pain. Six of Carfilhiot's men sagged to the ground in silence; three others took arrows in leg or shoulder. Carfilhiot's horse, with arrows in its neck and haunches, reared, screamed and fell. No one had aimed directly at Carfilhiot: an act of forbearance, alarming rather than reassuring.

Carfilhiot ran crouching to a riderless horse, mounted, kicked home his spurs and bending low to the mane, pounded away, followed by the survivors of his troop.

At a safe distance Carfilhiot called a halt and turned to assess the situation. To his dismay a mounted troop of a dozen men burst from the shadows of Dravenshaw. They rode bay horses and wore Kaber orange.

Carfilhiot hissed in frustration. At least six archers would be leaving the ambush to join the enemy troop: he was outnumbered. "Away!" cried Carfilhiot and put his horse once more to flight: up past the ruined fane, with the Kaber warriors barely a hundred yards behind. Carfilhiot's horses were stronger than the Kaber bays, but Carfilhiot had ridden harder and his heavy horses had not been bred for stamina.

Carfilhiot turned off the road into Dewny Swale, only to find another company of mounted men charging upon him from up-slope with leveled lances. They were ten or a dozen, in the blue and dark blue of Nulness Castle. Carfilhiot yelled orders and veered away to the south. Five of Carfilhiot's men took lances in the chest, neck or head and lay in the road. Three tried to defend themselves with sword and axe; they were quickly cut down. Four managed to win to the brow of the swale along with Carfilhiot, and there paused to rest their winded horses.

But only for a moment. The Nulness company, with relatively fresh horses, already had almost gained the high ground. The Kaber troop would be circling west along the old road to intercept him before he could gain Vale Evander.

A copse of dark fir trees rose ahead, where perhaps he could take temporary cover. He spurred the flagging horse into motion. From the corner of his eye he glimpsed bright red. He screamed: "Down! Away!" Over and down into a gulch he plunged, while archers in the crimson of Castle Turgis jumped up from the gorse and shot two volleys. Two of Carfilhiot's four were struck; once again chain-mail was penetrated. The horse of the third was struck in the belly; it reared over backward and fell on its rider who was crushed but managed to stagger, wild and disoriented, to his feet. Six arrows killed him. The single remaining warrior rode pell-mell down into the swale, where the Kaber warriors cut off first his legs, then his arms, then rolled him into the ditch to ponder the sad estate to which his life had come. Carfilhiot rode alone through the forest of firs, to come out on a wasteland of stone. A sheepherder's trail led through the rocks. Ahead towered the crags known as the Eleven Sisters.

Carfilhiot looked over his shoulder, then spurred his horse to its ultimate effort, through the Eleven Sisters and down the slope beyond into a dim gully choked with alders, where he drew his horse under a ledge and out of sight from above. His pursuers searched the rocks, calling and hallooing in frustration that Carfilhiot had escaped their trap. Time and time again they looked into the gully, but Carfilhiot, only fifteen feet below, was not seen. Around and around in Carfilhiot's head went an obsessive question: how had the trap been established without his knowledge? The map had shown only Sir Cadwal riding abroad; yet surely Sir Cleone of Nulness Castle, Sir Dexter of Turgis had gone out with their troops! The simple strategy of the signal system never occurred to him.

Carfilhiot waited an hour until his horse ceased to tremble and heave; then cautiously he remounted and rode down the gully, keeping to such shelter as was offered by alders and willows, and presently he emerged into Vale Evander, a mile above Ys.

The time still was early afternoon. Carfilhiot rode on into Ys. On terraces to either side of the river the factors lived quietly in their white palaces, shaded under pencil cypress, yew, olive, flat-topped pines. Carfilhiot rode up the beach of white sand to Melancthe's palace. A yard-boy came to meet him. Carfilhiot slid off the horse with a groan of relief. He climbed three marble steps, crossed the terrace and entered a dim foyer, where a chamberlain silently helped him from his helmet, his jupon and his chain cuirass. A maid-servant appeared: a strange silver-skinned creature, perhaps half-falloy.* She brought Carfilhiot a white linen shirt and a cup of warm white wine. "Sir, Lady Melancthe will see you in due course. Meanwhile, please command me for your needs."

"Thank you: I need nothing." Carfilhiot went out on the terrace and lowered himself into a cushioned chair and sat looking out over the sea. The air was mild, the sky cloudless. Swells slid up the sand to become a low surf, which created a somnolent rhythmic sound. Carfilhiot's eyes became heavy; he dozed.

He awoke to find that the sun had moved down the sky. Melancthe, wearing a sleeveless gown of soft white faniche,* stood leaning against the balustrade, oblivious to his presence.

Carfilhiot sat up in his chair, vexed for reasons indefinable. Melancthe turned to look at him, then a moment later gave her attention back to the sea.

Carfilhiot watched her under half-closed eyelids. Her self-

*Falloy: A slender halfling akin to fairies, but larger, less antic and lacking deft control of magic; creatures ever more rare in the Elder Isles.

*A fairy fabric woven from dandelion silk.

possession—so it occurred to him—if sufficiently protracted, might well tend to scrape upon one's patience... Melancthe glanced at him over her shoulder, the corners of her mouth drooping, apparently with nothing to say: neither welcome nor wonder at his presence unattended, nor curiosity as to the course of his life.

Carfilhiot chose to break the silence. "Life here at Ys seems placid enough."

"Sufficiently so."

"I have had a dangerous day. I evaded death by almost no margin whatever."

"You must have been frightened."

Carfilhiot considered. "'Fright'? That is not quite the word. I was alarmed, certainly. I grieve to lose my troops."

"I have heard rumors of your warriors."

Carfilhiot smiled. "What would you have? The land is in turmoil. Everyone resists authority. Would you not prefer a country at peace?"

"As an abstract proposition, yes."

"I need your help."

Melancthe laughed in surprise. "It will not be forthcoming. I helped you once, to my regret."

"Truly? My gratitude should have soothed all your qualms. After all, you and I are one."

Melancthe turned and looked off over the wide blue sea. "I am I and you are you."

"So you will not help me."

"I will give you advice, if you agree to act by it."

"At least I will listen."

"Change utterly."

Carfilhiot made a polite gesture. "That is like saying: 'Turn yourself inside-out.'"

"I know." The two words rang with a fateful sound.

Carfilhiot grimaced. "Do you truly hate me so?"

Melancthe inspected him from head to toe. "I often wonder at my feelings. You fascinate the attention; you cannot be ignored. Perhaps it is a kind of narcissism. If I were male, I might be like you."

"True. We are one."

Melancthe shook her head. "I am not tainted. You breathed the green fume."

350

"But you tasted it."

"I spat it out."

"Still, you know its flavor."

"And so I see deep into your soul."

"Evidently without admiration."

Melancthe again turned to look across the sea.

Carfilhiot came to join her beside the balustrade. "Does it mean nothing that I am in danger? Half of my elite company is gone. I no longer trust my magic."

"You know no magic."

Carfilhiot ignored her. "My enemies have joined and plan terrible acts upon me. Today they might have killed me, but tried rather to take me alive."

"Consult your darling Tamurello; perhaps he will fear for his loved one."

Carfilhiot laughed sadly. "I am not even sure of Tamurello. In any event he is very temperate in his generosity, even somewhat grudging."

"Then find a more lavish lover. What of King Casmir?"

"We have few interests in common."

"Then Tamurello would seem to be your best hope."

Carfilhiot glanced sidewise and searched the delicate lines of her profile. "Has Tamurello never offered his attentions to you?"

"Certainly. But my price was too high."

"What was your price?"

"His life."

"That is inordinate. What price would you demand of me?"

Melancthe's eyebrows raised; her mouth went wryly crooked. "You would pay a notable price."

"My life?"

"The topic lacks all relevance, and disturbs me." She turned away. "I am going inside."

"What of me?"

"Do as you please. Sleep in the sun, if you are so of a mind. Or start back to Tintzin Fyral."

Carfilhiot said reproachfully: "For one who is closer than a sister, you are most acrid."

"To the contrary; I am absolutely detached."

"Well then, if I may do as I please, I will accept your hospitality."

Melancthe, mouth pursed thoughtfully, walked into the palace, with Carfilhiot at her back. She paused in the foyer: a round chamber decorated in blue, pink and gold, and with a pale blue rug on the marble floor. She called the chamberlain. "Show Sir Faude to a chamber and attend to his needs."

Carfilhiot bathed and rested for a period. Dusk settled across the ocean and daylight faded.

Carfilhiot dressed in garments of unrelieved black. In the foyer the chamberlain presented himself. "Lady Melanthe has not yet appeared. If you like, you may await her in the small saloon."

Carfilhiot seated himself and was served a goblet of crimson wine, tasting of honey, pine needles and pomegranate.

Half an hour passed. The silver-skinned serving girl brought a tray of sweetmeats, which Carfilhiot tasted without enthusiasm.

Ten minutes later he looked up from his wine to find Melanthe standing in front of him. She wore a sleeveless black gown, cut with total simplicity. A black opal cabochon hung on a narrow black ribbon around her neck; against the black, her pale skin and large eyes gave her a look of vulnerability to the impulses of both pleasure and pain: a semblance to excite any wishing to bring her either or both.

After a pause she sat beside Carfilhiot, and took a goblet of wine from the tray. Carfilhiot waited but she sat in silence. At last he asked: "Have you enjoyed a restful afternoon?"

"Certainly not restful. I worked on certain exercises."

"Indeed? To what end?"

"It is not easy to become a sorcerer."

"That is your will?"

"Certainly."

"It is not overly difficult, then?"

"I am only at the fringes of the subject. The real difficulties lie yet ahead."

"Already you are stronger than I." Carfilhiot spoke in a jesting voice. Melanthe smiled not at all.

After a heavy silence she rose to her feet. "It is time for dinner."

She took him into a large chamber, paneled in the blackest of ebony and floored with slabs of polished black gabbro. Over the ebony a set of glass prisms illuminated the service.

Dinner was served on two sets of trays: a simple meal of

mussels simmered in white wine, bread, olives and nuts. Melancthe ate little, and apart from an occasional glance at Carfilhiot, gave him no attention, and made no effort at conversation. Carfilhiot, nettled, likewise held his tongue, so that the meal went in silence. Carfilhiot drank several goblets of wine, and finally set the goblet down with a petulant thump.

"You are beautiful beyond the dreams of dreaming! Yet your thoughts are those of a fish!"

"It is no great matter."

"Why should we know constraint? Are we not ultimately one?"

"No. Desmëi yielded three: I, you and Denking."

"You have said it yourself!"

Melancthe shook her head. "Everyone shares the substance of earth. But the lion differs from the mouse and both from man."

Carfilhiot rejected the analogy with a gesture. "We are one, yet different! A fascinating condition! Yet, you are aloof!"

"True," said Melancthe. "I agree."

"For a moment consider the possibilities! The vertexes of passion! The sheer exuberances! Can you not feel the excitement?"

"Feel? Enough that I think." For an instant her composure appeared to falter. She rose, crossed the chamber and stood looking into the sea-coal fire.

In a leisurely fashion Carfilhiot came to stand beside her. "It is easy to feel." He took her hand and laid it on his chest. "Feel! I am strong. Feel how my heart moves and gives me life."

Melancthe pulled her hand away. "I do not care to feel at your behest. Passion is a hysteria. In truth I have no yearning for men." She moved a step away from him. "Leave me now, if you please. In the morning, you will not see me, nor will I advance your enterprises."

Carfilhiot put his hands under her elbows and stood facing her, with firelight shifting along their faces. Melancthe opened her mouth to speak, but uttered no words, and Carfilhiot, bending his face to hers, kissed her mouth. He drew her down upon a couch. "Evening stars still climb the sky. Night has just begun."

She seemed not to hear him, but sat looking into the fire. Carfilhiot loosed the clasps at her shoulder; she let the gown slide from her body with no restraint and the odor of violets hung in the air. She watched in passive silence as Carfilhiot stepped from his own garments.

At midnight Melancthe rose from the couch, to stand nude before the fire, now a bed of embers.

Carfilhiot watched her from the couch, eyelids half-lowered, mouth compressed. Melancthe's conduct had been perplexing. Her body had joined his with suitable urgency, but never during the coupling had she looked into his face; her head had been thrown back, or laid to the side, with eyes focused on nothing whatever. She had been physically exalted, this he could sense, but when he spoke to her, she made no response, as if he were no more than a phantasm.

Melancthe looked at him over her shoulder. "Dress yourself."

Sullenly Carfilhiot donned his garments, while she stood in contemplation of the dying fire. He considered a set of remarks, one after the other, but each seemed very heavy, or peevish, or callow, or foolish and he held his tongue.

When he had dressed, he came to her and put his arms around her waist. She slipped back from his grasp and spoke in a pensive voice: "Don't touch me. No man has ever yet touched me, nor shall you."

Carfilhiot laughed. "Am I not a man? I have touched you, thoroughly and deep, to the core of your soul."

Still watching the fire Melancthe shook her head. "You occur only as an odd thing of the imagination. I have used you, now you must dissolve from my mind."

Carfilhiot peered at her in bafflement. Was she mad? "I am quite real, and I don't care to dissolve. Melancthe, listen!" Again he put his hands to her waist. "Let us truly be lovers! Are we not both remarkable?"

Again Melancthe moved away. "Again you have tried to touch me." She pointed to a door. "Go! Dissolve from my mind!"

Carfilhiot performed a sardonic bow and went to the door. Here he hesitated, looked back. Melancthe stood by the hearth, one hand to the high mantle, firelight and black shadow shifting along her body. Carfilhiot whispered to himself, inaudibly: "Say what you will of phantoms. I took you and I had you: so much is real."

And in his ear, or in his brain, as he opened the door, came soundless words: "I played with a phantom. You thought to control reality. Phantoms feel no pain. Reflect on this, when every day pain comes past."

Carfilhiot, startled, stepped through the door, and at once it closed behind him. He stood in a dark passage between two buildings, with a glimmer of light at either end. The night sky showed overhead. The air carried an odd reek, of moldering wood and wet stone; where was the clean salt air which blew past Melancthe's palace?

Carfilhiot groped through a clutter of rubbish to the end of the passage and emerged into a town square. He looked around in slack-jawed perplexity. This was not Ys, and Carfilhiot spoke a dour curse against Melancthe.

The square was boisterous with the sights and sounds of a festival. A thousand torches burnt on high; a thousand green and blue banners with a yellow bird appliquéd on high. At the center two great birds constructed of bound straw bundles and ropes faced each other. On a platform men and women costumed as fanciful birds pranced, bobbed and kicked to the music of pipes and drums.

A man costumed as a white rooster, with red comb, yellow bill, white feathered wings and tail strutted past. Carfilhiot clutched his arm. "Sir, one moment! Enlighten me, where is this place?"

The man-chicken crowed in derision. "Have you no eyes? No ears? This is the Avian Arts Grand Gala!"

"Yes, but where?"

"Where else? This is the Kaspodel, at the center of the city!"

"But what city? What realm?"

"Are you lost of your senses? This is Gargano!"

"In Pomperol?"

"Precisely so. Where are your tail feathers? King Deuel has ordained tail-feathers for the gala! Notice my display!" The man-chicken ran in a circle, strutting and bobbing, so as to flourish his handsome tail-plumes; then he continued on his way.

Carfilhiot leaned against the building, gritting his teeth in fury. He carried neither coins, nor jewels, nor gold; he knew no friends among the folk of Gargano; indeed Mad King Deuel considered Carfilhiot a dangerous bird-killer and an enemy.

To the side of the square Carfilhiot noted the boards of an inn: the Pear Tree. He presented himself to the innkeeper only to learn that the inn was occupied to capacity. Carfilhiot's most aristocratic manner earned him no more than a bench in the common-room near a group of celebrants who caroused, wrangled and sang such songs as *Fesker Would a-Wooing Go*, *Tirra-Lirra-Lay*, *Milady Ostrich and Noble Sir Sparrow*. An hour before dawn they tumbled forward across the table to lie snoring among gnawed pig's feet and puddles of spilled wine. Carfilhiot was allowed to sleep until two hours into the morning, when charwomen came with mops and buckets, and turned everyone outside.

Celebration of the festival already had reached a crescendo. Everywhere fluttered banners and streamers of blue, green and yellow. Pipers played jigs while folk costumed as birds capered and pranced. Everyone used a characteristic bird-call, so that the air resounded to twitterings, chirps, whistles and croaks. Children dressed as barn-swallows, gold-finches, or tom-tits; older folk favored the more sedate semblances, such as that of crow, raven or perhaps a jay. The corpulent often presented themselves as owls, but in general everyone costumed himself as fancy directed.

The color, noise and festivity failed to elevate Carfilhiot's mood; in fact—so he told himself—never had he witnessed so much pointless nonsense. He had rested poorly and eaten nothing, which served to exacerbate his mood.

A bun-seller dressed as a quail passed by; Carfilhiot bought a mince-tart, using a silver button from his coat for payment. He ate standing before the inn, with aloof and disdainful glances for the revelry.

A band of youths chanced to notice Carfilhiot's sneers and stopped short. "Here now! This is the Grand Gala! You must show a happy smile, so as not to be at discord!"

Another cried out: "What? No gay plumage? No tail-feathers? They are required of every celebrant!"

"Come now!" declared another. "We must set things right!" Going behind Carfilhiot he tried to tuck a long white goose quill into Carfilhiot's waist-band. Carfilhiot would have none of it, and thrust the youth away.

The others in the band became more determined than ever and a scuffle ensued, in which shouts, curses and blows were exchanged.

From the street came a stern call. "Here, here! Why this disgraceful uproar?" Mad King Deuel himself, passing by in a befeathered carriage, had halted to issue a reprimand.

One of the youths cried out: "The fault lies with this dismal vagabond! He won't wear his tail-feathers. We tried to help him and cited your Majesty's ordinance; he said to shove all our feathers up your Majesty's arse!"

King Deuel shifted his attention to Carfilhiot. "He did so, did he? That is not polite. We know a trick worth two of that. Guards! Attendants!"

Carfilhiot was seized and bent over a bench. The seat of his trousers was cut away, and into his buttocks were thrust a hundred quills of all sizes, lengths and colors, including a pair of expensive ostrich plumes. The ends of the quills were cut into barbs to prevent their detachment, and they were arranged to support each other so that the plumage, upon completion, thrust up from Carfilhiot's fundament at a jaunty angle.

"Excellent!" declared King Deuel, clapping his hands in satisfaction. "That is a splendid display, in which you can take pride. Go, now. Enjoy the festival to your heart's content! Now you are properly bedizened!"

The carriage rolled away; the youths appraised Carfilhiot with critical eyes, but agreed that his plumage captured the mood of the festival, and they too went their way.

Carfilhiot walked stiff-legged to a crossroads at the edge of town. A sign-post pointed north to Avallon.

Carfilhiot waited, meanwhile plucking the feathers one by one from his buttocks.

A cart came from town, driven by an old peasant woman. Carfilhiot held up his hand to halt the cart. "Where do you drive yourself, grandmother?"

"To the village Filster, in the Deepdene, if that means aught to you."

Carfilhiot showed the ring on his finger. "Look well at this ruby!"

The old woman peered. "I see it well. It glows like red fire! I often marvel that such stones grow in the deep dark of the earth!"

"Another marvel: this ruby, so small, will buy twenty horses and carts like that one which you ride."

The old woman blinked. "Well, I must believe your word. Would you halt me in my home-going to tell me lies?"

"Now listen carefully, as I am about to state a proposition of several parts."

"Speak on; say what you will! I can think three thoughts at once."

"I am bound for Avallon. My legs are sore; I can neither walk nor sit astride a horse. I wish to ride in your cart, that I may come to Avallon in comfort. Therefore, if you will drive me to Avallon, ring and ruby are yours."

The woman held up her forefinger. "Better! We drive to Filster, thence my son Raffin puts straw in the cart and then drives you to Avallon. So all behind-hand whispers and rumors at my expense are halted before they start."

"This will be satisfactory."

Carfilhiot alighted from the cart at the sign of the Fishing Cat and gave over the ruby ring to Raffin who immediately departed.

Carfilhiot entered the inn. Behind a counter stood a monstrous man half a foot taller than Carfilhiot, with a great red face and a belly which rested on the counter. He looked down at Carfilhiot with eyes like stone pebbles. "What do you wish?"

"I want to find Rughalt of the sore knees. He said that you would know where to find him."

The fat man, taking exception to Carfilhiot's manner, looked away. He worked his fingers up and down the counter. At last he uttered a few terse words. "He will arrive presently."

"How soon is 'presently'?"

"Half an hour."

"I will wait. Bring me one of those roasting chickens, a loaf of new bread and a flask of good wine."

"Show me your coin."

"When Rughalt comes."

"When Rughalt comes, I will serve the fowl."

Carfilhiot swung away with a muttered curse; the fat man looked after him without change of expression.

Carfilhiot seated himself on a bench before the inn. Rughalt at last showed himself, moving his legs slowly and carefully, one at a time, hissing under his breath the while.

With a frowning eye, Carfilhiot watched Rughalt's approach. Rughalt wore the fusty gray garments of a pedagogue.

Carfilhiot rose to his feet; Rughalt stopped short in surprise. "Sir Faude!" he exclaimed. "What do you do here, in such a condition?"

"Through treachery and witchcraft; how else? Take me to a decent inn; this place is fit only for Celts and lepers."

Rughalt rubbed his chin. "The Black Bull is yonder on the Square. The charges are said to be excessive; you will pay in silver for a night's lodging."

358

"I carry no funds whatever, neither silver nor gold. You must provide funds until I make arrangements."

Rughalt winced. "The Fishing Cat, after all, is not so bad. Gurdy the landlord is daunting only at first acquaintance."

"Bah. He and his hovel both stink of rancid cabbage and worse. Take me to the Black Bull."

"Just so. Ah, my aching legs! Duty calls you onward."

At the Black Bull Carfilhiot found lodging to meet his requirements, though Rughalt screwed his eyes together when the charges were quoted. A haberdasher displayed garments which Carfilhiot found consonant with his dignity; however, to Rughalt's dismay Carfilhiot refused to haggle the price and Rughalt paid the wily tailor with slow and crooked fingers.

Carfilhiot and Rughalt seated themselves at a table in front of the Black Bull and watched the folk of Avallon. Rughalt ordered two modest half-measures from the steward. "Wait!" Carfilhiot commanded. "I am hungry. Bring me a dish of good cold beef, with some leeks and a crust of fresh bread, and I will drink a pint of your best ale."

While Carfilhiot satisfied his hunger, Rughalt watched sidelong with disapproval so evident that Carfilhiot finally asked: "Why do you not eat? You have become gaunt as an old leathern strap."

Rughalt replied between tight lips, "Truth to tell, I must be careful with my funds. I live at the edge of poverty."

"What? I thought you to be an expert cut-purse, who depredated all the fairs and festivals of Dahaut."

"That is no longer possible. My knees prevent that swift and easy departure which is so much a part of the business. I no longer ply the fairs."

"Still, you are evidently not destitute."

"My life is not easy. Luckily, I see all in the dark and I now work nights at the Fishing Cat, robbing guests while they sleep. Even so, my clicking knees are a handicap, and since Gurdy, the landlord, insists on a share of my earnings, I avoid unnecessary expense. In this connection, will you be long in Avallon?"

"Not long. I want to find a certain Triptomologius. Is his name known to you?"

"He is a necromancer. He deals in elixirs and potions. What is your business with him?"

"First, he will supply me with gold, as much as I need."

"In that case, ask enough for the both of us!"

"We shall see." Carfilhiot stood erect. "Let us seek out Triptomologius."

With a cracking and clicking of the knees, Rughalt arose. The two walked through the back streets of Avallon to a dark little shop perched on a hill overlooking the Murmeil estuary. A slatternly crone with chin and nose almost making contact gave information that Triptomologius had gone out that very morning to set up a booth on the common, that he might sell his wares at the fair.

The two descended the hill by twisting flights of narrow stone steps, with the crooked old gables of Avallon overhanging: the swaggering young gallant in fine new clothes and the gaunt man walking with the stiff careful bent-kneed tread of a spider. They went out upon the common, since dawn a place of seething activity and many-colored confusion. Early arrivals already hawked their goods. Newcomers established themselves to best advantage amid complaints, chaffing, quarrels, invective and an occasional scuffle. Hawkers set up their tents, driving stakes into the ground with great wooden mauls, and hung bunting of a hundred sun-faded hues. Food stalls set their braziers aglow; sausages sizzled in hot grease; grilled fish, dipped in garlic and oil, was served on slabs of bread. Oranges from the valleys of Dascinet competed in color and fragrance with purple Lyonesse grapes, Wysrod apples, Daut pomegranates, plums and quince. At the back of the common, trestles demarcated a long narrow paddock, where the mendicant lepers, cripples, the deranged, deformed and blind were required to station themselves. Each took up a post from which he delivered his laments; some sang, some coughed, others uttered ululations of pain. The deranged foamed at the mouth and hurled abuse at the passersby, in whatever style he found most effective. The noise from this quarter could be heard over the whole of the common, creating counterpoint to the music of pipers, fiddlers and bell-ringers.

Carfilhiot and Rughalt walked here and there, seeking the booth from which Triptomologius sold his essences. Rughalt, uttering low moans of frustration, pointed out heavy purses easily to be taken, were it not for his debilities. Carfilhiot halted to admire a team of two-headed black horses, of great size and strength which had drawn a wagon upon the common. In front of the wagon a boy played merry tunes on the pipes, while a pretty blonde girl stood by a table directing the antics of four cats which danced to the tunes: prancing and kicking, bowing and turning, twitching their tails in time to the music.

The boy finished his tune and put aside the pipes; on a platform in front of the wagon stepped a tall spare young-seeming man, with a droll face and sand-colored hair. He wore a black mantle displaying Druidic symbols, a tall black hat with fifty-two small silver bells around the brim. Facing the throng he raised his arms for attention. The girl jumped up to the platform. She was dressed as a boy in white ankle-boots, tight trousers of blue velvet, a dark blue jacket with golden frogs on the front. She spoke: "Friends! I introduce to you that remarkable master of the healing arts, Doctor Fidelius!"

She jumped to the ground and Dr. Fidelius addressed the throng. "Ladies and Sirs: We all know affliction of one sort or another—the pox, or boils, or hallucinations. Let me state at the outset, my powers are limited. I cure goiter and worm, costive impaction, stricture and bloat. I soothe the itch; I heal the scabies. Especially I mourn the anguish of cracking and creaking knees. Only one who suffers the complaint can know its trouble!"

As Dr. Fidelius spoke, the girl moved about the crowd selling ointments and tonics from a tray. Dr. Fidelius displayed a chart. "Observe this drawing. It represents the human knee. When injured, as at the blow of an iron bar, the kneecap recedes; the joint becomes a toggle; the leg rasps back and forth like a cricket's wing, with clicks and cracking sounds."

Rughalt was profoundly stirred. "My knees might serve as models for his discourse!" he told Carfilhiot.

"Amazing," said Carfilhiot.

Rughalt held up his hand. "Let us listen."

Doctor Fidelius spoke on. "The affliction has its remedy!" He picked up a small clay pot and held it on high. "I have here an ointment of Egyptian source. It penetrates directly into the joint and strengthens as it relieves. The ligaments recover their tone. Persons creep into my laboratory on crutches and stride out renewed. Why suffer this debilitation when relief can be almost immediate? The ointment is valuable, at a silver florin per jar, but it is cheap when one considers its effects. The ointment, incidentally, carries my personal guarantee."

Rughalt listened with fascinated attention. "I must surely put the ointment to a test!"

"Come along," said Carfilhiot curtly. "The man is a charlatan.

361

Don't waste time and money on such foolishness."

"I have nothing better to waste it on," retorted Rughalt with sudden spirit. "Were my legs once more nimble I would have money to spare!"

Carfilhiot looked askance toward Dr. Fidelius. "Somewhere I have seen that man."

"Bah!" growled Rughalt. "It is not you who suffers the pangs; you can afford skepticism. I must grasp at every straw! Hey there, Dr. Fidelius! My kneecaps answer your description! Can you bring me relief?"

Dr. Fidelius called out: "Sir, come forward! Even from this distance I diagnose a typical condition. It is known as 'Roofer's Knee,' or sometimes 'Robber's Knee,' since it often comes from the impact of the knee against roof-tiles. Please step over here, so that I may examine your leg with care. I can almost guarantee your surcease in a very short time. Are you a roofer, sir?"

"No," said Rughalt curtly.

"No matter. A knee, after all, is a knee. If left untreated, it will eventually turn yellow, extrude bits of decaying bone and become a source of annoyance. We shall forestall these events. Step over here, sir, behind the wagon."

Rughalt followed Dr. Fidelius to the other side of the wagon. Carfilhiot impatiently turned away and went off in search of Triptomologius, and presently found the necromancer stocking the shelves of his booth with articles brought by dog cart.

The two exchanged greetings and Triptomologius inquired the reason for Carfilhiot's presence. Carfilhiot responded in oblique terms, hinting of intrigues and mysteries which might not be discussed. "Tamurello was to leave a message for me," said Carfilhiot. "Have you been in late contact with him?"

"As lately as yesterday. The message made no mention of you; he remains at Faroli."

"Then I will make for Faroli with all speed. You must provide me a good horse and ten gold crowns, for which Tamurello will reimburse you."

Triptomologius drew back in shock. "His message told me none of this!"

"Then send a new message, but be quick about it, as I must depart Avallon at once—tomorrow at the latest."

Triptomologius pulled at his long gray chin. "I can spare no more than three crowns. You must make do."

"What? Must I eat crusts and sleep under the hedge?"

After a period of undignified wrangling, Carfilhiot accepted five gold crowns, a horse, suitably furnished, and saddle-bags packed with provisions of carefully stipulated kind and quality.

Carfilhiot returned across the common. He paused by the wagon of Dr. Fidelius, but the side doors were closed and no one could be seen: neither Dr. Fidelius, the girl or boy, nor yet Rughalt.

Once more at the Black Bull, Carfilhiot seated himself at a table in front of the inn. He sprawled out his legs, drank the yellow wine of muscat grapes, and reflected upon the circumstances of his life. In recent days, his affairs had not gone well. Images thronged his mind: he smiled at some and frowned at others. Thinking of the Dravenshaw ambush, he uttered a small moan and clenched his hand on the goblet. The time had come to destroy his enemies once and for all. In his mind he saw them in the semblance of beasts: snarling curs, weasels, boars, black-masked foxes. Melancthe's image appeared to him. She stood in the shadows of her palace, nude save for a wreath of violets in her black hair. Calm and still, she looked through him, past and away... Carfilhiot straightened sharply in his chair. Melancthe had always treated him with condescension, as if she felt a natural ascendancy, apparently on the basis of the green fume. She had preempted all of Desmëi's magical apparatus, allowing him none. From compunction, or guilt, or perhaps only to stifle his reproaches, she had beguiled the magician Shimrod, so that Carfilhiot might plunder his magical appurtenances—which, in any event, due to Shimrod's cunning lock, had brought him no benefit. Upon his return to Tintzin Fyral he must surely... Shimrod! Carfilhiot's instincts prickled. Where was Rughalt, who had limped forward so confidently to take treatment from Dr. Fidelius?

Shimrod! If he had taken Rughalt, who would be next? Carfilhiot felt cold and his bowels went queasy, as if they needed relief.

Carfilhiot rose to his feet. He looked out across the common. There was no sign of Rughalt. Carfilhiot cursed between his teeth. He had neither coin nor gold, and would have none till the morrow.

Carfilhiot worked to regain his composure. He drew a deep breath and clenched his fist. "I am Faude Carfilhiot! I am I, the best of the best! I dance my perilous dance along the edge of the sky! I take the clay of Destiny in my hands and shape it to my will. I am Faude Carfilhiot, the nonpareil!"

With a firm light step, he set off across the common. Lacking a weapon of any sort, he halted to pick up a broken tent-stake: a length of ash something over a foot long, which he concealed under his cape, then proceeded directly to the wagon of Dr. Fidelius.

Once behind Dr. Fidelius' wagon, Rughalt spoke in a reedy voice: "You have mentioned sore knees, which I have in abundance, to the number of two. They creak and click and on occasion bend in reverse direction, causing me discomfort."

"Interesting!" exclaimed Dr. Fidelius. "Interesting indeed! How long have you been so troubled?"

"Forever, or so it seems. It came upon me during the course of my work. I was subjected to alternating heat and cold, dampness and dry. Meanwhile I was forced to great exertions, twisting, turning, pushing, pulling, and I feel that I weakened my knees in the process."

"Precisely so! Still, your case shows peculiarities. It is not typical of the Avallon sore knee."

"I then resided in South Ulfland."

"I am vindicated! For the South Ulfland disease we will need certain medicines which I do not keep in the wagon." Shimrod called to Glyneth; she approached, looking back and forth between the two men. Shimrod took her somewhat aside. "I'll be in conference with the gentleman for perhaps an hour. Close up the wagon, put the horses to their traces. Tonight we may be on the road to Lyonesse."

Glyneth nodded her head in assent and went back to Dhrun with the news.

Shimrod turned his attention back to Rughalt. "This way, sir, if you will."

Presently Rughalt put a plaintive question: "Why are we going so far? We are quite away from town!"

"Yes, my dispensary is somewhat isolated. Still, I think I can promise you total palliation."

Rughalt's knees began to click and creak in earnest, and his complaints became increasingly peevish. "How far must we go? Every step we take is a step we must retrace. Already my knees are singing a sad duet."

"They will never sing again! Surcease is absolute and final."

"That is good to hear. Still, I see no sign of your dispensary."

"It is just yonder, behind that alder thicket."

"Hmf. An odd place for a dispensary."

"It should serve our purposes very well."

"But there is not even a path!"

"So we ensure our privacy. This way then, behind the thicket. Mind the fresh pads of cow-dung."

"But there is nothing here."

"You and I are here, and I am Shimrod the Magician. You robbed my house Trilda and you burned my friend Grofinet over a flame. I have sought you and your comrade a very long time."

"Nonsense! Nothing of the sort! Absurd, every word...What are you doing? Stop at once! Stop! Stop!, I say!"

And later: "Have mercy! No more! I was commanded to the work!"

"By whom?"

"I dare not tell...No, no! No more, I will tell—"

"Who commanded you?"

"Carfilhiot, of Tintzin Fyral!"

"For what reason?"

"He wanted your magic stuff."

"That is far-fetched."

"It is true. He was encouraged by the magician Tamurello, who would give Carfilhiot nothing."

"Tell me more."

"I know nothing more...Ah! You monster! I will tell you!"

"What then? Hurry, do not stop to think. Do not gasp; talk!"

"Carfilhiot is in Avallon, at the Black Bull...What now are you doing? I have told you all!"

"Before you die you must toast a bit, like Grofinet."

"But I have told you everything! Have mercy!"

"Yes, perhaps so. I have no real stomach for torment. Die then. This is my cure for sore knees."

Carfilhiot found Dr. Fidelius' wagon closed, but the team of two-headed horses was hitched to the wagon-pole, as if in readiness for departure.

Carfilhiot went to the door at the back of the wagon and pressed his ear against the panel. Silence, so far as he could determine, with the noise of the fair behind him.

He walked around the wagon, and discovered the boy and girl beside a small fire where they toasted skewers of bacon chunks and quartered onion.

The girl looked up as Carfilhiot approached; the boy kept his attention on the fire. Carfilhiot wondered briefly as to his detachment. A shag of golden-brown curls fell over his face; his features were fine, yet decisive. He was, thought Carfilhiot, a boy of remarkable distinction. His age was perhaps nine or ten. The girl was two or three years older, in the early springtime of her life, as gay and sweet as a daffodil. She looked up, to meet Carfilhiot's gaze. Her mouth drooped and she became still. She spoke, however, in a polite voice: "Sir, Dr. Fidelius is not here just now."

Carfilhiot came slowly forward. The girl rose to her feet. The boy turned to look in Carfilhiot's direction.

"When will he be back?" asked Carfilhiot gently.

"I think very soon," said the girl.

"Do you know where he went?"

"No, sir. He had important business, and we were to be ready to leave when he returned."

"Well then, everything is quite in order," said Carfilhiot. "Jump into the wagon and we will drive directly to Dr. Fidelius."

The boy spoke for the first time. Despite his clear features, Carfilhiot had thought him pensive, or even a trifle daft. He was taken aback by the ring of authority in the boy's voice. "We cannot leave here without Dr. Fidelius. And we are cooking our dinner."

"Wait in front, sir, if you will," said the girl and turned her attention back to the sizzling bacon.

27

THE RIVER CAMBER, approaching the sea, joined the Murmeil and became an estuary some thirty miles long: the Cambermouth. Tides, swirling currents, seasonal fogs and sand bars which appeared and disappeared with changes of weather made for uncertain navigation in and out of Avallon Harbor.

Approaching Avallon from the south by Icnield Way, the traveler must cross the estuary, at this point two hundred yards wide, by a ferry, tethered to an overhead cable by a chain hanging from a massive pulley-block. At the south the cable was secured to the top of Cogstone Head beside the lighthouse. At the north it terminated at a buttress of concreted stone on River Scarp. The cable crossed the estuary at a skewed angle; the ferry leaving Cogstone landing was thereby propelled by the flooding tide across the estuary to the dock at Slange, under River Scarp. Six hours later, the ebbing tide thrust the ferry back to the south shore.

Aillas and his companions, riding north along Icnield Way, arrived at Cogstone halfway through the afternoon. Riding over the Cogstone ridge they paused to overlook the wide view which suddenly spread before them: the Cambermouth extending in a sinuous curve to the west where it seemed to brim over the horizon; the estuary to the east spreading wide to join the Cantabrian Gulf.

The tide was at the turning; the ferry lay at Cogstone Landing. Ships finding a fair insore wind drove into the estuary to the west spreading wide to join the Cantabrian Gulf.

The tide was at the turning; the ferry lay at Cogstone Landing. Ships finding a fair inshore wind drove into the estuary with all canvas spread, including a large two-masted felucca flying the flag of Troicinet. As they watched it edged toward the northern shore and docked at Slange.

The three rode down the road to the landing where the ferry waited departure only upon full flood of the tide.

Aillas paid toll for the passage and the three rode aboard the ferry: a heavy scow fifty feet long and twenty feet wide, well loaded with wagons, cattle, peddlers and mendicants on their way to the fair; a dozen nuns from Whanish Isle convent, on pilgrimage to the Holy Stone brought by St. Columba from Ireland.

At Slange Aillas went to the Troice felucca for news, while his friends waited. He came riding back in a state of despondency. He brought out the Never-fail, and exclaimed in frustration as the tooth pointed north.

"In truth," declared Aillas, "I don't know what to do!"

Yane asked: "So then, what is the news from Troicinet?"

"They say King Ospero lies sickly in his bed. If he dies and I am not on hand, then Trewan will be crowned king—which is as he planned...I should be riding full speed south at this instant, but how can I with Dhrun my son to the north?"

Cargus, after a moment's thought, said: "You cannot ride south in any event until the ferry takes you back to Cogstone. Meanwhile, Avallon is an hour's ride north, and who knows what we will find?"

"Who knows? Let us be off!"

The three rode hard along the final miles of Icnield Way, between Slange and Avallon, arriving by a road which bordered the common. They discovered a great fair to be in progress, though already it had gone into its waning stages. Beside the common Aillas consulted the Never-fail. The tooth pointed north to a target across the common and perhaps beyond. Aillas made a disgusted sound. "He might be out there on the common or a hundred miles north, or anywhere in between. Tonight we shall check to the edge of town, then tomorrow, willy-nilly, I ride south by the noon ferry."

"That is good strategy," said Yane, "and even better if we are able to find lodging for the night."

"The Black Bull yonder seems appealing," said Cargus. "A mug of bitter ale, or even two, will not come amiss."

"The Black Bull then, and if luck is with us, there will be room to lay down our bodies."

At their request for lodging the innkeeper first held out his hands in despair, then was nudged by one of the porters. "The Duke's Room is open sir. The company never arrived."

"The Duke's Room, then! Why not? I cannot hold a choice lodging the whole night through." The landlord rubbed his hands together. "We call it the 'Duke's Room' because Duke Snel of Sneldyke honored us with his custom, and not twelve years ago. I'll take silver for the rent. During the Grand Fair, and for the Duke's Room, we ask a premium fee."

Aillas paid over a silver florin. "Bring us ale, out under the tree."

The three sat at a table and refreshed themselves in the cool breeze of late afternoon. The throngs had dwindled to a trickle of late-comers hoping to drive hard bargains, and scavengers. Music was quiet; vendors packed their goods; acrobats, contortionists, mimes and jugglers had gone their ways. The Grand Fair formally ended on the morrow, but already pavilions were being struck and booths disassembled; carts and wagons trundled off the common to the road and so away: to north, east, south and west. In front of the Black Bull passed the flamboyant wagon of Dr. Fidelius, drawn by a pair of black two-headed horses, and driven by a dashing young gentleman of striking appearance.

Yane pointed in amazement at the horses. "See the marvels! Are they freaks, or works of magic?"

"For myself," said Cargus, "I would prefer something less ostentatious."

Aillas jumped to his feet to look after the wagon. He turned back to his fellows. "Did you notice the driver?"

"Certainly. A young grandee on a lark."

"Or some wild young dartling with pretensions to gentility."

Aillas thoughtfully resumed his seat. "I have seen him before—under strange circumstances." He raised his mug only to find it empty. "Boy! Bring more ale! We will drink, then we shall follow Never-fail at least to the edge of town."

The three sat in silence, looking across the traffic of street and common. The serving-boy brought them ale; at the same moment a tall sandy-haired man with a wild and somewhat distracted look came striding along the street. He halted and spoke urgently to the boy. "I am Dr. Fidelius; has my wagon passed by? It would be drawn by a team of black two-headed horses!"

"I have not seen your wagon, sir. I have been busy fetching ale for these gentlemen."

Aillas spoke. "Sir, your wagon passed only minutes ago."

"And did you notice the driver?"

"I took special heed of him: a man of about your own age, with dark hair, good features and a manner which was notably bold or even reckless. I feel that I have seen him before, but I cannot remember where."

Yane pointed. "He drove away yonder, south along Icnield Way."

"Then he will be stopped at Cambermouth." He looked back to Aillas. "If I used the name Faude Carfilhiot would that bring shape to your memory?"

"It would indeed." Aillas thought back across an age of toil, flight and wandering. "I saw him once at his castle."

"You have verified my worst fears. Boy, can you get me a horse?"

"I can go to the ostler, sir. The better the horse, the more coin he will ask."

Shimrod tossed a gold crown upon the table. "Bring his best, and in haste."

The boy ran off. Shimrod sat upon a bench to wait. Aillas appraised him sidelong. "What, when you catch him at Slange?"

"I will do what must be done."

"You will have your hands full. He is strong and no doubt well armed."

"I have no choice. He has kidnapped two children who are dear to me, and he might well do them harm."

"I would believe anything of Carfilhiot," said Aillas. He considered his own circumstances and came to a decision. He rose to his feet. "I will ride with you to Slange. My own quest can wait an hour or two." The Never-fail still dangled from his wrist. He glanced at the index, then again, incredulously. "Look you, at the tooth!"

"Now it points south!"

Aillas turned slowly to Shimrod. "Carfilhiot drove south with two children: what are their names?"

"Glyneth and Dhrun."

The four men rode south in the light of the westering sun, and folk along the road, hearing the pound of hooves, moved to the side to let the riders pass, then turned to wonder why men should ride so hard at sundown along Icnield Way.

Across the heath rode the four and up Riverside Heights where they drew their snorting horses up short. The Cambermouth glared incandescent in the light of the setting sun. The ferry had not waited for full ebb. In order to make full use of daylight it had left Slange at the turn of the tide and already was halfway across the river. Last aboard was the wagon of Dr. Fidelius. A man standing at the side of the wagon might have been Faude Carfilhiot.

The four rode down the hill to Slange, to learn that the ferry would turn north sometime after midnight, when the tide was once more at flood, and would not cross to Cogstone Landing until sunrise.

Aillas asked the dock attendant: "Is there no other way across the water?"

"Not with your horses; no indeed, sir!"

"Then, can we cross afoot, and at once?"

"Nor neither afoot, sir. There's no wind to fill a sail, and no one would row you across with the current at full ebb, neither for silver nor gold. He'd end up on Whanish Isle, or beyond. Come back by sunrise and ride in comfort."

Back on the heights they watched the ferry dock at Cogstone. The wagon rolled ashore, moved up the road and out of sight into the dusk.

"There they go," said Shimrod flatly. "We can't hope to catch them now, the horses will run all night. But I know his destination."

"Tintzin Fyral?"

"First he will stop at Faroli to visit the magician Tamurello."

"Where is Faroli?"

"In the forest, not too far away. I can communicate with Tamurello from Avallon, through one Triptomologius. At the very least he will see to the safety of Glyneth and Dhrun if Carfilhiot brings them to Faroli."

"Meanwhile they are at his mercy."

"So they are."

Icnield Way, parchment-pale in the moonlight, crossed a land dark and silent, with no glimmer of light to be seen on either hand. South along the way the two-headed horses pulled the wagon of Dr. Fidelius, with wild eyes and flaring nostrils, mad with hate for the being who drove them as they had never been driven before.

At midnight Carfilhiot pulled to a halt beside a stream. As

the horses drank and cropped grass beside the road, he went to the back of the wagon and opened the door. "How goes it in there?"

After a pause Dhrun spoke from the darkness: "Well enough."

"If you want to drink, or ease yourselves, come down, but try no tricks as I lack patience."

Glyneth and Dhrun whispered together, and agreed that there was no reason to ride in discomfort. Warily they descended from the back of the wagon.

Carfilhiot allowed ten minutes, then ordered them back into the wagon. Dhrun went first, silent and stiff with anger. Glyneth paused with one foot on the bottom step of the ladder. Carfilhiot stood with his back to the moon. She asked: "Why have you kidnapped us?"

"So that Shimrod, whom you know as Dr. Fidelius, works no magic against me."

Glyneth tried to keep her voice from trembling. "Are you planning to set us free?"

"Not immediately. Get in the wagon."

"Where are we going?"

"Into the forest, then away to the west."

"Please let us go!"

Carfilhiot studied her where she stood full in the moonlight. A pretty creature, thought Carfilhiot, fresh as a wildflower. He said lightly: "If you behave nicely, then nice things will happen to you. For now: into the wagon with you."

Glyneth climbed into the wagon, and Carfilhiot closed the door.

Once more the wagon set off along Icnield Way. Glyneth spoke into Dhrun's ear: "This man frightens me. I'm sure that he is Shimrod's enemy."

"If I could see, I'd stab him with my sword," muttered Dhrun.

Glyneth said hesitantly: "I don't know if I could do so—unless he were trying to harm us."

"Then it would be too late. Suppose you stood by the door. When he opened it, could you thrust through his neck?"

"No."

Dhrun sat silently. After a moment he picked up his pipes and began to blow softly: trills and runs, to help himself think. He stopped short and said: "That's rather odd. It's dark in here, is it not?"

"Very dark indeed."

down you will do the same."
said: "In truth, I am no longer in the mood for your
dy, so come down."
n from the wagon first."

id of you."
he help?"
some way. You don't know Dhrun."
hrew open the door. "Come out, you little lizard."
d overheard the conversation with great joy; it
Glyneth had evaded Carfilhiot. Feigning blindness,
r the door and descended to the ground, though
ard to control his exultation. How beautiful the
! How green the trees, how noble the horses! He
fore seen Dr. Fidelius' wagon: gaudy, tall and ec-
portion. And there was Glyneth, as dear and pretty
gh now she was pale and strained, and her blonde
ngled around dry twigs and oak leaves.
d by the wagon, peering into nothingness. Car-
the pallet into the wagon. Dhrun watched him
his was the enemy! Dhrun had imagined him older,
tures and a mottled nose, but Carfilhiot was clear-
ndidly handsome.
agon," said Carfilhiot. "Quick, the both of you."
ats must have a run!" cried Glyneth. "And some-
ll give them some cheese."
cheese, bring it here," said Carfilhiot. "The cats
and tonight all of us may eat cat."
ade no response, and gave Carfilhiot the cheese
ent. The cats took their exercise, and would have
occasion. Glyneth was compelled to speak sternly
ould return to their baskets. And once again the
south.
wagon Dhrun exclaim to Glyneth: "I can see!
bees flew from my eyes! They are as good as ever!
he bees."
Glyneth. "That is wonderful news! But we must
ot know! He is as crafty as he is terrible."
r be sad again," said Dhrun. "No matter what
think back to the time when the world was dark."
l happier if we were riding with someone else,"
istfully. "I spent all last night in a tree."

"Perhaps I've never played in the dark before. Or perhaps I've never noticed. But as I play, the golden bees fly in swoops and loops, as if they were annoyed."

"Perhaps you are keeping them from their sleep."

Dhrun blew into his pipes with more fervor. He played a jig and a merridown and then a caper of three parts.

Carfilhiot called back through the window: "Stop that damnable fifing; it puts my teeth on edge!"

Dhrun said to Glyneth: "Amazing! The bees dart and swoop. Like him"—he jerked his thumb forward—"they have no taste for music." He raised the pipes to his lips, but Glyneth stopped him. "Dhrun, no! He will do us harm!"

All night the horses ran, knowing no fatigue but nevertheless furious at the demon who drove them so mercilessly. An hour after dawn Carfilhiot allowed another ten-minute halt. Neither Dhrun nor Glyneth chose to eat; Carfilhiot found bread and dried fish in the larder at the back of the wagon; he ate a few mouthfuls and once more urged the horses into motion.

All day the wagon rumbled across the pleasant landscapes of south Dahaut: a flat country of endless expanses with a great windy sky overhead.

Late in the day, the wagon crossed the Tam River by a stone bridge of seven arches and so entered Pomperol, without challenge either by the single Daut border official or his corpulent Pomperan counterpart, both preoccupied by their chess game, on a table placed precisely over the boundary at the center of the bridge.

The land altered; forests and isolated muffin-shaped hills, each crowned with a castle, reduced the vast perspectives of Dahaut to ordinary human scale.

At sunset the horses at last began to flag; Carfilhiot knew that he could not drive another long night through. He turned off into the forest and halted beside a brook. While he gingerly unharnessed the horses and tied them where they could drink and graze, Glyneth built a fire, hung the iron pot from its tripod and cooked a makeshift soup from materials at hand. She released her cats from their basket and let them run here and there about a strictly circumscribed area. Sitting over their meager supper, Dhrun and Glyneth spoke together in subdued undertones. Carfilhiot, across the fire, watched them through half-closed eyelids, but said nothing.

Glyneth became increasingly disturbed by the quality of Carfilhiot's attention. At last, as twilight darkened the sky, she called her cats and put them into their baskets. Carfilhiot, seemingly lazy and passive, sat in contemplation of her slight yet unexpectedly rich contours, the easy graces and elegant little flourishes which made Glyneth her unique and endearing self.

Glyneth rinsed the iron pot, stowed it in the locker with the tripod. Carfilhiot rose to his feet, stretched. Glyneth eyed him askance as he went to the back of the wagon, reached within and brought out a pallet which he spread beside the fire.

Glyneth whispered into Dhrun's ear; together they went to the wagon.

Carfilhiot stood behind them. "Where are you going?"

"To bed," said Glyneth. "Where else?"

Carfilhiot seized Dhrun and lofted him into the wagon, then closed and barred the door. "Tonight," he told Glyneth, "you and I will bed by the fire, and tomorrow you will have much to think about."

Glyneth tried to run behind the wagon, but Carfilhiot seized her arm. "Save your energy," he told her. "You will find yourself becoming tired presently, but you won't want to stop."

Inside the wagon Dhrun snatched up his pipes and began to play, in a passion of fury and helpless grief for what was happening to Glyneth. The golden bees, about to relax for the night, with only an occasional warm buzzing to remind Dhrun of their presence, flew a set of resentful loops, but Dhrun played only the harder.

Carfilhiot jumped to his feet and strode to the wagon. "Put an end to the streedle! It grinds on my nerves!"

Dhrun played with an even greater fervor which almost lifted him from his seat. The golden bees flew in zig-zag courses, turned erratic somersaults and finally in despair flew from Dhrun's eyes altogether. Dhrun played all the louder.

Carfilhiot went to the door. "I will come inside; I will break your pipes and deal you such buffets as to silence you very still."

Dhrun played on and the piping excited the bees so that they flew back and forth across the wagon, careening from side to side.

Carfilhiot raised the bar from the door. Dhrun put down the pipes and spoke: "Dassenach, to hand!"

Carfilhiot threw open the door. The bees flew out and struck his face; he recoiled, and so saved his life, as the blade hissed

past his neck. He uttered a sta[...]
sword, wrested it from Dhrun's [...]
derbrush. Dhrun kicked at him [...]
and sent Dhrun reeling back int[...]

"No more noise!" panted Car[...]
piping, or I will do you harm!"

He slammed the door and th[...]
neth, only to find her scrambl[...]
massive old oak tree. He ran acr[...]
was out of his reach. He clim[...]
higher and out to the end of a [...]
her weight, and Carfilhiot dare[...]

He spoke, first cajoling, then [...]
she made no response, and sat [...]
filhiot spoke in a final threat, [...]
then he descended the tree. [...]
chopped away the branch which [...]
and let her die.

All the night long Glyneth h[...]
miserable. Carfilhiot, on the p[...]
sleep, although from time to ti[...]
the fire, and Glyneth was afra[...]

Inside the wagon Dhrun la[...]
his regained sight, but sick wit[...]
side by the fire.

Dawn slowly illuminated th[...]
pallet, and looked up into the [...]
be going."

"I don't care to come down[...]

"Suit yourself. I am leaving[...]

Carfilhiot harnessed the ho[...]
where they stood trembling [...]
tation for their new master.

With growing concern, Gl[...]
filhiot watched her from the [...]
up: "Come down and get into[...]
out and strangle him before [...]
tree and throw a rope over th[...]
the rope so that the branch b[...]
I won't and you will be sore[...]
you, to do as I like."

"If I com[...]
Carfilhio[...]
sour little b[...]

"Let Dhr[...]
"Why?"
"I am afr[...]
"How ca[...]
"He'd fin[...]
Carfilhiot[...]
Dhrun h[...]
seemed that[...]
he groped f[...]
he found it[...]
world looke[...]
had never b[...]
centric of pr[...]
as ever, thou[...]
curls were ta[...]

Dhrun st[...]
filhiot threw[...]
furtively. So[...]
with ropy fe[...]
eyed and sp[...]

"Into the [...]
"First my [...]
thing to eat!

"If there i[...]
can eat grass[...]

Glyneth m[...]
without com[...]
prolonged the[...]
before they [...]
wagon drove[...]

Inside the [...]
Last night the[...]
My eyes, not[...]

"Sh!" said [...]
not let Carfil[...]

"I will nev[...]
happens. I wi[...]

"I would fe[...]
said Glyneth [...]

"If he dares touch you, I will cut him in pieces," declared Dhrun. "Don't forget! I can see now."

"Perhaps it won't come to that. Tonight he may be thinking of other things . . . I wonder if Shimrod is trying to find us?"

"He can't be too far behind."

The wagon rolled south, and an hour after noon arrived at the market-town Honriot, where Carfilhiot bought bread, cheese, apples and a jug of wine.

In the center of Honriot, Icnield Way crossed the East-West Road; Carfilhiot drove to the west urging the horses to ever greater speed, as if he too anticipated the coming of Shimrod. Snorting, shaking their manes, heads low to the ground or sometimes raised on high, the great black horses plunged west, their soft tiger feet thrusting back the ground. Behind trundled the wagon, wheels bounding, the body swaying on its long laminated easy-ways. Occasionally Carfilhiot used his whip, cracking it upon the glistening black haunches, and the horses tossed their heads in rage.

"Take care, take care!" they cried back. "We obey the instruction of your reins, because that is the way it must be; but do not presume, or we might turn and rear over you and flail down our great black feet, and drag you to the dirt and stamp you into the ground! Hear, and have a care!"

Carfilhiot could not understand their speech and used the whip as suited his pleasure; and the horses tossed their heads in ever-mounting fury.

Late in the afternoon the wagon passed King Deuel's summer palace. For the day's entertainment King Deuel had ordained a pageant entitled: "Birds of Fantasy." With great artistry his courtiers had bedecked themselves in black and white feathers, to simulate imaginary sea-birds. Their ladies had been allowed more latitude and they promenaded along the greensward in total avian extravagance, using the plumes of ostrich, egret, lyrebirds, peacocks and vesprils. Some wore confections of pale green, others cerise or mauve or golden-ochre: a prospect of the most gorgeous complexity, and one enjoyed to its fullest by Mad King Deuel, who sat on a tall throne, costumed as a cardinal, the only red bird of the pageant. He was enthusiastic in his praises and called out compliments, pointing with tip of his red wing.

Carfilhiot, recalling his previous encounter with King Deuel, pulled the wagon up short. He considered a moment, then descended and called Glyneth down to the road.

He instructed her in terms which admitted of neither argument nor flexibility. She lowered the side panel to make a platform, brought out her basket, and with Dhrun playing the pipes, set her cats to dancing.

The ladies and gentlemen in their remarkable finery came to watch; they laughed and clapped their hands, and some of them went to call King Deuel's attention to the novel exercises.

King Deuel presently stepped down from his throne and sauntered across the sward to watch the display. He smiled and nodded, but he was not altogether uncritical. "I see here an ingenious effort, to be sure, and the antics are amusing enough. Ha! Excellent saltation there! That black cat is agile! Still it must be remembered that the feline is a lesser order, when all is said. Dare I ask why we have no dancing birds?"

Carfilhiot spoke up. "Your Majesty, I sequester the dancing birds within the wagon! We deem them too exquisite for the common view!"

Mad King Deuel spoke haughtily: "Do you then characterize my august vision as vulgar and common, or anything other than sublime?"

"Indeed not, your Majesty! You are welcome, and you alone, to inspect the extraordinary spectacle inside the wagon."

King Deuel, mollified, marched to the back of the wagon. "A moment, your Majesty!" Carfilhiot closed the side panel, cats and all, and went to the rear. "Glyneth, inside! Dhrun, inside! Prepare the birds for his Majesty. Now, sir, up these steps, and in with you!"

He closed and barred the door, and climbing to the front seat, drove away at a mad gallop. The befeathered ladies looked after in puzzlement; some of the men ran a few steps along the road but were impeded by their black and white plumage, and so, with wings trailing, they returned to the sward before the summer palace, where they tried to fit some pattern of logic upon the occurrence.

Within the wagon King Deuel shouted out orders: "Halt this vehicle at once! I see no birds whatever! This is a most insipid prank!"

Carfilhiot called down through the window: "In due course, your Majesty, I will halt the wagon. Then we shall discuss the plumes and quills that you decreed for my backside!"

King Deuel became silent and for the rest of the day made only fretful clucking sounds.

The day drew toward a close. In the south appeared a line of low gray hills; an outlying arm of Forest Tantrevalles lay dark across the north. Peasant huts became rare and the land tended toward the wild and melancholy.

At sunset Carfilhiot drove the wagon across a meadow to a copse of elms and beeches.

As before Carfilhiot unharnessed the horses and put them to graze on a long tether, while Glyneth cooked the supper. King Deuel refused to leave the wagon, and Dhrun, still feigning blindness, sat on a fallen log.

Glyneth brought soup to King Deuel and served him bread and cheese as well; then she went to sit by Dhrun. They spoke in low voices.

Dhrun said: "He pretends not to watch you, but everywhere you go his eyes follow."

"Dhrun, don't become reckless. He can kill us, but that is the worst he can do."

Dhrun said through clenched teeth: "I won't allow him to touch you. I will die first."

Glyneth whispered: "I've thought of something, so don't worry. Remember, you are still blind!"

Carfilhiot rose to his feet. "Dhrun, into the wagon with you."

Dhrun said sullenly: "I intend to stay with Glyneth."

Carfilhiot seized him, carried him kicking and fighting to the wagon and thrust him inside and barred the door. He turned toward Glyneth. "Tonight there are no trees to climb."

Glyneth backed away. Carfilhiot came after her. Glyneth sauntered to the horses. "Friends," she said, "here is the creature who drives you so hard, and whips your naked backsides."

"Yes, so I see." "I see with both heads at once."

Carfilhiot cocked his head to the side, and approached slowly. "Glyneth! Look at me!"

"I see you well enough," said Glyneth. "Go away, or the horses will trample you."

Carfilhiot halted and looked at the horses, their white eyes and stiff manes. Opening their mouths they showed long forked fangs. One of them suddenly rose on his hind legs and struck down at Carfilhiot with the talons of its front feet.

Carfilhiot retreated to where he could climb upon the wagon

if necessary, and stood glowering. The horses lowered their manes, sheathed their talons, and once more began to graze.

Glyneth strolled back to the wagon. Carfilhiot jerked forward. Glyneth stopped still. The horses raised their heads and looked toward Carfilhiot. Their manes began to rise. Carfilhiot made an angry gesture and climbed to the seat of the wagon.

Glyneth opened the back door. She and Dhrun made a bed under the wagon and rested undisturbed.

On a morning dreary with spatters of rain, the wagon passed from Pomperol into west Dahaut and entered the Forest of Tantrevalles. Carfilhiot, hunched on the front seat, drove at reckless speed, wielding his whip with abandon, and the black horses ran foaming through the forest. At noon Carfilhiot turned off the road to follow a dim lane which climbed the slopes of a rocky hill, to arrive at Faroli, the octagonal multi-leveled manse of Tamurello the Sorcerer.

By three sets of invisible hands Carfilhiot had been bathed and groomed, lathered head to toe with sweet sap of dimity. He had been scraped with a white boxwood paddle and rinsed in warm water scented with lavender, so that his fatigue had become no more than a delightful languor. He dressed in a shirt of black and crimson and a robe of dark gold. An invisible hand tendered him a goblet of pomegranate wine, which he drank, then stretched his beautiful easy limbs like a lazy animal. For a few moments he stood in reflection, wondering how best to have his way with Tamurello. Much depended upon Tamurello's mood, whether it were active or passive. Carfilhiot must control these moods as a musician controls his music. Finally he left the chamber and joined Tamurello in the center saloon, where on all sides tall panes of glass overlooked the forest.

Tamurello seldom showed himself in his natural similitude, preferring always a guise from among the dozens at his command. Carfilhiot had seen him in a variety of phases, more or less beguiling, but all memorable. Tonight he was an elderkin of the falloys, in a sea-green robe and a crown of silver cusps. He used white hair and silver-pale skin, with green eyes. Carfilhiot had seen this semblance before and had no great love for its extremely subtle perceptions and the delicate precision of its demands. As always, when confronted with the falloy elderkin, Carfilhiot adopted a manner of taciturn strength.

The elderkin inquired as to his comfort. "You are refreshed, I hope?"

"I have known several days of hardship, but I am once more comfortable."

The elderkin turned a smiling glance out the window. "This misfortune of yours—how curious and unexpected!"

Carfilhiot replied in a neutral voice: "For the whole of my inconvenience I blame Melancthe."

The elderkin smiled once more. "And all without provocation?"

"Naturally not! When have I, or you, concerned ourselves with provocation?"

"Seldom. But what will be the consequences?"

"None, or so I hope."

"You are not definite in your own mind?"

"I must give the matter thought."

"True. In such cases one must be judicious."

"There are other considerations to be weighed. I have had shocks and rude surprises. You will recall the affair at Trilda?"

"Well enough."

"Shimrod traced Rughalt through his disgusting knees. Rughalt instantly disclosed my name. Shimrod now thinks to avenge himself upon me. But I hold hostages against him."

The elderkin sighed and made a fluttering gesture. "Hostages are of limited utility. If they die they are a nuisance. Who are these hostages?"

"A boy and a girl who traveled in Shimrod's company. The boy plays remarkable music on the pipes and the girl talks to animals."

Tamurello rose to his feet. "Come."

The two went to Tamurello's workshop. Tamurello took a black box from the shelf, poured inside a gill of water, added drops of a glowing yellow liquid which caused the water to show films of light at various levels. In a leather-bound libram Tamurello located the name "Shimrod." Using the appended formula he prepared a dark liquid which he added to the contents of the box, then poured the mixture into an iron cylinder six inches tall and two inches in diameter. He sealed the top with a glass cap, then held the cylinder to his eye. After a moment he gave the cylinder to Carfilhiot. "What do you see?"

Looking through the glass, Carfilhiot observed four men riding at a gallop through the forest. One of the men was Shimrod.

He recognized none of the others: warriors, or knights, so he judged.

He returned the cylinder to Tamurello. "Shimrod rides pell-mell through the forest with three companions."

Tamurello concurred. "They will arrive within the hour."

"And then?"

"Shimrod hopes to find you here in my company, which will afford him cause to call on Murgen. I am not yet ready for a confrontation with Murgen; hence you must inevitably be judged and suffer the adjudication."

"So I must go."

"And quickly."

Carfilhiot strode back and forth across the chamber. "Very well, if that is the way of it. I hope that you will give us transport."

Tamurello raised his eyebrows. "You intend to retain these persons to whom Shimrod is attached?"

"What reason is there to do otherwise? They are valuable hostages. I will trade them for the locks on Shimrod's magic, and his retirement from the case. You may cite these terms to him, if you will."

Tamurello grudgingly agreed. "What I must do, I will do. Come!"

The two went out to the wagon. "There is another matter," said Tamurello. "One which Shimrod pressed upon me before your arrival, and which I cannot deny him. In the strongest terms I advise and in fact make demands upon you: do not injure, abase, abuse, torment, mistreat, harass, or make physical contact with your hostages. Cause them no travail, mental or physical. Do not allow them to be mistreated by others. Do not neglect them to their detriment or discomfort. Do not facilitate nor suggest, nor by any act of omission, allow them to suffer misfortune or hurt or molestation, accidental or otherwise. Ensure their comfort and health. Provide—"

"Enough, enough!" croaked Carfilhiot in anger. "I understand the gist of your remarks. I must treat the two children like honored guests."

"Exactly so. I do not choose to answer for harms done by you, from frivolity, lust, mischief, or spite; and Shimrod has made these demands upon me!"

Carfilhiot controlled the tumult of his feelings. He spoke in a terse voice. "I understand your instructions and they shall be implemented."

Tamurello circled the wagon. He rubbed the wheels and the rims with a blue jade talisman. He went to the horses, lifted their legs and wiped their feet with the stone. They stood trembling and rigid to his touch, but, recognizing his power, pretended not to see him.

Tamurello wiped the horses' heads, flanks, haunches and bellies with the stone, then rubbed the sides of the wagon. "Now! You are ready! Be off with you and away! Shimrod approaches fast. Fly low, fly high, but fly to Tintzin Fyral!"

Carfilhiot jumped to the driver's seat, took up the reins. He raised his hand to Tamurello, snapped the whip. The horses lunged forward into the air. Westward over the forest careened the wagon of Dr. Fidelius, high above the highest tree tops, and folk of the forest looked up in awe at the two-headed horses plunging across the sky, with the tall wagon trundling behind.

Half an hour later four horsemen arrived at Faroli. They dismounted from their horses, to stand swaying, limp with fatigue and frustration, for already, through Never-fail, they knew that Shimrod's wagon had gone.

A chamberlain came from the manse. "Your wishes, noble sirs?"

"Announce us to Tamurello," said Shimrod.

"Your names, sir?"

"He expects us."

The chamberlain withdrew.

At one of the windows Shimrod glimpsed a moving shadow. "He watches us and listens," Shimrod told the others. "He decides which guise he will show us."

"The life of a wizard is a strange one," said Cargus.

Yane asked in wonder: "Is he ashamed of his own face?"

"Few have seen it. He has heard enough; now he comes."

Slowly, step by step, a tall man approached from the shadows. He wore a suit of silver chain, the mesh so fine as to be near-invisible, a jupon of sea-green silk, a helmet surmounted by three tall prongs, like the spines of a fish. From the brow hung a row of silver chains concealing the face below. At a distance of ten feet he halted and folded his arms. "I am Tamurello."

"You know why we are here. Call back Carfilhiot, with the two children he has kidnapped."

"Carfilhiot has come and gone."

"Then you are his accomplice and share his guilt."

From behind the chains came a low laugh. "I am Tamurello. For my deeds I accept neither praise nor blame. In any case, your quarrel is with Carfilhiot, not with me."

"Tamurello, I have no patience for empty words. You know what I require of you. Bring Carfilhiot back, with my wagon and the two children he holds captive."

Tamurello's response came in a deeper, more resonant voice. "Only the strong should threaten."

"Empty words again. Once more: Order Carfilhiot to return."

"Impossible."

"You have expedited his escape from me; you thereby take responsibility for Glyneth and Dhrun."

Tamurello stood silent, arms folded. The four men felt his slow inspection from behind the silver chains. Finally he said. "You have delivered your message. You need not delay your going."

The four men mounted their horses and departed. At the edge of the glade they paused to look back. Tamurello had returned into the manse.

In a hollow voice Shimrod said: "So there we have it. Now we must deal with Carfilhiot at Tintzin Fyral. Temporarily at least, Glyneth and Dhrun are safe from physical harm."

Aillas asked, "What of Murgen? Will he intercede?"

"It is not so easy as you might think. Murgen constrains magicians to their own affairs, and so himself is constrained."

"I can wait no longer," said Aillas. "I am obliged to return to Troicinet. Already I may be too late, if King Ospero is dead."

28

FROM FAROLI BACK TO ICNIELD WAY rode the four men, then south through Pomperol, and across the breadth of Lyonesse to Slute Skeme on the Lir.

At the harbor the fishermen were chary of so much as discussing passage to Troicinet. The master of the *Sweet Lupus* told them, "A Troice warship patrols sometimes close along the shore, sometimes out by the horizon, and sinks any hull it can catch. It is a fast ship. To make the cheese more binding, Casmir keeps spies by the dozens. Were I to make the passage, news would reach Casmir and I'd be taken as a Troice agent, and who knows what might happen? What with the old king dying, we can expect change: for the better, or so I hope."

"Then he's not dead yet?"

"The news is a week old; who can say? Meanwhile I must sail with one eye for the weather, one eye for the Troice and one eye for the fish, but never more than a mile offshore. I'd need a fortune of money to tempt me to Troicinet."

Shimrod's ear had picked up a hint that the fisherman's resolve was flexible. "How long is the crossing?"

"Oh, if one left by night, to avoid spies and patrols, he'd arrive the next night. It's a good reaching wind and the currents are mild."

"And what is your price?"

"Ten gold crowns might tempt me."

"Nine gold crowns and our four horses."

"Done. When will you leave?"

"Now."

"Too risky. And I must prepare the boat. Come back at sunset. Leave your horses at the stable yonder."

Without noteworthy incident the *Sweet Lupus* made a brisk crossing of the Lir and put into Shircliff, halfway along the Troice coast, two hours before midnight, with lights still showing in the dockside taverns.

The master of the *Sweet Lupus* tied up to the pier with a notable lack of apprehension. Cargus asked: "What of the Troice authorities? Won't they seize your boat?"

"Aha! That is a tempest in a teapot. Why should we inconvenience each other over foolishness? We stay on good terms and do favors for each other and affairs proceed as always."

"Well then, good luck to you!"

The four applied to the ostlery for horses and woke the ostler from his bed on the straw. At first he was inclined to peevishness. "Why not wait for morning like sensible men? Why this bustling about at all hours and denying honest men their sleep?"

Cargus growled even more peevishly: "Hold your complaints, and provide us four sound horses!"

"If I must I must. Whither go you?"

"To Domreis, at best speed."

"For the coronation? You are starting late for a ceremony which begins at noon!"

"King Ospero is dead?"

The ostler made a reverent sign. "To our sorrow, for he was a good king, free of cruelty or vain display.

"And the new king?"

"He is to be King Trewan. I wish him prosperity and a long life, since only a churl would do otherwise."

"Hurry with the horses."

"You are already too late. You will founder the horses if you hope to arrive for the coronation."

"Hurry!" cried Aillas in a passion. "Bestir yourself!"

The ostler, muttering to himself, saddled the horses and led them to the street. "And now, my money!"

Shimrod paid over his price and the ostler retired. Aillas told his fellows, "At this moment I am King of Troicinet. If we arrive at Domreis before noon I will be king tomorrow."

"And if we are late?"

"Then the crown has been set on Trewan's head and he is king. Let us be off."

The four rode west beside the coast, past quiet fishing villages and long beaches. At dawn, with the horses stumbling from fatigue, they arrived at Slaloc where they changed horses and rode through the morning toward Domreis.

The sun rose toward the zenith, and ahead the road curved down a slope, across a park to the Temple of Gaea, where a thousand notables attended the coronation.

At the edge of the temple grounds, the four were halted by a guard of eight cadets from the College of Dukes, wearing blue and silver ceremonial armor, with tall scarlet plumes at the side of their helmets. They dropped halberds to bar the way of the four travelers. "You may not enter!"

From within came the peal of clarions, a processional fanfare signaling the appearance of the king-designate. Aillas spurred his horse into motion and broke past the crossed halberds, followed by his three companions. Before them stood the Temple of Gaea. A heavy entabulature rested on columns in the classical style. The interior was open to the winds. On a central altar burned the dynastic fire. From the vantage of horseback Aillas saw Prince Trewan mount steps, walk with ritual solemnity across the terrace and kneel on a cushioned bench. Between Aillas and the altar stood the quality of Troicinet in formal caparison. Those at the back turned in outrage as the four rode up behind them.

Aillas called out: "Make way, make way!" He sought to ride through the ranked nobility, but angry hands seized his bridle and jerked his horse to a halt. Aillas jumped to the ground and thrust forward, pushing the rapt and reverent onlookers roughly from his way, to their shock and disapproval.

The High Priest stood before the kneeling Trewan. He held high the crown and uttered a sonorous benediction in the ancient Danaan tongue.

Thrusting, dodging, side-stepping, careless of whom he shouldered aside, striking down the aristocratic arms which reached to stay him, swearing and gasping, Aillas gained the steps.

The High Priest brought forward the ceremonial sword and placed it before Trewan, who, as custom ordained, placed his hands on the cross-piece of the handle. The priest scratched Trewan's forehead with a knife, drawing a drop of blood. Trewan, bowing his head, pressed the blood to the sword handle, to symbolize his will to defend Troicinet with blood and steel.

The priest raised the crown on high, and held it over Trewan's head, as Aillas gained the steps. Two guards rushed to seize him; Aillas pushed them aside, ran to the altar, thrust the High Priest's arm aside before the crown could touch Trewan's head. "Stop the ceremony! This is not your king!"

Trewan, blinking in confusion, rose to his feet and turning, looked into Aillas' face. His jaw dropped; his eyes widened. Then, feigning outrage, he cried out: "What means this sorry intrusion? Guards, drag off this madman! He has committed sacrilege! Take him aside and cut him loose from his head!"

Aillas pushed the guards aside. He called out: "Look at me! Do you not know me? I am Prince Aillas!"

Trewan stood heavy-browed and indecisive, his mouth twitching and red spots burning in his cheeks. At last he called out in a nasal voice: "Aillas drowned at sea! You can't be Aillas! Guards, hither! This is an impostor!"

"Wait!" A portly old man, wearing a suit of black velvet, slowly climbed the steps. Aillas recognized Sir Este who had been seneschal at the court of King Granice.

Sir Este gazed a moment into Aillas' face. He turned and spoke to the assembled nobility, who had pressed forward to the steps. "This is no impostor. This is Prince Aillas." He turned to stare at Trewan. "Who should know it better than you?"

Trewan made no reply.

The seneschal turned back to Aillas. "I cannot believe that you absented yourself from Troicinet and gave us all to mourn from sheer frivolity, nor that you arrived at this instant merely to create a sensation."

"Sir, I have only just returned to Troicinet. I rode here as fast as horses could carry me, as my comrades here will attest. Before this time I was prisoner to King Casmir. I escaped only to be captured by the Ska. There is more to tell, but with the aid of my comrades I have arrived in time to preserve my crown from the murderer Trewan, who pushed me into the dark sea!"

Trewan gave a cry of rage. "No man may besmirch my honor and live!" He swung the ancient ceremonial sword in an arc to cleave Aillas' head from his body.

Nearby stood Cargus. He flung out his forearm; through the air flew his broad Galician dagger, to strike deep into Trewan's throat, so that the point protruded from the side opposite. The sword clattered to the stone floor. Trewan's eyes rolled upward to show the whites and he dropped in a spraddle-legged heap, to kick and convulse and at last lay quiet on his back.

The seneschal signaled to the guards. "Remove the corpse."

Then to the assembly: "Noble folk of Troicinet! I recognize Prince Aillas as the proper and rightful king. Who disputes or gainsays my judgment? Let him step forward to declare his impeachment!"

He waited half a minute.

"Let the ceremony proceed!"

29

AILLAS AND SHIMROD, departing the palace Miraldra before dawn, rode eastward along the coast road. Late in the afternoon they passed through Green Man's Gap, where they halted to look across the view. The Ceald spread away before them in bands of many colors: hazy black-green, grayed yellow and fusk, smoky blue-lavender. Aillas pointed across the distance to a glint of placid silver. "There is Janglin Water, and Watershade. A hundred times I have sat just here with my father; always he was happier to be coming home than going. I doubt if he was comfortable in his kingship."

"What of you?"

Aillas considered, then said: "I have been prisoner, slave, fugitive, and now king, which I prefer. Still, it is not the life I would have chosen for myself."

"If nothing else," said Shimrod, "you have seen the world from its underside, which perhaps might be to your advantage."

Aillas laughed. "My experience has not made me more amiable; that is certain."

"Still, you are young and presumably resilient," said Shimrod. "Most of your life lies ahead of you. Marriage, sons and daughters; who knows what else?"

Aillas grunted. "Small chance of that. There is no one I wish to marry. Except..." An image came to Aillas' mind, unbidden and unpremeditated: a dark-haired girl, slender as a wand, olive-pale of complexion, with long sea-green eyes.

"Except for whom?"

"No matter. I will never see her again...Time we were on our way; there are eight miles yet to ride."

The two men rode down upon the Ceald, past a pair of drowsy villages, through a forest, over old bridges. They rode beside a marsh of a hundred waterways, fringed with cat-tails, willows and alder. Birds thronged the marsh: herons, hawks perched high in the trees, blackbirds among the reeds, coots, bitterns, ducks.

The waterways became deeper and wider, the reeds submerged; the marsh opened upon Janglin Water, and the road, passing through an orchard of ancient pear trees, arrived at Watershade Castle.

Aillas and Shimrod dismounted at the door. A groom came up to take their horses. When Aillas had departed Watershade for the court of King Granice, the groom had been Cern the stable-boy. Cern now greeted Aillas with a broad, if nervous, smile of pleasure. "Welcome home, Sir Aillas—though now it seems it must be 'Your Majesty.' That doesn't come comfortable to the tongue, when what I remember best is swimming in the lake and wrestling in the barn."

Aillas threw his arms around Cern's neck. "I'll still wrestle you. But now that I'm king, you've got to let me win."

Cern tilted his head sidewise to consider. "That's how it must be, since it's only proper to show respect for the office. So then, one way or the other, Aillas—sir—Your Majesty—however you are to be called—it's good to see you home. I'll take the horses; they'll like a rub and a feed."

The front doors were flung open; in the aperture stood a tall white-haired man in black with a ring of keys at his waist: Weare, the chamberlain at Watershade for as long as Aillas could remember and long before. "Welcome home, Sir Aillas!"

"Thank you, Weare." Aillas embraced him. "In the last two years I've often wished to be here."

"You'll find nothing changed, except that good Sir Ospero is no longer with us, so that it's been quiet and lonely. How often I've longed for the good days, before first you, then Sir Ospero went to the court." Weare took a step back and gazed into Aillas' face. "You left here a boy, without a care, handsome and easy, with never a harsh thought."

"And I have changed? In truth, Weare, I am older."

Weare studied him a moment. "I still see the gallant lad, and also something dark. I fear you have known trouble."

"True enough, but I am here and the bad days are behind us."

"So I hope, Sir Aillas!"

Aillas once again embraced him. "Here is my comrade the

noble Shimrod, who I hope will be our guest long and often."

"I am happy to know you, sir. I've put you in the Blue Chamber with a nice view across the lake. Sir Aillas, tonight I thought you would prefer to use the Red Chamber. You'd hardly be for your old rooms, nor for Sir Ospero's chambers, quite so soon."

"Exactly right, Weare! How well you know my feelings! You've always been kind to me, Weare!"

"You've always been a good boy, Sir Aillas."

An hour later Aillas and Shimrod went out upon the terrace to watch the sun settle behind the far hills. Weare served wine from a stoneware jug. "This is our own San Sue which you liked so well. This year we've laid down eighty-six tuppets. I won't serve nut-cakes, because Flora wants you with your best appetite for supper."

"I hope she's not producing anything too lavish."

"Merely a few of your favorites."

Weare departed. Aillas leaned back in his chair. "I've been King a week. I have talked and listened from morning till night. I have knighted Cargus and Yane and invested them with property; I have sent for Ehirme and all her family; she will live out her life in comfort. I have inspected the shipyards, the armories, the barracks. From my spy-masters I have heard secrets and revelations, so that my mind throbs. I learn that King Casmir is building war galleys at inland shipyards. He hopes to assemble a hundred galleys and invade Troicinet. King Granice intended to land an army at Cape Farewell and occupy Tremblance up into the Troaghs. He might have succeeded; Casmir expected nothing so bold, but spies saw the flotilla and Casmir rushed his army to Cape Farewell and arranged an ambush, but Granice was warned by his own spies, and called off the operation."

"The war apparently is controlled by spies."

Aillas agreed that this might seem to be the case. "On balance, the advantage has been ours. Our assault force remains intact, with new catapults to throw three hundred yards. So Casmir stands first on one foot, then the other because our transports are ready to sail, and the spies could never warn Casmir in time."

"So you intend to prosecute the war?"

Aillas looked out across the lake. "Sometimes, for an hour or two, I forget the hole where Casmir put me. I never escape for long."

"Casmir still does not know who fathered Suldrun's child?"

"Only by a name in the priest's register, if even he has troubled to learn so much. He thinks me moldering at the bottom of his hole. Someday he will know differently . . . Here is Weare, and we are summoned to our supper."

At the table Aillas sat in his father's chair and Shimrod occupied the place opposite. Weare served them trout from the lake and duck from the marsh, with salad from the kitchen garden. Over wine and nuts, with legs stretched out to the fire, Aillas said: "I have brooded much on Carfilhiot. He still does not know that Dhrun is my son."

"The affair is complicated," said Shimrod. "Tamurello is ultimately at fault; his intent is to work through me against Murgen. He forced the witch Melancthe to beguile me that I might be killed, or marooned, in Irerly, while Carfilhiot stole my magic."

"Will not Murgen act to recover your magic?"

"Not unless Tamurello acts first."

"But Tamurello already has acted."

"Not demonstrably."

"Then we should provoke Tamurello to a demonstration more overt."

"Easier said than done. Tamurello is a cautious man."

"Not cautious enough. He overlooked a possible situation which would allow me to act in all proper justice against both Carfilhiot and Casmir."

Shimrod thought a moment. "There you leave me behind."

"My great grandfather Helm was brother to Lafing, Duke of South Ulfland. I have had news from Oäldes that King Quilcy is dead: drowned in his own bath-water. I am next in line to the Kingdom of South Ulfland, which Casmir does not realize. I intend to assert my claim by the most immediate and definite process. Then, as Carfilhiot's lawful king, I will demand that he come down from Tintzin Fyral to render homage."

"And if he refuses?"

"Then we will attack his castle."

"It is said to be impregnable."

"So it is said. When the Ska failed, they reinforced that conviction."

"Why should you have better luck?"

Aillas threw a handful of nutshells into the fire. "I will be acting as his rightful sovereign. The factors of Ys will welcome me, as will the barons. Only Casmir would oppose us, but he is sluggish and we plan to catch him napping."

"If you are able to surprise me—and you have—then you should surprise Casmir."

"So I hope. Our ships are loading; we are giving false information to the spies. Casmir presently will discover an unpleasant surprise."

30

KING CASMIR OF LYONESSE, who never took comfort in half-measures, had established spies in every quarter of Troicinet, including the palace Miraldra. He assumed, correctly, that Troice spies subjected his own activities to a scrutiny equally pervasive; therefore, when taking information from one of his secret agents, he used careful procedures to safeguard the agent's identity.

Information arrived by various methods. One morning at breakfast he found a small white stone beside his plate. Without comment Casmir put the stone in his pocket; it had been placed there, so he knew, by Sir Mungo, the seneschal, who would have received it from a messenger.

After taking his breakfast, Casmir swathed himself in a hooded cloak of brown fustian and departed Haidion by a private way through the old armory and out into the Sfer Arct. After ensuring that no one followed, Casmir went by lanes and alleys to the warehouse of a wine merchant. He fitted a key into the lock of a heavy oak door, and so entered a dusty little tasting room smelling heavily vinous. A man squat and gray-haired, with crooked legs and a broken nose, gave him a casual salute. Casmir knew the man only as Valdez; and he himself used the name "Sir Eban."

Valdez might or might not know him as Casmir; his manner at all times was totally impersonal, which suited Casmir very well.

Valdez pointed him to one of the chairs, and seated himself in another. He poured wine from an earthenware jug into a pair of mugs. "I have important information. The new Troice king intends a naval operation. He has massed his ships in the Hob

Hook, and at Cape Haze troops are moving aboard; an assault is imminent."

"An assault where?"

Valdez, whose face was that of a man clever and cool, ruthless and saturnine, gave an indifferent shrug. "No one has troubled to tell me. The shipmasters are to sail when the weather shifts south—which gives them west, east and north for their sailing."

"They are trying Cape Farewell again: that is my guess."

"It might well be, if defense has been relaxed."

Casmir nodded thoughtfully. "Just so."

"Another possibility. Each ship has been supplied with a heavy grapple and hawser."

Casmir leaned back in his chair. "What purpose would these serve? They can't expect a naval battle."

"They might hope to prevent one. They are taking aboard firepots. And remember, south wind blows them up the River Sime."

"To the shipyards?" Casmir was instantly aroused. "To the new ships?"

Valdez raised the cup of wine to his crooked slash of a mouth. "I can only report facts. The Troice are preparing to attack, with a hundred ships and at least five thousand troops, well armed."

Casmir muttered. "Balt Bay is guarded, but not that well. They could work disaster if they took us by surprise. How can I know when their first fleet puts to sea?"

"Beacons are chancy. If one fails, through fog or rain, the whole system fails. In any case there is no time to set up such a chain. Pigeons will not fly a hundred miles of water. I know no other system, save those propelled by magic."

Casmir jumped to his feet. He dropped a leather purse upon the table. "Return to Troicinet. Send me news as often as practical."

Valdez lifted the purse and seemed satisfied by its weight. "I will do so."

Casmir returned to Haidion, and within the hour couriers rode from Lyonesse Town at speed. The Dukes of Jong and Twarsbane were ordered to take armies, knights and armored cavalry to Cape Farewell, to reinforce the garrison already on the scene. Other troops, in the number of eight thousand, were despatched in haste to the Sime River shipyards, and everywhere along the coast watches were set. The harbors were sealed and all boats restricted to moorings (save that single vessel which would carry Valdez back to Troicinet), in order that spies might not apprise the Troice that the forces of Lyonesse had been mobilized against the secret assault.

The winds shifted south and eighty ships with six thousand soldiers took departure. Leaning to the port tack they sailed into the west. Passing through the Straits of Palisidra, the fleet kept well to the south, beyond the purview of Casmir's vigilant garrisons, then swung north, to coast easily downwind, with blue water gurgling under the bows and surging up behind the transoms.

Meanwhile, Troice emissaries traversed the length and breadth of South Ulfland. To cold castles along the moors, to walled towns and mountain keeps, they brought news of the new king and his ordinances which must now be obeyed. Often they won immediate and grateful acquiescence; as often they were forced to overcome hatreds fomented by the murders, treacheries and torments of centuries. These were emotions so bitter as to dominate all other thought: feuds which were to the participants as water to a fish, vengeances and hoped-for vengeances so sweet as to obsess the mind. In such cases logic had no power. ("Peace in Ulfland? There shall be no peace for me until Keghorn Keep is broken stone by stone and Melidot blood soaks the rubble!") Thereupon, the envoys used tactics more direct. "You must, for your own security, put aside these hatreds. A heavy hand rules Ulfland, and if you will not conform to the order, you will find your enemies in favor, with the might of the realm at their call, and you will pay a hard price for worthless goods."

"Ha hmm. And who is to rule Ulfland?"

"King Aillas already rules, by right and might, and the old bad times are gone. Make your choice! Join with your peers and bring peace to this land, or you will be named renegade! Your castle will be taken and burned; you, if you survive, will live out your life as a thrall, with your sons and daughters. Cast your lot with us; you cannot but gain."

Thereupon, the person so addressed might try to procrastinate, or declare himself concerned only with his own domain, without interest in the land at large. If his nature were cautious, he might assert that he must wait to see how others conducted themselves. To each case the envoy replied: "Choose now! You are either with us in law, or against us, as an outlaw! There is no middle way!" In the end almost all the gentry of South Ulfland gave acquiescence to the demands, if only out of hatred for Faude Carfilhiot. They arrayed themselves in their ancient armor, mustered their troops, and rode out from their old keeps with banners fluttering above their heads, to assemble on the field near Cleadstone Castle.

In his workroom Faude Carfilhiot sat absorbed in the moving figures on his map. What could such a conclave portend? Certainly nothing to his advantage. He summoned his captains and sent them riding down the valley to mobilize his army.

Two hours before dawn the wind died and the sea became calm. With Ys close at hand the sails were brailed and the oarsmen bent their backs to the sweeps. Point Istaia and the Temple of Atlante interposed their silhouettes across the pre-dawn sky; the ships slid over pewter water, close by the steps descending from the temple to the sea, then turned where the beach curved down from the north into the estuary of the Evander and grounded upon the sand to discharge troops, then the transports eased close up to the docks at Ys to unload cargo.

From their garden terraces the factors of Ys watched the debarkation with no more than languid interest, and the folk of the town went about their affairs, as if incursions from the sea were a daily occurrence.

At the balustrade of her own palace Melanthe watched the ships arrive. Presently she turned and slipped into the dim interior of her palace.

Sir Glide of Fairsted, with a single companion took horse and rode at speed up the vale, through fields and orchards, with mountains rising steep to right and left. Through a dozen villages and hamlets the two men rode, with no one giving so much as curiosity to their passage.

The mountains converged upon the valley which finally terminated under that flat-topped height known as Tac Tor, with Tintzin Fyral to the side. A taint on the air grew ever stronger and presently the two riders discovered the source: six poles fifty feet tall, supporting as many impaled corpses.

The road passing under the poles crossed a meadow which displayed further evidences of Carfilhiot's severity toward his enemies: a gantry twenty feet high from which hung four men with heavy stones dangling from their feet. Beside each stood a marker, measured off in inches.

A sentry-house guarded the way. A pair of soldiers in the black and purple of Tintzin Fyral marched out to cross halberds. A captain followed them and spoke to Sir Glide. "Sir, why do you make approach to Tintzin Fyral?"

"We are a deputation in the service of King Aillas," said Sir Glide. "We request a conference with Sir Faude Carfilhiot, and we solicit the safety of his protection before, during and after this conference, in order to achieve the full freedom of our expression."

The captain performed a somewhat casual salute. "Sirs, I will transmit your message at once." He mounted a horse and rode up a narrow way cut so as to traverse the cliff. The two soldiers continued to bar the road with crossed halberds.

Sir Glide spoke to one of the guards. "You have served Sir Faude Carfilhiot over a long period?"

"Only a year, sir."

"Your nationality is Ulf?"

"North Ulf, sir."

Sir Glide indicated the gantry. "What is the reason for this exercise?"

The guard gave an indifferent shrug. "Sir Faude is persecuted by the gentry of the region; they will not abide his rule. We scour the land, keen as wolves, and whenever they go abroad, to hunt or inspect their lands, we take them into custody. And then Sir Faude makes an example to deter and frighten the others."

"His punishments show ingenuity."

Again the guard shrugged. "It makes no great difference. One way or another it is death. And simple hangings or even impalings at last become a bore for all concerned."

"Why are these men measured by markers?"

"They are great enemies. You see there Sir Jehan of Femus, his sons Waldrop and Hambol, and his cousin Sir Basil. They were taken and Sir Faude sentenced them to punitive display, but also showed clemency. He said: 'Let markers be placed; then when these miscreants have stretched to double their length, let them be released, and allowed to run freely back over the fells to Castle Femus.'"

"And how goes it with them?"

The guard shook his head. "They are weak and suffer anguish; and all have at least two feet still to grow."

Sir Glide looked back along the valley and up and down the mountainsides. "It would seem no great matter to ride up the valley with thirty men and effect a rescue."

The guard, grinning, showed a mouthful of broken teeth. "So it would seem. Never forget, Sir Faude is a master of crafty tricks. No one invades his valley to escape free and harmless."

Sir Glide again considered the mountains rising steep from the valley floor. No doubt they were riddled with tunnels, vantages and sally-holes. He told the guard: "I would suspect that Sir Faude's enemies gather faster than he can kill them."

"It may be so," said the guard. "Mithra keep us safe!" The conversation, from his point of view, had run its course; perhaps already he had been too garrulous.

Sir Glide joined his companion, a tall man dressed in a black cloak and broad-brimmed black hat pulled low over his forehead to shadow a spare long-nosed face. This person, though armed only with a sword and lacking armor, nonetheless carried himself with the ease of a nobleman, and Sir Glide treated him as an equal.

The captain came down from the castle. He addressed Sir Glide. "Sir, I have faithfully delivered your message to Sir Faude Carfilhiot. He gives you entrance to Tintzin Fyral and warrants your safety. Follow, if you will; he can receive you at once." So saying, he put his horse through a grand caracole and galloped away. The deputation followed at a more moderate pace. Up the cliff they rode, back and forth, and at every stage discovered instruments of defense: embrasures, traps, stone-tumbles, timbers pivoted to sweep the intruder into space, sally-ports and trip-holes.

Back, forth, again and again, and the road widened. The two men dismounted and gave over their horses to stable-boys.

The captain took them into the lower hall of Tintzin Fyral, where Carfilhiot waited. "Gentlemen, you are dignitaries of Troicinet?"

Sir Glide assented. "That is correct. I am Sir Glide of Fairsted and I carry credentials from King Aillas of Troicinet, which I now put before you." He tendered a parchment, at which Carfilhiot glanced, then handed over to a small fat chamberlain. "Read."

The chamberlain read in a reedy voice:

"To Sir Faude Carfilhiot
At Tintzin Fyral:

By the law of South Ulfland, by might and by right, I
have become King of South Ulfland, and I hereby require
of you the fealty due the sovereign-ruler. I present to you
Lord Glide of Fairsted, and another, both trusted council-
lors. Sir Glide will enlarge upon my requirements and in
general speak with my voice. He may be entrusted with
whatever messages, even the most confidential, you may
care to impart.

I trust that you will make quick response to my demands
as expressed by Sir Glide. Below I append my signature
and the seal of the kingdom.

Aillas
Of South Ulfland and
Troicinet: King."

The chamberlain returned the parchment to Carfilhiot, who
studied it with a thoughtful frown, obviously arranging his
thoughts. At last he spoke in tones of great gravity. "I am naturally interested in the concepts of King Aillas. Let us conduct
this business in my small saloon."

Carfilhiot led Sir Glide and his companion up a low flight of
steps, past a kind of aviary thirty feet high and fifteen feet in
diameter, equipped with perches, nests, feeders and swings.
The human denizens of the aviary exemplified Carfilhiot's
whimsy at its most pungent; he had amputated the limbs of
several captives, both male and female and had substituted iron
claws and hooks, with which they clung to the perches. Each
was adorned with plumage of one sort or another; all twittered,
whistled and sang bird-songs. Chief among the group, splendid
in bright green feathers, sat Mad King Deuel. Now he hunched
on his perch, an aggrieved expression on his face. At the sight
of Carfilhiot he became alert and hopped briskly along the perch.
"One moment, if you will! I have a serious complaint!"

Carfilhiot paused. "Well, what now? Of late you have been
querulous."

"And why should I not? Today I was promised worms. In spite of all, I was served only barley!"

"Patience," said Carfilhiot. "Tomorrow you will have your worms."

Mad King Deuel muttered peevishly, hopped to another perch and sat brooding. Carfilhiot led his company into a room paneled in pale wood, with a green rug on the floor and windows overlooking the valley. He gestured to a table. "Be seated, if you please. Have you dined?"

Sir Glide seated himself; his companion remained standing at the back of the room. "We already have taken our meal," said Sir Glide. "If you like, we will go directly to our business."

"Please do so." Carfilhiot leaned back in his chair and thrust out his long strong legs.

"My message is simple. The new king of South Ulfland has arrived in force at Ys. King Aillas brings a strong rule to the land and all must obey him."

Carfilhiot gave a metallic laugh. "I know nothing of this. To the best of my information, Quilcy left no heirs; the line is dead. Where then does Aillas derive his right?"

"He is King of South Ulfland by collateral lineage and by proper law of the land. Already he comes up the Vale, and he bids you to descend and meet him, and to give over any thoughts of resisting his rule from the strength of this, your castle Tintzin Fyral, since in this case he will reduce it."

"That has been tried before," said Carfilhiot, smiling. "The assailants are gone and Tintzin Fyral remains. In any event King Casmir of Lyonesse will not allow a Troice presence here."

"He has no choice. We have already sent a force to take Kaul Bocach and so deny Casmir his thoroughfare."

Carfilhiot sat brooding. He gave his fingers a contemptuous flick. "I must move with deliberation. The circumstances are still uncertain."

"I beg to contradict you. Aillas rules South Ulfland. The barons have acceded to his rule with gratitude, and they have marshaled their troops at Cleadstone Castle, in case they are needed against Tintzin Fyral."

Carfilhiot, startled and stung, jumped to his feet. Here was the message of the magic chart! "Already you have incited them against me! In vain! The plot will fail! I have powerful friends!"

Sir Glide's companion spoke for the first time. "You have a single friend, your lover Tamurello. He will not help you."

give you assurances, but their falsity will be easy to detect. One last time: give me my possessions and my two children."

"I submit to no man's orders."

Shimrod turned away. He crossed the terrace and mounted his horse. The two emissaries rode down the zig-zag way, past the gantry and the four taut men from Femus Castle, and so down the road toward Ys.

A band of fifteen ragged mendicants straggled south along the Ulf Passway. Some walked hunched; others hopped on crippled legs; others wore bandages stained by festering sores. Approaching the fortress at Kaul Bocach, they noted the soldiers on guard and shambled forward at best speed, groaning piteously and demanding alms. The soldiers drew back in distaste and passed the group through quickly.

Once beyond the fort the mendicants recovered their health. They straightened, discarded bandages and hobbled no more. In a forest a mile from the fortress they brought axes from under their garments, cut poles and built four long ladders.

The afternoon passed. At dusk another group approached Kaul Bocach: this time a troupe of vagabond entertainers. They made camp in front of the fort, broached a keg of wine, set meat to cooking on spits and presently began to play music while six comely maidens danced jigs in the firelight.

The soldiers of the fort went to watch the merriment and to call out compliments to the maidens. Meanwhile the first group returned in stealth. They raised their ladders, climbed unseen and unheard to the parapets.

Quickly and quietly they knifed a pair of luckless guards whose attention had been fixed on the dancing, then descended to the wardroom, where they killed several more soldiers at rest on their pallets, then leapt upon the backs of those who watched the entertainment. The performance came to an instant halt. The entertainers joined the fight and in three minutes the forces of South Ulfland once more controlled the fortress at Kaul Bocach.

The commander and four survivors were sent south with a message:

CASMIR, KING OF LYONESSE: TAKE NOTE!

The fortress Kaul Bocach is once more ours, and the interlopers from Lyonesse have been killed and expelled.

Neither trickery nor all the valor of Lyonesse will again take Kaul Bocach from us. Enter South Ulfland at your peril!

Do you wish to test your armies against our Ulfish might? Come by way of Poëlitetz; you will find it safer and easier.

I sign myself

Goles of Cleadstone Castle,
Captain of the Ulf armies
At Kaul Bocach.

The night was dark and moonless; around Tintzin Fyral the mountains bulked black against the stars. In his high tower Carfilhiot sat brooding. His attitude suggested impatience, as if he were waiting for some signal or occurrence which had failed to show itself. At last he jumped to his feet and went to his workroom. On the wall hung a circular frame something less than a foot in diameter, surrounding a gray membrane. Carfilhiot plucked at the center of the membrane, to draw out a button of substance which grew rapidly under his hand to become a nose of first vulgar, then extremely large size: a great red hooked member with flaring hairy nostrils.

Carfilhiot gave a hiss of exasperation; tonight the sandestin was restless and frolicsome. He seized the great red nose, twisted and kneaded it to the form of a crude and lumpy ear, which squirmed under his fingers to become a lank green foot. Carfilhiot used both hands to cope with the object and again produced an ear, into which he uttered a sharp command: "Hear! Listen and hear! Speak my words to Tamurello at Faroli. Tamurello, do you hear? Tamurello, make response!"

The ear altered to become an ear of ordinary configuration. To the side a nubbin twisted and curled to form a mouth, shaped precisely like Tamurello's own mouth. The organ spoke, in Tamurello's voice: "Faude, I am here. Sandestin, show a face."

The membrane coiled and twisted, to become Tamurello's face, save for the nose, where the sandestin, from carelessness, or perhaps caprice, placed the ear it had already created.

Carfilhiot spoke earnestly: "Events are fast in progress! Troice armies have landed at Ys and the Troice king now calls himself King of South Ulfland. The barons have not stayed him, and I am isolated."

Tamurello made a reflective sound. "Interesting."

"More than interesting!" cried Carfilhiot. "Today two emissaries came to me. The first ordered that I surrender myself to the new king. He uttered no compliments and no guarantees, which I regard as a sinister sign. Naturally I refused to do this."

"Unwise! You should have declared yourself a loyal vassal, but far too ill either to receive visitors or come down from your castle, thereby offering neither challenge nor pretext."

"I obey no man's bidding," said Carfilhiot fretfully.

Tamurello made no comment. Carfilhiot went on. "The second emissary was Shimrod."

"Shimrod!"

"Indeed. He came in company with the first, skulking in the shadows like a ghost, then springing forth to demand his two children and his magic stuff. Again I gave refusal."

"Unwise, unwise! You must learn the art of graceful acquiescence, when it becomes a useful option. The children are useless to you, as are Shimrod's stuffs. You might have ensured his neutrality!"

"Bah," said Carfilhiot. "He is a trifle compared to you—whom, incidentally, he maligned and scorned."

"In what wise?"

"He said that you were undependable, that your word was not true and that you would not secure me from harm. I laughed at him."

"Yes, just so," said Tamurello in an abstracted voice. "Still, what can Shimrod do against you?"

"He can visit an awful magic upon me."

"So to violate the edict? Never. Are you not the thing of Desmëi? Are you not possessed of magical apparatus? Thereby you become a magician."

"The magic is locked in a puzzle! It is useless! Murgen may not be convinced. After all, the apparatus was stolen from Shimrod, which must be regarded as provocation of one magician by another."

Tamurello chuckled. "But remember this! At that time you lacked magical implements and so were a layman."

"The argument seems strained."

"It is logic; no more, no less."

Carfilhiot was still dubious. "I kidnapped his children, which again could be construed as 'incitement.'"

Tamurello's response, even transmitted through the lips of the sandestin, seemed rather dry. "In that case, return Shimrod his children and his goods."

409

Carfilhiot said coldly: "I now regard the children as hostages to guarantee my own safety. As for the magical stuffs, would you prefer that I use them in tandem with you, or that Shimrod use them to support Murgen? Remember, that was our original concept."

Tamurello sighed. "It is the dilemma reduced to its starkest terms," he admitted. "On this basis, if no other, I must support you. Still, under no circumstances may the children be harmed, since the chain of events would at the end certainly confront me with Murgen's fury."

Carfilhiot spoke in his usual airy tones. "I suspect that you exaggerate their significance."

"Nevertheless you must obey!"

Carfilhiot shrugged. "Oh I shall humor your whims, right enough."

The sandestin precisely reproduced Tamurello's small tremulous laugh. "Call them what you like."

31

WITH THE COMING OF DAYLIGHT the Ulf army, still a mutually suspicious set of small companies, struck camp and mustered in the meadow before Cleadstone Castle: two thousand knights and men-at-arms. There they were shaped into a coherent force by Sir Fentaral of Graycastle who, of all the barons, was most generally respected. The army then set off across the moors.

Late the following day they established themselves on that ridge overlooking Tintzin Fyral from which the Ska had previously attempted an assault.

Meanwhile, the Troice army moved up the vale, encountering only incurious stares from the inhabitants. The valley seemed almost uncanny in its stillness.

Late in the day the army arrived at the village Sarquin, within view of Tintzin Fyral. At the behest of Aillas, elders of the town came to a colloquy. Aillas introduced himself and defined his goals. "Now I wish to establish a fact. Speak in candor; the truth will not hurt you. Are you antagonistic to Carfilhiot, or neutral, or do you support him?"

The elders muttered among themselves and looked over their shoulders toward Tintzin Fyral. One said: "Carfilhiot is a man-witch. It is best that we take no stance in the matter. You are able to strike off our heads if we displease you; Carfilhiot can do worse when you are gone."

Aillas laughed. "You overlook the reason for our presence. When we leave Carfilhiot will be dead."

"Yes, yes; others have said the same. They are gone; Carfilhiot remains. Even the Ska failed so much as to trouble him."

"I remember the occasion well," said Aillas. "The Ska retired because of an approaching army."

"That is true; Carfilhiot mobilized the valley against them.

We prefer Carfilhiot, who is a known if erratic evil, to the Ska, who are more thorough."

"This time there will be no army to succor Carfilhiot: not from north or south or east or west will help come."

The elders again muttered among themselves. Then: "Let us suppose that Carfilhiot falls, what then?"

"You will know a just and even rule; I assure you of this."

The elder pulled at his beard. "It makes good hearing," he admitted; then, after a glance at his fellows, he said: "The situation is of this nature. We are staunchly faithful to Carfilhiot, but you have terrified us to the point of panic, and therefore we must do your bidding, despite our inclinations, if Carfilhiot ever should ask."

"So be it. What, then, can you tell us of Carfilhiot's strength?"

"Recently he has augmented his castle guard, with wolf-heads and cutthroats. They will fight to the death because they can expect nothing better elsewhere. Carfilhiot forbids them to molest the folk of the valley. Still, girls often disappear and are never again heard from; and they are permitted to take women from the moors, and they also practice indescribable vices among themselves, or so it is said."

"What is their present number?"

"I guess between three and four hundred."

"That is not a large force."

"So much the better for Carfilhiot. He needs only ten men to hold off your entire army; the others are extra mouths to feed. And beware Carfilhiot's tricks! It is said that he uses magic to his advantage, and he is an expert at his ambushes."

"How so? In what fashion?"

"Notice yonder: bluffs extend into the valley, with little more than an arrow-flight between. They are riddled with tunnels; were you to march past a hail of arrows would strike down and in one minute you would lose a thousand men."

"Just so, if we were rash enough to march under the bluffs. What else can you tell us?"

"There is little else to tell. If you are captured you will sit a high pole until your flesh rots away in rags. That is how Carfilhiot pays off his enemies."

"Gentlemen, you may go. I thank you for your advice."

"Remember, I spoke only in a hysteria of fear! That will be the way of it."

Aillas marched his army another half-mile. The Ulf army occupied the heights behind Tintzin Fyral. No word had yet arrived from the force which had set out to take Kaul Bocach; presumably it had succeeded.

The exits and entrances to Tintzin Fyral were sealed. Carfilhiot must now trust his life to the impregnability of his castle.

In the morning a herald carrying a white flag rode up the valley. He halted before the gate and cried out: "Who will hear me? I bring a message for Sir Faude Carfilhiot!"

On top of the wall stepped the captain of the guard, wearing Carfilhiot's black and lavender: a massive man with gray hair flowing back on the wind. He cried out in booming tones: "Who brings messages to Sir Faude?"

The herald stepped forward. "The armies of Troicinet and South Ulfland surround the castle. They are led by Aillas, King of Troicinet and South Ulfland. Will you convey the message I bring, or will the miscreant descend to hear with his own ears and answer with his own tongue?"

"I will convey your message."

"Tell Faude Carfilhiot that, by order of the king, his rule at Tintzin Fyral is ended, and that he remains in occupation as an outlaw, without franchise from his king. Tell him that his crimes are notorious and bring great shame to him and his henchmen, and that a requital is forthcoming. Tell him that he may ameliorate his fate by surrendering at this instant. Tell him further that Ulf troops control Kaul Bocach, to bar the armies of Lyonesse from Ulfland, so that he may expect no succor from King Casmir, nor anyone else."

"Enough!" cried the captain in a vast roaring voice. "I can remember no more!" He turned and jumped down from the wall. Presently he could be seen riding up the road to the castle.

Twenty minutes passed. The captain returned down the road and once more ascended the wall. He called: "Sir Herald, listen well! Sir Faude Carfilhiot, Duke of Vale Evander and Prince of Ulfland, knows nothing of Aillas, King of Troicinet, and does not acknowledge his authority. He requires the invaders to leave this domain which is alien to them, on pain of bitter war and awful defeat. Remind King Aillas that Tintzin Fyral has known a dozen sieges and has succumbed to none."

"Will he or will he not surrender?"

"He will not surrender."

"In that case, make announcement to your fellows and all

those who bear arms for Carfilhiot. Tell them that all who fight for Carfilhiot and shed blood on his behalf will be deemed no less guilty than Carfilhiot and will share his fate."

Dark moonless night fell across Vale Evander. Carfilhiot climbed to the flat roof of his high tower and stood in the wind. Two miles down the valley a thousand campfires created a flickering carpet, like a drift of red stars. Much closer a dozen other fires rimmed the northern ridge and suggested the presence of many more across the ridge, away from the wind. Carfilhiot turned and, to his startled dismay, at the top of Tac Tor he saw three more fires. They might well have been built only to daunt him, and so they did. For the first time he felt fear: first, a gnawing edge of wonder if possibly, by some tragic failure of fate, Tintzin Fyral might, on this occasion, fall to a siege. The thought of what would happen were he captured sent a clammy coldness down through his bowels.

Carfilhiot touched the harsh stone of the parapets for reassurance. He was secure! How could his magnificent castle fall? In the vaults were stores for a year or even longer; he had ample water from an underground spring. A gang of a thousand sappers, working night and day, in theory, might excavate the base of the cliff so as to topple the castle; practically the idea was absurd. And what could his enemies hope to achieve from the top of Tac Tor? The castle was protected by the width of the chasm: A long bow-shot. Archers on Tac Tor might cause a harassment until screens were raised against the arrows, whereupon their efforts became futile. Only from the north would Tintzin Fyral seem vulnerable. Since the Ska attack Carfilhiot had augmented his defenses, providing ingenious new systems against any who might hope to use a battering-ram.

So Carfilhiot reassured himself. Further, and superseding all else, Tamurello had avowed support. Should supplies run short, Tamurello could replenish them by magic. In effect, Tintzin Fyral might stand secure forever!

Carfilhiot looked once more around the circle of night, then descended to his workroom, but Tamurello, through absence, neglect, or design, would not talk with him.

In the morning Carfilhiot watched as the Troice army advanced almost to the base of Tintzin Fyral, evading his ambush by marching single-file behind a screen of shields. They cut down his impaling poles, released the stretched men of Femus Castle from their weights, and set up camp on the meadow. Trains of supplies moved up the valley and along the ridge, preparations of an unhurried and methodical sort, which caused Carfilhiot new apprehension despite all logic to the contrary. There was peculiar activity on top of Tac Tor and Carfilhiot watched the skeletons of three enormous catapults take shape. He had thought Tac Tor a place of no danger, by reason of its steep slopes, but the cursed Troice had found the trail and with ant-like industry, piece by piece, had carried to the summit the three great catapults now rearing against the sky. Surely the range was too far! Thrown boulders would simply bounce away from the castle walls and menace the Troice encampment below. So Carfilhiot assured himself. On the north ridge six other siege-engines were under construction, and again Carfilhiot felt queasiness to see the efficiency of the Troice engineers. The engines were massive, designed with great precision. They would in due course be brought close to the edge of the cliff; in just such a fashion the Ska had ranged their engines...As the day wore on Carfilhiot began to doubt, and the doubts deepened to rage: the engines were set up well to the safe side of his collapsible platform. How had they learned of this danger? From the Ska? Reverses from all directions! A thud and a shock as something struck the side of the tower.

Carfilhiot swung around aghast. On Tac Tor he saw the arm of one of the great catapults swing up and snap to halt. A boulder climbed high into the air, made a slow arc and slanted down toward the castle. Carfilhiot threw his hands over his head and crouched. The stone missed the tower by five feet and hissed past to land near the drawbridge. Carfilhiot took no pleasure in the miss; these were ranging shots.

He ran down the stairs and ordered a squad of archers to the roof. They went to the battlements; they placed their bows to the merlons, lay back and held the bows with a foot. They drew to the fullest draught and loosened. The arrows arched high across the gulf, then slanted down to strike the slopes of Tac Tor. A futile exercise.

Carfilhiot cried out a curse and waved his arms in defiance. Two of the catapults launched together; two boulders hurtled high, completed their arcs, slanted down their final courses and plunged into the roof. The first killed two archers and broke the roof; the second missed Carfilhiot by ten feet, to plunge through the roof and into his high parlor. The surviving archers scrambled down the stairs followed by Carfilhiot.

For an hour boulders struck down upon the roof of the tower, destroying the battlements, bursting in the roof and breaking the roof-beams, so that they protruded half in the air, half-down to the floor below.

The engineers altered the aim of their machines and began to break in the walls of the tower. It became clear, that in a period of time to be measured in days, the engines on Tac Tor alone could batter the tower of Tintzin Fyral to its foundation.

Carfilhiot ran to the frame in his workroom and now succeeded in making contact with Tamurello. "The army is attacking from the heights with enormous weapons; help me or I am doomed!"

"Very well," said Tamurello in a heavy voice. "I will do what must be done."

On Tac Tor Aillas stood where he had stood before, during a different era of his life. He watched as the flung stones crossed the gulf to batter Tintzin Fyral, then spoke to Shimrod: "The war is over. He has nowhere to go. Stone by stone we dismantle his castle. It is time for another parley."

"Let's give him another hour of it. I feel his mood. It is fury but not yet despair."

Across the sky moved a crepuscule. It settled to the top of Tac Tor and exploded with a small sound. Tamurello, taller by a head than ordinary men, stood facing them. He wore a suit of gleaming black scales and a silver fish-head helmet. Under black brows his eyes glared round with rings of white surrounding the black iris. He stood on a ball of flickering force which subsided, lowering him to the ground. He looked from Aillas to Shimrod and back to Aillas. "When we met at Faroli I failed to recognize your high estate."

"At that time I lacked such estate."

"Now you expand your grasp across South Ulfland!"

"The land is mine by right of lineage and now by force of conquest. Both are valid entitlements."

Tamurello made a sign. "In peaceful Vale Evander, Sir Faude Carfilhiot maintains a popular rule. Conquer elsewhere, but stay your hand here. Carfilhiot is my friend and ally. Call away your armies, or I must exert my magic against you."

Shimrod spoke. "Desist, before you cause yourself embarrassment. I am Shimrod. I need speak a single word to summon

416

Murgen. I was forbidden to do so unless you made prior interference. Since you have done so I now call on Murgen to intercede."

A flash of blue flame illuminated the mountain-top; Murgen stepped forward. "Tamurello, you violate my edict."

"I protect one dear to me."

"You may not do so in this case; you have played a wicked game, and I tremble with the urge to destroy you at this moment."

Tamurello's eyes seemed to glare with black radiance. He took a step forward. "Do you dare such threats to me, Murgen? You are senile and flaccid; you cringe at imaginary fears. Meanwhile I wax in strength!"

Murgen seemed to smile. "I will cite first, the Wastes of Falax; second, the Flesh Cape of Miscus; third, the Totness Squalings. Reflect; then go your way, and be grateful for my restraint."

"What of Shimrod? He is your creature!"

"No longer. In any event, the offense was engendered by you. It is his right to restore the equipoise. Your deeds were not overt, and I punish you thus: return to Faroli; do not in any guise venture from its precincts for five years, on pain of expunction."

Tamurello made a wild gesture, and disappeared in a whirl of smoke, which became a crepuscule drifting eastward with speed.

Aillas turned to Murgen. "Can you help us further? I would hope not to risk the lives of honest men, nor yet my son."

"Your wishes do you credit. But I am bound by my own edict. No more than Tamurello may I interfere for those whom I love. I walk a narrow way, with a dozen eyes judging my conduct." He laid his hand on Shimrod's head. "Already you have altered from my concepts."

"I am as much Dr. Fidelius the mountebank as I am Shimrod the magician."

Murgen, smiling, drew back. The blue flame in which he had arrived came into being and enveloped him; he was gone. On the ground where he had stood remained a small object. Shimrod picked it up.

Aillas asked: "What is it?"

"A spool. It is wound with a fine thread."

"To what purpose?"

Shimrod tested the cord. "It is very strong."

Carfilhiot stood in his workroom, shuddering to the shock and thud of boulders striking down from the sky. The circular frame altered to become the face of Tamurello, mottled and distorted with emotion. "Faude, I have been thwarted; I may not intercede for you."

"But they destroy the fabric of my castle!" And next they will tear me to pieces!"

Tamurello's silence hung more heavy in the air than words.

After a moment Carfilhiot spoke on in a voice breathless, soft and exalted with emotion: "So great a loss and then my death— is it tolerable to you, who so often have declared your love? I cannot believe it!"

"It is not tolerable, but love can not melt mountains. All reasonable things, and more, will I do. So now, make yourself ready! I will bring you here at Faroli."

Carfilhiot cried out in a piteous voice: "My wonderful castle? I will never leave! You must drive them away!"

Tamurello made a sad sound. "Take flight, or give surrender: which will you do?"

"Neither! I trust you! In the name of our love, help me!"

Tamurello's voice became practical. "For best terms, surrender now. The worse you hurt them, the harder will be your fate."

His face receded into the gray membrane, which now snapped away from the frame and disappeared, leaving only the beechwood backing-panel. Carfilhiot cursed and dashed the frame to the floor.

He descended to the floor below and walked back and forth with hands clasped behind his back. He turned and called to his servant. "The two children: bring them here at once!"

On top of Tac Tor the captain of the engineers suddenly leapt in front of the catapults. "Hold your fire!"

Aillas came forward. "What goes on?"

"Look!" The captain pointed. "They have put someone up on what is left of the roof."

Shimrod said: "There are two: Glyneth and Dhrun!"

Aillas, looking across the gulf, for the first time saw his son. Shimrod, beside him, said: "He is a handsome boy, and strong and brave as well. You will be proud of him."

"But how to make rescue? They are at Carfilhiot's mercy. He

has canceled our catapults; Tintzin Fyral is once more invulnerable."

Glyneth and Dhrun, dirty, bewildered, unhappy and frightened, were seized from the room where they had been confined and ordered up the spiral staircase. As they climbed they became aware of a recurrent impact which sent vibrations down the stone walls of the tower. Glyneth stopped to rest, and the servant made urgent gestures. "Quick! Sir Faude is in haste!"

"What is happening?" Glyneth asked.

"The castle is under attack; that is all I know. Come now; there is no time to waste!"

The two were thrust into a parlor; Carfilhiot paused in his pacing to survey them. His easy elegance was absent; he seemed disheveled and distraught. "Come this way! At last you will be of use to me."

Glyneth and Dhrun recoiled before him; he urged them up the staircase, into the upper levels of the tower. Above a boulder plunged down through the broken roof to batter at the far wall. "Quick now! Up with you!" Carfilhiot shoved them up the sagging and broken staircase, out into afternoon sunlight, where they stood cowering in expectation of another projectile.

Dhrun cried out: "Look to the mountain yonder!"

"That's Shimrod up there!" cried Glyneth. "He's come to rescue us!" She waved her arms. "Here we are! Come get us!" The roof groaned as a beam gave way and the staircase sagged. "Hurry!" cried Glyneth. "The roof is falling under us!"

"This way," said Dhrun. He led Glyneth close to the broken battlements, and the two gazed in fascinated hope across the chasm.

Shimrod came to the edge of the cliff. He held a bow in one hand and an arrow in the other. He gave them to an archer.

Glyneth and Dhrun watched him in wonder. "He's trying to signal us," said Glyneth. "I wonder what he wants us to do?"

"The archer is going to shoot the arrow; he's telling us to be careful."

"But why shoot an arrow?"

The line from Murgen's spool, so fine as almost to float in the air, could not be broken by the strength of human arms. Shimrod carefully laid the thread along the ground, back and forth in ten-foot bights, so that it might extend freely. He held up bow and arrow so that the two wistful figures, so near and yet so far, might divine his purpose, then tied an end of the thread to the arrow.

Shimrod turned to Cargus. "Can you flight this arrow over the tower?"

Cargus fitted arrow to bow. "If I fail, pull back the cord and let a better man make the attempt!"

He drew back the arrow to arch the bow, raised it so that the arrow might fly its farthest course, and released. High through the sky, down and over the roof of Tintzin Fyral, flew the arrow, the thread floating behind. Glyneth and Dhrun ran to catch the thread. At Shimrod's signal they tied it to a sound merlon at the far side of the roof. At once the thread thickened, to become a cable of braided fibers two inches in diameter. On Tac Tor a squad of men, putting their shoulders to the rope, pulled up the slack and drew it taut.

In the parlor three floors below, Carfilhiot sat glumly, but relieved that he had so ingeniously halted the barrage. What next? All was in flux; conditions must change. He would exercise his keenest ingenuity, his best talents for agile improvisation, that from this dreary situation he might salvage the most and best for himself. But, despite all, a dismal conviction began to ease across his mind, like a dark shadow. He had very little scope for maneuver. His best hope, Tamurello, had failed him. Even if he could keep Dhrun and Glyneth on the roof indefinitely, he still could not endure a siege forever. He made a petulant sound of distress. It had become a time for compromise, for amiability and a clever bargain. What terms would his enemies offer him? If he surrendered his captives and Shimrod's goods, might he be left in control of the Vale? Probably not. Of the castle itself? Again, probably not . . . Silence from above. What might be happening on Tac Tor? In his mind's eye Carfilhiot imagined his enemies standing at the edge of the cliff, calling ineffectual curses across the wind. He went to the window and looked up. He stared at the line across the sky and uttered a startled cry. Already from the edge of Tac Tor he detected men preparing to slide down the rope. He ran to the stairs and bellowed down to his captain. "Robnet! A squad to the roof, in haste!"

He ran up to the wreck of his private quarters. The stairs to the roof sagged under his weight, groaning and swaying. With a tread as light as possible, he climbed up. He heard Glyneth's exclamation, and tried to hurry, and felt the stairs give way beneath his feet. He lunged, and, catching a splintered roof-beam, pulled himself up. Glyneth, white-faced, stood above him. She swung a length of broken timber and struck at his head with all her strength. Dazed, he fell back and hung with one arm over the roof-beam; then, making a wild grasp with the other arm, he caught Glyneth's ankle and pulled her toward him.

Dhrun ran forward. He held his hand into the air. "Dassenach! My sword Dassenach! Come to me!"

From far across the Forest of Tantrevalles, from the thicket into which Carfilhiot had flung it, came Dassenach the sword, to Dhrun's hand. He raised it high and thrust it down at Carfilhiot's wrist and pinned it to the roof-beam. Glyneth kicked herself free and scrambled to safety. Carfilhiot gave a poignant cry, slipped to hang by his pinned wrist.

Down the rope, riding a loop, came a squat broad-shouldered man, with a dark dour countenance. He dropped upon the roof, went to look at Carfilhiot. Another man slid down from Tac Tor. They lifted Carfilhiot to the roof and bound his arms and legs with rope, and then turned to Glyneth and Dhrun. The smaller of the two men said, "I am Yane; that is Cargus. We are your father's friends." This was said to Dhrun.

"My father?"

"There he stands, next to Shimrod."

Down the line slid man after man. Carfilhiot's soldiers tried to fire arrows from below but the embrasures were set unsuitably in the walls and the arrows went astray.

Tintzin Fyral was empty. The defenders were dead: by sword, fire, asphyxiation in sealed tunnels and the executioner's axe. Robnet, captain of the guard, had climbed atop the wall which enclosed the parade grounds. He stood spraddle-legged, wind blowing his gray locks. He roared challenge in his vast hoarse voice. "Come! Who will meet me, sword in hand? Where are your brave champions, your heroes, your noble knights? Come! Clash steel with me!"

For a few moments the Troice warriors stood watching him. Sir Cargus called up. "Come down, old man! The axe awaits you."

"Come up and take me! Come test your steel against mine!"

Cargus made a motion to the archers; Robnet died with six arrows protruding from neck, chest and eye.

The aviary presented special problems. Certain of the captives fluttered, dodged and climbed to high perches to avoid those who came to release them. Mad King Deuel attempted a gallant flight across the cage, but his wings failed him; he fell to the floor and broke his neck.

The dungeons yielded stuff forever to haunt the thoughts of those who explored them. The torturers were dragged screaming out on the parade ground. The Ulfs cried out for the impaling poles, but King Aillas of Troicinet and South Ulfland had proscribed torment, and their heads were taken by the axe.

Carfilhiot occupied a cage on the parade ground at the base of the castle. A great gibbet was erected, with the arm sixty feet from the ground. At noon on a raw overcast day, with wind blowing strangely from the east, Carfilhiot was carried to the gibbet; and again passionate voices were heard. "He escapes too easily!"

Aillas paid no heed. "Hang him high."

The executioner bound Carfilhiot's hands behind him, fitted the noose over his head, and Carfilhiot was taken aloft to dangle kicking and jerking: a grotesque black shadow on the gray sky.

The impaling poles were broken and the fragments set afire. Carfilhiot's body was cast on the flames, where it twitched and crawled as if dying a second time. From the flames rose a sickly green vapor which blew away on the wind, down Vale Evander and over the sea. The vapor failed to dissipate. It clotted and coalesced, to become an object like a large green pearl, which fell into the ocean where it was swallowed by a turbot.

Shimrod packed into cases his stolen apparatus, and other items as well. He loaded the cases into a wagon and with Glyneth beside him drove the wagon down the vale to old Ys. Aillas and Dhrun rode on horses to the side. The cases were loaded aboard the ship which would convey them back to Troicinet.

An hour before sailing, Shimrod, motivated by caprice, mounted a horse and rode north along the beach: a way he had come long ago in dreams. He approached the low palace beside the sea, and found Melancthe standing on the terrace, almost as if she had been awaiting him.

Twenty feet from Melancthe Shimrod halted his horse. He sat in the saddle, looking at her. She said nothing, nor did he. Presently he turned his horse about and rode slowly back down the beach to Ys.

32

EARLY IN THE SPRING OF the year, envoys from King Casmir arrived at Miraldra and requested audience with King Aillas.

A herald announced their names: "May it please your Highness to receive Sir Nonus Roman, nephew to King Casmir, and Duke Aldrudin of Twarsbane; and Duke Rubarth of Jong; and Earl Fanishe of Stranlip Castle!"

Aillas stepped down from the throne and came forward. "Sirs, I bid you welcome to Miraldra."

"Your Highness is most gracious," said Sir Nonus Roman. "I carry with me a scroll indited with the words of His Majesty, King Casmir of Lyonesse. If you permit, I will read them to you."

"Please do so."

The squire tendered Sir Nonus Roman a tube carved from the ivory of an elephant's tusk. Sir Nonus Roman withdrew a scroll. The squire stepped smartly forward and Sir Nonus Roman handed him the scroll. Sir Nonus Roman addressed Aillas: "Your Highness: the words of Casmir, King of Lyonesse."

The squire, in a sonorous voice, read:

For His Majesty, King Aillas,
In His Palace Miraldra, Domreis,
These Words:

    I trust that the occasion finds you in good health.

    I have come to deplore those conditions which have adversely affected the traditional friendship existing between our realms. The present suspicion and discord brings advantage to neither side. I therefore propose an immediate cessation to hostility, said truce to persist for at least one year, during which time neither side shall engage in armed effort or military initiatives of any sort without prior consultation with the other side, except in the event of exterior attack.

After one year the truce shall continue in effect unless one side notifies the other to the contrary. During this time I hope that our differences may be resolved and that our future relations shall be in terms of fraternal love and concord.

Again, with compliments and best regards, I am

> Casmir
> at Haidion, in
> Lyonesse Town

Returning to Lyonesse Town, Sir Nonus Roman delivered the response of King Aillas.

To Casmir, King Of Lyonesse,
These Words From Aillas, King
Of Troicinet, Dascinet And
South Ulfland:

I accede to your proposal of a truce, subject to the following conditions:

We in Troicinet have no desire to defeat, conquer or occupy the Kingdom of Lyonesse. We are deterred not only by the superior force of your armies, but also by our basic disinclinations.

We cannot feel secure if Lyonesse uses the respite afforded by a truce to construct a naval force of a strength sufficient to challenge our own.

Therefore, I agree to the truce if you desist from all naval construction, which we must consider as preparation for an invasion of Troicinet. You are secure in the strength of your armies, and we in the force of our fleet. Neither is now a threat to the other; let us make this mutual security the basis for the truce.

> Aillas

With the truce in effect, the Kings of Troicinet and Lyonesse exchanged ceremonial visits, Casmir coming first to Miraldra.

Upon meeting Aillas face to face, he smiled, then frowned and looked in puzzlement. "Somewhere I have seen you before. I never forget a face."

Aillas returned only a noncommittal shrug. "I will not dispute your Majesty's powers of recollection. Remember, I visited Haidion as a child."

"Yes, perhaps so."

During the remainder of the visit Aillas often found Casmir's gaze upon him, curious and speculative.

Sailing across the Lir on their reciprocal visit to Lyonesse, Aillas and Dhrun went to stand on the bow of the ship. Ahead Lyonesse was a dark irregular outline across the horizon. "I have never spoken to you of your mother," said Aillas. "Perhaps it is time that you knew the tale of how things went." He looked to the west, to the east and then once more to the north. He pointed. "Yonder, perhaps ten or twenty miles, I cannot be sure, I was pushed into the water of the gulf by my murderous cousin. The currents carried me ashore, as I hung on the very verge of death. I came back to life and thought that indeed I had died and that my soul had drifted into paradise. I was in a garden where a beautiful maiden, through the cruelty of her father, lived alone. The father was King Casmir; the maiden was the Princess Suldrun. We fell deeply in love and planned to escape the garden. We were betrayed; I was dropped by Casmir's orders into a deep hole, and he must yet believe that I died there. Your mother gave birth to you, and you were taken away that you might be secure from Casmir. In grief and utter woe, your mother gave herself to death, and for this anguish visited upon someone as blameless as moonlight I will forever in my bones hate Casmir. And that is the way of it."

Dhrun looked away across the water. "What was my mother like?"

"It is hard to describe her. She was unworldly and not unhappy in her solitude. I thought her the most beautiful creature I had ever seen..."

As Aillas moved through the halls of Haidion he was haunted by images of the past, of himself and Suldrun, so vivid that he seemed to hear the whisper of their voices and the rustle of their garments; and as the images passed the two lovers seemed to glance sidewise at Aillas, smiling enigmatically with eyes glow-

425

ing, as if the two had been playing in all innocence no more than a dangerous game.

On the afternoon of the third day, Aillas and Dhrun departed Haidion through the orangery. They went up the arcade, through the sagging timber portal, down through the rocks and into the old garden.

Slowly they descended the path through silence which like the silence of dreams was immanent to the place. At the ruins they stopped while Dhrun looked around him in awe and wonder. Heliotrope scented the air; Dhrun would never smell the perfume again without a quick clutch of emotion.

As the sun settled among golden clouds the two went down to the shore and watched the surf play over the shingle. Twilight would soon be coming; they turned up the hill. At the lime tree Aillas slowed his steps and stopped. Away from Dhrun's hearing he whispered: "Suldrun! Are you here? Suldrun?"

He listened and imagined a whisper, perhaps only a stirring of wind in the leaves. Aillas spoke aloud: "Suldrun?"

Dhrun came to him and hugged his arm; already Dhrun deeply loved his father. "Are you talking to my mother?"

"I spoke. But she does not answer."

Dhrun looked about him, down to the cold sea. "Let's go. I don't like this place."

"Nor do I."

Aillas and Dhrun departed the garden: two creatures, living and quick; and if something by the old lime tree had whispered, now it whispered no more and the garden throughout the night was silent.

The Troice ships had sailed. Casmir, on the terrace in front of Haidion, watched the sails grow small.

Brother Umphred came up to him. "Sire, a word with you."

Casmir regarded him without favor. Sollace, ever more fervent in her faith, had suggested the construction of a Christian cathedral, for the worship of three entities she called the "Holy Trinity." Casmir suspected the influence of Brother Umphred, whom he detested. He asked: "What do you want?"

"Last night I chanced to notice King Aillas as he came in for the banquet."

"Well then?"

"Did you find his face familiar?" An arch and meaningful smile trembled along Brother Umphred's lips.

Casmir glared at him. "As a matter of fact, I did. What of it?"

"Do you recall the young man who insisted that I marry him to the Princess Suldrun?"

Casmir's mouth sagged. He stared thunderstruck, first at Brother Umphred, then out across the sea. "I dropped him into the hole. He is dead."

"He escaped. He remembers."

Casmir snorted. "It is impossible. Prince Dhrun is all of ten years old."

"And how old do you make King Aillas?"

"He is, at a guess, twenty-two or twenty-three, no more."

"And he fathered a child at the age of twelve or thirteen?"

Casmir paced the floor, hands behind his back. "It is possible. There is mystery here." He paused and looked out to sea, where the Troice sails had now disappeared from view.

He signaled to Sir Mungo, his seneschal. "Do you recall the woman who was put to question in connection with the Princess Suldrun?"

"Sire, I do so remember."

"Fetch her here."

In due course Sir Mungo reported to Casmir. "Sire, I have tried to implement your will, but in vain. Ehirme, her spouse, her family, each and all: they have vacated their premises and it is said that they have removed to Troicinet, where they are now landed gentry."

Casmir made no response. He leaned back in his chair, lifted a goblet of red wine and studied the dancing reflections from the flames in the fireplace. To himself he muttered: "There is mystery here."

EPILOGUE

WHAT NOW?

King Casmir and his ambitions have temporarily been thwarted. Aillas, whom once he attempted to kill, is responsible, and Casmir already has developed a great detestation for Aillas. His intrigues continue. Tamurello, fearing Murgen, refers Casmir to the wizard Shan Farway. In their plotting they use the name "Joald" and both fall silent.

Princess Madouc, half-fairy, is a long-legged urchin with dark curls and a face of fascinating mobility. She is a creature of unorthodox habits; what will become of her? Who is her father? At her behest an adventurous boy named Traven undertakes a quest. If he succeeds she must grant him whatever boon he demands. Traven is captured by Osmin the ogre, but Traven saves himself by teaching his captor chess.

What of Glyneth, who loves Watershade and Miraldra, but yearns for her vagabond life with Dr. Fidelius? Who will woo and who will win her?

Aillas is King of South Ulfland and now he must reckon with the Ska, who wage war against the world. When he thinks of the Ska he thinks of Tatzel, who lives at Castle Sank. He knows a secret way into the fortress Poëlitetz: how will this knowledge serve him?

Who nets the turbot who swallowed the green pearl? Who proudly wears the pearl in her locket and is impelled to curious excesses of conduct?

Many affairs remain unsettled. Dhrun can never forget the wrongs done him at Thripsey Shee by Falael, even though Falael has been punished well by King Throbius. From motives of sheer perversity Falael provokes the trolls of Komin Beg to war, in which they are led by a ferocious imp named Dardelloy.

What of Shimrod? How does he deal with the witch Melancthe?

And what of the knight of the Empty Helmet, and how does he comport himself at Castle Rhack?

At Swer Smod Murgen works to elucidate the mysteries of Doom, but each clarification propounds a new puzzle. Meanwhile, the adversary stands back in the shadows smiling his smile. He is potent and Murgen must presently tire, and in great sorrow concede defeat.

GLOSSARY I

IRELAND AND
THE ELDER ISLES

Few definite facts are related of Partholón, a rebel prince of
Dahaut, who after killing his father fled to Leinster. The Fomoire
derived from North Ulfland, then known as Fomoiry. King
Nemed, arriving with his folk from Norway, fought three great
battles with the Fomoire near Donegal. The Ska, as the Nemedians called themselves, were fierce warriors; the Fomoire, defeated twice, gained final victory only through the magic of three
one-legged witches: Cuch, Gadish and Fèhor: a battle in which
Nemed was killed.

The Ska had fought with honor and valor; even in defeat they
commanded the respect of the victors, so that they were allowed
a year and a day to make their black ships ready for an onward
voyage. At length, after three weeks of banquets, games, songs
and the drinking of mead, they set sail from Ireland with Starn,
first son of Nemed, as their king. Starn led the surviving Ska
south to Skaghane, northernmost of the Hesperians, at the western verge of the Elder Isles.

Nemed's second son, Fergus, sailed to Amorica and assembled an army of a Celtic people known as the Firbolg, which he
led back to Ireland. Along the way the Firbolg put into Fflaw at
the tip of Wysrod, but so vast an army came to confront them
that they left without a battle and continued to Ireland, where
they became preeminent across the land.

A century later the Tuatha de Danaan, after an epic migration
from central Europe through Asia Minor, Sicily and Spain, crossed
the Cantabrian Gulf to the Elder Isles, and established themselves in Dascinet, Troicinet and Lyonesse. Sixty years later the
Tuatha split into two factions, one of which moved on to Ireland,
to fight the Firbolg at the First and Second Battles of Mag Tuired.

The second Celtic surge which propelled the Milesians into

Ireland and the Brythni into Britain bypassed the Elder Isles. Celts nonetheless migrated into Hybras in small groups and spread everywhere, as Celtic place-names across the isles attested. Tribes fleeing Britain after the defeat of Boudicaa forced their presence upon the rocky northern foreshore of Hybras, and established the Celtic kingdom Godelia.

THE FAIRIES

Fairies are halflings, like trolls, falloys, ogres and goblins, and unlike merrihews, sandestins, quists and darklings. Merrihews and sandestins both may manifest human semblance, but the occasion is one of caprice and always fugitive. Quists are always as they are, and darklings prefer only to hint of their presence.

Fairies, like the other halflings, are functionally hybrids, with varying proportions of earth-stuff. With the passage of time the proportion of earth-stuff increases, if only through the ingestion of air and water, though occasional coition of man and halfling hastens the process. As the halfling becomes "heavy" with earth-stuff it converges toward humanity and loses some or all of its magic.

The "heavy" fairy is abusively ejected from the shee as a boor and lummox, to wander the countryside and eventually merge into the human community, where it lives disconsolately and only rarely exercises its fading magic. The offspring of these creatures are peculiarly sensitive to magic, and often become witches or wizards: so with all the magicians of the Elder Isles.

Slowly, slowly the halflings dwindle; the shees grow dark, and the halfling life-stuff dissipates into the human race. Every person alive inherits more or less halfling-stuff from thousands of quiet infusions. In human inter-relationships the presence of this quality is a matter of general knowledge, but sensed subliminally and seldom accurately identified.

The fairy of the shee often seems childlike by reason of intemperate acts. His character varies of course from individual to individual, but is always capricious and often cruel. Similarly, the fairy's sympathies are quickly aroused, whereupon he becomes extravagantly generous. The fairy is inclined to be boastful; he is given to dramatic postures and quick sulks. He is sensitive in regard to his self-image and cannot tolerate ridicule, which prompts him to a prancing demonstrative fury. He admires beauty and also grotesque oddity in the same degree; to the fairy these are equivalent attributes.

The fairy is erotically unpredictable and often remarkably promiscuous. Charm, youth, beauty are not cogent considerations; above all the fairy craves novelty. His attachments are seldom lasting, in common with all his moods. He quickly shifts from joy to woe; from wrath through hysteria to laughter, or any of a dozen other affections unknown to the more stolid human race.

Fairies love tricks. Woe to the giant or ogre the fairies decide to molest! They give him no peace; his own magic is of a gross sort, easily evaded. The fairies torment him with cruel glee until he hides in his den, or castle.

Fairies are great musicians and use a hundred quaint instruments, some of which, like fiddles, bagpipes and flutes have been adopted by men. Sometimes they play jigs and knockabouts to put wings on the heels; sometimes mournful tunes by moonlight, which once heard may never be forgotten. For processions and investitures the musicians play noble harmonies of great complexity, using themes beyond the human understanding.

Fairies are jealous and impatient, and intolerant of intrusion. A boy or girl innocently trespassing upon a fairy meadow might be cruelly whipped with hazel twigs. On the other hand, if the fairies were somnolent the child might be ignored, or even showered with a rain of gold coins, since the fairies enjoy confounding men and women with sudden fortune, no less than with sudden disaster.

![] GLOSSARY III: ![]

THE SKA

For ten thousand years or longer the Ska maintained racial purity and continuity of tradition, using the same language so conservatively that the most ancient chronicles, both oral and written, were intelligible at all times across the years without archaic flavor. Their myths recalled migrations north behind the Würm glaciers; their oldest bestiaries included mastodons, cave bears and dire wolves. Their sagas celebrated battles with cannibal Neanderthals, with a culminating victory of extermination where the red blood ran deep over the ice of Lake Ko (in Denmark). They followed the glaciers north into the virgin wilderness of Scandinavia, which they claimed as their homeland. Here they learned to smelt bog-iron, forge tools, weapons, and structural pieces; they built seagoing boats and guided themselves by the compass.

About 2500 B.C. an Aryan horde, the Ur-Goths, migrated north into Scandinavia, driving the relatively civilized Ska west, to the fringes of Norway and eventually into the sea.

The remnants of the Ska descended upon Ireland and entered Irish myth as "Nemedians": the Sons of Nemed. The Ur-Goths adopted the Ska folkways, and became ancestors to the various Gothic peoples, most notably the Germans and the Vikings.

From Fomoiry (North Ulfland) the Fomoire migrated into Ireland, and engaged the Ska in three great battles, forcing them to depart Ireland. This time the Ska moved south to Skaghane, which they vowed never to leave. Molded by bitter adversity, they had become a race of aristocratic warriors and considered themselves actively at war with all the rest of the world. All other peoples they deemed subhuman and only marginally superior to animals. With each other they were fair, mild and reasonable; with others they were dispassionately pitiless: this philosophy became their tool for survival.

Their culture was unique and unlike any other of Europe; in certain aspects spare or even austere, in other ways richly detailed. Every person was trained to be potentially capable of any achievement; no one would think to admit himself or herself a dullard, or inept at any conceivable skill; as a Ska his universal competence was taken for granted. Words like "artist" and "creativity" were unknown: each man and woman crafted beautiful handiworks without thinking the activity unusual.

On the battlefield the Ska were fearless in the fullest meaning of the word, for a variety of reasons. An "ordinary" might become a "knight" only by destroying three enemies. No Ska could survive in the contempt of his fellows; under such circumstances he would sicken and die through sheer self-loathing.

Despite Ska conviction of basic equality, Ska society was highly stratified. The Ska king was privileged to appoint his successor: usually but not always his eldest son. After a year the new king must be approved by a moot of the upper nobility, and once again after three years of reign.

Ska law by contempoary standards was reasonable and enlightened. The Ska never used torture and a slave was treated with the tolerant if impersonal kindness a farm animal might be given. If obstreperous he was punished either by a flogging of no great severity, imprisonment in a pen on bread and water, or sudden death. Among themselves the Ska were open, generous and nakedly honest. Duels were illegal; rape, adultery, sexual perversions were considered bizarre aberrations and the offenders were killed to sustain the general welfare. The Ska regarded themselves as the only enlightened folk of the age; others saw them as merciless brigands, thieves and murderers.

The Ska knew no organized religion, though they recognized a pantheon of divinities representing natural forces.